# DEITY

THEY'RE NOT ONLY THE KINGS

OF RAVENWOOD HEIGHTS

THEY'RE MY EXECUTIONERS.

# CHAPTER 1

The bright halo of flames behind me stretches my shadow across the hard ground, distorting it against the trees and elongating it, morphing it into something girls like me only see in nightmares. But when it comes to girls like me, there's no such thing as nightmares—only the harsh reality otherwise known as life.

My feet pound against the hard earth, pushing me further away from the flaming cabin behind me, a cabin that not thirty seconds ago was supposed to be my salvation. It was supposed to keep me safe, keep me alive and away from the evil in this world. Only now, it's in a million broken pieces, just as fractured and broken as the devastated remains of my heart.

Sharp pants tear through my lungs as I focus on nothing but running, desperate to get away. My rapid pulse thumps loudly in my ears, getting faster and faster by the second. I match my strides to its sound, forcing myself on as I fly through the woods, launching myself over fallen branches and cutting up my arms and face from the sharp bushes around me. But nothing matters now, only that I get away.

I can't … I don't understand how this is happening. I'm so fucking confused. Why? Why would they do this? *How* could they do this? One second, I was searching through the cabin trying to figure out the best room to blow their minds, and the next, I'm bolting through the woods, my skin burned, bloodied, and bruised.

How could they betray me like that?

*I trusted them.*

This isn't right. I thought they loved me, but all this time, it's just been a game to them. They led me to believe that I was their world. They spun an intricate, complex web around me, and I fell straight into it, handing over my fragile heart on a silver platter.

I'm so fucking stupid.

I should have known life was never supposed to be that good for me. From the day I was born, the world has been plotting against me. Every single person who has entered my life has proved untrustworthy. I thought Ember was the final nail in my coffin. I should have known.

In this world, there's always room for another betrayal. People say not to kick someone when they're down, but Dynasty doesn't give a shit about ethics and morals. If you're down, they're going to stand by and demand you dig your own fucking grave, and only then will they push you headfirst into it, making sure you stay down for good.

I bet the boys are halfway back to Ravenwood Heights already, laughing about the way they took that dagger and slammed it straight through my broken heart and tore me to shreds. I bet they love just how easily they were able to fool me.

The only ray of sunshine in my world is the knowledge that Cruz's guilty conscience is probably eating him alive, but the darkness in his eyes before he closed that goddamn door ... was any of it real? Did I even know them at all?

They told me they loved me. They said they'd do anything to protect me and keep me safe, and time and time again, they proved that to be true, but here I am, my feet pounding against the uneven ground, branches cutting up my skin as I frantically run, desperate to get away.

I was such a fool to believe them.

How many times did they warn me not to trust anyone in this twisted world? How was I to know that they were talking about themselves?

FUCK.

I push myself faster, my hands covering my face, protecting it from the sharp twigs and branches sticking out at every angle. My wrists and forearms are cut up and bleeding while my leather pants are doing a poor as fuck job of protecting my legs.

Why the fuck did I have to wear heeled fucking boots tonight? My old ripped-up Queen shirt is twisted around my body, now showing a shitload more than just a little side boob, and fuck, what I wouldn't give for a goddamn bra right now ... or my fucking phone that sits safely in Cruz's pocket. I bet that was part of their sick little plan all along—make sure that I don't have anywhere to go, no one to trust, and no way to call for help.

I'm fucking screwed.

The flames roar from the cabin and I look back over my shoulder, watching how the bright halo spreads out through the woods, but that halo doesn't reach me anymore. It's just me, alone in the thickening woods, lost and bloodied. I can barely see two feet in front of me as every step takes me deeper into the darkness.

My heart continues to hammer and the tears flow down my cheeks, staining my dirty skin and mixing with the soot from the explosion.

A migraine quickly settles in as tonight's shit storm quickly catches up with my body. I'm fucking exhausted. I've been running for what feels like a lifetime, but in reality, it's only been a few months. Five, maybe six? I can't tell anymore. It's been one thing after another since the second I got to Ravenwood Heights. One disaster just blurring into another like a constant stream of bad luck.

How could my parents want me to fight for this? I get that it was something to fight for eighteen years ago, but not anymore. There's too much corruption, too much pain and betrayal that runs far too deep. I can't trust a single person. Going back there would be a suicide mission.

I should disappear, let them think I'm dead and just slink away into the world to live a miserable, lonely life. Sure, I'll probably hate it, constantly looking over my shoulder and watching my back, but I'll be alive and sometimes, that's all a girl can ask for.

I look back ahead of me but see nothing in the darkness. As my foot catches on a fallen branch, I go sprawling to the ground, dropping down into a shallow ditch and cutting up my knees more than they already are.

I hit the ground with a loud thump, winding myself in the process, narrowly avoiding smacking my head right into the base of a massive tree trunk.

"Owwwww, fuck," I growl under my breath, clenching my jaw to keep myself from screaming out in pain.

I roll back onto my ass, cringing and grunting as the rocks and fallen twigs dig into my sides. This is so far from how I had planned my night to go.

How the fuck did I end up sitting in a shallow ditch? Hell, knowing my luck, it's most likely a pre-dug shallow grave the boys had planned on dumping me once they got a hold of my dead body. It's out in the middle of the thick, dark woods, right where I'll never be found. Perfect.

I wonder how many other shallow graves I've run past.

I guess they owe me now. I just saved them all the time and effort of getting me here. I might as well just stay and let the devastation catch up to me. It's not like my life is going to get any better from here.

I bring my knees up, ignoring the pain that shoots through both my ass and my feet with the movement. This is more exercise than I've done since … well, ever, and I'm going to be paying for it later.

I squint into the darkness, trying to get a good look at my bloodied knees and get to work, picking out shit from the dirty ground and trying to wipe away anything that doesn't belong.

My heart continues pounding and I take a short moment to try and catch my breath. I can still see the faint halo from the flames in the distance which means that I'm not nearly far enough away. I need to get gone and I need to do it now. Hell, I should get used to it. Running is about to become my life.

My hands come back covered in blood, but I can't think about it. I need to grin and bear it. I can worry about all my injuries later. For now, I need a fucking game plan.

It's only been ten minutes since the cabin went up in flames, but that ten minutes has changed it all. Surely the boys will turn around soon enough to come and check me off their hit list, and when that happens, I need to be as far away from here as possible.

They'll come for me just as they went for every other target. They don't miss. They don't make mistakes, so why the hell am I still breathing?

How am I going to get myself out of here? I don't even know how long these woods go on for, let alone what I'll find when I reach the other end. Am I up for days of walking through the thick trees and sleeping in shallow graves or do I need to just push myself for another ten minutes to find civilization?

Fuck that. I have to stay away from roads or anywhere that they could find me. I need to stay hidden until I'm sure they're not looking for me. Who am I kidding? They'll never stop searching. We've been through too much together. They won't let this be the end.

As for now, I need to keep moving.

I tip my head up, looking at the cloudy, dark sky above. The smoke from the explosion is thick in the air, masking the stars that beg to be seen. My breath comes in shallow gasps, and as I sit here with my head up to the sky, I slowly feel my heart calming to a normal pace. The exhaustion of the day hits me like a wrecking ball and I know that I won't be able to last much longer.

I need to find somewhere safe to spend the night and I need to do it now.

Taking a deep breath, I push myself back to my feet and climb out of the ditch. I've only been sitting here for a few minutes, but in that short time, darkness has completely overwhelmed the woods. Though it's nearly impossible to see, I have to try. Staying in this little ditch all night is just asking for trouble, and from here on out, I rely on only me.

As the adrenaline fades, a chill washes over me, making my skin prickle and the little hairs on my arms stand straight up. I've never been one for the cold. I fucking hate this, but if I don't keep moving, I might just freeze to death before Paris or the boys even get a chance to get their slimy little hands on me.

I perch my foot against the hard earth, and as I push myself out of the small ditch, I hear the faint sirens in the distance.

Well, shit. If it's not one thing, it's another.

Should I really be surprised? Of course the cops are on their way. There was a massive fucking explosion. It'd be just my luck to get arrested on arson charges and make myself a sitting duck. I wonder who would come for me first, Paris or the boys?

Ignoring the way my body begs for relief, I force myself forward through the woods again. Every step I take gets harder, but I can't give up. I have to put some epic space between me and the cops.

I focus solely on putting one foot in front of another. From now on, the cold doesn't exist and the pain sure as hell doesn't exist. It's just the fear I have to conquer now.

I hear a branch breaking deep in the woods and I come to a startling standstill, my back straightening as I strain to hear through the thick bushes.

My heart thunders in my chest and I look around, trying to determine which direction the sound came from. There's another soft creak followed by the sound of something or someone brushing past leaves. A shiver shoots right down my spine, sending my blood cold.

I'm not alone in these woods.

I try to calm my racing heart, straining to hear through the trees, over the sound of my heavy pulse booming in my ears.

"Oh, Winter," a chilling voice calls out through the bushes, his tone muffled by distance. "Come out, come out, little rabbit. I know you're hiding in here."

Fuck me in the royal asshole.

No, no, no. It can't be.

I'm done for. I don't stand a fucking chance. Not now. I thought I had more time.

I'd recognize that perfect, deep, tormenting voice anywhere— Dante fucking Carver.

"Come on, baby. Just tell me where you are. You don't need to be scared of me. Let's just talk and straighten this shit out," he calls, that familiar velvety tone speaking right to the broken pieces of my heart.

"I promise I won't hurt you. It was just an accident."

Yeah fucking right. I bet he thinks poisoning Tobias King was just an *accident* too. After everything we've suffered through over the past few months, does he really think I'm just going to show myself and fall back into his trap? He's a fucking idiot and I've allowed him to play his game for far too long, I've allowed them *all* to play a game, but not anymore. If tonight has taught me anything, it's to trust no one. The only person I have in my corner is me.

I bite down on my tongue, hating the taste of blood that comes with it, but if anything, it's helping me to keep my fucking mouth shut. I'd give anything to be able to call out to him, to tell him how he hurt me and how all four of them broke my heart, but I can't. My time will come to put these motherfuckers in their place, but that time isn't now. I need to play this smart.

I suck in a deep breath and prepare myself. I can't see shit and my body is aching, but I need to push through it. I need to survive.

I start moving, my hands shaking with the overwhelming fear that at any second, Carver could catch up to me. All it would take is one single branch cracking under my boot and I'll be a dead woman.

Carver has a set of skills that, until meeting the guys, I didn't even realize were physically possible. I thought it was all shit you see in stupid romantic suspense movies where the hero saves the girl. It's all fantasy, but people like that really do exist, and right now, I have one of them bearing down on me, intent on finishing what he started.

I creep through the woods, unable to reel in the paralyzing fear. Tears silently stream down my face as I all but tiptoe through the darkness, as step by step, he gains on me.

My mind is so messed up that it's nearly impossible to tell just how far back he is until his chilling tone rips through the silence once again. "Come on, little rabbit. Where are you?"

My eyes bug out of my head as my heart all but fucking stops.

He's closer than I thought.

I take off at another sprint, racing ahead, my feet slamming against the hard ground as my fists pump out in front of me, and just like that, I hear him moving through the woods behind me.

He's got me. It won't be long now.

I'm never going to survive this. He's too fast, too lethal.

I give it everything I have, desperately trying to put distance between us, but he's gaining too fast and my body is quickly giving out. I'll never survive like this.

I have to stop.

I have to hide.

As long as he can hear me tearing through the woods, it's like sending up a neon sign with an arrow pointing right at me. Running isn't playing it smart, all I'm doing is painting a bigger target on my back. All he would need is one single glance of me breaking through the woods and I'll have a bullet in the back of my head. He's just that good.

My only shot at freedom is dead silence.

I stop running, coming to a complete standstill as I desperately try to control my rapid breathing, knowing that it would give me away in seconds.

I hear Carver's run come to a stop a short distance behind me, and now more than ever he's listening intently, trying to figure out my game plan.

Looking around, I strain to find somewhere to hide. If this were anyone but Carver, I'd try to fight my way out, but against a man like him, I have no chance.

A fallen tree sits just to my right and I snake through the woods to get to it, being as silent as humanly possible as I hear Carver slowly making his way toward me. "Winter? Where are you, girl? We need to talk this out."

I drop down behind the fallen tree and lay down in the dirt right beside it, keeping myself as close as possible while letting the main part of the tree trunk conceal me. I'm not stupid, I know there's a big possibility that he could still find me here, but right now, this is my best shot.

Closing my eyes, I focus on trying to calm my racing heart and find some level of control over my rapid, loud panting. I haven't come this far to let my basic human need for oxygen give me away.

I listen to the noises of the woods, taking note of every step Carver takes toward me. He's nearly silent. He's always been that way, especially back at home. I've never been able to hear him coming but there's a distinct crunch of fallen leaves that not even Dante Carver can conceal beneath his feet.

"Alright, babe. You've made your point," Carver taunts. "You don't trust us, that much is clear, but I need to get you out of here before the cops find you. They'll put you in another cell and I know how you hate that. I won't let you go through that again."

I ball my hands into fists, desperate to keep myself under control. I'm lying out in the cold woods, my body both shivering and aching while my heart hammers away with fear. The last thing I need is to be reminded of the few times that I've been thrown in cells. They're not exactly my fondest memories and he knows that. He's trying to flush me out and he's using my trauma to make it happen.

That asshole. Is trying to blow me up not bad enough? Now he's going to stoop to this level? Fuck him. Fuck them all.

The seconds tick by and I bite down on my tongue even harder, knowing that having decent self-control is a low point for me. I'm reckless and stupid and that's gotten me in more than enough trouble over the past few months, but now is not the time to allow that recklessness to get the best of me.

He's banking on it though.

It takes only a minute for me to hear him right on the other side of the fallen tree trunk and I sink down lower, willing myself to dissolve into the ground beneath me. Each step he takes is like a shot straight to the heart.

If Carver is making his way through the woods, does that mean the others are too? The SUV drove away without a body in sight, but that doesn't mean shit in this world. I watched King, Cruz, and Grayson get into the car, but I never saw Carver get in.

Fuck.

Of course they left him behind.

I bet he watched me get thrown through the air. He probably

watched as I looked after the disappearing SUV and laughed as he saw the betrayal sink heavily into my bones. I bet the bastard even took a second to get off on the thought before coming after me. He probably thought he was doing me a solid by letting me have a head start.

The fear paralyzes me, and I hold my breath, terrified that he's able to hear me breathing.

Carver stops and my heart pounds even faster.

He knows I'm here.

He creeps in closer to the tree trunk and I suck in a shallow breath, desperately trying to keep myself calm while knowing that had it been daylight, he would already have me thrown in the back of a car.

There's a short pause where he hovers above the tree trunk, looking out at the woods around him, slowly scanning as I fret and panic below. "I can smell you," he murmurs, knowing I'm close. "I might not be able to see you, but don't be fooled, Winter, I know you're here."

Fuck. Fuck. Fuck. FUCK.

How did this become my life?

I start counting backward from one hundred, keeping my eyes closed as his familiar, warm scent washes over me and messes with my head. I have to keep myself in control and letting my reckless flag fly free is not exactly a smart move right now.

I get down to thirty-six before Carver finally steps back from the tree trunk and scans the opposite side of the woods.

If only he was smart enough to look down.

He stays here for a minute, knowing I'm close, but unable to pinpoint my exact position in the darkness before he finally takes a step deeper into the woods to keep looking, giving me just the slightest fraction of relief.

"I'm going to find you, Winter," he promises as he moves another step away. "It's only a matter of time."

# CHAPTER 2

A minute passes and then another before I hear Carver even further away and I finally allow myself to take a deep breath. He doesn't stop calling for me, doesn't stop taunting me with the promise of finding me, and for that, I keep myself still and hidden. It'll only be a matter of time before he can't smell me anymore and he'll double back, searching all night if he has to.

He won't give up but neither will I.

The minutes turn into hours and my sense of time becomes warped in the cold night. Tugging my arms inside my Queen tank, I curl them around my aching body.

I hear noises all around me. Owls calling out in the darkness, rodents scattering through the leaves, and the occasional murmur from Carver, non-stop searching for me well into the dark night.

The sirens soon fade away and the smoke begins to clear, leaving nothing but misery and betrayal in its wake.

"I can't fucking find her," I hear murmured through the woods just as the first rays of sunshine hit the very tops of the trees, shedding a dim brightness through the darkened woods and allowing me, for the first time in hours, to see what lies around me.

Have I really been out here all night?

It takes me all of two seconds to realize that Carver's on a phone call, most likely to the boys and it cuts me like never before. Fuck, I'd prefer the pain of his bullet tearing through my body than this constant reminder of their betrayal. But that's not important right now. What's important is that his voice is far across the woods, putting enough space between us to allow me the chance to run.

"I know. I know. I'll fucking get her," he says, his tone dark and angry, a version of himself that once made me so unbelievably hot, but now only sends chills shooting down my spine. "I won't let her get away. I'm going to end this."

Fucking asshole.

God, how is it possible to be so in love with someone while equally hating them? It's not natural.

"Yeah ... bye."

I don't wait a second longer.

I fly to my feet, knowing that this could be my only shot at freedom, and I fucking run.

Branches scrape along my fragile skin as I tear through what's left of the bushes, the dim sunlight barely lighting my way, but it's all I need to be able to launch myself over fallen branches and avoid falling into any more shallow ditches.

My body still aches from last night's ordeal, but the few hours of stillness went a long way to re-energize my exhausted body.

My gaze darts from left to right, desperately seeking out Carver, and every step I take that I'm not discovered, I count as a win. But I'm no fool, I know he's not far and it will only take a second for him to realize that I'm running. Hell, I'm sure the sound of me tearing past the low bushes has already alerted him and I have to assume that he's already coming for me.

This may be my only shot and that knowledge pushes me faster.

As I run, I give myself a short minute to grieve for the four new relationships that I allowed to overwhelm my heart with happiness. Things will never be the same. How could they?

I let them into my life, I foolishly trusted them, and they betrayed me in the worst possible way.

I'll never forgive them for this.

Realizing that the more I think about them and their stupidly beautiful faces, my pace begins to slow. I shake it off, and as I hear the branches and bushes crunching in the distance behind me, I push myself to my absolute limits.

"You can't outrun me." Carver's voice comes tearing through the woods, and with every single word he throws my way, my determination only grows. I've allowed the guys to rule over me these past few months, but not anymore.

The old Winter is back and I won't be backing down. From here on out, Elodie Ravenwood ceases to exist, just as it was always meant to be. From here on out, I own my shit, and I have four targets standing in my way.

I push myself faster for everything that's right in the world, for my parents and for all the innocent victims of Dynasty.

I will be making it out of this alive, and when I do, I'm going to thrive, the boys be damned.

Five minutes turn into ten, and with every step I take, I hear Carver in the distance, quickly closing in on me. But all too soon, I break out into a small clearing with a beautiful log cabin that sits high at the top of a small hill, overlooking the wide expanse of woods around it.

It's fucking perfect.

That slight glimmer of hope that resides deep inside my gut begins to burn just a little bit brighter as I race toward it, hoping to whoever lives above that I can disappear before Carver breaks out of the woods. It's a slim chance, but I have to try.

I give it everything I've got. My legs burn from the run, but I'm not at the end yet. I can't give up. I won't. My life depends on it.

"WINTER."

Fuck.

I look back over my shoulder to see Carver flying out of the woods, looking as though he's just woken from a peaceful twelve-hour nap, while I, on the other hand, look like I've been squeezed through a bull's asshole.

Carver has the stamina to do this all day and night, but I'm on borrowed time. I can't do this much longer. I have to find an escape and I have to do it sooner rather than later.

I reach the log cabin a minute later and race around to the side, not willing to waste time going to the front door only to find it locked and impossible to break down. Without thinking, I scoop up a large gnome statue and launch it right through the back window and dive straight through after it, narrowly avoiding slicing a large gash through my thigh.

I scramble to my feet, only having seconds to save my fucking ass.

My eyes dart around the cabin and I can barely think over the sound of my heartbeat pulsing rapidly in my ears. I need to hurl. That was too much exercise for me, but I don't have time for that. I need to hold it together.

I have all of two seconds to put a plan into place and I better make it good.

I run into the kitchen and wrap my hand around a knife before darting straight out again. He's going to expect the obvious. Most people would hide in the bottom of the pantry or race up the stairs to the furthest bedroom and put themselves under the bed, but I'm not in the business of making things easy.

I run into the open living room and dive down behind the couch before crawling across to a small side table and folding myself inside the bottom part of the cupboard, a space that none of the guys could even dream about getting themselves into.

I close the door just as a loud BANG sounds around me and the front door of the luxury cabin splinters right off the hinges. I hear the wood slamming against the adjoining wall, and I peer out through the small keyhole, realizing how fucked I would have been had this little cupboard been locked.

An imposing Carver steps through the doorway of the cabin and I swallow back fear, watching as he comes to a standstill and slowly scans the empty room.

I hold my breath, not ready to be caught so soon. If he wants to fuck around and play twisted little games, then we will, but he should be warned that I don't like to lose.

Carver steps deeper into the cabin and I shrink impossibly further into the small cupboard as I watch him. His eyes rake over the living room, scanning over each piece of furniture, knowing that I'm not as stupid as I look. I've been running all my life. I'm not about to make this easy for anyone.

"Come on, little rabbit," he says, his tone thick and velvety, making me wish that things could be different. But side note—what the fuck is this little rabbit thing he's got going on at the moment? I don't think he's ever called me that.

He slowly starts walking through the living space, checking behind every piece of furniture in the room. "You can't hide in here forever. There's only so many places your tight little body can fit. I will find you. Why don't you just save us all a little bit of time and come out? There's a few things we need to … talk about."

In his fucking dreams, but he's right. There are more than a few things that need to be discussed, but that's not going to happen until I have him chained to a fucking chair … and not in the good way.

Carver steps closer to the cupboard and I tighten my grip on the knife as I pull back from the keyhole, knowing that even through this tiny little hole, he'd be able to point out my eyes anywhere. But what am I really willing to do with this knife?

I killed his bastard of a father with a dagger right through the gut. Can I make it two for two? I don't know. It's one thing wanting revenge for their betrayal, but ending them would be like ending myself. They still own my heart, no matter how badly I wish they didn't. If I were to hurt them in any way, I don't know if I'd be able to live with myself after.

I listen and feel for the soft vibrations of his steps as he moves past the small cupboard, disregarding it because of its size, and as I hear him move past me and move deeper into the cabin, I lean forward again and watch as he goes.

Carver grabs the side of the couch and in one smooth motion, flips it away from him before moving onto the next and making my heart pound furiously inside my chest, pumping so hard and fast that it's bound to give out soon.

Not able to find me, he moves onto the dining room, but I don't dare move. I need a few minutes to catch my breath before I keep going. Besides, this cabin is fucking huge—it's going to take him a while to search every nook and cranny. So instead, I focus on putting a plan in place.

As Carver moves into the kitchen, I watch as he takes note of the missing knife and grabs one for himself, making my stomach sink. "This isn't a game you want to play, Winter. I don't want to hurt you, but if you strike against me, I'll have no choice but to react."

He continues searching through the kitchen as my stomach attempts to right itself. I've been stabbed before and it wasn't nice, but Carver was the one there to save me. I saw the guilt in his eyes when he thought he wasn't fast enough, and the pain on his face when he watched me quickly fading. There's no way he'd inflict that kind of pain on me, but then, for so long I thought there was no way he'd ever try to blow me up … so there's that.

In my world, trust is just an illusion.

Carver moves through the kitchen with precise movements, and as he does, I take a second to look around, seeing only the few angles I can get to from the small keyhole of the cupboard. I spy a door across the hall and my back straightens as much as this small cupboard allows.

I try to remember what the front of the cabin looked like, but I only got a brief glimpse before I ran straight around it. My desperation makes the details more than just a little bit fuzzy. I'm pretty sure there was a garage … or maybe it was just another living space or a private office.

Fuck, I don't know, but I have to check. It's the only shot I've got, otherwise, I'm screwed. We're in the middle of the woods. Perhaps there's a hunting rifle or something that will increase my chances of survival.

My gaze swings back to the kitchen to watch as Carver slowly steps out of it and creeps across the open living space toward the beautiful wooden staircase. His footsteps are deathly silent and I bet he thinks that he's about to get the jump on me, but he's got another thing coming.

His hand gently falls to the handrail and I watch as he all but glides up the stairs, not making a single creak in the floorboards. This cabin is huge, and assuming that there's at least three bedrooms and bathrooms upstairs, I have a few minutes to figure out what the fuck I'm going to do. With that in mind, I slowly push the cupboard door open, feeling more vulnerable than ever before.

I keep my eyes trained on the stairs as my heart thunders in my chest. The slightest noise will have Carver's toned as fuck ass down here in the blink of an eye. I've never been one to do things quietly. I've always wanted to go out with a bang, so this doesn't come naturally to me, but when the door completely opens without a sound, a small sliver of relief pulses through me.

Now all I have to do is crawl out of this fucking thing.

I get my ass out of the cupboard and get to my feet only to keep myself crouched down as much as possible. I rise up onto my tippy-toes because for some reason, my brain tells me that tippy-toes equals silence, and after letting out a shaky breath, I bolt across the room, terrified of giving myself away.

My fingers curl around the door handle and I quickly push it open, holding my breath because … why not?

The door pushes back into a darkened room and I quickly step down into it, feeling my whole world beginning to right itself when I realize that I was right. It's a fucking garage, and more than that, it's fully stocked. So fucking stocked that it'll be hard to find what I'm looking for—not that I even know what that is.

It's a four-car garage and in the space directly in front of me, there's an old car sitting pretty, and for a second, my heart races into gear, more than ready to throw myself into it and barge through yet another garage door until I realize that the whole fucking motor is in pieces on the ground to my right.

"Fucking hell," I mutter to myself, flicking the lock on the back of the door and putting the smallest barrier between me and Carver, despite the fact that he could knock this door down just by looking at it the wrong way.

My gaze shifts over the garage as my hands shake at my sides.

What should I do? What the mother-effing hell do I do?

Hurrying over to the shelving, I release the knife and start scrambling through boxes, coming up with nothing but tools and old rags. The guy who owns this must be some sort of mechanic. Coming up blank, I spin around and look over the rest of the garage. I hurry past a second row of shelving when my gaze lingers on a stack of old cardboard boxes, but it's not exactly the boxes I'm looking at, more the oddly familiar, weatherproof fabric sprawled across the floor behind them.

My brows crease as I make my way around the boxes and take in the way the weatherproof fabric is draped over something almost like a cover … a fucking motorcycle cover.

I race toward it, gripping the fabric with both hands before tearing it off and fearing the worst. There's a good possibility that whatever is under this cover is in just as many pieces as the car motor behind me.

The cover drops to the ground beside me revealing an old road bike that looks as though it's been sitting here for years.

Fuck, yes.

It could be in better condition, but for now, it's a solid escape plan.

I step into the side of the bike, looking over it and checking for a key, only there isn't one.

My head snaps up to the workbench across the garage and I race to it, desperately searching, a little more recklessly than I should be. Tools clatter around, but hopefully with the internal door closed, Carver can't hear me upstairs … but the real question is, is he even still up there? Maybe he's finished looking.

I have to make this fast.

I tear open drawers, leaving a mess behind, but my desperation soon pays off as I find the bike key hanging from a small hook on the side of the workbench. "Sweet baby Jesus. Yes," I hiss under my breath, curling my hand around the keys, feeling myself one step closer to freedom.

I'm nearly there. I just have to figure out how to turn the fucking bike on, open the garage, and get the fuck out of here without alerting the mega ass upstairs.

It's impossible.

This bike is bound to rumble through the whole fucking cabin with vibrations rocking through the foundations as the garage door peeling back will most likely squeal or hum, or fuck, knowing my luck, it'll probably set off a goddamn alarm that specifically says, 'The bitch is getting away. The bitch is getting away. The bitch is getting away.'

Hell, not to mention that there's a good chance that the bike won't even start. It could be out of gas or it could just choke and die in the ass. There are so many risks involved with making some kind of bullshit escape plan, all of which draw Carver's attention right to me, but it's the only shot I've got.

Let's face it, even if I did find a hunting rifle hidden in here somewhere, would I really be able to use it on him? No. Hell to the no. I've always prided myself on making hard decisions, having to do what a girl has to do just to get by, but hurting Carver is a no-go zone. Don't get me wrong, I'm more than happy to kick his legs out from under him and watch his bitch ass go tumbling to the ground, but hurting him to the point of risking death … no. Just the thought kills me.

It shouldn't. He sure as fuck didn't give it a second thought when King's cabin exploded into a million pieces around me, but Carver has had a hard life. He's lived a life where emotion and purpose are put aside for the cause, leaving you to come to terms with the bullshit at a later time. He's a fucking robot. He's learned how to remove emotion from a situation, unlike me, but it's something that I'm quickly being forced to figure out.

Knowing that every second counts, I fly over to the disaster of a workbench and scramble through everything until my fingers curl around the one thing that now sits between me and my freedom.

The automatic garage door controller.

I have one shot at this and I have to time it just right.

My leg flies over the seat and I get comfortable on the old bike before taking the handlebars and placing both feet down on the ground. I lift the bike off its stand and gently rock it side to side, listening to the soft splash of the gas inside the tank. There's not a lot in there but hopefully it's enough to get me out of here.

The nerves spark deep inside me as I let out a shaky breath and kick my heel up, pushing the stand up with it. The key effortlessly slides into the ignition as I look up at the garage door and slowly roll the bike a little closer to it.

"Winter, baby. Where the fuck are you?" I hear from deep inside the house, telling me that Carver is still in the upstairs bedrooms.

It's now or fucking never.

I hit the button for the garage door at the same time that I twist the key in the ignition. "Come on," I beg under my breath as the bike begins to rumble beneath me, the sound already deafening, meaning that Carver is already on his way. "Please, please, please, please."

I twist the handlebar, giving the bike a little more gas and just like that, it comes alive like a reader at the biggest book signing event of the century.

The bike hums smoothly, the sound completely giving me away as the garage door takes it's sweet fucking time. "Hurry up and open your bitch ass," I screech at it as I hear a loud bang coming from the internal door just moments before it's torn right off its hinges.

Carver takes one look at me on the bike and I see the fear of losing me flashing through his ridiculously, electrifying eyes. "WINTER. NO," he roars as he takes off at a hard sprint, racing toward me with everything that he's got.

My eyes widen and I watch him almost in slow motion, knowing that if I don't make the decision to leave right fucking now, I might not live to make another fucking decision ever again.

Without hesitation, my foot drops down on the rest, clicking the gear into first as my hand violently twists the handlebar. The tires screech against the ground, and not a second before Carver reaches me, I fly out of the garage, ducking my head to avoid the rising door, and breaking out into the wide-open world with my freedom only just intact.

My head flies back over my shoulder as I take off with a loud roar down the dirt drive, finding Carver standing in the open garage door, his hands knotted in his hair, slowly shaking his head as he watches me get away.

A wide grin stretches across my face and just to rub salt in the wound, I raise my hand behind me and lift a less than manicured middle finger until it's flying high and proud. "FUCK YOU, DANTE CARVER," I call out, knowing that even over the roar of the bike, he can make out my every word.

And just like that, I turn back to the dirt road, knowing all too well that this game of cat and mouse is only just getting started, and while I've escaped with my freedom, he's still coming for my life.

Getting this far already is a miracle but getting much further would be unheard of. Dante Carver isn't one to give up, and I need to be prepared. This isn't just a battle the boys have started, but a whole fucking war.

# CHAPTER 3

$G$as syphons out of an old F-150 as my gaze shifts around the dodgy parking lot. I stand in the dark corner of the lot, my attention constantly travelling back to the biker bar across the road, knowing all too well that dark corners like this aren't exactly a great place for a petite girl in torn, raggedy clothing to be found.

I can only imagine the bullshit that's gone down in this very corner. Drug deals. Murder. Rape. Anything. If you can think of it, I'm sure it would have gone down here. Hell, I don't even know where *here* is, but I don't need to. All that matters is getting gas so that I can keep riding and hopefully figure out where the hell I'm going.

I've been on the road all fucking day and so far, it hasn't been going great. I've nearly ridden straight off the highway and crashed into oncoming traffic after nearly falling asleep out of sheer exhaustion. I bet the boys would have gotten a kick out of that.

My near crash prompted me to pull off the side of the road at a truck stop where I hid my bike behind a couple of bushes and laid down in the grass. My stomach rumbled the whole time smelling the food coming from the shitty truck stop, but I didn't dare risk going in there and showing my face.

I wouldn't be surprised if Carver's got Cruz and Grayson using all that expensive technology to try and find me. I won't risk it, not until I'm ready to face them.

I slept in the grass for half an hour before getting on my bike and not stopping until now when my gas light came on and warned me not to fuck around.

So, here I am, making my way through the country, one dive bar at a time.

Gas spills out and I pull back, quickly capping the tank and pulling out the old plastic hose from the old F-150. I couldn't believe my luck when I found it in the back of the truck. I was more than prepared to go dumpster diving to find something to do the trick, but my luck must be turning around.

Not wanting to spend more time here than necessary, I throw my leg over my bike and climb back on, hating the ache in my ass from riding all day. I can't say that I've ever ridden my Ducati for this many hours straight, but I can guarantee that it would be a shitload better than this thing, and I sure as fuck wouldn't be having to stop every two hours to massage my ass cheeks.

I miss my fucking bike. I hate that Knox made sure to destroy it when he nearly killed Cruz, but I hate it even more that my selfishness allowed him to get away. Knox deserves to be buried in a shallow grave and I want to be the one to put him there. Fuck Cruz. I know I've always said that Cruz would be awarded the honor of ending Knox, but then his stupid ass attempted to blow me up so all those happy little promises that I once made don't mean shit anymore.

The bike roars to life, and as I take off like a bat out of hell, I spy two men slipping down the side alley of the biker bar and everything inside of me screams to stop. They look like the kind of assholes that I would have gotten a kick out of beating just a few short months ago.

Every instinct inside of my body is telling me to jump off this ridiculous bike and put my brass knuckles to use for the first time in so long, but the exhaustion is quickly creeping through my bones, and at some point, I'm going to have to find somewhere to spend the night.

But where? Park benches aren't really my thing.

I hit the gas and take off, leaving the biker dudes to their bullshit while hoping that tonight isn't the night that they decide to take it too far with a young, drunk girl, otherwise, I'd never forgive myself. But where do I draw the line? I can't save everybody. Hell, what the fuck am I even talking about? It's hypothetical. There is no girl who needs saving, unless I count myself, then I guess I have a valid reason for taking off.

I need to save myself. I need to get out of here and figure out where to go.

The bike flies down the highway and for being old, it's doing a pretty decent job of getting me from point A to point B, wherever the hell point B is. Though, the engine is starting to get pissed that it hasn't been rewarded with a good rest. After all, it's probably thirty years older than my Ducati. This thing is practically a grandpa.

My eyes quickly begin to get droopy when a street sign flashes past me with the name Santa DeClara sprawled across it, telling me to take the next right.

My back straightens and my eyes widen with a million and one different memories, most of them good apart from one that tears me to shreds every time I think about it.

Without hesitation, I take the next right and fly towards Santa DeClara, hoping that I'm making the right decision, but who the hell knows? Lately, I haven't been able to trust myself when it comes to making decisions. I'm just lucky that the last few I've made seem to be paying off.

I ease up on the gas as I drive into the small familiar town and make my way through the streets that I used to walk every day on my way to one of my many schools.

This place used to symbolize hope. It gave me a reason to keep going, but had I known what was in store for me over the following few years, I would have run when I had the chance.

I ride up onto the short driveway and the bike putters with relief as I cut the engine. I glance up at the modest home and hope to whoever lives above that I'm not about to knock on the door only to find an unfamiliar face staring back at me.

Not wanting to wait a second longer, I scramble off the bike and make my way around to the front door, feeling my hands starting to shake. I haven't been here in five years and so much has changed since then. I'm not the same girl that I used to be. Hell, I don't even recognize myself anymore, how is she supposed to?

I'm not used to not trusting my own judgment. Feeling that decaying unease spreading through me, I shake it off and try to find that little piece of myself that always tells me to go ahead and strive for greatness, even if the whole world is against me.

My fist raises and I knock against the flimsy metal door frame that looks like one good storm could have it flying down the street. I take a hesitant step back, preparing to come face to face with my past.

A shuffling comes from inside followed by a low groan before I hear someone on the opposite side, fiddling with the locks.

The door opens before my face, and not a second later, I stare up at the one woman who always had my back.

Karleigh Jensen, the one good foster parent I ever had.

"Winter?" she breathes, looking up and down at the state of me covered in cuts and bruises, twigs in my hair, blood all over my clothes, exhaustion clear on my face, and my skin stained with dirt.

"Yeah …"

She watches me for a second, hardly able to believe what she's seeing but not a moment later, she takes a step back and waves me in. "Come on, sweet girl. I'll whip you up some spaghetti and meatballs while you shower, then we'll talk."

I nod, and just like that, she draws me into her arms and holds me tight. "It's all going to be alright," she tells me before pulling back and nodding down the hallway. "You know where the towels are."

I give her a tight smile, hating just how fond I am of her. Apart from the boys, she's the only person I've allowed to get to know the real me. She saw me while the rest of the world couldn't, especially at a time when I needed it most. I first came to Karleigh when I was nine years old and had some of the best years of my life here. Don't get me wrong, I was trouble when I first arrived with nothing but a broken duffle bag. Instead of sending me away like everyone else did, she persisted and taught me some of the most important lessons of my life.

That I am worthy of love.

Being with Karleigh was the first time I truly longed to have parents of my own. Every time I imagined what my mother would be like, I pictured Karleigh's loving heart, caring nature, warmth, and her patience. I knew that's what I always wanted my own mother to resemble.

Karleigh was the closest thing I ever had to a mother and I hope that one day, when I have kids of my own, I'm just like her. Seeing her now only reminds me that over the past five years, while I've changed and turned into a woman, I'm still that lost little girl who was delivered to her doorstep a lifetime ago.

At thirteen, I was taken away, and still to this day, I count that as the worst thing that has ever happened to me. The pain of losing her sits high above the pain of killing a man for the first time, or the fear of constantly having a target painted on my back. This place was my salvation and I'm hoping to God that just for tonight, it can be that again.

I trudge down to the bathroom, stopping on the way to grab a towel out of the hallway cupboard, and as I do, I can't help but notice the four sets of eyes staring back at me from each open doorway of the four small bedrooms that line the far side of the house.

A million memories fly through my head. I used to be one of these kids. The need to tell them that things will get better flitters through my chest, but I can't work out if I'd be lying or not, so I don't say anything at all. I just grab my towel and keep on walking.

The shower is shit. The water pressure sucks and it's a mess from already having four kids through it this evening, but after the past two days that I've had, it's like stepping into heaven.

The hot water sails over my bruised skin, washing away the dirt under my nails while cleaning up the dried blood that's been caked all over me, allowing me for the first time to get a good look at my injuries.

My fingers massage my skin, trying to ease the pain of my exhausted muscles as the shampoo rinses from my long hair. Being conscious of the limited water supply, I end my shower about three hours sooner than I would have liked. The floor mat is damp under my feet as I wrap the thin towel around my body.

A soft knock sounds at the bathroom door before I hear Karleigh's gentle tone muffled through the wood. "Open up. I've got some fresh clothes here for you."

My gaze shifts down to my ruined, dirty clothes on the bathroom floor and I realize that I'm never going to see them again. My fingers close around the door handle and I pull it open just enough for

Karleigh's hand to slip through the gap as she thrusts a pile of clothes my way. "Make it quick," she tells me. "Your dinner is on the table."

I take the clothes from her as a joyful happiness comes through me at seeing the brand-new pair of panties sitting right on top. There's nothing better than clean underwear.

Not wanting my dinner to get cold, I rummage through the clothes, finding a pair of charcoal sweats that are about two sizes too big. I pull them up and have to fold them over at the top to keep them from falling down before squeezing into a black tank that looks like it belonged to me as a thirteen-year-old kid, but it still fits.

I twist my hair up into a bun before rubbing a little bit of moisturizing cream into my face. My gaze travels over myself, and when I realize that it's not going to get any better, I let out a sigh and step out of the bathroom, preparing myself to face the music.

Karleigh stands in her modest kitchen, my bowl of spaghetti and meatballs in her hand as she walks across to the dining table. She places it down and turns to really take me in. Her face drops as she presses her lips into a tight line, her heart on her sleeve. "Oh, sweet girl. Come and sit down, then you're going to tell me everything."

Out of habit, I do exactly what I'm told, moving across the kitchen until my ass is falling down onto the hard wooden chair. Any other time, I'd be happy to sit at her table, having a home cooked meal, but after sitting on that old bike for so long, my ass is screaming at me to get right back up again. I wouldn't dare disrespect her like that though. Karleigh deserves better.

I dig into my dinner, each bite I take somehow bigger than the last. "When was the last time you ate?" she questions as she crosses the kitchen and opens a cupboard.

I shrug my shoulders, my mouth too full to speak yet. "I don't know," I tell her after swallowing. "Maybe two days ago."

Karleigh's soft sigh is heard right across the kitchen as she grabs something from the cupboard and comes to sit down beside me. She places a small bottle of ointment down in front of her before reaching across and taking my free arm in her hands. She starts rubbing the ointment into my wounds and I hiss in pain. There's nothing worse than Karleigh playing nurse.

I scoop another spoonful of pasta into my mouth as her thumbs massage soothing circles into my sore arms. "Start talking, Winter," she insists.

I press my lips into a hard line as I turn to look at her, knowing with every ounce of my being that what gets discussed here tonight will never leave this table. "Elodie Ravenwood," I tell her, watching as her brows drop and her thumbs stop moving.

"Huh?"

"It's my name," I explain. *My real name.* I don't use it though. I still go by Winter. At least, the majority of the people in my life call me Winter," I add almost as an afterthought, thinking of the way that the name 'Ellie' was always slipping from Grayson's delicious lips.

"Elodie Ravenwood," she murmurs, trying the name out on her tongue. "Sounds fancy."

"It is," I grumble. "And so is the lifestyle that goes with it."

Karleigh focuses heavily on me, her gaze boring into mine. "Why do I feel like this isn't a good thing?"

"It's not … well … most of it isn't. I was able to find my parents."

"Oh, that's great news," she beams, her eyes wide.

I give her a blank stare. "They were brutally murdered by the very men who vowed to protect and follow them."

"Oh." Her face twists into an awkward cringe and I can't help but laugh. "You've got to look on the bright side," she continues. "At least you now know where you come from and get a good idea of the people that they once were."

"Yeah, that's the whole reason I'm in this mess in the first place." Her brows drop and I decide to put her out of her misery and lay it all out on the table. "My father, Andrew Ravenwood, was the leader of a prestigious secret society that was on the verge of corruption. They value their traditions, and when my mother gave birth to a baby girl instead of a son to carry on the leadership as my father's heir, all hell broke loose."

"Wait … wait, wait, wait. Let me just catch up. You're telling me that you're the heir of a secret society."

I nod. "And a billionaire."

Karleigh's mouth drops. "No fucking way," she breathes, making my fork pause halfway to my mouth at her rare display of foul language. Over the four years that I stayed here, I don't think I ever heard her curse once. She takes a second to right herself before leaning back in her chair. "Okay, Miss Billionaire Heiress, I'm struggling to see where your issues lie. Because to me, it sounds like you have everything a girl could need."

"You know that corruption I mentioned?" she nods and I continue. "Well, there are sixteen other families that make up Dynasty, and some of them … aren't so great. They didn't approve of my parents going against tradition and didn't approve of the leadership being handed off to a girl. There's a whole bunch of other bullshit, but basically it ended up with both of my parents being murdered and me being shipped off into foster care, but they were always watching me, always ready to strike against me, and once I turned eighteen, I was of legal age to take over my father's reign."

Her brow arches high. "So, you're now the leader of this corrupted secret society?"

"Yup."

"And these people who murdered your parents are now after you?"

"Well … they were. Most of them are dead now."

Karleigh's eyes bug out of her head. "Holy fuck," she mutters to herself, pushing back from the table and crossing the kitchen once again. She comes back with a bottle of wine and instantly takes a swig. "Did you …. did you kill somebody, Winter?"

My lips press into a hard line and she takes another swig of wine before letting her head fall into her hands. She massages her temples as she becomes deep in thought. "I'm going to go ahead and assume that was done out of self-defense," she states, not wanting a response as she comes to terms with what she's just learned.

She lets out a breath and looks back up at me, wanting to move right on with the conversation. "So, you're a big deal, huh?"

I shrug my shoulders. "I guess. Sort of."

"Okay," she says, getting comfortable. "So, if most of these bad guys are dead, then what's your problem? Why are you here looking like you've just taken a trip to hell and back?"

"Because along the way, I met four of the most incredible guys. They are lethal and dangerous, and in my own stupidity, I fell in love with each and every one of them. They had my back. They took out the threats that stood against me, and together, the five of us were finally making the changes that Dynasty desperately needed. Until two days ago when they tried to blow me up."

Karleigh just stares. "I, ummm … I don't even know what to say to that. You're in love with four different guys?"

"Seriously? That's what you took from that?"

"Well, I mean … it's certainly a strange little arrangement you've got there."

"Can we just focus on the important parts? They tried to kill me. These guys are unstoppable and they know that I'm still alive. I trusted them with everything and they betrayed me and, now they're not going to stop until I'm dead. They've shown their cards now. There's no going back."

Karleigh slides the bottle of wine to me and I take a well-needed sip. "What are you going to do?" she questions. "I'm happy to give you my couch for the night, you know that, but I have four children staying here. I can't take you in. I can't risk their lives just to save yours. I'm sorry."

I nod. "I know that, and I wouldn't expect you to. I just … I was hoping you could help me figure out what the fuck to do, because I am so fucking lost. I don't know what to think or where to go … who to trust. My head is a mess."

She leans back into her seat and looks back at me. "This Dynasty thing … what does it mean to you?"

"It's … it's my legacy. It's a part of who I am, even if it took me a really long time to realize that. It's all I have of my parents and I want to make them proud. I don't want them to have died for nothing."

"So, you don't want to lose it?"

I shake my head and she lets out a heavy sigh, taking the bottle of wine right back. "Then the way I see it, you have two choices." I sit up straighter, listening intently. "You can run away. I'll give you some cash and some clothes. Disappear into the night, change your hair, and just keep driving until you're sure they won't be able to find you and then live the best life you can possibly live."

"Or?" I prompt, knowing that running isn't an option. They will never stop searching for me. After all, there's only one true leader of Dynasty, and its people will do whatever it takes to get her back.

Karleigh's tongue rolls over her bottom lip as she focuses intently on my gaze. "Look," she says. "I don't know the kind of woman you've grown into, but the little girl that I once knew was a fighter. She used to stand out in my yard belting the crap out of a punching bag. That little girl didn't take crap from anyone. She stood up to her bullies, and she made a name for herself. She was strong and fearless, and I know that while you may be scared right now, that fearless little girl is still inside of you begging to come out. So, Miss Elodie Ravenwood, you can either run away, or you can go back there, straighten your goddamn crown, and take the reins."

"You really think I can do it?"

Karleigh nods. "Dynasty is your legacy, your rightful home, and you're going to go back there and show those fuckers what you're made of. I know you can do it because I didn't raise a quitter. And as for those four guys—make them hurt."

# CHAPTER 4

My eyes peel open into the early morning sunshine that streams through Karleigh's living room window to find four little faces staring back at me.

My body straightens.

"Ummmm … hey," I say, my groggy morning voice cracking as I speak, a reminder of how I don't do mornings well.

They just keep staring and I push up on the couch, my body aching from head to toe while my neck screams for a decent massage. It's not the first time that I've slept on this old couch, but I hope that it's the last. I could feel the springs digging into my back from every angle.

Karleigh and I sat and talked all night and she made me realize that she was right. My parents gave up everything for Dynasty, and while they maybe didn't know that at the time, I've come to realize it for them. So, I'm not going back there for myself, I'm going back to fight for my parents because they deserve it.

They didn't die in vain and I'm going to make sure of that, and just as Karleigh said, I'm going to straighten my crown and take the goddamn reins, the boys be damned. Though, first things first, the second I get home and to my laptop, I'm ordering Karleigh a brand-new couch and having it delivered stat. She couldn't possibly want to hold onto this thing. It's on its last leg. Actually, it's well past that stage.

I rub my hands over my face, dreading what I have to do today, but I'm not going to give up. I've had a home cooked meal, fresh clothes, and a hot shower. That's all I need to find myself and get back on track. It'll be a long drive home, but a girl has to do what a girl has to do.

"You snore," a voice comes from the living room floor before me. I glance up to find a little girl who somehow reminds me of myself. It must be the chip on her shoulder.

My face twists into a sneer. "Do not."

"Do too," she rushes out. "You drooled as well."

My eyes narrow and just to be sure, I glance down at the cushion that my face has been squished into for the last six hours to find a perfect round drool patch.

Fuck.

Karleigh's voice comes hollered through the kitchen. "Don't start with her, Racquel. Winter will whoop your miniature butt into next week if you push her buttons just right."

The little girl's eyes widen and I poke out my tongue just to prove a point. Her eyes narrow and before another comment can come flying out of her mouth, Karleigh calls out again. "All of you rascals, get yourselves seated at my table before breakfast gets cold. You too, Winter."

I grumble and pull myself up, following the kids as they rush out of the living room.

Bacon and eggs line the dining table and my stomach grumbles. I had plans on skipping out early to get a head start on my suicide mission, but I guess one more meal wouldn't go astray.

I sit down directly opposite Racquel just so I can press her buttons the whole way through breakfast and when we're done and cleaning up the table, a heaviness sinks into my stomach, wishing I had more time with Karleigh.

She wraps her arms around me, pulling me in tight when we finish loading the dishwasher. "Don't be a stranger," Karleigh tells me. "I'm going to spend every day worrying about you until I get the call telling me that you kicked all their bitch asses."

Loud, shocked gasps come from behind us before the kids burst into overwhelming fits of laughter at Karleigh's casual use of words they could only dream to get away with using.

"I promise," I tell her. "The second I can, I'll call, and if you don't hear from me, then you can safely assume that their bitch asses kicked mine."

"Hey," she snaps. "Last night I gave you a free pass, but no one gets away with using that kind of language in my house except for me. Is that understood? I don't care that you're all grown now. You could be a hundred years old, and I'll still see you as the distressed little nine-year-old girl who smashed my great-grandmother's glass vase when she lost her TV privileges."

My eyes widen as a cringe cuts across my lips. "You still remember that?"

She points to her temple, narrowing her eyes on me. "This thing is like a storage pit, filled with all the awful things you guys have done to me over the years. I don't forget anything. You'll do well to remember that."

I can't help but laugh and she instantly pulls me back in. "Be safe, Winter. You've come so far. I'd hate to see anything happen to you. You deserve the world."

"Thank you," I murmur. "It was great seeing you again."

"You too, sweet girl. Now get out of here before you turn me into a blubbering mess."

I pull back and give her a tight smile, hating that I have to leave my past behind again, but in order to have a future, I have no choice. I grab the key for the bike off the counter and start to make my way to the door when Racquel meets my stare and I can't help but stop. "Have you ever made Karleigh really, really mad?" I ask her.

Racquel shakes her head and a sly grin twists across my lips. "Don't even think about it, Winter," Karleigh warns.

What can I say? Old habits die hard.

I lean down to whisper in Racquel's ear, desperately holding onto the laughter that threatens to pour out. "Be careful. Once, I made her so angry, that she turned bright red and horns came out of her head. I swear, she even had a tail and a forked tongue. I think she's some kind of devil-woman."

Racquel's mouth drops as her eyes go wide, and with those few parting words, I all but skip out the front door as Karleigh's low, familiar groan sounds behind me.

Laughter bubbles out of me as I push my way out the door, feeling as though I made the right decision to come here last night. I feel empowered. I feel as though I can do anything, and I hope to God that I'm right.

I make my way around my bike, and just as I go to throw my leg over the seat a figure steps out from the shadows behind me. My head snaps around and I suck in a loud gasp.

Dante Fucking Carver.

His hands fly up, acting all innocent, and before I can even get a scream out, my fingers curl into a tight fist and I throw it forward, catching the bastard right in the jaw.

"Fuck," he grunts, his hands flying up to his face as I silently praise myself for never taking my brass knuckles off, but it's not over yet. His moment of distraction is all I need and I take the opportunity to bring my knee up and slam it right between his legs.

Pride shoots through me as I watch him crumble, doubling over in pain. I've never been able to get the drop on Carver. Maybe things really are starting to look up for me.

His pained groans sound through Karleigh's front yard, but I'm not about to hang back and check that he's alright. I need to get the fuck out of here.

I throw my leg over the bike and all but slam the key into the ignition before twisting it as fast as I can, only nothing happens. The bike just dies.

I try again and again, my desperation quickly catching up to me as I spy Carver out of the corner of my eye getting back to his feet. "Do you really think I'm stupid enough to let you get away twice?" he grumbles, the pain still clear in his tone, though I'm not surprised. His balls are probably up in his throat right about now.

Seeing no other options, I throw myself off the bike and go to run but his thick fingers curl around my wrist like a vice. "Sorry, baby. You're not going anywhere."

I pull against him, tugging as hard as I can, but he's too strong, even with his injury slowing him down. "FUCK. LET ME GO, ASSHOLE."

Carver yanks hard on my wrist and I fall back into him. He catches me around my waist and holds tight, keeping my back pressed up against his strong chest. "Would you stop fucking pushing me away. I'm not going to hurt you."

"Forgive me if I don't believe you," I spit, ignoring that familiar, manly scent that wraps around me and breaks my heart all at the same time. "After all, you and your asshole friends tried to blow me up two nights ago."

"If you stopped fucking squirming and give me a second, I could explain it to you."

I laugh, clawing at his arm around my waist. "Right. Like any bullshit excuse you throw at me is supposed to make any of this okay. I don't fucking trust you, Carver. I'll never trust you again. Any of you."

"Stop Winter. You're drawing attention," he growls in my ear.

"What's the matter?" I spit. "Scared your little plan is going to shit itself?"

I slam my ass back into his groin and he crumbles again, the low groan in his throat almost enticing me to forgive him and jump his fucking bones. He doesn't dare release his hold on me, and if anything, it gets impossibly tighter.

"FUCK," he roars. "I get it, okay. I fucking get it. I deserve it. I know that, but seriously? Why the fucking balls? Anything but the balls. I swear, once I get you home, I'll let you do whatever the fuck you want to me, but LEAVE MY FUCKING BALLS OUT OF IT."

I try to fight out of his hold, doing anything and everything I can possibly think of, but he's too fucking strong. "You're stupider than I thought if you think I'm about to go anywhere with you. YOU TRIED TO BLOW ME UP."

"Would you just … FUCK. STOP. I know it's hard for you to see around your own big fucking head, but this is bigger than you. I've already told you that, I need a second to explain why we did what we did, so either peacefully get your ass inside the car, or I'll fucking make you. What's it going to be?"

"Neither, asshole. I'm your fucking leader and I'm demanding that you let me go."

Carver laughs. "Seriously? You think that bullshit is going to work on me? I'm not one of those family heads who's going to drop to my knees at your feet. You know that. You're being a fucking brat. Get in the car."

I let out a breath, trying to calm myself before I take another cheap shot at his balls. "You tried to blow me up," I say, lowering my tone. "I can't forgive that. I won't. The four of you broke my trust. You betrayed me. You told me that you would always keep me safe, always protect me. It was all lies."

"I swear to you," he murmurs, his face lowering beside mine until his lips are right beside my ear. His hold loosens around my waist until it's more like a caress rather than a steel vice. "I fucking love you, Winter. I would never have done that unless I had to. Please, just let me get you out of here and we can go somewhere to talk. There's more going on than you know."

I turn in his arms, letting him see the clear betrayal in my eyes, but more so I can see what's reflected in his. "I don't trust you. Any of you."

He nods, not removing his arm from around my waist. "I know and I'll do anything it takes to earn that trust back, but right now, I'm your only shot at staying alive. So, whether you trust me or not, you're coming with me."

I clench my jaw and raise a brow. "You must think I'm such an idiot. Do you honestly think I'm going to let you play me like that? Get me nice and close just to give you another shot at taking my life? Yeah, fucking right," I say, placing my hand against his arm around my waist and giving it a hard shove until it finally falls away. "I'll find my own way home, and when I do, the four of you better be fucking ready, because I'm coming for you and I won't stop until I have each of you begging for your lives."

Hurt flashes in Carver's dark eyes and I have to brace myself to keep from bawling like a fucking toddler having a tantrum. He steps into me and I back up. "I fucking hope that you hold us accountable," he mutters, matching each of my steps with one of his own, stalking me like a proud lion, "and I fucking hope that you make it hurt. I hate what we've had to put you through, but right fucking now, this bullshit between us isn't working for me."

Without warning, Carver reaches out and grabs me, his strength knowing no bounds. He throws me over his thick shoulder as I squirm for freedom. I belt my hands against his back, but it's as though I'm swatting a fly.

He takes off at a run, darting back behind the property before launching himself over Karleigh's back fence. "WHAT THE ACTUAL FUCK DO YOU THINK YOU'RE DOING? PUT ME DOWN, RIGHT FUCKING NOW, DANTE CARVER. YOU'RE GOING TO DROP ME."

Carver's only response is to spank my ass which only makes me want to nut punch him again.

He darts through the neighboring properties until he gets to an empty street and aims for a black SUV that sits on the lonely road. He reaches the car and I'm pulled off his shoulder only to be pinned between his ripped body and the side panel of the door.

Carver reaches around me and opens the back door before leaning in and grabbing a roll of fucking duct tape. "No," I demand, shaking my head. "Don't you fucking dare."

"Sorry, babe," he says, wrestling against my hold until he has both of my wrists securely in his big hand. "Just remember that this is for your own good." And just like that, the bastard starts binding my hands together.

"I hate you," I mutter as he twists the duct tape around my wrists, making sure that I won't be able to break free.

"I know," he tells me. "But a part of you still loves me, and until you can honestly tell me that you don't, I'm not going anywhere."

"I don't."

"You're a terrible liar, Winter."

I just glare, and not a second later, he starts to bind my ankles as well. When he straightens up, he meets my eyes, and for good measure, he presses a piece of tape over my mouth so that I can't spend the next few hours ranting and raging at him.

Carver scoops me off the side of the car and all but tosses me across the back seat. The door slams behind him, a door that I'm sure has the child lock on, and all I can do is shoot daggers his way as I watch him walk around to the driver's door.

He climbs in and looks back at me, double checking that I haven't managed to escape in the last three seconds.

"Fucking asshole," I spit, only with the tape, it comes out more like 'Mufking nastoll.'

"I'm sorry, babe," he tells me as the engine roars to life. "It'll all make sense soon enough." And just like that, Carver takes off like a rocket, leaving Santa DeClara behind and along with it, all my hopes and dreams of having any kind of future.

# CHAPTER 5

Carver hits a bump and my head rebounds off the backseat, forcing a low groan to travel up my throat. "Shit," he laughs from the front. "I didn't mean to actually hit that one, but the last three ... yeah, consider them payback for making me spend the night in the fucking woods. I swear, I fell asleep in a fucking ant's nest. The little fuckers were crawling over me all night."

I clench my jaw, not impressed with his bullshit commentary in the least. We've been driving for less than two hours and the fucker just won't shut up. It's as though he's getting some kind of sick, twisted enjoyment out of this. Though, why wouldn't he? Our whole relationship has been a lie. I bet he's been waiting for this day since the second I showed my face in Ravenwood Heights.

His phone rings on the front passenger seat and he reaches across to grab it, glancing down at the name that flashes up on the screen. "About fucking time," he grunts, placing the phone down on his lap and hitting speakerphone. "I've been trying to call you for the past two hours. Where the fuck have you been?"

King's deep tone tears through the phone. "Chill the fuck out man. We've been making funeral arrangements with Cruz's mom. She's going all fucking out, but she's a mess. It's too fucking much for her to handle."

Funeral? What the fuck? They don't mean *my funeral,* do they? Fucking hell. I'm not even dead yet and they're already making plans. Unless something else went down while I was away.

"Are you fucking kidding me?" Carver roars, the anger in his tone speaking volumes. "Why the fuck are you wasting time on that shit? That's not important. You should be spending every fucking second searching for them."

There's a slight scuffle through the phone before Grayson's familiar roar breaks through the small SUV. "We fucking are but if we're not acting the part, they won't buy it. Every minute wasted is another minute that they're gone. Just focus on finding Ellie and leave us the fuck alone to do what we have to do. I should have been the one to stay. I never would have let her get away."

Fuck me.

Anger bubbles deep inside of me. How can they just talk about it so easily, as though what they did means absolutely nothing? They tried to blow me the fuck up and now they're acting as though it was as easy as picking out their favorite dish.

I start rubbing my face against the leather seat of the SUV, trying to be discreet as the duct tape slowly peels back off my face. I cringe and moan, hating how obvious I'm being but fuck Carver. I don't care if he knows. He'd be stupid to assume that I wouldn't try anything.

"Come on, bro," I hear Cruz mutter, his voice softer and further away, making my heart break all over again. I think his betrayal was the worst. "We're all fucking stressed. You know Winter, she would have put up a big fucking fight. She would have made it hell for him."

"Too fucking right," Carver murmurs as he glances back at me, his eyes narrowing on the duct tape that's nearly off my face. "She had me jumping through fucking hoops, but I found her this morning. That's why I'm calling. She's in the back being as fucking stubborn as ever."

I scoff. What the fuck was he expecting?

"My girl is there?" Cruz asks, his voice a little louder as if he had stolen the phone right out of Grayson's hands. "Is she alright? Why hasn't she been cursing us out this whole time? Babe, are you there? Let me explain... it's just ..."

I scoff to myself. *His girl?* It'll be a cold day in hell when I'll be his girl ever again.

Carver just laughs, cutting him off and I watch as his eyes sparkle through the rearview mirror. "She's uhhhhh ... she's a little tied up right now."

"Fucking hell, man," King interjects, with an irritated sigh. "What the fuck did you do?"

"I did what I had to do. She wasn't going to come easily," he explains. "She's a fucking fire cracker, you know that, but she's safe.

I'm going to take her somewhere and try to ... explain what's been going down, that's assuming she lets me."

"Why wouldn't she?"

The tape finally comes free and I screech out, my anger knowing no bounds. "Because you fuckheads tried to blow me up. Are you fucking kidding me? I hate you. All of you can go to hell and suck my fucking dick while you're at it. You're not going to get away with this. I'm going to fuck you all up. I trusted you and you all fucking betrayed me, but never again."

"Babe, come on. I swear to you, if there was another way ..." Cruz says, trailing off, the hurt in his voice almost enough to have me taking back every word I said, but fuck him. His bullshit isn't going to work on me this time. I won't ever fall for that crap again. Any of their crap.

Carver glances back at me with unease in his eyes and before I get a chance to tell Cruz to go to hell, he cuts me off, his deep voice filling the cab. "Gotta go," he says as I bring my bound wrists up to my mouth and start gnawing at the thick tape. "I'll let you guys know what's going down once I have a plan."

I groan low, pulling my hands away for a brief second. "If you're going to fucking kill me, just get it over and done with. I'm done playing your bullshit games."

Carver's gaze shifts to mine in the rearview mirror. He rolls his eyes as though my little outburst is below him, and that one look has the anger building up inside me once again.

I don't fucking hesitate.

I throw myself up onto the seat and without a second of warning,

I loop my bound wrists over his head and bring them down around his neck. I pull tight, giving it everything I have as I press his throat into the back of his seat. "I fucking hate you, Dante Carver. You're just like your father. Corrupted, sick, and twisted."

The asshole has the audacity to laugh as I try to choke him. "Are you done?" he questions, his Adam's apple bobbing up and down over my wrists. His hand comes up and with a quick flick, his fingers break straight through the duct tape at my wrists and the momentum of suddenly being free as I pull back against his throat has me falling back into the seat, sprawling out across the soft leather with a loud oomph.

His laugh infuriates me more.

"What the fuck is wrong with you?" I screech, quickly trying to right myself. "Do you really think this is funny? Haven't you humiliated me enough?"

"Babe," he chuckles. "You're humiliating yourself enough on your own, you don't need my help."

My gaze narrows as I reach across to try the door handle, only to get absolutely nowhere. Though what the hell was I going to do if it opened? Roll out onto the middle of the highway while traveling a million miles an hour? Yeah, fuck that. I know I have a bad habit of being reckless, but that's even pushing it for me. Though, the road rash and a few broken bones might be worth it just to get away from Carver.

I fall back against the seat, my arms crossed over my chest as I feel my inevitable end creeping closer and closer with absolutely no way out. "Fuck you," I snap, hating just how easily he was able to put me right back under his hold.

Carver sighs and pulls off the side of the road and into the parking lot of a small diner. The SUV comes to a stop out front and it takes me all of two seconds to realize just how secluded this place is. There are only two other cars in the lot and I can guarantee that one of them belongs to the cook while the other is most likely the underpaid waitress who probably wishes she could be anywhere but here.

"Wow," I say, glancing through the front windshield at the dodgy diner. "What a perfect place to finally take me out. You've always been one for theatrics. How do you want to do this? Do you want me to try and escape so you can get a kick out of chasing me through the kitchen with a knife, or are you just going to go with an old-school bullet through the head at the counter trick?"

Carver turns around, a heavy scowl on his face. "Shut the fuck up with the dramatics. I'm not going to fucking kill you. I stopped so we could get some lunch. After all, you need to have energy if you're going to bitch and whine at me for the rest of the day."

"You're such an ass."

"Don't act so surprised," he mutters, cutting the engine and pushing out the door. I watch as he walks around to the back passenger door and pulls it wide. Carver reaches into the car and grabs my ankles, tearing them up onto the backseat and smirking to himself as the momentum has my body flying back against the chair.

"The fuck do you think you're doing?" I spit, trying to pull my legs free and sit back up at the same time, but Carver's grip is too strong and instead I just end up looking like a fish out of water, flopping around on the back seat of the expensive car.

Carver scoffs at my performance and pulls a knife from … I don't know where, and for a slight moment, my heart sinks. This is it. I'm going to be killed in the backseat of a stolen SUV … at least, I assume it's stolen.

If I knew this is how I was going to go, maybe I would have stayed back at King's cabin and allowed myself to perish in the explosion. At least that's a better story than this shit.

"Would you hold still?" Carver snaps. "I don't want to cut you."

I pause, my brow raising. "You don't want to cut me, yet you have absolutely no issue trying to blow me up? Holy shit, Carver, do you ever hear yourself? I always knew you were fucked in the head, but I didn't realize that you were that stupid."

Carver just groans and presses his weight down over me, seeing as I refuse to keep still on my own. The tip of the blade lowers toward me and in one smooth flick of his wrist, the knife slices straight through the remainder of the tape.

Carver climbs off me and I stare at him in confusion.

What the fuck is going on here?

"Come on," he mutters, stepping away from the open door to allow me space. "We're going to go inside, order some burgers, and talk."

My brows furrow as I scoot closer to the open door while trying to peer around him for some kind of escape. "Talk?"

"Yes. Talk," he states, rolling his beautiful dark eyes. "There are a few things that clearly need to be discussed, and my hopes are to do that without you trying to make a run for it or stab me in the eye with your fork. I just want to eat and talk."

The very second the word 'eat' pours out of his mouth, my stomach grumbles and I know that I won't be able to resist. I glance over his shoulder, getting a good look at our surroundings. The diner is secluded, and the fact that we're in a near empty lot with nothing else around us tells me that I'm completely fucked. I won't be able to run anywhere without him catching me first.

I let out a sigh and move out into the fresh air, watching the way Carver hovers close by my side. "Fine. We'll eat, but don't expect me to play the role of your doting girlfriend. If I see an out while I'm in there, I'm taking it. I'm more than happy to leave your bitch ass behind."

"Jesus Christ," he murmurs, placing a hand on my lower back and leading me toward the diner. "Why does everything have to be so dramatic with you? Just sit your ass down in the booth and let me feed you so we can talk without your bullshit attitude."

I scoff, hating the feel of his hand on my back. "Put yourself in my shoes, Carver. Imagine if the boys tried to fucking kill you and it came out of nowhere."

He shakes his head. "They wouldn't. We're family."

"Yeah," I mutter. "Up until two days ago, I thought the same fucking thing."

Carver grips my wrist and spins me so fucking fast that I barely have a chance to gasp before my back is slammed up against the glass window of the diner and his fury is bearing down on me. "Don't you fucking say that," he roars. "You know they would lay their lives down for you."

"Then tell me that they had nothing to do with that fucking bomb. Tell me King didn't set it, that they didn't just turn their backs and drive away while my body was catapulted through the air. They betrayed me. You betrayed me. You're not my family anymore. You're as bad as Paris."

His hand snaps around my throat and he pushes me back into the window even harder, yet for some reason, I know he won't kill me. "We did what we had to fucking do to save your stupid ass. Don't you confuse that with betrayal. We're nothing like Paris."

My brows furrow and my hands slam against his chest, forcing him back a step. And while my strength is no match for his, I'm grateful when he actually releases my throat and backs up. "What do you mean you had to do it to save me? We were safe in the cabin. That's why we were there. The guys chasing us were all dead. We were fine."

Carver presses his hands to his temple and steps back again, turning his back on me as he stares out at the empty lot. "FUCK," he roars in despair, his anger bubbling up inside of him and getting the better of him. He turns back and the pain in his eyes is enough to have me falling back against the window again. "You weren't fucking safe. None of them were."

"That's bullshit. I was always safe with you guys," I demand. "What the hell are you talking about?"

Carver sighs and his hands fall to his sides as he steps in close to me. His hands find their favorite position on my waist as his forehead drops to my shoulder. "The car chase, the shooting, the fucking raid on your house, it was all a distraction. Paris knew we were never going to let her get close to you again, so she devised a sick fucking plan to get us all out of Ravenwood Heights, and we fell straight into her damn trap."

I shake my head, my hand pressing against his chest to feel his heart racing. Despite how much I want to hate him, I just can't. He draws me in. His pain is like a beacon screaming my name. "What happened?" I breathe, the fear rising up in my chest. Anything that could have a man like Dante Carver breaking has to be bad … so fucking bad.

He takes a deep breath and pulls back as his hand falls from my waist and digs into his pocket. He pulls out his phone and turns it to face me. "Right after we walked out of the cabin to do the perimeter search, all four of us got this exact same message."

My brows furrow as I take the phone from him and glance down at the screen to find all seven of the boys' siblings held in a dark and dirty room. Their eyes are blindfolded and their precious little mouths gagged with rope as they sit in straight back chairs all in a line, their wrists and ankles strapped down to keep them from running.

A sharp gasp tears from within me as my hand flies to my mouth. Carver's little sisters are only seven and nine, and despite the blindfolds that cover most of their faces, their fear is as clear as day. Cruz's brothers are a little older and look as though they're trying to be brave for the rest of them, but it's not working. They're scared for their lives, and they should be. Paris isn't the kind to willingly spare them. She'll kill each of them just to teach the boys a lesson.

King's brother and sister, Caitlin and Cody sit side by side, their pinky fingers interlocked as they desperately try to hold onto hope. They're only six. They shouldn't be facing this, especially Caitlin who's still healing from the explosion during the ball.

This isn't fair.

Grayson's little brother has his face turned and it's impossible to make out what he's feeling, but I have a pretty good guess. He's older than the rest, maybe fifteen or sixteen, and I don't doubt that he's heard the whispers going around about Paris Moustaff. They all know they're in danger, but he's the only one who would know just how much.

I read the caption below the photo.

*'Either she dies or they do. Take your pick.'*

I shake my head, unable to believe what I'm seeing. "We have to do something," I say, tears instantly staining my cheeks.

"We are doing something," he insists, the intensity in his eyes urging me to hurry up and realize that. "We faked your death. The second we saw you race out of the cabin, we blew it up. We had no fucking choice. We did what we had to do to save them, and I'm so fucking sorry that we lost your trust in the process, but I'd do it a million times over if it means saving my little sisters."

I stare up at him, my mind twisting and turning with all this information. "I ... I don't even know what to say. Did you ... Are they safe?"

Carver shakes his head. "She didn't fucking release them. She wants your fucking body as proof."

My heart shatters and in a split second, I know what I have to do.

I step into Carver and raise my chin to press a kiss against his cheek, the rage and betrayal that sits heavily inside my chest quickly fading away. Reaching around him, I grip the gun that rests in the back of his jeans and press it into his hands. "It's okay," I tell him, the tears welling faster and faster in my eyes. "Just promise me that you'll make it quick. They come first. Save your sisters."

# CHAPTER 6

"The fuck is wrong with you?" Carver snaps, snatching the gun far away from me and tucking it back into the waistband of his jeans. "No one is fucking dying, especially not you. Paris isn't going to win like that."

"You have no choice," I remind him. "She needs my dead body, otherwise all your siblings are as good as dead. Don't pretend like you don't know that."

"You don't think that's the only fucking thought that's gone through my head for the past forty-eight hours? It's not an option. You are my family now."

I shake my head, seeing no other way around it. "Then what the hell are you going to do? Chasing me through the fucking woods for two days isn't helping anyone."

"Chasing you through the woods meant that you were running in the opposite fucking direction of Ravenwood Heights, and the longer she thinks that you're dead, the greater chance we have of getting each of them back alive. So yeah, chasing you through the woods is helping everyone."

Carver grabs my wrist and tugs it hard, pulling me toward the entrance of the diner as he lets out a frustrated groan. "Come on," he snaps. "I said we're stopping to eat and talk and that's exactly what we're going to do."

I hurry along, sure that if I were to stop, he'd probably just tug my whole fucking hand right off my body. We walk through the dirty glass door and head straight for the counter. Carver sits first and I slide into the space beside him as he looks up at the young waitress who eats him up with her sultry gaze. "We'll take two burgers with fries," he tells her, not noticing the way she eye-fucks him with every chance she gets.

I settle in beside him and he takes my hand, slowly rubbing his thumb across the top of my knuckles. "I'm sorry," he murmurs once the waitress scurries off to put in our order. "You don't know how fucking badly I wish that we could have done things differently, but we had a split second to make a decision and we went with the one that would guarantee you staying away."

I shake my head. "You could have told me and I would have gone. I could have hid out in a run-down hotel until it was safe to come home."

Carver squeezes my hand, his eyes expressing what he refuses to say out loud. "But you wouldn't have," he murmurs, his voice lowering to a near whisper as he meets my eyes with a knowing, broken stare. "You would have come storming back into Ravenwood Heights with a fucking vengeance, demanding retribution. You're reckless, and while most of the time I absolutely love that fearlessness about you, it would have fucked us all this time. We had to keep you out of it. Dynasty needed to see the real guilt and self-loathing on the boys' faces when they returned without us. They needed to buy the lie that we both perished in that explosion, and Paris needed to see the fear in yours when you were left behind and the boys blew the cabin."

"What do you mean she needed to see it? Were you recording it, like her own private snuff film of me being blown to pieces?"

Guilt twists over his face as he slowly nods. "Gray was to film it and send it to Paris as proof of death, but it wasn't enough for her. She wants to feel your lifeless body in her hands."

I shake my head, my gaze on the table for a long, drawn out moment. A sigh pulls from my lips. "So, what now?"

Carver shrugs his shoulders. "I don't know," he says, the raw honesty in his tone crippling my will to go on. "The boys have been working on tracking them and are planning a raid. They're ready to go at a moment's notice, but so far, we've got nothing. Paris has done a pretty fucking good job at keeping herself hidden. Anything that could have traced their location was removed and destroyed. So at the moment, all we've fucking got is that damn picture."

I throw myself to my feet and start pacing behind him, my head a complete mess. "We have to do something. We can't just sit here and wait. I mean … fuck. How are you just sitting here?"

"We have no choice," he reminds me. "One of us had to stay back and watch over you. Who fucking knows if Paris had her men out in those woods as well. Just because she's got all of our siblings doesn't mean that you're miraculously not a target anymore. You'll keep being a target until we can show her proof of death, but that's never going to happen. She'll always be after you."

"Yeah … until I put a fucking bullet in her head," I mutter under my breath, meeting his heavy stare with one of my own. "Why you? Why'd you pull the short straw and have to stay back to look after the untrustworthy train-wreck?"

Carver stands and presses into me, hating my conclusion of how they see me, but responding nonetheless. "Because I'm the one who has nothing to lose, no one to mourn for me, no one to grieve when they learn of my death. The boys … their families are already going through so much having just lost their children to a woman like Paris. Me staying behind, it causes the least damage."

My chin raises. "You're wrong about that," I murmur. "The whole fucking world would mourn if it lost you."

Carver watches me for a long tension-filled moment before letting out a heavy sigh just as our burgers and fries are placed down on the counter. "Come on," Carver says, scooting back into his seat and patting the space beside him. "Sit your ass down and eat. There's nothing for us to do. We've done our part and now we have to trust the boys to do theirs."

I reluctantly take my seat, feeling as though the past two days have been a colossal waste of time. The boys should have been upfront and honest about the plan. I would have done anything it took to help get their brothers and sisters back, but the fact that they thought my recklessness was going to destroy their plans, that really fucking hurts.

My stomach rumbles as I take my first bite of my burger and my eyes close in satisfaction. All this running has certainly worked up my appetite, but I didn't realize just how hungry I was until this very moment. I've been focusing on bigger things, things that are now proving to be something completely different.

Within seconds, my burger is gone and I start picking at my fries knowing that I'll get a stomachache from eating so fast, but I can't seem to care. I'll deal with it later, as for now, there are far too many questions plaguing my mind.

"How did you find me this morning?" I ask, glancing across at Carver who hasn't stopped watching me. "I thought I was being pretty fucking smart going to Karleigh's place."

A soft smile pulls up the corners of Carver's lips. "Don't get me wrong, going to Karleigh's place was a good idea. You were safe there. You got fed, were given clean clothes, a shower, and somewhere to sleep that wasn't full of fucking ants biting your goddamn ass, but if the aim was to go somewhere I couldn't find you, then yeah … your plan sucked. Before coming to Ravenwood Heights, Santa DeClara was the one town where you were happy. Checking Karleigh's place was my first thought and it paid off."

I let out a defeated sigh, only now just realizing how well the boys know me. Fuck, I think they know me better than I know myself.

My gaze drops back to my plate and I start pushing my fries through my ketchup. "I think once I get back to Ravenwood Heights and all this bullshit blows over, I'd like to do something for Karleigh. She's got it rough and I have all these resources at my fingertips that could help her out. She did so much for me, and I was just an ungrateful kid who didn't know better, but now … I don't know. I want to thank her for giving me a home when I had nothing."

Carver's hand falls over my shoulder and he pulls me in before pressing a soft kiss to my temple. "I think that's a great idea," he tells me, but I quickly pull out of his hold, not ready to fall back into the same old patterns. What the boys did to me was unforgivable, and while I now understand why they did it, it's going to take a minute to be able to move past it, and as usual, Carver doesn't miss a goddamn thing.

His gaze drops and the tiny sliver of hope quickly burns out. "I'm sorry," he whispers, turning to face me better while doing everything he can to avoid my hard stare, though I'm not surprised, apologies aren't exactly Carver's strong point. They're like two ends of a magnet always pulling away from each other. "I fucking hate that we did that to you, and believe me, the guys are feeling it too, especially Cruz. Betraying your trust like that … it's not something we're taking lightly. We know we fucked up and we'll do everything we can to make up for it, but I won't apologize for doing what I had to do to try and save my sisters."

"I know," I whisper. "I'm not looking for an apology. I understand why you did what you did, all of you. But it doesn't take away the hurt of watching the SUV drive away from me. The cabin was up in flames and I was waiting for you guys to realize and turn back for me, but you never did. That was the worst part, realizing that you guys had tried to kill me, that I put my trust in the wrong people."

"But you didn't," he urges, grabbing both of my hands and staring deep into my eyes, his desperation to win me over knowing no bounds. "We didn't try to kill you. We knew you were safe, we watched you come running out of the cabin before we blew it, and I stayed behind to watch over you. We knew you were going to be okay. You have to know that."

"I get that," I snap back at him, stealing my hands back. "But it doesn't hurt any less."

I stand and let out a frustrated sigh and my hands start pumping at my side, our conversation quickly working me up. I start pacing once again, moving back and forth behind Carver as he watches me with caution, each step I take being monitored as though I'm about to break, but honestly, I kinda feel like I am.

The more I think about it, the harder it gets and my control quickly starts to slip.

They betrayed me. They blew up the cabin even though I was standing right in front of it. They took off as though nothing happened. They let Carver stalk me through the woods with no explanation in the hopes of keeping me scared and away. But what hurts the most is that they kept me out of it. We were supposed to be a family. They were the loves of my life and they so easily kept this from me. Their little brothers and sisters are in danger and instead of coming to me to explain the situation, they made shitty decisions that are going to stay with me the rest of my life.

They didn't trust me to be able to help them get their family back and that one tiny piece of knowledge tears me apart from the inside out.

My pacing gets faster as my strides get longer and soon enough, I'm practically storming up and down the length of the diner. I'm on my eighth lap before I notice my huffing is so loud that the dude cooking the amazing burgers in the kitchen can hear me. My hands ball into fists again, pissed off with myself for not being able to control my emotions.

Maybe the guys were right not to trust me with saving their siblings. I probably would have fucked it up.

I storm right out the glass door and toward the SUV, my fists so tight that my brass knuckles hurt around my fingers. I just need to … fuck. I need to get it out. I need to …

"WINTER!"

I spin around to find Carver flying toward me, his brows drawn in concern. "You good?" he asks, moving in closer. Only with every step he takes, the realization gets clearer.

I shake my head and clench my jaw, desperately wishing I could drop to my knees and scream until all of it goes away. I don't say a damn word, but I don't need to. Carver has always been able to read me so clearly.

Without skipping a beat, he takes my hand and pulls me toward the side of the diner, away from the prying eyes inside. He comes to a stop and I stare up at him in confusion until he pulls off his shirt and stands before me with his arms out wide. "Give it your best shot."

My eyes narrow and I slowly begin to shake my head. "Are you insane?" I demand, my lips pulling up in a confused sneer. I'm too fucking worked up to play his stupid games right now. "I'm not going to hit you. I just … I need …"

"You need to fucking hit something, so what the hell are you waiting for? I'm standing right here. Let's get it over and done with so we can get out of here."

"Despite the fact that you tried to blow me up, I don't want to hurt you."

Carver scoffs and I roll my eyes, knowing exactly what his scoff was for—the asshole doesn't think I'm capable of hurting him. "Come on, Winter," he says, his voice dropping low. "I know you don't want to hurt me because even though you're desperately trying not to feel it right now, you still fucking love me, and despite the hell you've put me through over the past two days, I'm still madly in love with you, which is exactly why I need you to do this."

"That doesn't make any sense."

"Sure it does," he mutters, taking my hand and folding it into a tight fist. "Every fucking minute of every fucking hour all I can think about is that cabin blowing up and your fragile little body flying through the sky. I have to live with myself knowing that I had a part in that, knowing that my selfish need to put my sisters' safety above yours nearly cost you your life. You and I are too fucking stubborn. We'll never get past this unless we force ourselves to do it. So here I am, in the flesh. You need this, and God knows I fucking deserve it."

I let out a heavy breath and clench my jaw as I stare up at him. "Such a fucking martyr."

"It's a win-win situation, Winter. We're both going to get what we need. We can't lose."

"I could slip and knee you in the balls again," I mutter, the idea sounding better and better by the second.

"Okay," he says, taking a slight step back. "In that case, let's set some ground rules."

I roll my eyes and stare up at him, hating that it has come to this, but I should have seen it coming. Carver is the king of self-loathing. He will find any excuse to blame himself for shit that was out of his control, then he'll punish himself for years just to prove something, but in my experience, it's usually something stupid. Hell, I'm sure he still hasn't forgiven himself for accidentally shooting me, but as usual, it was out of his control. "Go on then," I say, unable to resist the allure of releasing this wild rage building within me.

He gives me a hard stare. "Balls are out of bounds. They've already suffered enough for one day."

I groan, the devastation all too real. "Anything else?"

He shrugs. "I mean, my face is pretty fucking gorgeous. It'd be a shame to mess it up."

"Right," I say, raising my hand and starting to pull off my brass knuckles. "Got it. I'll aim for the heart."

Carver stops me, placing his hand over mine and pushing my brass knuckles back into place. "Leave them," he tells me, the darkness in his eyes shining brighter than ever before.

I watch him for a second. "You have some pretty fucked up demons living inside of you."

"You don't know the half of it," he mutters under his breath, standing tall and nodding at me, letting me know he's ready whenever I am.

I save his comment for another time and let out a shaky breath. I don't know how something so incredibly wrong can feel so right at the same time. There's always been an understanding between Carver and me, and though this isn't the first time he's offered his body as a punching bag, our relationship has changed so much since then. "It's not too late to change your mind."

He shakes his head as a soft glimmer of excitement sparkles in his dark eyes. "Do your fucking worst, babe."

I don't hesitate, rearing back and letting my fist fly free.

I give it all I've got, letting out every frustration as I slam my fists into his chest and abs over and over again. I avoid his ribs at all costs despite knowing that, with the thick layer of muscles protecting his body, I probably won't be able to do any real damage, but I'm not taking any chances.

My breath comes in short, hard pants as I let it all out and with each punch, the built up frustration inside of me slowly begins to ease. Carver's torso turns an angry shade of red, but he doesn't flinch once, not even when my brass knuckles slam against his chest and the hard metal pinches against his beautiful sun-kissed skin. Instead, he simply reminds me to correct my form and not bother him with lousy punches.

His jaw clenches and his eyes close, taking and accepting each one of my blows, and as the minutes drag on, my punches lose momentum.

I stumble back as it all becomes too much and catch myself against my knees, breathing heavily as I try to gain control. "Holy shit," I pant, glancing up. "Are you alright?"

Carver's face twists as though he doesn't understand the question then simply tugs his shirt out of his pocket and pulls it over his head. "You good now or do you need to scream behind the dumpster while I pretend not to hear you?"

I roll my eyes and mutter a string of curses under my breath as I follow Carver back around to the SUV. "I'm good," I finally tell him. "I'm still pissed off and the moment I see them, I'm fully prepared to pull their testicles out through their eyeballs and feed them to each other in a fancy salad with Italian dressing."

Carver arches a brow as he glances my way. "That … uhhh. That was oddly specific."

I shrug my shoulders, more than proud of the plan that's been swirling around my brain since lying on the cold ground in the woods. "Yeah, well I've had a lot of time to think about revenge over the past few days."

"Did you come up with anything solid?"

I smirk and glance across at him just before he opens the driver's door and sinks down into the SUV. "You're not ready to hear about those plans yet. I think I'll keep them locked away until you all fuck up again. After all, it's inevitable."

"Trust me, babe," he mutters as I drop down in the passenger seat beside him. He starts the engine and glances at me as he reverses out of his parking space. "I won't be fucking up like that ever again, especially where you're involved."

I look out the window, the heaviness creeping back into my soul. "You also told me that you'd never hurt me and always keep me safe, but look how that turned out."

Carver sighs and I know he must feel that right down in his gut, but he'll never admit it. So instead, he focuses his attention on the highway, speeding down the road with absolutely no destination in mind.

Twenty minutes pass when my eyes start getting heavy and I notice Carver out the corner of my eyes, gently rubbing at his chest. It was never my intention to actually hurt him while I was busy losing control and using him as a punching bag, but I'm not going to lie, after everything the guys have put me through, knowing that I was at least able to make him think twice about allowing me to do that again has the satisfaction swelling deep inside me.

"How does it feel getting beat up by a girl?" I ask, side-eyeing him and letting him see the proud smugness pouring out of me.

Carver scoffs and quickly moves his hand away from his chest. "What? That?" he chuckles, the amusement pouring out of him in waves. "That's not my version of getting beat up. That was the equivalent of letting a little rabbit have a tantrum on my chest."

A cocky grin rests across his stupid lips and the wider it gets, the narrower my eyes become. He glances my way, laughing at his own stupid wit and seeing the fresh hell building in my eyes, he quickly darts the SUV off the side of the road and brings the car to a stop just in time for me to launch myself at him, determined to show him exactly what it means to get beat up by a girl.

# CHAPTER 7

Flames spread through the cabin, licking up the walls and getting hotter by the second, trapping me inside with absolutely no escape. I run from room to room, banging on the windows, trying to break my way out, but it's no use.

I'm going to die here today.

My heart thunders in my chest, the fear becoming all too real. I need to get out before I'm roasted like a marshmallow over a campfire.

The ticking continues and I flick my gaze back to the explosives that sit in the very center of the living room, directly in the center of the cabin. It tells me there's only thirty seconds left before it takes my life and there's not a damn thing I can do about it.

Twenty-nine.

Twenty-eight.

Damn it. What do I do? I need to get out of here. I don't want to die like this. I wasn't supposed to die here. I was supposed to have a long happy life with the boys, getting dicked every second of the day. This isn't how my story is supposed to end.

I race through the kitchen and start searching through the drawers, desperate to find something to break through the solid windows, the soft ticking of the bomb somehow following me from room to room, even over the sound of the flames overtaking the cabin.

I scramble through the drawers, not finding anything that will help. It's all plastic utensils and tea towels. Nothing that can help. The panic sets in full force and I grab the espresso machine off the counter and launch it at the window, only for it to rebound back at me, breaking into a million pieces on the hot floorboards.

I should jump away from the wreckage, but I'm too caught up in the images I see out the window. The four boys stand by an SUV, pointing and laughing at my misery. They did this to me. How could they? I trusted them. I loved them.

Grayson holds a phone, capturing my demise for the world to see while King wears that normal hard expression, but the smugness in his eyes speaks volumes. Cruz though, he really breaks my heart, the way he howls with laughter as though watching me die is the best damn entertainment he's ever had. But where's Carver? He was just here a second ago, but now he's gone.

The soft ticking continues and I put the boys to the back of my mind, doing everything in my power to forget them as I race back into the living room. My gaze shifts toward the bomb.

Fuck. Eight seconds left.

I wasted too much time in the kitchen.

Tick. Tick. Tick.

I'm out of time. All I can do is try to save myself when the bomb goes off. It's inevitable. I'm all out of options.

I scan the room, the ticking telling me that I have only mere seconds to make a decision.

Five.

Four.

Three.

FUCK.

I dive behind the old couch and duck my head down, my eyes clenching in fear as my whole body shakes. The flames are burning so hot that my skin is covered in sweat. It's hard to breathe, the smoke is so thick, but that doesn't matter now. All that matters is the ticking telling me that my life is about to be over.

"WINTER?"

I hear the boys' laughter clouding my mind and I wrap my arms around my head, desperately trying to keep myself protected, but it's too late. This is the end.

BOOM!

My eyes spring open into a dark room to find Carver hovering over me, his hands at my shoulders, violently shaking me awake. "Winter, babe. Wake up."

My eyes begin flickering around the room, searching every dark corner, every shadow, and crevice, checking for the flames that threaten to consume me. "You're safe," Carver tells me, his eyes boring into mine with a desperate panic. "It was just a dream."

I let out a heavy sigh and take slow, calming breaths, keeping my eyes focused on his until the fear finally begins to ease. "Where are we?" I ask, taking another moment to glance around. The last thing I remember is giving Carver shit from the passenger side of the stolen SUV, and now I'm here in someone else's bed in a room that I don't recognize.

"You crashed in the car so I pulled into a cheap motel," he explains. "We don't have to stay here if you don't like it, but I thought you'd be more comfortable in a bed."

I nod and relax back into the bed, unable to deny the fact that even though it's the worst bed I've had the displeasure of sleeping in, it's the best option I've had since first arriving at the now non-existent cabin nearly three days ago.

Carver drops back beside me and pulls me into his arms, his warm hand rubbing up and down my side. "Are you alright?" he asks, noticing just how freaked out I am by the nightmare that felt so damn real. "I thought you didn't get nightmares when you're with me."

"I thought I didn't either," I murmur, placing my hand against his chest and listening to the steady rhythm of his heart. "But for the first time, you're the reason for the nightmare, not the solution."

A soft, broken sigh sounds through the cramped room as his hold tightens around me. "I hate that you can't trust me anymore," he whispers. "I'd do anything to change that."

I raise my chin to meet his broken stare and my lips press against his. "I know," I tell him. "You don't know how badly I wish things were different. I just want everything to go back to how it was before all of this shit, before … everything."

"Before me?"

I shake my head ever so slightly. "No, never before you." I pull out of his arms and climb over him until I'm straddled over his hips and looking down at his devilish face. "I hate this weird place that we're in. I hate the thought of not being able to trust you, and I hate that I've spent the past few days fearing that everything I had with each of you was all a lie."

Carver's fingers knot into my hair and he slowly brings me down to him, his lips cautiously brushing over mine. "Never."

I can't resist him a second longer and press deeper into him, my lips locking with his in a sensual dance. He's been close to me this whole time, stalking me like his next victim, yet at this moment, I've never missed him so much.

My heart screams for more while my brain tells me to keep my distance until I'm certain that I can trust him again. Who knows, maybe this was all a part of his wicked plan, but there's no denying it, sex with Carver has always been mind-blowing, and if he really does turn this shit back on me and end my life, then I might as well have been thoroughly fucked first.

His hand curls down around my body as our tongues fight for dominance, but after a few relentless moments, Carver surrenders, letting me take control. Though, he would have felt my wrath had he not. I've been through enough pain and suffering to not get exactly what I need right now.

I feel him hardening beneath me and I grind my pussy against him, the satisfaction tearing through me like a rocket. I've got to have it all. I need to feel him deep inside of me, but more than that, I need him to submit to me, to give me whatever I ask of him, to please me until I can't possibly take it any longer.

I tear my lips away and sit up as I rock my hips back and forth over his throbbing erection. His hands fall to their favorite spot on my hips, his fingers digging into my skin. I reach down and grip the hem of my black tank before slowly peeling it up, watching Carver's gaze heat as his focus drops to the feminine curves of my body in the soft moonlight coming in through the motel window.

"Touch me, Carver," I demand. "Make me come harder than ever before."

The desire sweeps through him and he sits up, wrapping his arm around my back and holding me close as I continue to grind against him. My tits sit right by his mouth and he wastes no time sucking my pert nipple between his warm lips as his other hand slides up my body, teasing my skin with his feather-soft touch until it's cupped around my other breast. His fingers roam over my nipple, gently flicking and pinching until I'm panting for more.

His tongue glides over my nipple with practiced skill and my pussy clenches, feeling more than left out. "Fuck, Carver. I need that tongue on my clit."

Carver's hands drop away, and in one smooth move, he grabs both of my legs and flips me off him until my back is slammed against the hard bed and my legs are up in the air. He hovers over me and grips my panties before tearing them clean from my body as though the flimsy material was made out of nothing more than cheap tissue paper.

He takes my knees and spreads them wide, making my pussy drip with readiness from the pure need and desire pulsing through my body.

Carver meets my eyes as his tongue rolls over his bottom lip, the hunger pulsing through his stare enough to cripple me. "Do your fucking worst," I insist, using the same words that he'd used against me beside the diner before allowing me to fuck him up, only now the tables have turned and I hope to whoever exists above that Carver fucks me up in all the right ways.

His gaze sparkles as his lips pull into a wicked one-sided grin, but as stunningly wicked as it is, I can't focus on it as every part of my being is locked on the way his thick fingers trail down my needy skin. Then without warning, he finds my pulsating cunt and thrusts two fingers deep inside me, making me cry out as his gaze hungrily locks on my weeping pussy, watching the show with desire.

Carver's fingers draw out of me and I clench down on them, desperate to keep him inside of me, but he doesn't disappoint as he thrusts them straight back in, curling his fingers at just the right angle, finding that one spot that has my eyes rolling to the back of my head.

His fingers move deep within me and I curse myself for being so damn obvious. I need him more than anything. Not even an attempt on my life could keep me away from him.

Carver's gaze heats as he watches his thick fingers slowly move in and out of my cunt, glistening with my arousal. His tongue roams over his lips in hunger and as his heavy stare shifts to meet mine, my heart seems to race so much faster.

"You fucking love it," he tells me, his deep tone speaking right to my soul.

I bite down on my lip and break into sobs as he pulls his thick fingers from my pussy, but the devastation is short lived as he moves his drenched fingers toward his plump lips. He sucks them into his mouth and the way his eyes close in the sweetest pleasure, knowing it's my arousal on his tongue—fuck. It's easily the hottest thing I've ever seen.

When his eyes open, they're flaming with need. "So fucking sweet," he tells me before thrusting those same two fingers back inside of me with a whole new ferocity that drives me wild with need.

Carver adjusts himself at the end of the bed and lowers his lips to my clit as his fingers continue working my cunt. My fists knot into his hair and I cry out, bucking beneath him when his warm, skilled tongue flicks over my sensitive clit.

He laps up my arousal as though it's a potent elixir with the purpose of keeping his heart beating. He teases me, his tongue roaming over my cunt as he sucks my clit between his lips, gently pinching it and sending me into overdrive as he makes up for each of his misdemeanors over and over again.

I'm his fucking queen, and goddamn, he knows it. He's not just fucking me with his mouth, he's fucking worshiping me and I'm so here for it.

Carver's fingers hit the spot again and again, and I clench down around him, desperately needing this release. "Fuck, Carver. Make me come."

My fingers knot tighter in his hair as he applies more pressure to my clit, lapping his tongue back and forth, circling, flicking, teasing. His fingers assault me with an erotic dance, moving gently inside of me, massaging my walls and making me long for his hard, thick cock.

My hips buck beneath him but he holds me down, forcing me to take every bit of pleasure he's giving until it's all too much and I come undone beneath his tongue. My orgasm tears through me, pulsating and shaking my whole damn body.

My legs tighten around his head, holding him there as my high rocks through me. I come on his fingers and I feel the way he pulls out of me, not wanting to waste a drop as his tongue dips into my tight cunt, taking it all.

When my convulsions ease, he crawls up between my legs and drops his lips to mine, his tongue diving deep inside my mouth and sharing those last drops of my arousal. He grinds his hard cock against my spent pussy and it's like an electric bolt, shooting straight to my core and bringing her back to life.

"Fuck, Carver," I pant as his lips move down my jaw and find that sensitive spot just below my ear. His hand travels down the curve of my body, stopping on its way to clutch my breasts and pinch my already pebbled nipple, exactly the way that King does, reminding me just how perceptive this man really is. I cry out and he continues down past my thigh before grabbing my leg and hitching it high over his hip.

Carver lines himself up with my entrance and without skipping a beat, gives me what I've been craving this whole time. He fills me like never before, stretching my walls and sinking deep inside of me and as I clench around him, his head drops into the curve of my neck as a loud, grumbly groan pulls from deep within his chest, his satisfaction and overwhelming pleasure clear in his tone.

Carver's cock flinches inside me and I gasp, gripping his face and bringing his lips back to mine. He kisses me eagerly as he starts to fuck me like a loyal servant giving in to my every need. "Fuck, Winter. I thought I was never going to feel you like this again."

"Don't you forget that," I whisper against his lips. "Now fuck me like it truly is the last time you'll ever touch me."

Carver meets my stare, his eyes burning with the challenge and in the very next second, he takes my knee that's curled around his hip and brings it right up to his shoulder before pushing up on his hands and really fucking me.

I watch his body roll with each movement as his long, thick cock moves all the way back before slamming deep inside of me. My fingers trail down my body, past my waist and down past my clit until I feel his hard cock thrusting in and out of my tight cunt. I wrap my fingers around him and squeeze, feeling my arousal begin to soak my hand.

He hammers into me, both of us moaning and panting with need, but I'm not ready for this to end just yet. I curl my arm around his neck and push him off me, allowing myself to roll with his movements. He remains upright and scoots back against the headboard of the bed and I immediately grip onto it, knowing that what I have in store for him is going to require us both to hold on for dear life.

Carver's arm curls around my waist, holding me close to him and sucking my nipple into his mouth as I start to fuck him, taking out all my frustrations on his cock. I throw my head back and groan low as his cock pushes deep inside me while my pussy grinds, rubbing my clit against his warm skin.

His free hand curls around my ass and spanks it hard before moving lower and teasing my hole. I push back against his touch, telling him to go for fucking gold.

I squeeze down on his cock as I move up and down, rocking my hips and feeling like a fucking goddess.

Pushing. Pulling. Giving. Anything I can get I'm taking it like the greedy, selfish bitch that I am.

Carver's fingers tighten on my body. "Fuck, babe," he pants, raising his hips to meet my thrusts and groaning with every one of them. "Your sweet little pussy is like a fucking dream. It's too good to be real."

"Trust me," I say, dropping down over him and squeezing even tighter. "It's as fucking real as it gets."

He growls low and the sound spurs me on, but Carver has other plans. His hold around my waist tightens and he raises me up, holding me still and before I even know what's going on, he thrusts up into me, fucking me from below, his jaw clenched and his need written all over his handsomely rugged face.

I grip onto the headboard even tighter, my fingers starting to hurt from just how hard I'm holding on, but if I were to ease up, I'd surely crumble and fall. "FUCK. FUCK. FUCK," I cry out, my head thrown back. "RIGHT THERE. MORE. HARDER."

He pushes himself to his limits, his jaw clenching even harder as I squeeze down on his cock. I'm almost sure that his fingers are bruising my skin, but I need it. I need to feel his pain, I need it rough, and I need it right fucking now.

"FUUUUUCK," Carver roars before spanking my ass once again.

I reach down between us, risking letting go of the headboard, but every girl knows that sometimes you have to risk it for the biscuit. My fingers press down over my throbbing clit and I rub it furiously, feeling an electric current pulsing straight through my core, building faster and higher.

Carver works my cunt and ass, his lips all over my body and as he thrusts up into me one last time, I clench my eyes and my orgasm explodes through me.

"CARVER," I cry, dropping down over him and feeling him still deep inside of me, filling me with his hot cum as my body shatters around him, squeezing his thick cock like never before as the rest of my body shakes and trembles under his incredible touch.

My head drops into the warm curve of his neck as he holds me tight, refusing to let me go. Carver pants heavily in my ear and I feel the rapid beat of his heart pounding against my tits. "Holy shit, babe," he breathes, his fingers gently stroking over my exhausted body as his cock remains buried deep inside of me. "Who would have known that a few days away from you would have resulted in that?"

I smile against his warm skin. "Just wait until the guys find out that while they've been busy panicking over me hating them, that I've been fucking you like nobody's business."

"Cruz would have my balls if he found out."

"Then I'll be sure to let him know," I laugh, my lips softly brushing over his warm skin before letting out a breathy sigh. "I'll give them all a chance to make it up to me, don't worry about that."

"Oh, I'm not worried," he murmurs in the darkened room. "I'm counting on it, and hopefully you might even let me watch."

I pull back and meet his warm stare and press my lips to his. "You really are a dirty perv, aren't you?"

"You've got no fucking idea," he tells me, flinching his cock that's still deep inside of me before scooting down in the bed until I'm lying flat on his chest, his cum slowly dripping out of me and making a mess of the sheets, but a mess that feels so damn good.

I prop myself up on his chest and meet his tired stare as I slowly begin rocking my hips up and down, feeling him coming alive beneath me once again.

His knuckles brush down the side of my face and he pushes the hair away from my eyes, needing to see all of me. "You know, Dynasty already thinks we're dead. We could escape this bullshit, just you and me. We could make a life for ourselves away from all of this."

I sit up just a little bit higher and his cock goes deeper. "You know," I whisper, still slowly rocking. "The guys can all go and suck my big dick. I have a score to settle with each of them, and no matter how angry I am with them right now, they're still all the loves of my life. I can't leave them. We've been through too much, and deep down, you couldn't leave them either. They're your brothers."

His thumb brushes over my lips as his gaze bores into mine. "I know," he murmurs. "I'm nothing without my brothers, but you can't deny that getting the hell out of there sounds like a pretty good fucking idea."

"There's no denying that," I say, my voice lowering with the blissful pleasure rocking through my body. "But if you took me away, you know they'll come for me. They won't stop until they get me back, which is exactly why we're going back there the second the sun rises in the sky. We can't let them do this by themselves. They're our family and I know you want to keep me safe, but I know you too damn well, Dante Carver. You need to be there to save your sisters and make Paris pay. I won't have it any other way. Besides, those precious little girls are going to need your warm arms wrapped around them, and I'm not about to allow you to let them down."

Carver shakes his head, his gentle fingers dropping to my waist. "That's not part of the plan," he tells me, the brief flicker of sadness in his eyes telling me that I'm right—he wants to storm into that shithole of a room that Paris has them in and be the hero his little sisters have always seen him as, and fuck it, I want to see it too.

"Who gives a shit about the plan?" I demand. "Paris took your family. The plan was fucked from the very beginning. So, what do you say? Are we going to hole up in this shitty motel twiddling our thumbs and waiting for the boys' call to say that it's over, or are we going to show a united front and kill the fucking bitch? I don't know about you, but I refuse to let her slip through our fingers again. Either way, I'm taking back Dynasty."

Carver watches me a second longer, deep in thought, struggling between sticking to the carefully laid out plan the boys had crafted and doing what his heart is telling him to do. "Okay," he finally says. "It's a seven-hour drive home, so the second I'm finished reveling in your sweet pussy, we'll leave, but I have one condition."

I raise my brow, my movements pausing as I wait for what's most likely something I'm not going to like, wondering when the hell he thought he was in the position to make demands. "What's your condition?"

"When you get home, you need to give each of the guys the time of day to earn your forgiveness. We're never going to be how we were before if you're forever holding onto that resentment, and fuck, babe, I was really getting used to this whole group sharing bullshit."

I press my lips into a hard line, studying his flawless features, and quickly realize that he's right, and while I have every intention to try and get us back to where we used to be, it's not just going to happen overnight. "Okay," I finally whisper, starting to slowly fuck him again. "I'll let them argue their case, but it's not going to be easy, and it's not going to happen in the blink of an eye. All four of you are going to have to work your asses off to get back in my good graces."

"Oh yeah?" he questions, his arm snaking around my waist as a devilish smirk tears across his handsome face. "Why don't I start working off my debt right fucking now?"

# CHAPTER 8

Carver's phone blares through the stolen SUV just as the sun peeks over the mountains in the distance. We've been on the road for the past two hours and so far, the whole long-distance road trip thing is starting to wear on my nerves.

I hate road trips, and I hate them more when I have a broody as fuck man sitting beside me who refuses to let me blast music and sing at the top of my lungs because apparently, it's too fucking early in the morning for that bullshit.

Fuck him though. There's no other way to road trip, otherwise it's not a road trip—it's just sitting in a metal box with wheels for hours on end. Though, if I'm being completely honest with myself, the reason for his sour mood probably has something to do with me asking him to stop at the first gas station we passed, claiming I got my period and asking him to go in to get me hoochy-coochy wipes and glow in the dark tampons. He didn't look too fucking impressed when he came striding out of the gas station, telling me he had to ask the chick behind the counter to help him find it, only to have her laugh in his face, but fuck, it was some great entertainment and went a long way in making me feel better.

I think I'm going to get 'Petty Bitch' tattooed across my ass just to remind the guys where my true nature lies, but if I really think about it, perhaps the petty train is the way to go. The boys are big enough to handle it, and damn, it would make me feel a shitload better than the one-on-one sit-down chat about feelings the guys would prefer to give me.

Carver scoops his phone up and winces as he looks over the screen. "Fuck, the boys want to video chat."

I scoff, listening to the irritating sound of his ringtone. "They're probably checking that I didn't try to kill you in your sleep."

Carver chuckles to himself before quickly glancing my way. "You couldn't kill me," he mutters, "even if you tried, but the idea is amusing so thanks for that."

"Would you wipe that ridiculous smirk off your face and answer the damn call? Your ringtone is the equivalent of nails on a chalkboard."

"In that case, I might just wait a second."

"Fuck me in the ass," I grumble, snatching the phone out of his hands and pressing accept on the call before fixing my face with an irritated scowl for good measure.

Cruz's face appears on the screen and before I can even get out a snappy, bullshit threat, he rushes out with a desperate, "How's my girl?" before his eyes go wide, realizing that the girl in question is staring back at him and isn't too fucking happy about it.

"Ah, fuck," Carver mutters under his breath. "Here we go."

"YOUR FUCKING GIRL?" I demand, the fury bubbling deep within me. "Where the fuck do you get off calling me your girl? Maybe you've forgotten, but only a few short days ago, your bitch ass tried to blow me up, you betrayed me, you turned your back on me and left me in the dark, scared for my fucking life. I'm not your fucking girl anymore. You don't get the right to call me that."

"Fuck, babe. I'm sorry. I thought Carver explained everything to you."

I choke on my own breath. "He sure as fuck explained everything to me, and if you think that's magically just going to take away the betrayal that sits in my chest every time I think of you guys, you've got another thing coming. Nothing will change the fact that you blew up the cabin and left me behind, broken, bloodied, and bruised. I can't magically forget about all of that. Whether or not you had good intentions and were doing everything in your power to save your brothers and sisters, it doesn't change anything."

Cruz just stares, unsure of what to say as I watch his heart break before me. "Babe, please," he begs, the guys' faces coming into view behind him. "You have no fucking idea how sorry I am for all of that, we all are, but we had three seconds to come up with a plan, and yeah, it was a fucking shitty one, we get that and will spend the rest of our lives trying to make up for that. Every fucking second since the cabin went up in flames, all I've been able to think about is how badly we fucked up."

My gaze shifts out the window, unable to handle the pain that comes pulsing out of Cruz's heavy gaze. I give myself a second, desperately trying to compose myself before losing control … Well, more so than I already have. "Why'd you call, Cruz? Carver's driving. He can't video chat right now."

"Driving?" King cuts in, shoving his face right in the frame to steal the spotlight which only manages to irritate me further. I mean, not even a little attempt at begging for forgiveness? He's just going to jump right in with demanding answers. Fucking cocksucking swamp turd. "Why the fuck are you driving? You were to stay at the motel until the threat passed. We can't risk anybody seeing you. You're supposed to be dead. You're a ghost."

"I'll be a fucking ghost to you if you don't stop demanding answers out of me," I snap back at him. "You have to back off. All of you. It's not your place to be assholes to me right now."

Carver sighs beside me and I roll my eyes as he cuts in, giving them the answers that I wasn't prepared to give. Well at least the answers that we already pre-planned to give, seeing as though telling them that we're on our way back to Ravenwood Heights was a no-go. "Chill out, bro. We're hungry. The food at the motel is fucking shit. It's practically shit on toast with a side of diarrhea. We'll just pick something up and then head back."

"Good," Grayson says, stepping in on Cruz's other side, the three of them all squishing together like a muscle orgy. "I don't need to remind you what's at stake here."

Carver screeches to a stop, the tires skidding off the side of the road as he tears the phone out of my hands. "Where the fuck do you get off with that bullshit? These are my little fucking sisters too. Don't fucking question me. I will always do what's fucking right for them, no matter what."

Cruz steps away from King and Grayson and stares down Carver through the phone. "Look, we're all feeling it, alright? We just want them back safe."

"Don't fucking let me down, Cruz. They're the only family I've got left."

"I've got you, bro," Cruz murmurs, lowering his tone to keep the conversation somewhat private despite the fact that we can all still hear exactly what's being said, though I'm sure Carver appreciates the gesture. "We might be onto something," Cruz adds. "We're closing in, just waiting for a few things to come through."

Carver nods and hands me the phone before pulling back out onto the highway, Cruz's words giving Carver the slight bit of hope he needs to get our asses back home as soon as possible.

Cruz's heavy stare comes back to mine and the tension sits between us like a knife slicing straight through to my heart. "Winter," he says, his voice soft and low, warning me that whatever is about to come out of his mouth is something I'm not yet ready to hear. A beep sounds through the phone and I watch as Cruz cuts himself off with a sigh. "Shit, sorry babe, it's my mom. I have to take this. She's been inconsolable since learning that not only were her babies taken, but that I had a hand in ending both yours and Carver's lives. You know how fond she is of you, and she thinks of Carver as an adopted son. She's been trying to put the funerals together as well, seeing as though there's nobody else, but … it's a lot for her. I'd do anything to be able to tell her that it's not true, but we have to have Dynasty believing you're gone otherwise Paris won't buy it."

Shit. I'm going to have to really make it up to her, but how? I have no fucking idea.

I nod and before I get another word out, Cruz gives me a sad smile. "Love you," he mutters awkwardly before quickly ending the call and leaving me feeling so much heavier than before.

I flop back into my seat and glance across at Carver as he speeds down the road, knowing that the boys' idea of 'closing in' means that they could have information on his sisters' whereabouts any minute and he wants to be there when they do. "That sucked," I murmur, once again finding myself wishing that things could be different.

"You were going to have the awkward first conversation at some point, just be thankful that you got to do it over the phone where he couldn't see the way your hands were balling into fists."

I roll my eyes. "Good point."

"Plus," he continues, "had you been at home, you would have inevitably tried to storm away and they all would have followed you until you lost control and nut-punched them … or gave in."

I prop my feet up on the dash, scooching down in my seat and getting comfortable. "No way in hell I would have given in that easily. They're going to have to fight for my attention, especially Cruz."

"Why especially Cruz?"

"Because he's the kind one. The rest of you assholes are more than capable of doing shit like this. In fact, I'm surprised you haven't already tried it just for shits and giggles. But Cruz is different. Out of all of you, he actually has a conscience. He's nurturing and always walks on the bright side, unlike the rest of you who were practically born in hell. He does things with his heart, not out of obligation. I just … I don't know."

"His betrayal hits the hardest," Carver finishes for me. I nod and he goes on. "So, how come you were so quick to forgive me?"

A loud, howling laugh tears out of me. "Oh, that's cute. You think you've been forgiven because I allowed you to fuck me into oblivion? Not even close, Carver. You just caught me at a time of weakness and happened to have the right equipment and skillset to make me forget about the world around me."

An offended gasp tears out of him and I hesitantly glance his way. "I … I don't know what to say," he baffles. "I feel so used."

"Oh, yeah?" I grin, stretching across the center console and palming his dick through his sweatpants, loving the way he comes alive under my touch. I release my seatbelt and climb across until I'm straddled in his lap, his engorged cock pressing up against my pussy as he continues to drive. "Just you wait and see my next party trick."

And without giving him a second to wipe the shock off his face, I reach down between us and free his cock before settling myself over him and riding him the whole way back to Ravenwood Heights.

"**N**o fucking way," I breathe, gaping at Carver as he smirks beside me, the smugness pouring out of him in waves, pleased to be able to shock me right to my core. I mean, after everything we've been through, this shouldn't come as a surprise, but damn, it caught me off guard.

"I swear," he tells me. "You know that I make it my mission to have dirt on each of these bastards, and this … this is what I got on him."

"But that's … I don't even know what that is. Everyone else has fraud or drug smuggling buried in their closet, but this? I'll never be able to look at him the same again. Are you sure there wasn't a different secret you could exploit to make this happen? I really could have gone without knowing about this."

Carver shrugs his shoulders. "I mean, there probably is, but this is definitely the easiest way to get us back through the gates undetected."

"Are you one hundred percent sure?"

Carver nods and looks down at his watch. "He should be pulling up right about now," he says just as an expensive black sedan pulls into the empty lot across the road. Carver grins wide, his pride knowing no bounds. "Like fucking clockwork," he tells me. "Brooks has a standing appointment with Missy at 10 am every second Wednesday for the past six years."

"No way."

Carver nods. "I made it my business to meet with Missy a few years back. She's part of the trans community and absolutely rocking it in this industry. She's completely booked out as well, though she would be seeing as though she's the only person in the area who specializes in weird kinks and requests. She's a fucking legend around here."

My eyes bug out of my head. "What kind of weird kinks and requests are we talking about?"

Carver grins, knowing that whatever is about to come out of his mouth is going to shock me all over again. "Baby kinks."

"Baby kinks? What the fuck is that supposed to mean? Is Brooks into child fucking?"

"No," Carver laughs, shaking his head. "Baby kinks like … he'll dress up as one, diaper and all, and that's about as far as my research went before I got a mental picture and had to bail."

"Okay," I muse, my eyes narrowing as I try to figure out the logistics of one of Brooks' meetings with Missy. "What does she actually do for him? Change his diaper, tell him he's been a very naughty boy and then fuck? Does he get a warm bottle of milk afterwards?"

"I …" Carver cuts himself off and shakes his head. "I'm trying really hard not to think about what else goes down in there and you're making it really hard."

I can't help but laugh, imagining all the possibilities while knowing that I could never take Earnest Brooks seriously again. Don't get me wrong, I'm not one to kink shame. Choke, spank, spit, and whip; I'm down with it all. To each their own, but using a diaper and having some poor girl clean up after you is where I draw the line.

I bet Missy gets paid a shitload to act out his unique fantasies. It makes a girl wonder just how much money we're talking about here. In fact, maybe

I need to have a sit down with Missy and get all her trade secrets. I'm sure she'll have a few suggestions of new ways that I can rock the guys' worlds. Hell, I'll even settle for some good stories. Either way, she sounds like a fucking rock star with her priorities sorted right the fuck out. She's a girl after my own heart.

Forcing myself to concentrate, we watch as Earnest pushes his way out of his fancy black sedan and cautiously looks around, though today, he's clearly not cautious enough as his gaze sweeps straight past our stolen SUV and he starts sauntering toward the building that looks suspiciously like a Chinese restaurant.

"Wait here," Carver says. "I'll be back in ten. When you see me come out, we run."

"What?" I rush out, hating that he's taking the lead on this when only a few nights ago, I promised myself that wasn't going to happen again, that I was going to be the leader of my own fate from here on out. "No. I'm going in."

Carver's eyes bug out of his head. "You can't go. You're supposed to be in hiding, remember? Besides, if you walk into that place, you'll be confused as a sex worker, and knowing your luck, you'll probably end up covering for Missy. But if I go in, I just look like a curious customer having a look at the merchandise."

"Damn it," I groan, flopping back into my seat. He has a good point.

He grins wide, that stupid pride of his shining brightly once again so I flip him off just to be a petty bitch. Carver flies out of the car and looks back at me through his open door. "Don't go anywhere," he tells me. "I mean it."

I roll my eyes and make a show of locking my car door and Carver just winks, his stupidly beautiful face making everything clench deep inside me. Without another word, he closes the door and pulls his hood over his head, trying to conceal himself from the people around us.

He breaks into a light jog and I watch as he slips around the side of the building, bypassing the main entrance with the kind of confidence that would have anyone thinking that he was supposed to be there.

Carver disappears out of sight and I rest back into my seat, keeping my eyes on the building, and ten minutes later, just as promised, Carver comes racing out of the building, his face as white as a ghost telling me that he saw more than his fair share and it's not something he ever wanted burned into his mind.

I laugh as I watch him before realizing that he's not heading this way. "Oh, shit," I panic, remembering that I'm supposed to be running with him. I scramble out of the car and race across the street to the empty lot. Carver reaches the black sedan ages before I do and by the time my ass is crashing down into the front passenger seat, Carver is already peeling out of the parking lot.

"What happened?" I rush out, hating that blank expression on his face.

He just shakes his head. "I just … wrong room, okay?"

"Wrong room?"

"I don't want to talk about it," he spits. "Ever. Got it? Don't ever bring it up again, okay? Promise me. Never again. Promise, Winter."

"But like … what did you see? Was he in his diaper or did he change it up and go with a dog kink? Did he have a collar and a leash? OH! Was he hardcore head-to-toe in latex with a ball gag?" I laugh, grinning back at

Carver while watching his face drain of color by the second, while knowing that I will probably never see him like this ever again. Though, a guy like Carver has seen it all so I can only imagine what kind of fresh hell he just walked in on, but damn it, my curiosity knows no bounds. Though, why I'm so desperate to know what Earnest is into, beats me.

"ELODIE FUCKING RAVENWOOD. NEVER AGAIN."

I just laugh, sinking back into the seat as Carver speeds down the narrow streets of Ravenwood Heights. I try to go over our plan, which really isn't a plan at all. We've already done the hard part—stealing a car that will get us through the gate without detection and seeing as though at least three of the Dynasty families possess this exact same car, we figured it was a safe bet, as long as we keep our faces concealed.

Next up, actually getting through the gate, getting down to my property, and through the front door without a damn person seeing us.

Piece of cake. I think.

It takes all of two minutes to reach the main gates of Ravenwood Estate and Carver slowly approaches with his phone in hand. He stops by the keypad and searches something before grinning to himself and confidently entering a code.

The gate pulls back, just as it should. "Whose code was that?" I ask, glancing at him as we roll on through the gate.

"Earnest's," he laughs. "Apparently his car key wasn't the only thing I was going to steal today."

I roll my eyes as I shake my head but as we approach the big house at the end of the street, my nerves quickly bubble up and wreak havoc in my gut. "Are we doing the right thing?" I question, slipping my hands under my legs to keep them from shaking.

"Who fucking knows?" Carver grumbles, "But if it all goes south, just remember that coming back here was all your idea."

"Be serious," I tell him. "Should we call it quits and leave now while we still have the chance, or are we doing the right thing?"

"I can't answer that for you, babe. All I know is that the whole way here, all I've been able to think about is getting my sisters back, and that we probably should have given the boys a heads up that we were coming back. You know them, they're not so big on surprises."

"Yeah, well, there's nothing we can do about that now," I remind him. "Besides, the guys didn't give much thought to the fact that I don't like surprises either and that didn't stop them from blowing me up, so surprise, I guess. Call it an eye for an eye, though this is hardly the same thing. It's more like a pinky finger for an eye."

Carver sighs and glances my way. "You're never going to tire of reminding us just how badly we fucked up, are you?"

"You might as well embrace it," I grin. "That reminder is going to be hanging over your heads for the rest of your lives."

"Fuck me," Carver mutters before the car falls silent.

He pulls into my driveway and my heart breaks looking up at my home to find the windows all boarded up and the yard a mess from the raid a few days ago, but now isn't the time to get upset about it. There will be time to fix my home, along with Carver's once this shit is over, but right now, we have bigger fish to fry. There's no time for tears.

"Alright," he says, stopping by the keypad for my home and nervously looking up at the gate. "Let's hope they're too fucking busy to watch the gate today."

He enters what looks like Grayson's new code, knowing that had he entered his own, the guys would be notified. We both hold our breaths, despite not having to. We've both done dumber shit than this, and besides, the worst that could happen is being caught by the boys, or Paris could be inside with them all tied up just waiting for me to come flying through the front door so she can put a bullet through my head, but hey, I'm all about that positive thinking now.

The gate slowly peels open and Carver hits the gas, taking us closer and closer to our doom because, let's face it, Carver was right, the guys aren't going to appreciate this one bit, but what's done is done. No one saw us sneaking in, so there's absolutely no reason why we can't hide out here until it's all over. At least that way we'll all be together.

Carver drives up around the side of the house and parks in between the bushes and a big tree, concealing the sedan as best he can, though I'm sure at some point we'll remember to return it ... or not.

We climb out of the car and we both freeze for a second, our eyes coming to one another's. "Front or back?"

"Well," he winks, making me squirm with need, "I thought you'd never ask."

"Carver," I snap.

He laughs off his stupid joke and shrugs his shoulders. "I guess it really doesn't matter at this point, but if you really want to fuck with them, I'd sneak in through your bedroom window."

# CHAPTER 9

Carver and I laugh like a bunch of delinquent children as he makes a brace for my foot and I hold on to his shoulders. "Don't fucking miss," he whisper-yells as we both look up at the second story roof. It's one thing getting the guys up there, but me? Fuck that. This is definitely not something that I would ever try by myself, yet somehow Paris got her bitch ass up here so if she can do it, then so can I.

"Oh yeah," I grumble, searching deep within me for every little bit of sarcasm I can possibly muster. "I'm really going to go to all this effort just to miss the fucking ledge, but it wouldn't be an issue if I actually had someone who wasn't such a bitch trying to haul me up. Heard of a gym? How much do you bench anyway? Ten, maybe pushing twenty pounds?"

"Well, maybe if you didn't knock back so many fucking burgers, we wouldn't be having this issue," he teases, more than capable of throwing me around whenever the fuck he wants; a point he's proven far too many times. "For real though," he continues. "Are you ready?"

I nod, focusing all my attention on the ledge that I have to cling onto for dear life. "Make a bitch fly."

And fly, I do.

Carver launches me up, maybe a little too high as my whole body lands flat on the second story roof, no clinging for dear life needed. "Whoops," he chuckles below as I scramble to get my legs securely on the roof. "You good?"

"Good," I laugh, getting myself in a safe position before looking back down at him to watch him turn this mission into the gun show as he flexes his biceps and looks them over with pride.

"Damn," he says with a stupid grin. "I don't even know my own strength."

"Shut up and get your ass up here, little rabbit," I say, mocking the ridiculous new nickname he has for me. "And besides, I weigh all of three pounds. Now, if you launched a semi up here with me, then I'd be impressed."

Carver lets out a frustrated huff and with one smooth move, he bends and jumps like nothing I've ever seen before. His fingers grip onto the ledge and he pulls himself up as though he was on Ninja Warrior. He takes my hand and helps me to my feet before guiding me toward my bedroom window, clutching my hand tightly, terrified that I'll misstep and tumble to my fifth or sixth death of the week.

We reach my window in no time and he makes quick work of

removing the boards with his bare hands. "What's the whole 'little rabbit' thing you've got going on at the moment?" I ask as he indicates for me to go first.

He shrugs his shoulders. "I don't know, it sounded right at the moment and I think it's going to stick. You'll hereby be deemed little rabbit for all eternity. Besides, we were out in the wilderness, it seemed fitting," he explains as a dark, twisted sparkle hits his eyes. "Plus I've come to learn that cute little pet names always have a certain … intimidation factor when stalking someone through the woods. It reminds your prey that they're not even a player in the game. You're just fucking with them and could take them out at a moment's notice."

"Juuuuuust perfect," I mutter under my breath, very ungracefully maneuvering myself through the half-broken window with a few omphs, gahs, and groans, wondering if he sees me that way.

"It really is," he tells me, basically flying through the window after me like some kind of gazelle. "It's a special moment that will bond us forever, something the guys will never be able to share with you, just me."

"You mean that particular time in my life that I'd do anything to forget? The time where I thought you were a crazed serial killer stalking me through the dark, cold woods, like some kind of twisted *Snow White and the Huntsman* bullshit?"

"To be fair, I am a crazed serial killer who was stalking you through the dark, cold woods," he beams. "Our own little fairytale."

"Keep in mind, Mr. Serial Killer, I was right under your nose the whole time and you couldn't find me," I remind him. "But for the record, you're an ass."

"You're welcome," he says with a cheesy wink before picking up an empty photo frame, completely ignoring my little reminder. I watch as his eyes sparkle with excitement, speaking right to that wicked part of myself that I was always told to keep hidden, that is until I met the Kings of Ravenwood Heights. "Game time."

Carver drops the photo frame and the glass shatters into a million pieces. I tiptoe over the smashed glass and drape myself over the bed as dramatically as possible. Carver comes and stands by my bedside, his hand resting peacefully on my shoulder like some bullshit staged photograph from a million centuries ago.

We listen, and we wait.

The noise coming from the lower part of the house comes to an immediate stop and within seconds, loud grunts and curses are heard as the rumble of feet sprinting up the stairs echo through my parents' home. If I listen close enough, I could probably make out which footstep belongs to who, but instead, I relax and enjoy this rare moment of catching them off guard.

"Three," Carver whispers as a satisfied smirk settles over my lips. "Two. One."

The door barges open and the three starring assholes of my latest nightmares come storming in, guns in their hands, pointing proud and true right at my chest. Their eyes bug out of their heads almost in unison, and if I wasn't so filthy with them, I might even laugh.

A million emotions flicker through their stormy gazes. Love. Regret. Pain. Indecision. Betrayal. Each one of them hits me like a ton of bricks falling from the sky, but so much has to go down before we can come out the other end. A million hard conversations that are bound to kill me faster than that goddamn cabin explosion.

Their guns lower and it takes me all of two seconds to realize that all of them are dressed head-to-toe in black combat clothing. "What's going on? Why are you dressed like that?" I demand, flying to my feet only to have Carver pull me back down to avoid me stepping on the broken glass.

Grayson recovers first and pushes his way between King and Cruz's shoulders, taking point on this shit storm. "Excuse me? You break into your own goddamn house and have the nerve to demand answers? What the fuck are you doing here? We had a plan. You were to stay concealed until this shit was over."

"No," I demand. "You four assholes had a plan that you refused to let me in on, so I made my own goddamn plan. I don't play by your rules anymore. This is my home you're standing in, my leadership, and my fucking life. Nobody saw us, we were careful. I had Carver covering me the whole time, but that's beside the point. You should never have excluded me from this in the first place. I get that the four of you want to keep me safe, but that doesn't mean that you get to dictate the details of my life. Is that clear?"

"No, it's not fucking clear," King roars, pushing deeper into my bedroom. "You're fucking pissed, I get that. I'd be fucking livid if I were you too, but this is our family at stake, not yours. So yeah, call me a cold-hearted asshole, but when it comes to protecting my little brother and sister, I'll do whatever the fuck it takes, even if it means hurting you in the process."

Fuck Carver and the glass. I throw myself up. "You don't think I know that?" I demand, stepping right in front of King and shoving my hand hard into his chest. "You don't think that after everything we've been through that I don't see all of your siblings as my own? I stood in front of Carver with a fucking gun and begged him to take my life so he could deliver my dead body to Paris and see the safe return of your siblings. So, fuck you, Hunter King. Don't underestimate my loyalty, and don't fucking make excuses for your betrayal. You made a split-second decision without thinking it through and it was the worst one you could have made. You put my life at risk. You fucking gutted me, made me question whether I could trust the four men who swore to protect me, the four men who told me that they loved me. You couldn't trust me to help save your family, so you fucking broke me instead. You all fucking did."

King clenches his jaw, his eyes swimming with a sea full of regret and pain, knowing I'm damn right as Grayson stands straighter, a rare show of emotion pouring out of his broken gaze, but I don't linger on it. Instead, I turn toward Cruz, the one whose betrayal cut the deepest.

"You," I say, stepping toward him and focusing on the way his pained green eyes focus heavily on mine. "You broke my fucking heart. You were the one who was always supposed to have my back. They're all cold, shallow, and heartless, but you … you were pure. You were the one I thought would never break me."

His heart shatters before my very eyes and the sight almost has me breaking into tears, but I don't dare shed a tear for him, for any of them. I won't allow myself to be vulnerable like that until they can earn my trust back, but it won't be easy. I fell for them too quickly the first time, but now, I have my wits about me. I won't be fooled so easily.

Fool me once, that's on you. Fool me twice, and that's going to weigh on me for the rest of my life.

Carver steps into my back, placing a hand on my shoulder like I'm some kind of rabid animal needing to be tamed. He pulls me back a step and gives Cruz a moment to pull himself together as he looks at Grayson and King. "Let's just take a minute to chill out," he says. "What's going on with the kids? You're dressed for a fucking raid."

Grayson nods. "We are," he confirms. "We think we've got them. We're just waiting for one more bit of intel to come through to confirm, and then we're going in. Fuck Paris and her demands, I want my brother back where I know he's safe."

"Fucking hell," Carver says, running his fingers through his hair and nodding. "How much longer?"

King shakes his head. "No idea. We've been waiting all fucking morning, but seeing as though you're here, you might as well suit up. We're going to need every set of hands available."

"Cover your face, though," Grayson adds. "The whole fucking town thinks you're dead along with Ellie. You can't be seen, unless you've already blown your damn cover gallivanting through Ravenwood Heights like you haven't got a fucking care in the world."

Carver's fist slices through the air and slams against Grayson's jaw like a fucking freight train. No warning, no wind up, not another fucking word spoken between them. Though nothing needs to be said,

Carver said everything with that one punch.

Grayson simply nods, accepting his errors and taking responsibility for speaking out of line. Carver is a tough guy and can handle a hell of a lot more than most, but speak ill about his intentions and loyalties, and you better start counting your days. I've learned that the hard way, but right now, I have every right to question him. Grayson is different though. The boys share a brotherhood that allows them to get away with murder, but if they're pushed too far, someone might just end up knocked out for a few good days.

Not wanting to hang around for their bullshit, I cut through the guys and peel off my old shitty clothes, throwing them in a pile on the ground before searching through my closet for my favorite black leather high waisted pants, combat boots and a long-sleeved cotton shirt.

"The fuck do you think you're doing?" King asks, his gaze swiftly shifting over my cut-up body, just as Grayson and Cruz do, getting a good look at the fresh hell they put me through.

My hands stop on my shelving as my gaze slices to King's, the tension in the room growing to impossible heights. "Excuse me?" I question, pausing a second to let my glare truly sink in. "What does it look like I'm doing? Grayson said it was all hands on deck. So, I'm coming with you whether you like it or not."

King chokes back a laugh, staring at me as though he can't actually figure out if I'm joking or not. "You're kidding, right?" he finally says, his words falling from his mouth cautiously, almost as though he's terrified of offending me.

What. A. Fucking. Joke.

"Look me in the eye, King," I implore. "Does it look like I'm kidding?"

Cruz recovers from his earlier heartbreak and takes a hesitant step toward my massive walk-in closet. "Babe, I know you've gone through hell over the past few days, and I swear to you, each of us will do whatever it takes to make it up to you, but it's too fucking dangerous. We don't know what we'll be walking into, and on top of that, we can't risk you getting pinched by Paris. Taking you there is literally hand-delivering you into the lion's den."

I slap a stupid smile across my face. "How sweet. All of a sudden you care if I live or die. That's nice, but I've made up my mind. I'm coming, so either start including me in your plans, or I'll find my own way there. And trust me, you won't appreciate my version of busting in there. Take your pick."

Grayson clenches his already bruising jaw. "Ellie, please. These are our little brothers and sisters. This isn't just some simple raid where I can hold your hand the whole way through. I'm sorry, babe. It's really not my intention to make things worse right now. Believe me, if there was something I could say to make it all go away, I would, but you can't even hold a gun without shaking."

I don't skip a beat, tearing the gun out of the back of Carver's jeans, and shooting a bullet straight between Grayson and King's heads, watching as it sails directly between them and lodges into the wall behind my bed.

Cruz flinches, staring at me as though I'm some kind of stranger while I stand unmoving, Carver's gun held firmly out before me as my aim remains true and my hand unwavering.

I meet Grayson's surprised stare. "Do you need a second to reevaluate just how pathetic you think I am?" I question. "I am the rightful leader of Dynasty. I am *your* leader, and no longer your girl who can be pushed around by your bullshit egos. Whether you like it or not, your actions at the cabin changed me. Laying alone in the cold dirt, surrounded by woods and the unknown, I had more than enough time to reevaluate the person I wanted to be. Call it a little bit of soul searching, but I have realized that I am not weak. I am not afraid, and I am sure as fuck not some dumb bitch who can be led around by the tits. You four may be the Kings of Ravenwood Heights, but I'm your goddamn queen. From here on out, I am your equal, and you will treat me as such. So man the fuck up, get out of my room and offer me just a shred of privacy so that I may ready myself to help save the young lives of Dynasty, like any other leader should do."

The boys just stare and after a long moment, Carver steps into me and takes the gun from my hand. He meets my eyes as he stands before me, pride surging through his gaze as he nods. "Okay," he says. "You are our equal. Be ready in fifteen minutes and meet downstairs to discuss the plan. You'll need a face covering like me. I know you don't approve of this 'you're dead' plan, but it's what we're working with and we're going to use it to our advantage. You'll stay concealed behind it unless you physically cannot anymore."

I nod and Carver takes my chin between his fingers before leaning into me and gently murmuring against my lips, keeping his comments low and private. "Is it wrong for me to be so fucking turned on right now?"

I pull out of his grip and roll my eyes. "Go. Get out of here and take your band of douche canoes with you."

Carver simply nods and strides out of my room, leaving the three assholes behind. "Winter," Cruz starts, only to be met with a firm shake of King's head. "She's not ready, man. Just give her some time."

Both King and Grayson watch me with sorrow-filled gazes before finally taking the few steps to the door and leaving me be until it's just Cruz left staring, his heart so heavy on his sleeve that I fear it may fall off. "I'm sorry," he whispers, his voice breaking in despair.

"I know," I murmur, wishing I could just run straight into his warm arms and tell him that everything is going to be okay, but right now, I just don't know if that's true. "I just …"

"Time," Cruz finishes for me.

I nod and his gaze drops to the ground, his heart completely torn apart by not only his own betrayal and guilt, but my rejection and inability to just put it behind me.

He walks out of my room and takes my heart right along with him before I remember who the fuck I am and straighten my back.

Knowing that we're pressed for time, I get busy changing into my combat gear, pulling my clothes into place, tying my hair up into a slicked-back long ponytail and pocketing a black bandana that will eventually be wrapped around my face, just below my eyes.

*Goodbye, weak bitch.*

*Hello Tomb Raider—Winter style.*

# CHAPTER 10

My combat boots clunk against the stairs, descending into my living room like a warrior into hell. My slow steps give the guys a moment of warning to brace themselves before having to face me again.

I'm almost drunk on the power. I have those bitches shaking in their boots, at least, I'd like to think that I do. In reality, nothing scares them, especially not me.

I make it to the bottom of the stairs, ignoring the holes in the walls, the shattered glass, and all of my parents' broken possessions that lay discarded at my feet, evidence of the raid that Paris initiated. She will make up for it, even if it means picking up every single piece of shattered glass with her bare fingers.

Carver's home was destroyed only a few short weeks ago and I really feel for him, but now, I feel it on a much higher level. I feel his pain, understand the torture of having someone else in your home, tearing it down with malicious intent. It fucking sucks, but I'm a big girl now. I have bigger fish to fry. All that matters now is getting those kids back home to the safety of their mother's arms. We'll deal with the rest after, and we won't stop until it's done. Besides, I kinda got the better end of the deal when it comes to comparing mine and Carver's home situation. At least I still get to call my home my own. Carver's bitch of a mother took it upon herself to move into his trashed house, leaving us with yet another mess to clean up.

I can't wait to shove it to that woman. Every time I think of her, I can picture the way her face twisted in disgust when she threatened to kill any unborn child that Carver and I may have in the future. I remember it so clearly, it was right before she threatened to slit her son's throat if I were to speak a damn word of our hushed conversation. She's fucking awful. When you take both of Carver's parents and smoosh them together, you don't expect the result to be someone as incredible as Dante Carver. It's a miracle that he turned out so well. You know, when he's not trying to blow up his girlfriend.

My hand curls around the end of the railing as I hit the bottom step and I swing myself around to face the living room. I see all four of the guys busily getting themselves ready, shoving guns into holsters and tightening straps as blueprints are being spread out on the table.

I rush into the room, pissed off for taking so long to get myself ready. Clearly I've missed something. "What's going on?" I demand, jogging toward the table and glancing over Cruz's shoulder as he points out something on the blueprints, though I won't even pretend to know what I'm looking at. Blueprints really aren't my area of expertise, especially when I don't even know what the blueprints are for.

"We got them," Grayson says, stepping in beside me and glancing down at the blueprints as he continues loading himself with weapons. "They've been right under our fucking noses this whole time."

"What?" I rush out, my eyes wide as my head snaps up to his. "What do you mean?"

"Paris has them stashed in one of Dynasty's underground bunkers, not even a fucking mile from here."

My eyes bug out of my head, but I don't get another word in as King's warm hand curls around my elbow and yanks me back away from the table. He doesn't skip a beat, grabbing a utility belt and strapping it around my waist. "Are you fucking sure about this?" he questions, his tone harsh and straight to the point, leaving absolutely no room for me to get a read on his emotions, though something tells me that will all change once we have his brother and sister back. The groveling will start after that. "Once we bust in there, there's no going back. Bullets will be flying at your fucking head. Do you understand that? If you get yourself in trouble, you're on your own. We all have a fucking job to do. Grayson won't be babysitting you this time. So which is it? You're either going to stand on your own, or you're going to be a fucking liability."

I reach across to the table and grab a gun before shoving it deep into the holster at my hip. "Question my ability to do this one more time and I'm going to take this gun and shoot the tip off your dick."

King's brow arches as he watches me and I see his snappy retort busting to come flying through his lips but he bites his tongue. He reaches for another belt that he tightens around my thigh, shoving a knife into it and meeting my hard stare with a narrowed gaze. "Don't accidentally stab yourself with it."

"Careful," I warn. "I might miss and get you instead."

King huffs as he turns back around to focus on the blueprints, and as he steps away I find Carver directly behind him, shaking his head. "At some point, you're all going to have to get over your bullshit."

I give him a blank stare. "I'm the only one who has shit that needs to be made up for. He has no reason to be all pissy."

King doesn't turn back but his scoff is so fucking loud that it basically bounces off the wall. "Do I need to remind you that you just tried to shoot me upstairs? That bullet went zooming right past my fucking face. You could have killed me. You're not nearly practiced enough to be pulling stupid pranks like that."

A booming laugh comes tearing out of me. "That's rich coming from the guy who set off the bomb that nearly killed me. Feels good, doesn't it? Nearly being killed by the person you love. Though, at least I had the decency to look you in the eye when I did it."

"Knock it off," Cruz mutters, loading himself up and checking over his guns. "We get it. You hate each other right now and there's all sorts of shit to be unpacked from all of this, but now's not the time. Get your heads in the game. You can tear each other apart when we get back."

"My head is in the fucking game," King snaps back at him at the same time that I mutter, "You're damn right, I'll be tearing all of you apart when we get back."

Carver groans. "All of you shut the fuck up," he says before looking up at Grayson. "What's the plan?"

"Alright," Grayson responds, pointing down at the blueprints. "We're going in here."

I step in between King and Grayson to get a good look, and despite how angry I am with King right now, I can't help but love the feel of his fingers brushing against mine, even more so when his pinky finger locks around mine, telling me that hopefully soon, we'll be able to get back to where we used to be.

My gaze drops down to the blueprints and I follow Grayson's finger as it travels over the papers, committing every step of the plan to memory. I won't be the reason the boys don't get their brothers and sisters back.

I hold my hand out to Carver. "Phone."

His brows furrow in confusion, but nonetheless, he hands over the goods. I pull up the photo of the kids that Paris sent and focus on the surroundings, taking note of where everything lies in the room, how big it is and just how hard it would be to get them all out of there. "Where is this room?" I ask, lowering the phone beside the blueprints and getting a good mental idea of what we're about to walk into.

"It's hard to tell from just this picture, but my guess is that they're being kept in one of these three rooms," Grayson explains, his finger moving across the papers. "If it were me, I'd have put them in the room furthest from the exit, but this is Paris and so far, she's surprised us every step of the way so we're going in with absolutely no expectations. Anything goes. Just keep your chin up and your eyes open. It'll most likely be dark and dirty, hard to see, and probably scary as fuck. Keep your gun up at all times. Shoot first, ask questions later."

I nod. "Got it."

"Good," he says, his eyes softening for just a moment before hardening with the knowledge of the task ahead of us. "Everybody else sweet on the plan?"

The guys all nod and finish loading themselves up with weapons, and I don't miss the way Cruz adds a few more knives and another gun to my other hip.

"Let's roll," Carver says once everyone is ready.

He pulls his balaclava over his head, hiding his face just as the guys asked him to do as Cruz reaches for the black bandana hanging around my neck. He pulls it up over my face and rests it just below the bridge of my nose so only my eyes are visible. "I don't want you getting hurt," he murmurs, the pain still heavy in his eyes from my earlier rejection. "You know that King is just talking shit. You're not going to be on your own there. We'll protect you no matter what."

"I know," I whisper, "but I don't need your protection. I can handle myself. I know what I'm getting into. I'll be okay."

"I know you can handle yourself, I've seen it. But I don't want your stubborn need to prove some bullshit point to get you in trouble. If you're backed into a corner, you fucking call for help. Got it?"

I roll my eyes and nod. "Got it."

His eyes brighten with the slightest bit of hope but it's short lived as the guys start filing out of the room. I turn and stalk them, following close on their heels knowing damn well that if I don't get into the car quick enough, they'll leave without me.

We all pile in and Grayson makes a point of Carver and I getting squished into the trunk space. After all, we're supposed to be dead, and while our faces are covered, seeing two extra bodies getting around with the boys would be suspicious as fuck.

It's only a quick drive, and hell, I don't even know whose fucking car this is. All my father's cars were destroyed. Carver's Escalade was damaged when Knox decided to throw Cruz off his bike and I'm pretty sure the SUV we'd stolen from Cruz's mom was covered in bullet holes. I mean, we really shouldn't be trusted with cars at the moment. We have a really bad track record. Take my Ducati for example. I don't even know what's going on with that anymore, but I wouldn't mind having it back so I can have some kind of escape when the boys start begging for forgiveness.

Carver pulls me into his chest as the rest of the car remains silent. "You good?" he questions as I listen to the steady rhythm of his heart, wondering why the hell it isn't pounding like mine.

"Will be once we get them all out," I murmur. "I hate that they're in this situation because of me."

"This isn't your fault, Winter," he insists, his tone rising so that the guys can all hear our conversation. "Paris is fucked in the head. This is on her. I don't want you resting this on your shoulders. If something happens to any one of them, it'll fucking kill you and I don't want you carrying that type of guilt. Trust me, it's not fun."

I let out a sigh, and before I even get the chance to argue or question him, Grayson is bringing the car to a stop. "We're here," he says, his tone low as the guys look out the window at the sleek high-rise office building that sits before us, the hundreds of occupants within having absolutely no idea of the horrors that have been going on in the bunker below their building.

Grayson hits the gas again, driving straight through to the underground parking lot as I look around, wide-eyed, trying to figure out how the hell we get from the parking lot into this bunker, but as Grayson continues going down the levels, it starts to become a little clearer.

We reach the very bottom and must be at least five floors down when he brings the car to a stop outside a black metal door labeled 'Maintenance.'

"This has got to be it," Cruz murmurs, his voice so low that perhaps he's talking to himself.

"Only one way to find out," King mutters as his eyes swing back to me with concern, looking as though he wishes to have chained me to my father's desk in the hopes of keeping me safe. But we've all learned that the only true way for me to keep safe is to remain by their sides.

Silence fills the car as the boys shift their gazes from one end of the parking lot to the other, searching for cameras, threats, or other entrances. Coming up blank, we all pile out of the car, determined not to let those kids spend another minute terrified and alone in there.

Grayson leaves the car running for a quick getaway as we all rush toward the metal maintenance door. It's locked, but I'm not surprised.

As if some idiot is going to leave this open for the public to come walking in.

All eyes fall on King. We're going to have to blow it, but in doing so, we give ourselves away which will only mean trouble for us. Who knows what kind of orders Paris has given her men. If they know we're coming, they could harm the kids. There will no doubt be a wild shootout, and to be honest, if it's going to go down like that, then I'd prefer the kids to be out of here before it happens.

King tracks back to the car and just as he starts searching through a big bag of goodies, we hear the familiar sound of the metal lock sliding out of place.

My heart stops as King quickly dives behind the car.

Grayson and Carver fall in beside the door on the left as Cruz yanks me to the right and slaps his hand over my mouth for good measure.

The heavy door scrapes along the concrete floor and a guard steps out from the hidden bunker. There's still a chance that this room is just a maintenance room, but one look at this guard and it's clear that he's one of Paris' men.

He freezes, seeing our car parked right by the door and without hesitation, his hand flies to his gun at his hip, but he didn't count on Carver stepping out of the shadows behind him. No one ever does.

Before the guy can even gasp or shit his pants, Carver's hands circle his head and violently twist, snapping his neck. We all watch as he silently crumbles to the ground, and just like that, we gain entry into Paris' secret little lair.

Both Grayson and Cruz catch my eyes, making sure that I'm all good after witnessing Carver snap that dude's neck, and to be honest, I'm really fucking grateful that they can't see the wicked grin that's stretched across my lips below my bandana. I've seen far too much death over the past few months and I'm starting to enjoy it. I must be sick or twisted … hell, I'm probably both.

Either way, I'm about to revel in some more.

The five of us slip through the big metal door and into a long tunnel, just as we had thought, and the further we go along, the more familiar it becomes, shaping up exactly as it was drawn out in the blueprints.

Despite wanting to run, we keep at a slow pace knowing that guards could jump out at any time and that the sound of us running through the tunnel is bound to give us away. Now is the time to play it safe. My coveted recklessness can fly free once the kids are out of here.

There's a light up ahead and we all come to an immediate stand still as a guard crosses in front of it and comes to a stop in front of another heavy, metal door completely oblivious to the five of us deep in the tunnel.

"Mine," Grayson murmurs, his eyes narrowing in excitement as he reaches down beside his hip and draws his gun. He takes a second and I watch as he twists something onto the end. As his hand falls away and I get a good look at the new addition to his gun, understanding dawns. I've seen enough scary movies to know that it's a silencer which makes this all so much more intriguing.

He raises his gun and I find myself watching in anticipation, my breath held as my eyes widen. My heart starts to race, and as he squeezes the trigger, the bullet flies straight through the guard's forehead with a soft *pew*, dropping him like a sack of shit. A thrill fires through my veins and the need to slam Grayson up against the wall of the tunnel overwhelms me.

Shit.

Head in the fucking game.

We work quickly, rushing up to the door in case there are any other guards around to alert the people inside of our presence.

Cruz grabs the guard's body and flips it over until we find a keychain connected to his belt. I dive down and unhook it, my gaze shifting to each of the boys.

I take a heavy breath and slide the key into the lock, knowing that the second I open this door, all hell is going to break loose. "Get your gun ready," King reminds me. "There's no turning back now."

# CHAPTER 11

With a hard pull, I slide the heavy lock back on the door and Grayson shoves past me, pushing the door hard, knowing that I would have struggled with its weight. It swings back, dragging across the concrete just as the door out in the parking lot had done.

The boys rush in before me, leaving me for last, and while they claim that this is all equal, I know they're wanting to assess the room before giving me a chance to come into the mess, but I won't be holding back. I don't need to be treated with kid gloves anymore. I know the consequences of living in a world surrounded by corruption. I know exactly what I'm getting myself into, and when I told the boys that I could handle it, I fucking meant it.

I race in after them, my gun held out, ready to shoot as I force myself in between Grayson and Carver. It's only been a second or two since the boys rushed the room, but the guards are only now just realizing something is off.

Their heads begin raising, assuming the scraping of the door had come from one of the guards, but seeing us standing before them, ready to rain down hell, they quickly jump into action.

Not fucking quick enough though.

My gaze sweeps across the room, trying to determine where the kids would be kept and I hardly get the whole way around before the first bullets ring out, way before the guards have a chance to even reach for their guns, most of them are still getting to their feet.

They all duck for cover as the boys handle the fucking room like the kings that they are. Bullets rain down around the bunker, ricocheting off the metal walls.

One thing is clear though, Paris Fucking Moustaff is not here.

The bunker is much bigger than the blueprints suggested, making me wonder if Dynasty was trying to keep this hidden or if Paris had gone to the effort to expand it. Seeing as though we're underground and absolutely nothing looks new about it, my guess is that Dynasty had the blueprints drawn up incorrectly.

A bullet zooms straight past my head and instead of fretting and panicking about it, it just pisses me off. I stare back at the guy who had let his bullet loose at my face and without hesitation, I squeeze down on the trigger and truly join the party.

He drops to the ground and as I go to find my next target, my gaze shifts to a part of the back wall that doesn't quite look right. "There," I call out to Cruz who somehow is now right beside me. "They've got to be in there. There are no other doors."

"GO," he yells back at me. "I'll cover you."

I run for my fucking life, darting through flying bullets and avoiding the assholes who want to put a bullet through my head. I reach the door and just as I grip the heavy chain that keeps it locked, two guards come racing at me, both anger and fear in their eyes. I don't get a chance to say hello though, as they both drop to the ground when bullets send their brains spurting out the front of their heads, splashing all over me.

I hold back vomit as my gaze flicks to Cruz. He looks back at me, double-checking that I'm okay before concentrating on the room around him. We can deal with the brains later, right now I have to get this fucking door open.

The boys start to spread out, wanting to keep me protected from all angles as I grip onto the chains and desperately try to free them, but there's no use. I'll never get them open with my bare hands.

I look around the fallen guards, but none of them seem to have keys connected to their belts like the guy at the last door had. I guess this one is up to me.

Lining myself up with the door, I hold my gun and clench my jaw. This is probably the stupidest thing I've ever done, but it's all I've got right now, and it seems to work in the movies. So before I get the chance to hesitate, I shoot, letting the bullet fly free.

It completely misses and a frustrated squeal tears out of me. I try again and again until I have no bullets left and only then I realize that while I haven't achieved exactly what I wanted, I was able to nick the chains enough to destroy the integrity of the loop. I turn the gun around and use the butt to smash the loop and I don't dare let up, I keep at it, letting out all the rage I feel for the boys as I duck and weave while trying to avoid getting shot in the back.

A shadow appears at my side and I raise the gun, ready to smash this guy's skull when I find Carver creeping in beside me. "I'm not strong enough," I call to him, hoping he can hear me over the thundering sound of the bullets echoing through the metal bunker.

Without hesitation, he grabs the gun from my hand and I shuffle out of the way. He brings it down so hard, the chain falls away. He drops the gun to the bloodied floor and reaches for the other that Cruz had shoved into my belt.

He hands it over and with the door unchained and a good handful of the guards down, King rushes toward us. "They're going to be ready for us," Carver reminds him.

"Not as fucking ready as I am."

Cruz and Grayson shuffle toward the main door, preparing themselves for when we get the kids out of here, wanting a clear path for them to be able to run out and back into the tunnel, but first things first—finding and freeing them.

Carver presses his strong body against the door as his firm grip circles the lock. He meets King's gaze as he steps directly in front of the door, the two of them ready to do this as a team. I keep away from the door, knowing that there's no way in hell that I'll be able to move fast enough to be helpful. This is exactly what King was talking about back at my place. I have to know my limits so that I won't be a liability.

"Ready?" Carver questions.

King nods. "Go."

The door swings open so fast that I nearly miss the fucking action of King racing forward into the dark room. Bullets fly at his face, but he avoids them like a fucking rockstar and fires back, only needing one shot to take the fucker out.

Bullets come flying from every direction as Carver stands with King, taking on the enemy, proudly ready to die for their cause.

Two more guards go down and King calls out, glancing back at me. "Now."

I don't hesitate, darting into the room. My gaze quickly scans the area to find the row of kids still seated in the hard chairs up against the dirty wall. Their eyes are covered, hands and ankles bound while their mouths are gagged with dirty material. It's probably been days since they've been let up from these chairs, having to soil themselves with no food or water.

Devastation tears through me but I have to put it aside until later, though one thing is for sure, seeing their little brothers and sisters like this sure as fuck has our hearts breaking and our motivation skyrocketing.

I drop down in front of Grayson's brother, the eldest of the kids, and tear the knife out of the holster at my thigh. I slip the tip of it under the material wrapped around his mouth and hope to God that I don't cut him as I try to break it free.

My hand works back and forth and as it does, I tear the blindfold off his eyes, letting him know that he's safe. "You're okay," I urge.

"Grayson is here. We're all here."

His face is dirty and the fear is overwhelming, but as I free him of the material around his mouth, I see his determination. He pulls at the binds on his ankles and wrists. "Get me out of here," he spits. "I'm going to fucking kill them."

I grab his chin and force his stare to mine. "Let your brother handle them. Our real fight is with Paris Moustaff, not hired goons. I need you here. We have to free these kids."

Hesitation shines in his eyes and I see the hope of killing his attackers fade from his eyes. "Okay," he rushes out, his determination so much like his big brother's. "Anything."

I cut him free and grab another knife from my belt before pressing it into his hand. He drops to his knees beside me despite his exhaustion and gets to work, desperately helping me free the other kids.

With the kids so damn scared and pulling away from us despite our words of encouragement, it's taking way too long. King rushes in to help free his brother and sister while Carver takes control of the remaining guards in the room.

The kids all get free and we start racing toward the door, King staying behind to eliminate the threats and cover our backs with Carver. We break out of the shitty room they were held in and I push them faster, racing toward the exit and into the tunnel knowing that Grayson and Cruz will have my back, even more so now that I stand with their siblings.

"Go, go, go," Grayson yells out, his words nearly drowned out by the sound of the guns. "Stay with them. Make sure they get out of here."

Despite how badly I want to stay behind with the guys, I have a job to do and I won't dare let them down. I run with the kids, breaking out into the tunnel while holding the hands of the younger ones, making sure they don't get left behind.

We run, our feet slamming against the hard concrete of the tunnel, the little light at the end is our only beacon of hope. We get halfway through the tunnel, each step just a little bit closer to freedom as the sound of the guns behind us echo through the tunnel with a haunting chill that these kids will never be able to forget.

I can almost make out the dead guard at the parking lot entrance when hands knot into my hair, yanking me back with a ferocious pull. I go down hard with a loud scream as a guard drops down on top of me. "I don't fucking think so, bitch," he spits, his dirty stench consuming me.

The kids all stop, looking back at me in horror as I shove my knee into the guard's junk with everything that I've got, but from this angle, I get his thigh, which only serves to piss him off. "Keep going," I yell at the kids, hoping to God that Grayson's brother has the brains to take charge and get them all out of here.

The kids squeal as the guard grabs at me, pressing his weight over me and punching me right in the fucking ribs. I cry out in pain as I hear the horrified echoes of the children's gasps flowing down the tunnel.

"Get off her," I hear cried before a younger-looking Grayson comes bearing toward the guard and nails him in the jaw.

"FUCK," the guy roars, flying back just enough for me to bring up my boot and shove hard against his chest. I scramble to my feet and grab the miniature Grayson by the elbow, shoving him hard toward the terrified children. "Go. Leave me," I spit as the guard gets back to his feet and starts stalking me down the tunnel. "Run. The keys are in the fucking car. Head count before you go. Six kids, seven including you. Don't look back until you're back behind the gates of Ravenwood Estate."

"Are you sur—"

The guard lunges at me. "RUN."

He takes off like a fucking rocket, scooping up the kids as he goes and shuffling the rest in front of him, proving that he is, after all, going to one day be a hero just like his big brother.

I dart out of the way, not prepared to let this asshole get the drop on me a second time. My hands fall to my belt, feeling around for something to use when I find a small dagger, one I didn't even know was there. I tear it out of the holster and flip it to my right hand, right where it belongs, while reminding myself to thank the boys for saving my life once again.

The excitement bubbles within me, feeling as though I'm finally back to my roots, but I hold back, listening to the sound of the kids escaping and making sure that they're far enough away before taking this fucker out. Though I have to play it safe, too much confidence could end with him whooping my ass and getting to the kids before they can get out of here.

I need to bide my time and play it smart.

I listen to the sound of the guns. There's still rapid fire but it's not as consistent as it was five minutes ago. Perhaps this thing is finally coming to an end.

Bored of my waiting game, the guard lunges at me again, but this time, I'm ready.

I pull back and bring my knee up, just as he flies at me. My knee lands right in the center of his stomach, winding him, but his momentum is enough to throw me backward. I stumble, hardly catching myself before going back at him.

The dagger shoots out, but he has his wits about him enough to pull back, narrowly avoiding the sharp blade. I go again, slicing out in front of me, this time cutting a shallow arc across his chest. "Fuck, you little bitch. You'll pay for that."

I just laugh. "Fucking try me, asshole."

He races toward me, going for the dagger, but I duck and slam my knee back into his stomach before dodging out of the way, letting his momentum move past me, only to step in beside him and slam his face straight into the concrete wall of the tunnel.

Blood spurs from his nose as he cries out, but I keep on him, determined to finish this.

I kick him hard in the ribs before getting him in the back of his knees, forcing him down to the ground. He falls forward, only just catching himself and the thought enters my mind—how easy would it be to slit his throat?

Am I truly losing any goodness that I had inside of me? Am I crossing some kind of invisible line?

The sound of tires screeching echoes through the tunnel and

relief pulses through me.

The kids got away, but now I need to.

Not wanting to test my boundaries, I step around the side of the guard and nail him in the temple with the tip of my boot, knocking him the fuck out as I tuck the dagger back into my belt where I won't be tempted to slit any more throats. Besides, slitting throats is a messy sport and I'm already covered in brains. I'm going to have to shower for at least an hour to get the stench of this shit off me.

Knowing the kids are safe and hearing the sound of the gunshots echoing down the long tunnel, I turn back to the bunker and stare toward it, seeing the small shadows of the few remaining men inside.

That room is hell on earth and everything inside of me is telling me to sprint back toward it and help the guys where I can, but they would be able to concentrate better if I wasn't there. Right now, they think I'm safe in the car, speeding back toward Ravenwood Estate. They don't need to know that I'm still here. Besides, if I ran back in there, guns blazing, it's only going to increase the tension between us, and as much as I want to hate on them for the rest of my life, at some point, I would really love to get back to where we were in our relationships.

Despite my better judgment, I turn away and walk out of the stupid tunnel. The second I step out into the parking lot, I feel relief wash over me. It's over. At least, for me it is.

I drop my ass down onto the cool ground, staring back through the tunnel just in case another guard makes it past my boys and I have another ass to kick.

The exhaustion is real, and while I was only inside that bunker for maybe fifteen minutes, I feel like I've been running a marathon. I lean back on my hands in the empty lot, feeling deflated. I knew there was a chance that Paris wasn't going to be there, but I had hoped. I had hoped that I could put a perfectly round bullet through her head and that this was all going to be over, but as usual, she is three steps ahead of us.

This shit is never going to end.

The gunshots slow and as the minutes tick by, it eventually fizzles down to silence.

Bodies start making their way through the tunnel and I peer through, watching the boys make their way toward me. They're still so far away and all I see are fuzzy silhouettes in the distance, but as they creep closer, it becomes clear that maybe the guys coming toward me aren't my guys at all. What if these are Paris' hired muscle making their way out of the tunnel? What if my boys didn't make it?

My heart starts to race as every inch of me becomes alert and ready for an attack. I fly to my feet, my dagger in my hand while desperately wishing that I hadn't lost my other gun.

The people in the tunnel get closer and with each passing second, I feel myself getting sweatier and sweatier.

I should take off while I still have a chance, but my heart is telling me that the boys would have made it. They have to. They're too good to perish in a bullshit shootout like that. They're gods, impossible to defeat.

My hands start to shake, but as the guys in the tunnel pass the guard that I'd knocked out, they pause, looking over him for a short second. The fear inside my chest increases, but when one last gunshot rings out and a bullet slams right through the back of the guard's skull, everything eases within.

The guys make their way out of the tunnel, each of their confused gazes hitting me like a wrecking ball. "What the fuck are you doing here?" Grayson demands, glancing around the parking lot for the car and the kids. "What happened? You were supposed to leave with them."

I point back in through the tunnel at the guy lying dead in a pool of his own blood. "He happened. He grabbed me while we were trying to get out and then your stupid brother tried to fight him off. I told them to just keep running, get in the car, and go. If the guard had killed me and they were waiting …"

Carver nods and lets out a breath, leaving the rest of my comment unspoken. After everything we just went through to save them, I don't think any of us are willing to even entertain the idea of what could have happened had the guard gotten past me. "They got away? They're safe?"

"Assuming Grayson has taught his brother how to drive, they should already be home in their mother's arms."

Soft sighs of relief sound through the empty parking lot, but they die down when King meets my stare. "I was wrong to give you such a hard time about coming. You handled yourself well."

I stare back at him, my hurt shining so much brighter than anything else. It's one thing for the guys to betray my trust, but to doubt that I'd make such a reckless decision to tag along to something like this if I didn't think I would be able to handle it.

My gaze meets each of theirs as my chin raises. "You all want to make it up to me, then teach me how to fight."

"Fight?" Carver questions. "You can fight. It's scrappy, but effective."

I shake my head. "I want to fight like you guys. I want to be a warrior. I'm sick of being weak. I'm sick of being the girl who needs her douchebag boyfriends to always protect her. I'm sick of being the poor orphaned girl who can't take care of herself, who isn't strong enough to lead a group like Dynasty, and who doesn't have a damn person who thinks she's worthy of ruling. So, you're going to teach me how to fight. You're going to make me stronger, and you're going to turn me into someone whom the other fuckheads of Dynasty will respect without question."

They each watch me a second longer before finally nodding, but it's Grayson who finds the balls to actually speak. "The second you're ready, we'll start training."

I don't bother responding. There's no point. They know I'm grateful, but far too stubborn to fall in line with my praises of thanks. Instead, I turn and start making my way toward the ramp to lead us out of this bullshit parking lot maze.

Twenty minutes later, the latest stolen car comes to a stop inside my family's garage. We all bail out and both Carver and I head for the internal door of my home, seeing as though the rest of Dynasty thinks we're dead. King, Cruz, and Grayson take off to their homes to check on their siblings, and in this moment, I truly feel for Carver. He'd do anything to go and check on his sisters, but he can't, not until we tell the world that we're still alive. Until then, he's stuck hidden away in my home, just like me.

The garage door draws down and I make my way up to my room, feeling Carver following me up the stairs. Once inside my room, I close the door behind me, a silent message that I want to be left alone—whether he'll respect that or not is a mystery for now.

Within seconds, my clothes are on the bathroom floor and the hot stream of the shower is rushing down over my skin, washing away the chunks of brain and making me gag as I see them hitting the shower tiles and falling down the drain.

I take my time, scrubbing my body clean until I finally feel like myself again and only then do I turn off the shower and wrap my towel around me. I turn out the light and walk into my darkening bedroom to find Carver already half asleep in my bed.

I drop my towel and slide in between the sheets with him, letting him pull me into his warm, inviting arms. As the exhaustion quickly begins to claim me, I do everything I can not to think of the horrors still yet to come.

# CHAPTER 12

Hands rest against my shoulder before gently shaking me awake. "Babe," Cruz's voice seeps through my sleep-deprived mind. "Wake up."

"Get lost," I grumble, pulling away and falling back into Carver's arms, feeling as though I've only slept for a minute or two, but the brightness of my room that has my eyes clenching with irritation tells me otherwise.

"Okay, I can go," he says in a teasing tone. "But I kinda thought your morbidly inclined mind would wanna sneak into your own funeral and watch everyone sob for you. Plus, it's after midday. I mean, if it were nine in the morning, I'd get it, but you've been asleep for at least fifteen hours."

My eyes ping open to find a gorgeous face grinning down at me.

I push up onto my elbow, earning a groan out of Carver who clearly doesn't feel the same excitement, but if Cruz is right and we have been asleep for that long, then Carver can shove it and deal with the real world. "My funeral's today?"

"Uh-huh," he rumbles. "I don't know about you, but I've been waiting fucking days to watch the big fake sob-fest that Ember puts on for her fallen bestie."

"Shit," I laugh, pushing up until I'm sitting cross-legged. I rub my hands over my face, wishing these people could have organized the Elodie Ravenwood day of mourning for a much healthier hour. "Did you really have to go and mention her name? I kinda forgot that she existed for a while."

"Sorry," he mutters, a cheeky grin stretching across his delicious face and momentarily making me forget that we're in a weird place right now. "You know me, fuck ups are my number one talent."

I give him a hard stare as his gaze drops to my body, only to remind me that I went to bed stark naked last night. "Seriously?"

Cruz just laughs. "Come on. Get up. I'm sure we could find you something perfectly appropriate to wear."

"Damn it, Cruz," I mutter, throwing the blankets back and getting a slight thrill out of the way Carver flinches at the cold before forcing myself out of bed and onto my tired legs. "Why does that have to sound so freaking good?"

Cruz steps right into me, cutting me off with that fine, ripped body that has me drooling with need. It's been far too long since I've felt his touch, when in reality, it's only been a few painful days. His hands fall to my waist and I tilt my head to meet his intense stare, unable to keep myself from leaning into his hold. "It's always fucking good when it comes from my mouth."

I raise a brow, desperately willing myself not to crack a smile as I try to remember that I'm still so angry with him, but Cruz Danforth comes fully equipped with a set of special skills to make any woman fall at his feet and forget her own damn name. Hell, right now, I don't even think I remember why I was angry in the first place. All that matters is drowning in a sea of green as I stare up into his hypnotic gaze. "That cocky confidence of yours is going to get you in trouble one day."

Cruz winks and everything below the border clenches. "I'm counting on it."

I pull myself away from the ticking time bomb, needing that bit of space to keep my head screwed on correctly. He caught me in a weak moment. I was more than content living in my dreamland where I had four perfectly behaved men worshipping my body as though they'll never get to taste it again. It was magical and has left me more than willing to forgive and forget just to feel that same magic all over again.

But I won't. They won't be getting off that easily. I'll just have to kick the boys out of my room, visit the drawer beside my bed, and dust off a few toys. Though, the last time I tried to get myself off, I ended up with Paris breaking into my room and nearly getting stabbed for what must be the third or fourth time.

Fuck, maybe my pussy is cursed.

I shake off the thoughts and pull out of Cruz's arms before cutting across my room to the massive walk-in closet. "How much time do we have?"

"Twenty minutes or so," Cruz murmurs, walking into the doorway of the closet and leaning up against the frame.

My eyes bug out of my head. "Twenty minutes?" I demand. "Holy fuck, Cruz. You should have woken me like an hour ago. I can't get ready in twenty minutes. There's too much to do. How the hell am I supposed to make myself look like your worst nightmare who just stepped out of hell in twenty minutes?"

Cruz laughs and steps deeper into the closet. "Babe, you look like the fucking angel of death any day of the week. You could turn up dressed as a fucking clown wearing a pink tutu and they would still kneel before you."

I shake my head. "No, you don't get it. I can't just look like my usual fucked up self in leather pants, sexy boots, and a goddamn chip on my shoulder. This whole faked death thing is a chance for a new start. I get to be reborn today, and I get to do it in the image I want the rest of Dynasty to see me as. This is a big, defining moment for me, and I want it to be so fucking perfect that kids will talk about it for the rest of their lives."

Carver grumbles from the bed. "Babe, you're coming back from the dead. Go naked if you want to. No matter what you wear, people are going to talk about it."

I grab a heel from my shoe rack, shove my head out of my closet and launch it at his stupid head. "You're such a guy. You don't get it."

Carver narrowly avoids the shoe and climbs out of bed, his cock standing at attention as he stretches and runs his hand down his chest. His other hand falls to his hard cock and he smirks across the room at me. "You and I are already dead, so what do you say about one last good fuck before we rise from the ashes and blow their fucking minds?"

I glance away from his gorgeous cock and focus on the rack of clothes before me. "You're on your own," I tell him. "But if you stop by King's room, I bet he'd be willing to help you out. He could use something shoved down his throat to keep those bullshit comments from flying out of his damn mouth."

"The fuck did you just say?" King's voice comes booming through my room.

I cringe, sinking deeper into my closet. "Fuck," I mutter, glaring across at Cruz. "Thanks for the heads up."

Cruz's hands fly up. "Hey, I'm in the fucking closet with you. I didn't see him either. That shit is all on you."

Carver walks by the closet door and straight out of my room, his dick still in his hand. When King doesn't say another word, I happily assume that he left with Carver to get their asses ready for my big, shining moment ... or to follow through on my suggestion.

My eyes shuffle over my clothes, stopping on a dark red latex dress that I haven't had the pleasure of trying on before. "Perfect," I grin, taking the dress off the hanger and looking over it. This is going to be a bitch to get into, but it'll be so worth it. But how?

My gaze shifts to Cruz who still stands right beside me and my grin only stretches wider. "What?" he questions, knowing the look in my eyes all too well.

"I'll make you a deal," I tell him. "You help me get into this thing and while you do, I'll give you a chance to plead your case."

His eyebrows shoot straight up as he all but snatches the dress out of my hands and studies it closely, trying to figure out how the hell to get it on. "You got yourself a deal, babe, but I don't know how helpful I'm going to be, like how the fuck does this even work? Do you step into it or does it go over your head? I mean, it's a little stretchy, but … fuck."

I shrug my shoulders, looking over it with the same complex confusion. "Trial and error?" I suggest.

"Your funeral," he jokes before laughing even harder at his ridiculous little pun. "Arms up. Let's do this shit."

Cruz gathers the dark red latex in his hands, making a hole for my head to slip through as I twist my hair up into a bun, not willing to let it get tangled in the material, not unless I want to lose chunks of it on my big coming back from the dead day.

He double-checks that he's holding it the right way with the underwired cups and the coochy high slit at the front before shoving the tight material over my arms and head. It gets stuck on my shoulders. "Fucking hell," he mutters to himself, getting busy trying to yank it down into place.

The underwired cups plaster across my face as the latex slaps across my skin, every time Cruz pulls it out just a little, it sounds better than one of King's amazing ass spanks. "Holy fuck, dude. Hurry up. I'm going to need a fucking facelift after this."

"I'm getting there," he murmurs, concentrating hard. "Wait," he says, stopping. "You're fucking naked. Didn't you want panties or something first?"

"No," I scoff. "Not in this thing. Best to go without. Just make sure I don't trip and fall and flash my fucking cooch to all of Dynasty."

Cruz chuckles to himself, probably committing the vision to memory as he gets back to work. "They'd be honored to see such a perfectly tight pussy, although, its beauty is bound to give some of those old fuckers a heart attack," he muses. "Wouldn't that be the best way to go? Death by pussy? You know, I'd be fucking honored to be smothered to death by that thing. Any fucking day, babe. Just say the word and you can come and sit on my face."

A massive, smitten grin stretches across my lips and I let it fly strong and proud knowing that he can't see it. I fucking love Cruz's humor. His chilled, relaxed light is the perfect match to balance out the boys' darkness. At first, I thought it was just Grayson and Carver who struggled on the dark side, but the more I've gotten to know them, the more I've realized just how dangerously close King is to toeing that line, just like me. Cruz is a must in our group. He keeps us all sane, all down to earth and grounded. Without him, we'd all be locked up and fighting our demons.

He pulls the latex a little harder and my eyes pop out the top. "Cruz," I whisper with the underwire cups pressing against my lips.

His eyes meet mine, softening as he recognizes the white flag flying high in my tone. "I know," he whispers, stepping in closer and pressing a soft, lingering kiss to my forehead. "You just need time."

I nod, realizing that he isn't about to drop to his knees and start groveling for forgiveness like Grayson and King are bound to do. He doesn't need to because I know his heart just as he knows mine. I know he didn't intend to blow me up. He was backed into a corner just like the rest of them, and I know deep in my heart that he's spent every second since hating himself for his part in it.

"It just hurts," I tell him. "I understand why you did it and I respect that, I would have done the same thing had I been in your position, and I forgive you for having to make such a hard call, but as much as I want to forgive and forget, it doesn't just magically take the pain away."

He steps into me again, getting the dress over my face and curling his arms around me, rubbing his thumbs back and forth over my ass cheeks. "You know that I'm going to spend every day of my life making it up to you?" he tells me. "Every fucking time I close my eyes, I see your body being thrown through the air. I begged them to stop. I broke two of King's fucking ribs with my knee, but we had to keep going. We trusted Carver to take care of you, and while I knew he wouldn't have done it in the same way that I would, I know that he wouldn't have let any harm come to you. I know you didn't feel it, but you were safe."

I nod and raise my chin, silently begging him to kiss me. "I'm starting to realize that."

Cruz brings his lips down to mine and it's like coming home. He gives me everything and just as always when it comes to Cruz, I feel all of his emotions through his warm kiss. The regret that sits heavily in his chest, the relief to have me home, the self-hate for not staying with his brothers in the first place. I might have been the one wronged by the boys, but they're harboring their own pain and it's a deep, guttural pain that I'll never be able to take away.

Cruz pulls back and rests his forehead against mine. "I fucking love you, Winter. You're my whole fucking world and while I know it's hard for you to hear that right now, just know that I'm not going anywhere. I will wait as long as it fucking takes to get you right back where I had you."

My eyes close with his sweet, overwhelming words and I let out a soft breath. "I'm counting on it."

His lips drop back to mine and I soak up every second of this perfect moment with him, knowing that it'll be short-lived, and like clockwork, a throat clears by my closet door and I glare at Grayson for ruining it. "I'd hate to break up the party, but we're leaving in like six fucking minutes and Ellie is still half-naked, not that I'm complaining."

I roll my eyes and Cruz looks back at Grayson. "Then help me get this dress on her. It's fucking impossible."

Grayson scoffs as though he holds all the secrets of the universe and strides into my closet, studying the dress as though it's a challenge set out just to fuck with his head. His finger and thumb rub over his lips as he gets lost in deep thought. "Alright," he finally says. "We pull out from all sides and then yank it down."

Cruz nods and the boys get into place, one on either side just as Carver and King show up in the doorway, stupid amused smirks on their faces as they watch my humiliation. Cruz and Grayson meet each other's gaze and with a nod, they get to work.

They each grab a handful of latex and just as planned, stretch it out before yanking it down into place. "Ahhhh, fuck," I screech as the underwired cups sit awkwardly over my tits, squishing them half to death. "My titties."

My hands dive into the front of the skin-tight dress, readjusting the goodies until they sit comfortably in the cups, and damn, does it do them justice. My tits are pushed up, plump, and fucking ripe for the taking. They look like they've been hand-delivered to my chest by the devil himself. In fact, the whole fucking dress looks like it came from the darkest pits of hell.

I match it with my black thigh-high boots—a new pair, seeing as though my other ones were destroyed from running through the woods for two fucking days. I spritz a bit of perfume, one that King gave to me just to drive him wild with need, and put my hair into a high, slicked-back ponytail. I could go the extra length by adding the matching latex gloves that came with the dress, but that just screams Halloween BDSM whore, and that's not quite the look I'm going for today … close, but not quite.

I excuse myself to race into the bathroom to pee, brush my teeth, and find my favorite dark red lipstick, and in hindsight, I probably should have peed before getting into this dress, but it's too late now.

I make my way downstairs to find the four boys waiting for me at the bottom in the most jaw-dropping suits that I've ever seen and I realize that this is becoming a little tradition of ours. Their eyes all pulse with a million different emotions, but pride and hunger are shining the brightest. They look like the best kind of meal.

I wonder if we should skip this whole thing and I can slowly undress them instead.

I shake off the thought, knowing just how bad of an idea that really is. "Alright," I say, hitting the bottom step as Grayson moves into my side and takes my arm. "Let's go to my funeral."

# CHAPTER 13

The dress is way too tight to even attempt letting the boys squish me into the trunk again, so I sit up front with my head down as Grayson drives through the streets of Ravenwood Heights. Nerves filter through me. I haven't exactly prepared a speech for this or have any experience with rising from the dead, but I'm assuming it's going to be a little something like 'Hey, joke's on you, I'm not dead. Let's go get fucked up back at my place!'

Actually, with Paris still haunting our town, maybe a party at my place isn't such a great idea, but it's the thought that counts.

Grayson slows the car and I raise my head to see the same cathedral where we said our final goodbye to Tobias King and a smugness settles through me. Tobias' funeral was fucking awesome. It was the royal treatment and seeing as though mine is being held here too, I guess that means they're going all out for me.

It's a shock to see how many people have come to say goodbye to me as the crowd of darkly dressed figures all cram through the cathedral doors. I haven't exactly been the nicest person in my short eighteen years, so I suspect that quite a few of these guests are here out of duty instead of grief.

Grayson drives straight past the cathedral and guilt settles into my soul at seeing Cruz's mom standing with her husband and newly saved sons, sobbing with grief. "Shit," Cruz murmurs from behind me, knowing just how hard all of this is on her, but she'll pull through. It won't be long until our secret is out and all her grief will vanish. Though I don't doubt that Cruz is going to get one hell of an ass-whooping.

Grayson finally brings the car to a stop behind the massive church where we can sneak in through the back undetected. We all clamber out of the car and Carver grabs my hand, darting across the lot to keep us out of sight.

The boys take off through the backdoor with more than enough excuses to be there, though they have to stop before walking through to wipe the stupid grins off their faces and pretend that today is the worst day of their lives. At least, I hope that's how they'd feel about being at my funeral—my real funeral, that is.

They quickly disappear out of sight, and knowing that there are bound to be people that way, Carver and I sneak through the shadows until we find one of the many back rooms. He breaks the window right off its tracks and gently places it down, not wanting the bad juju that's bound to come from vandalizing a cathedral.

Carver takes my waist and hoists me up through the window and while there aren't any people in this little back room, I do what I can to keep my legs glued together. Again with the bad juju. I'm sure getting my pussy out in a church isn't going to end well for me.

Carver comes straight through behind me, grabbing hold of my waist to balance me as he comes flying through so fast. We get to work.

We sneak out through the back room and through the long corridors, doing our best not to get caught. We hear the boys talking to someone, keeping them distracted, and we don't waste our opportunity to run.

We take off until we reach a door and Carver stops. "This is it. This leads out to the main part of the church. Are you ready for this? There's going to be people everywhere. We have to be discreet."

I nod. "Discreet isn't really my specialty."

"No shit," he mutters under his breath.

We meet each other's stare and with a small nod, Carver slowly pulls the door open.

We look in to find the cathedral filled with bodies. There must be hundreds of people here so far, and with every passing second, more come through the massive doors.

We stand right up at the front of the cathedral and I can see perfectly where my casket is going to sit. "Wow, this really is morbid," I say as a strange unease settles over me. "What a shame, I kinda thought this was going to be fun."

"Look at the bright side," he tells me. "At least people actually showed up. You could be staring out at an empty church. Now that would fucking suck."

"Good point," I mutter, nodding toward the massive vases of beautifully arranged flowers that all but cover the space behind the casket stand. "Do you think anyone will catch us behind there?"

Carver grins. "Hope not."

He takes my hand once again and with our heads down, we sneak out into the cathedral, doing our best to keep hidden despite being the most obvious people in the room. I mean, I must be the only person in here not wearing black.

We reach the big vases in no time, and when no one in the crowd screeches, gasps, or squeals, we each let out relieved sighs and drop down, hoping to God that no one decides to take a stroll back here.

We sit for at least ten minutes before the soft music starts and Earnest Brooks stands and approaches the dais. "Please stand," he asks the congregation, making my stomach drop.

"Him?" I whisper-yell as a sickly, paleness comes over Carver at seeing the guy who he last saw in a brothel doing who the hell knows what. "Why the hell does he get the honor of running this shit?"

"Good fucking question," he grumbles beside me, doing everything he can to not look Earnest's way.

"Is now a good time to quiz you on what you actually saw in there?"

His jaw clenches and he glares back at me. "I fucking told you to never bring it up again. I thought we were clear on that."

I laugh to myself but it quickly fades away as I watch Grayson,

Cruz, and King, along with other heads of Dynasty carrying a black casket down the long aisle, their heads all bowed in devastation. "Ah, fuck," I murmur as Carver's fingers slip into mine, hearing the sobs come from all corners of the cathedral. "Maybe we should have just run away when you suggested it."

"Sounds pretty fucking good now, huh?"

"You're damn right, it does," I say, eyeing the casket a little more closely. "Who the fuck is in there?"

Carver shakes his head. "I've got no fucking idea."

I roll my eyes and watch as the casket is placed upon the table in front of us. The men all take a second, paying their respects before turning and walking back to their wives to take their seats. Grayson, King, and Cruz linger though, letting their grief shine through just in case Paris has some of her men seated in the crowd. Though, I guess it doesn't matter. It'll only be a matter of time before they all know my death was faked.

The boys turn to take their seats with their families and I watch as Cruz sits beside his mother only to be snubbed and ignored, and while I hate that for him, I'm not going to lie—it kinda feels good. After all, Cruz would have been as honest as he could be with his mother and told her that it was his actions that killed me, and she would have punished him for it, even if it meant saving her other sons.

"It is with a heavy heart that I stand before you today to bid farewell to our great leader, last of her line, Elodie Ravenwood," Earnest starts. "She was a rising star who valued honesty and change and no doubt, given the time, would have achieved many incredible successes that those who follow could have only dreamed about. She had a fighting spirit, but her time was brutally cut short and that spirit will forever remain in the hearts of her people. It has come time for us to say farewell to the true heir of Dynasty and remember all that she has done for us in her short reign. We will not mourn. We will not shed a tear of grief. Instead, we celebrate her one last time, knowing that she is home with her loving parents, Andrew and London Ravenwood."

My eyes grow watery and I blink back the tears, desperately trying not to get emotional over something that hasn't even happened.

"Many of you did not get the chance to know Elodie on a personal level, you did not get the opportunity to know her story or her heart. So, I invite Grayson Beckett, a close acquaintance of Elodie's, who has prepared a few words in the hopes that Elodie's people could have known where she came from and how she became such a strong and caring leader."

There's nothing but silence through the cathedral as Earnest moves away from the dais and takes his seat. Grayson stands and makes his way to the stage, buttoning his suit jacket as he goes with a stack of papers in his hands, no doubt the eulogy that he wrote for me.

"You didn't tell me Grayson had written a speech," I mutter to Carver, unable to tear my eyes off Grayson as he looks out at the sea of bodies before him.

"I didn't know," Carver fires back.

"Elodie Ravenwood was a survivor," Grayson starts, standing proud and tall while making my heart shatter into a million pieces. Maybe I was wrong to come here today. It's too real, all these people grieving and sobbing for me and Grayson saying goodbye despite knowing that I'll be sleeping in his arms tonight. It's too much. "At the young age of two months old, Elodie was torn from her loving parents in a callous attack, one that we as a community will feel until our dying days. That night, Andrew and London Ravenwood were brutally murdered by the very people they trusted, leaving their baby girl alone and unprotected in this world filled with corruption. I don't know how she survived that night, but someone was watching over her.

"Unknown to the rest of Dynasty, Elodie was put into foster care. She traveled from home to home, not knowing her true identity as she battled being in the system. It wasn't kind to her, but she wasn't kind in return. Foster care is where she grew up, where she gained her strength and her no-bullshit attitude. Despite how she hated it, it molded her into the fierce, relentless, and often reckless woman that I had the pleasure of falling in love with."

Ahhhh, fuck. I need to be in his arms.

I stand, raising my chin with pride, and walk out from behind the massive vases keeping me concealed. Grayson notices me straight away and a wide grin stretches across his face as gasps of horror and confusion start filling the cathedral.

I ignore every little sound and walk straight into Grayson's welcoming arms and stretch up onto my tippy-toes, pressing my lips to his in a long-awaited kiss. "I love you too," I murmur. "I couldn't let you say the rest of that speech. That's our story, not theirs."

Relief shines in his eyes as he looks down at me. "Thank fuck for that."

The gasps get louder and louder and I pull out of his arms and look toward the crowd, only I didn't come here to let them know that I was alive, I came here to fucking rule.

I walk across the front of the stage and up the small step leading to the casket, but I don't dare stop. My heeled boot presses against the top of the casket and just as I go to step straight up onto it, Carver's hand slips into mine, helping me up.

I turn to face the crowd, standing before them like the fucking bad bitch that I am, my dark red latex dress speaking volumes. "Who's that?" I hear a kid in the front ask his mother.

The mother gasps, her eyes wide as I meet her horrified stare. "That's … that's Elodie Ravenwood."

The kid screams, his high-pitched wail setting off every other kid in the cathedral, the sound bouncing off the high ceilings like a haunting echo. "GHOST!"

The screams and shrieks are horrendous as kids start bolting for their lives, while their parents sit in shock, staring at me as though they can't believe what they're seeing.

I can't help but laugh as I watch the chaos unfold around me, but the laughter fades away as I find Ember Michaelson … or Harding, whichever the fuck she's going by now, staring up at me in panic. Her gaze drops and she starts scrambling through her bag. I meet Carver's stare. "Quick. Grab her before she gets a chance to tell Paris."

He moves like lightning, flying down from the front of the church and quickly burying himself in the crowd. People move out of his way, knowing exactly what would happen if they tried to stop him. She tries to run, but she should know better when it comes to Dante Carver.

Ember is dragged out of the pew and brought to the front, away from the crowd as Grayson's booming voice draws the crowd's immediate attention. "Ladies and gentlemen, your leader, the very much alive, Elodie Ravenwood."

Cheers holler around the cathedral as some remain sobbing, their emotions already too wound up to comprehend what's happening right before their eyes. I give it a moment before raising my hands, asking for silence.

The room falls quiet and I notice the other heads of Dynasty discreetly moving away from their families to come and stand with me, making a show of support despite not knowing a damn thing that's been going on, though I'm sure I'll be hearing all about their disappointment in that as soon as this is over.

Grayson moves away from the dais and stands by Carver's side as both King and Cruz move to my other side, the whole council and my boys creating a strong, united front, showing the whole community that we are stronger than ever before.

"You have no idea how grateful I am to be standing here before you today, though odd as it may be, I'm glad that I have this opportunity to share some truths with you all." I meet King's stare and he gives me a proud nod of encouragement and that one small gesture has my chin raising even higher. "There have been many whispers over the past few months and I have come here to set the record straight. I am sure by now that you have all heard of my mother, London Ravenwood, heard of the stories, her brilliance, courage, and beauty, but what some of you don't know is that my mother was a twin."

Gasps are heard all around but I don't let that deter my speech. I'm on a roll and it's going to stay that way. "Paris Moustaff is my aunt and she is everything that my mother wasn't. She's jealous, bitter, and has a dark heart. It was her involvement that saw my parents murdered, and it has been by her hand that I spent years jumping from foster home to foster home. She has followed me my whole life, inserting herself into my world, waiting for the right moment to strike. It was her intention to fool us all. She had planned on stealing my mother's identity and ending my life, to slot straight into the role that my mother left behind. She inserted people into my life," I say, pointing out Ember. "But every single one of her plans have failed, until recently. Paris kidnapped seven of our children and the price of their safe return was my death."

The gasps continue, like a chorus of shock. People stand in outrage while others just watch on in confusion. "I was prepared to hand myself over. I had the gun, loaded and ready, but we were not going to give in that easily. My death was faked. The King's cabin up in the woods was blown up and I along with it. Dante Carver and I went into hiding while the incredibly talented men of Dynasty found our kidnapped children and brought them home safely, but during the raid, Paris was not found, meaning our people are no longer safe. Paris will stop at nothing. She is responsible for multiple attacks and she will not get away with it."

The people roar their encouragement and I continue on, my voice getting louder by the second. "We will end her and we will take back what is ours. We will not fall under her hold. Dynasty will not perish.

We will forever thrive."

"KILL THE BITCH," comes from a booming voice in the crowd, making a wicked grin stretch across my face.

"That's exactly what I intend to do," I tell them, looking across the front row of bodies to find Cruz's mom wiping her tears and standing proud. "As for now, we celebrate another victory because tomorrow, when she realizes that my body is not rotting ten feet below ground, the real war begins."

# CHAPTER 14

"We should never have been kept in the dark," Harlen Beckett demands, his hand slamming down on the table in the council chambers.

I take a deep breath, remembering my resolve not to be so reckless and to think things through before going off on these assholes. "If there was a need to tell you all, I would have. However, it was a split-second decision. We had less than a minute to act and we did what we had to do," I say, not ready to admit that I was left in the dark as well, but the truth of that will die with me. Besides, I'm not about to throw the boys to the wolves when I haven't even finished clawing at them myself. "Sure, it was messy and we took risks, and before you argue that they are your children and that you had the right to know, I completely agree, but we made the call to keep it quiet. Paris needed to believe I was dead and to do that, we had to have all of Dynasty believing the lie, mourning and making funeral preparations until the last minute."

Harlen slowly nods, the anger still clear on his face, but he turns his attention toward Ember who stands in the corner of the room with Cruz at her back, her hands bound. "This conversation is not over, but speaking of not letting Paris in on the secret. What do you suppose we should do with her offspring?"

My gaze swivels around the room until it lands on Ember's pissed-off stare. "If it were up to me, I'd have slaughtered her just like her father, but apparently we have to allow her to plead her case and take a vote."

Earnest Brooks nods beside me and I muster up every ounce of will power to stop picturing him in adult diapers. "That is true, Miss Ravenwood. If the girl has been accused of wrongdoings and holds a seat on the council, she must be rewarded the opportunity to plead her innocence."

Ember fights against Cruz's hold. "Wrongdoings? I haven't done anything wrong except being related to her. You can't do this. Stop being such a fucking bitch. What are you even accusing me of doing?"

"Aiding and abetting a known fugitive," Carver throws back at her, leaning back in his seat like he was watching a movie play out before him. "Intent to cause bodily harm. Corruption. Or how about just being a shitty person?"

"Intent to cause who bodily harm?" she spits. "I haven't hurt anyone."

I scoff. "Well, I have a war coming down on me, so I don't exactly have much time to sit around trying to figure out what you did and didn't do. I think we should just throw you in a cell until we can squeeze a trial into our busy schedules, though you should be warned, our schedules are really packed at the moment. It might be a while before you can get in to settle this."

"THAT'S FUCKING BULLSHIT," she roars, thrashing against Cruz.

I fly out of my seat, unable to hold back my reckless nature. I storm across the chamber, practically running at her. My hand curls around her hair and I tear her head back before pressing my knife to her throat. "YOU KNOW WHAT'S FUCKING BULLSHIT?" I spit, my throat hurting from the deep growl of my tone. "THAT I CAN BET EVERYTHING THAT I HAVE THAT YOU KNEW PARIS WAS KIDNAPPING THOSE KIDS. YOU FUCKING KNEW WHERE THEY WERE AND YOU DIDN'T SAY SHIT."

"I DIDN'T."

I scoff. "I don't fucking believe you."

"I … I …"

"You were at that party, right where all those kids were. How the fuck did they get kidnapped, huh? The only thing that makes sense is that you had something to do with it."

Mr. Danforth stands, his jaw clenched as fury burns in his eyes. "IS THIS TRUE? DID YOU HAVE SOMETHING TO DO WITH THIS? SPEAK NOW, GIRL."

"I … fuck. Okay. I unlocked the door. I let them in, but I swear,

I didn't know they were going to kidnap those children," she says, her eyes wide with fear. "If I'd known, I never would have done it. I didn't know. You have to believe me. Please, Winter, come on. You know me better than anyone else here."

The knife drops from my hand and I rear back, slapping her so fucking hard that my hand stings, the pain throbbing in my palm. She cries out but I don't wait around to hear her sobs. "You're right, I do know you better than anyone else here. Which is why I know better than to trust a damn word that comes spewing out of your mouth." My gaze shifts to Cruz's. "Take her to the cells. She can rot down there for all I care."

Ember drops to her knees, her arms sliding out of Cruz's grip and momentarily taking him by surprise. Hell, I'm pretty damn shocked too. I've never been able to slip out of his hold—any of the guys for that matter. So, either Cruz is getting rusty on his hostage skills or Ember is even more slimy than we thought.

"Please, no, Winter," she begs, crawling along the dirty floor to my feet. "I can't go there. I'm not cut out for a cell. Please, don't do this to me. I swear, I'll do better. I'll tell you anything you want to know. You can't ... you can't do this to me. I have rights."

She grabs my leg, clawing onto me as though that's supposed to change my mind, but in all honesty, seeing a bitch on her knees begging just makes me feel all kinds of gross. "You're so fake," I mutter, kicking her off me as Cruz steps in behind her and hauls her to her feet. "Get her out of here. She's just embarrassing herself now."

Cruz nods and starts dragging her out of the room as she screams and fights against his hold, showing the other men around the table just how much she doesn't belong here. Though, it wasn't that long ago that I was causing scenes in this very room. Maybe it's my ego talking, but I'm the leader and that means that I'm entitled to have as many tantrums as I want. I can only imagine the shit that was going through the other council members' minds. Though, that's all in the past. I'm stepping up and making my father proud of not only the woman I've grown to be, but as the new leader of Dynasty. I'm going to pull my shit together and soar.

The second the door closes behind Cruz and Ember, I let out a sigh and drop back into my seat, glancing around the table and noting that every one of the men who sit before me look just as exhausted as I feel. "Look," I start, taking a risk, knowing that what I'm about to suggest could come back and bite me on the ass. I meet each of their curious stares. "I know you're all about your traditions and policies, but what's it going to take to get this bitch out of here? I can't sit across this table from her and have her living just down the road for the rest of my life. I mean, can we just vote out the whole Harding line? Is that even a thing?"

Loud sighs of relief come from all around the table. "Thank fuck for that," Matthew Montgomery says, his tone way out of line for such a formal table, but it shows just a sliver of his true personality, one that I appreciate and would probably get along with if it weren't for the fact that he's also a dick. He glances around the table. "I don't know about you guys, but Elodie is enough drama for me. I don't want to deal with Harding's offspring for the next twenty years. I don't trust her one bit."

"I agree," Harlen Beckett says to my left. "The girl is only going to bring us trouble."

Earnest shakes his head beside me. "I'm sorry, but we can't. As much as I cannot stand the vile creature, our by-laws specifically state that no founding family line can be removed from leadership unless done voluntarily."

My lips pull up into an irritated sneer. "So, change the by-laws," I state. "They were written a million years ago when every family stood as one. My grandfather could not have foreseen what would go down fifty years after writing the laws. Had he known of the corruption and disaster that would have come from his life's work, he would never have written that. We owe it to him to rebuild Dynasty in his true vision and to turn this sinking ship around. It used to be something great. We truly were a Dynasty, but now we're just scrambling to keep our heads above water. So, what's stopping us? Is there some bullshit rule that states the by-laws cannot be ruled against or are we going to allow Ember Harding to sit across from us every fucking day, giving her and her psychotic mother access to our world, to our kids?"

"Fuck the by-laws," Mr. Danforth says. "That bitch is the reason my sons were taken from me. She tortured and humiliated them. They're just children. They've sat in my wife's arms sobbing since their return and I will not allow it to happen again. I say we remove Ember Harding and scrub the Harding stain from our great organization, and the second we're done with that, we go after Paris. Who is with me?"

Carver stands, raising his hand, leading the pack. "I vote to have her removed."

King follows, standing tall. "I vote to have her removed."

Harlen Beckett goes next, quickly followed by Matthew Montgomery and soon enough, every man at the table is standing, their eyes locked on mine. "Then it's sorted. Ember Harding will be removed from Dynasty along with any blood relation. It will be as though the Harding line never existed. However," I say, my eyes skimming around the room as each of the men start taking their seats. "With Paris still out there, I am not comfortable releasing Ember from our cells. She will remain locked up until Paris Moustaff has been eliminated, only then will she be escorted out of Ravenwood Heights and out of the country."

Heads nod all around the table, all but the one directly to my right. "The by-laws state that there must be sixteen families represented at all times. We are already down to fifteen with the Scardoni line being wiped out. This puts us at fourteen."

My gaze narrows into a harsh glare, probably too harsh but my patience is being threatened. "Are there any by-laws in your precious book that tell me how exactly I'm supposed to rectify that?"

"I, umm …" he shakes his head, momentarily stumbling over his words before pulling himself together. "No, Miss Ravenwood, there is not. The by-laws were put together to avoid such certain situations."

I turn back to the faces that watch me all too closely. "I have a feeling that my own suggestions as to who should replace those family lines would not go down well, so how about this? Each man sitting around this table will be given three days to consider an applicant which will be presented to the table. Each applicant must be willing and able to take over such a role, they must be clean and trustworthy, no bullshit skeletons in their closets. I want background searches, financial checks, family history, and medical searches done. I want every little bit of dirt on these applicants. I want to know about your guy's first grade teacher who had an affair with the gym instructor. Nothing is off limits. I refuse to have something come and bite us in the ass five years down the track. Is that clear?"

"Yes, ma'am," comes from Matthew Montgomery, making my stomach clench with unease, not liking the way he seems to be sucking up to me more than usual.

"Then what?" Harlen Beckett questions.

I shrug my shoulders, not having thought this far through but it couldn't be too hard. "Then we do what we usually do, we vote. I'll narrow the list of applicants down to roughly five or six, and from there we will decide as a group, who shall be awarded with the two open seats at our table. Then, I'm sure all the wives would want to throw some elaborate party so we need to be ready for that. I don't want any surprises. We'll have to double security, passcodes for entry, RSVPs, that way every single body inside the party is accounted for."

"Perhaps we shall postpone any celebrations until after Paris has been dealt with," Mr. Danforth suggests just as his son comes striding back through the door looking incredibly lost as to why we're talking about celebrations.

Just as I go to agree with him, Carver cuts me off. "Trust me," he starts. "I'm usually the first to agree with postponing a party, but in this case, it may work against us. The families of Dynasty are already scared. They see us all falling one by one. We need to show them that we're not backing down, that we're not going into hiding over this, and that we're the ones with control."

"But we're not in control," I insist. "Paris has beat us at every turn."

"But the second we admit that to our people, all hell would break loose. We need to stand as a fucking force now more than ever," he says, awakening that fighting spirit within me. "Besides, what better opportunity to draw her out? Paris wouldn't be able to resist a public display at a party."

Damn it. The boy has a point.

I take a breath and nod. "I'll think about it."

Carver nods in return and just as I go to dismiss the meeting, Mr. Danforth clears his throat. "May I have the floor?"

My brows furrow and I quickly shoot my gaze to Cruz, who seems just as clueless as me. I wave my hand apathetically, giving Mr. Danforth free rein to speak his mind. "By all means. Go ahead."

"Rest your mind. It is nothing of importance," he tells me, a soft fondness spreading through his gaze. "In fact, quite the opposite, just an observation." He straightens his shoulders and raises his chin with pride. "I would like to take a moment to acknowledge how well I think you are handling yourself, today in particular. You have shown respect for your fellow members, a fierce protectiveness over your people, and demonstrated just how far you would go to honor the great founder of Dynasty. Today, Elodie Ravenwood, you have earned my respect, and I assume, the respect of the men sitting around you. You're still growing and learning your position here, while also making some impactful mistakes, but I do suspect that you are going to blossom into a fine leader, perhaps even the leader that Dynasty truly needs right now."

I stare, my stomach flip-flopping from side to side, unsure of what to say. Karleigh always told me that I was shit at accepting a compliment and I guess she was right. "Umm … thank you," I tell him, my gaze falling away. "If I knew I was getting graded on my performance, I would have tried to smile a little more."

"I wholeheartedly agree," Matthew Montgomery says, standing and meeting my hard stare. "I must admit that at the beginning, I had my doubts, as many of these men did. You were reckless, wild, and unpredictable, and yes, you still are those things, but today in light of recent events, you have shown restraint. You have gained my respect and I now proudly look at you as my leader. It is because of this that I feel it is my duty to inform you that over the past few days, as your people grieved your loss, others were rallying for your position, and I believe this puts yet another target on your back."

My brows furrow as my gaze shifts to Carver and King sitting around the table.

"Elaborate," Grayson cuts in from his position behind me, not giving me a chance to question it myself.

Matthew's gaze flicks to Grayson's before slicing across the table to Harlen's and finally, settling back on mine. "Harlen Beckett," Matthew says solemnly. "From the moment news spread of your death, he has been campaigning to take hold of leadership, and I fear that this has been going on long before your 'death.'"

I lean back into my seat, silently dismissing Matthew while still wondering why he's trying to creep so far up my ass. The usual Matthew is a dick. He's constantly fighting my decisions and doing his best to make me look like an incompetent idiot in front of these guys, and now, all of a sudden, he's my brand-new bestie. Move over Ember, there's a new snake on the loose.

My gaze settles on Harlen who's quick to straighten in his seat. His hand shoots out, holding it up as he begins to explain himself. "You must understand," he starts as his son steps in closer to my back. "We all thought that you had perished in the woods. It was my duty as one of the heads of Dynasty to ensure that our organization was not left defenseless, especially with the threat of Paris looming over our heads. I was doing my duty."

I nod. "Of course. I would expect no less from the men sitting around this table. Dynasty needs a leader to thrive. Though I have to admit, I am surprised that while your son was being kidnapped and tortured, you still managed to find a spare moment to campaign for your own selfish desires. Don't be fooled, Harlen Beckett. I see you over there, lurking in the shadows. You are on my radar and have been from the very start. I suggest that you be very careful about the next moves that you make."

He shakes his head. "You have me confused with someone else, Miss Ravenwood. I am loyal, and now that we can all celebrate your safe return home, I have no need to campaign for leadership."

A fake smile tears across my face as I hold back every wild emotion swarming through me. "Wonderful," I tell him, not doubting for a second that Matthew Montgomery is going to have a very unpleasant visitor in the late hours of the night.

And just like that, the men at the table stand and start filing out of the room, leaving me behind with the four broody assholes, who now have nothing to do but grovel for forgiveness.

# CHAPTER 15

## PARIS

Steam clouds my bedroom as I step out of the luxury bathroom in my champagne silk dressing gown. I'm living the fucking life, but I haven't got it all. Not yet, at least. Everything that once belonged to my spoiled bitch of a twin sister is soon going to be mine.

I've been waiting eighteen long years for this and I'm nearly at the end. I'm almost exactly where I always wanted to be—Andrew Ravenwood's wife.

He was always supposed to be mine. I saw him first, I wanted him first, I gave myself to him first, but he wanted her. He wanted the one with the bubbly attitude, the one who kissed his ass and catered to his every need. She was weak. She was never strong enough to stand by his side. Never strong enough to stand by the leader of Dynasty. He picked the wrong girl and that bitch never let me forget it.

She took everything that was supposed to be mine.

Joke's on her.

If she were alive now, I bet she would regret the day that she ever crossed me, but how could she? She's dead. I made sure of that. Just thinking about it gets me hot. Poor little London Ravenwood.

It was all too easy to build my army and get inside Royston Carver's corrupted little mind. Hell, it was even easier to get inside his bed. What a shame that little bitch had to go and slaughter him. He truly was a good fuck, much better than Harding.

His wife though, she really is a bitch, but what does it matter now? That was eighteen years ago and all I needed was to get on my knees just once and that man was putty in my hands. Though, I can guarantee that's the last time his dick ever got sucked. Ida Carver is way too precious to get on her knees.

What a fucking fool. They're all fucking fools. Since the second I had my twin sister and her husband slaughtered, every single person was gunning for leadership. I don't know how they could have been so stupid to assume that I was not going to take the position for myself.

London Ravenwood was going to rise from the dead, but this time, her rule was going to be all mine. If only her little offspring didn't have to go and set me back eighteen years. Just the thought of the hell I've had to endure from that girl has me grinding my teeth, but at least I know she was gifted her father's strength and endurance. Her mother was far too weak to have given her any decent qualities.

But the bitch is dead now. I'm not going to lie, I'm salty as fuck that I didn't get the pleasure of ending her life myself, but that's on me. I let her slip through my fingers one too many times. I had no choice but to play her precious boyfriends against her.

It was all too easy. In hindsight, I wish it had been just that bit more challenging. I wish they had put up more of a fight, but those shallow-minded, Calvin Klein wannabes caved to my will all too easily. Betraying the one that they swore to protect came as second nature.

It was like watching primetime television. No, scrap that, it was like being the only girl in a fucking sausage fest orgy getting gang banged over and over again. Pure fucking bliss.

As much as I would have loved to see the life drain out of her eyes, watching the playback of her body being thrown into the air as the cabin exploded into flames around her was all too good. Those boys really do know how to put on a spectacular show. Granted, I never got to see her body, but that was never going to happen. Dead or alive, they were never going to hand her over.

All I know is that Dynasty would never have gone to the effort of such an extravagant funeral just to appease me.

Elodie Ravenwood is dead. The leader of Dynasty is dead, and now it's my time to rise from the ashes. They know I am not London, but that doesn't matter anymore. I will rise as my own true self and rule in my own image. Fuck Andrew Ravenwood. I don't need him anymore.

I hold the power now. I am a fucking phoenix.

I mean, sure. The people of Dynasty are going to take a while to come around to me, seeing as I kidnapped their children from right under their noses, but it's not like I was going to kill them or anything. At least, I hadn't planned on it, but I knew they were safe … mostly.

Those doorknob guys were going to come for them. It was a guarantee that they would rescue their brothers and sisters while leaving Elodie's body behind. It was only a matter of time, which is why I got my ass out of there before they got a chance. Though I have to admit, they really did a number on my guards, but they were expendable. I can rebuild my security and I will.

I drop back onto my futon as the overwhelming power pulses through my veins. I'm a fucking queen now, born from the ashes with the sole intention to fly. I am unstoppable. I'm a fucking force.

No one can stand in my way, and if they do, they better be prepared to meet their maker because I will slaughter anyone who dares to stop me.

A soft breeze blows through the open window and I can't resist gently roaming my fingers over my body. I push the soft champagne silk off my shoulder and glance up to the guard standing by the door. His eyes are on me, mesmerized by my beauty and enraptured by desire.

"Fuck me," I demand, my stare boring into his as I untie my gown and slide my fingers down my excited body.

His eyes harden, snapping up from my hand to my eyes. "I … I'm sorry, Paris," he says, caught off guard as he shakes his head. "I cannot. I am married."

I let out a disappointed sigh and reach behind me to my bed, really wishing that it didn't have to come to this. My fingers curl around my gun and I raise it, my stare falling back on his as I spread my legs wide.

"I'm your fucking queen and I get what I want. So drag your useless ass over here, drop to your knees and eat my pussy until I come on your face. Is that understood?"

He swallows hard and I ignore the disdain in his eyes. "Yes, Paris. Of course, anything you want."

The guard starts making his way across my room, removing his utility belt as he goes, gently placing it down before peeling off his shirt and showing off his ripped body that he's been keeping from me all this time.

He gets down on his knees and curls his arms around my legs, dragging me down my futon to get me right where he wants me. His tongue hits my clit almost immediately and I shudder under his touch. It's amazing but it's not the same as that one blissful night that I got to be with Andrew, all the way back before London had to come and ruin it all. Nothing ever compares to him.

I glance across the room at the guard who stands stationed by my side entrance and flick the gun towards him. "You," I snap. "Touch me." He simply nods his head and starts moving toward me, removing his belt and shirt just as the other guard had done.

As he grows nearer, I look down at his body. It's definitely not as impressive as the other guy, but I bet his secrets lay somewhere else. "Remove your pants. I want to see what you're working with."

He nods and removes his pants, revealing a long, thick snake that has my mouth watering. "Come to me."

He steps in beside me, kneeling on the futon and I curl my fingers around his hardening cock. My fist roams up and down his velvety skin and I feel the small bead of excitement at his tip. "Play with me," I insist, reveling in the feel of the married guy's tongue working my clit.

Damn, what is it about a married man that gets me off so good?

Guard number two bends down and curls his mouth over my waiting nipple, flicking it as I work his cock and sending me right into an intense pleasure. My blood pulses rapidly through my body. It's been far too long since I was touched last, but let's face it, Harding didn't have the skill to do me like this.

My orgasm builds and everything clenches inside of me and just when my world is about to be thoroughly rocked, my bedroom door barges open, the doorknob slamming into the wall behind it and puncturing the drywall.

"YOU PROMISED THAT LITTLE BITCH WAS DEAD," Ida Carver demands, storming into my bedroom like a raging whore only to pull herself up short as she looks over me with my guards. "Ugh, fucking pathetic. My husband did not die so that you could fuck around with the help. Have some class about yourself."

The guards stop and my glare drops down at the man between my legs. "Did you hear the word 'stop' come from my lips? I don't think so. You were told to eat my fucking pussy until I came, and after that, you're going to fuck me until I scream. You both are."

They get back to work and a shallow laugh comes tearing up my throat, even more so when I take in the disgust etched across Ida's face. "Stop being such a prude," I laugh at her. "Come and join me. God knows it's been millennia since you've got your rocks off. It's time to celebrate. We've won."

"WON?" she shrieks. "We haven't won anything. You got played. The funeral was a sham. Elodie Ravenwood is alive and breathing, shitting all over your attempt at world domination while you're here letting your guards fuck you senseless. *She won.* You just proved yourself to be a joke. Again."

My foot slams against the chest of the guard on his knees, throwing him back at least three feet while clenching my fist around the other man's cock. "WHAT THE FUCK DID YOU JUST SAY?" I roar, my hard glare snapping up to Ida's as the man falls apart beneath my tight grip.

"You heard me," Ida spits, striding deeper into my room. "You fucked up. Elodie showed herself during the funeral and told every last person what had been going on. They're never going to follow you. You have no shot at leading Dynasty. You're screwed."

"She's not alive. I saw the video myself."

"Did you see her dead body?" Ida returns. "Did you watch the life drain out of her eyes? I don't think so. You let those boys fool you."

"But … your son. Dante. He perished right along with her."

"He did no such thing."

"FUCK." A loud, ear-shattering shriek tears out of me and I throw myself to my feet. "No. No. No. No. This isn't right. She's dead. I know she's dead."

Rage burns within me and in a split second, I reach down to the futon and grab the discarded gun before letting off two perfect shots, each bullet lodging right between the eyes of my two guards—my now very dead guards.

"FUCCCCCK," I squeal, my hands shaking as I launch the gun at the window, letting it shatter the glass into a million pieces.

"Seriously?" Ida grumbles, her lips pulling up in disgust at the sight of the two men lying dead on my floor, their blood seeping into the carpet. "A tantrum? That's how you want to handle this? You're losing it, Paris. You're getting dangerously low on players while she keeps gaining more. Elodie has you beat and there's nothing you can do about it. I might as well jump ship."

"Shut up. Shut up. SHUT UP," I screech, my hands going into my hair and fisting into tight knots as my mind takes me over every possible scenario. "It's just a temporary setback. I'll blindside her."

"Right," Ida laughs. "Haven't you tried that already? You failed. You keep failing. It's time to face the music, Paris. You're washed up. You're never going to make it into leadership. Let's just cut ties now and I'll try to save myself before they find out we've been working together."

"No," I rush out, my heart racing in my chest as I silently go over all my options. "It isn't over. My daughter. Ember. We still have her."

"Ember was captured and thrown into the cells. You have no leg to stand on. You're scrambling. Just leave it alone and run. Move out of state, go somewhere else and save yourself. They're going to kill you. It's only a matter of time."

I storm forward, meeting her face to face. "I'm not giving up," I roar. "I'm going to finish what I started and take back what's rightfully mine."

Ida shakes her head, looking at me as though I've completely lost my mind. "You're going crazy," she laughs. "By all means, keep going on this reckless path, but you're done dragging me down with you. I have a family to think about."

I scoff, clutching onto her wrist to stop her from leaving. "Says the woman who knowingly allowed my men to kidnap her children," I remind her. "If you walk out that door, I'll make sure they know all about you. We're seeing this through if it's the last thing we do."

Ida narrows her gaze, not appreciating my threat one bit. "You can't win this."

"Mark my words, Ida. I will win, even if it means taking you down to do it. Nothing will stop me from finishing her pathetic life and taking back what's mine. I'm going to slit her throat and listen to how she drowns in her own blood. I'm going to revel in it, bathe in it, thrive with it. Elodie Ravenwood will die by my hand, and when she does, all of Dynasty will know about it. Then they will bow down to me until my dying days."

# CHAPTER 16

My arms twist around my body as I desperately attempt to pull myself free from the red latex dress. Don't get me wrong, it's sexy as fuck and I feel like an absolute boss in it, but getting in and out of it has been an absolute nightmare.

I shouldn't have sent the boys away. They were right there, standing at the bottom of the stairs begging to be the one to come up with me and finish this incredibly weird day off right, but I pushed them all back as there are just too many emotions clouding my mind to think straight.

I don't even know what to think anymore. I don't want to be angry with them, but a part of me simply can't help it. I want to scream and let loose. I want to make them feel what I felt when I watched them drive away. I want them to fear for their lives the way I feared for mine in those woods, but mostly, I want them to feel the overwhelming grief I felt when I thought they didn't love me. But I can't. I can't do that to them. The idea of them feeling those things terrifies me.

Shit, look at me going all soft. Don't tell me that after years of bullshit that has turned my brittle heart to stone, I suddenly fall in love, not once, but four times, and now I lack the ability to make them bleed. If it were anyone but my four guys, they'd already be dead and buried six feet underground.

Crap. I have to figure myself out. Maybe it's just this day. I mean, how many people get to attend their own funeral? It's not the easiest thing to witness. It was like having a bucket of ice water tipped over my head, forcing me back to reality. Add Ember's bullshit plus the off-putting compliments thrown at me from Danforth and Montgomery and it's definitely been a weird day.

A throat clears in my doorway and I stop struggling with the red dress and turn around to find Grayson leaning up against the door frame. His eyes rake up and down my body, the hunger deep within them making me crave for everything we once had.

"Can I help you?" I question, my eyes hardening, despite the love I feel for him, even more so since hearing what he had to say during the funeral.

He pushes off the door frame and starts walking deeper into my closet. "No," he rumbles, his voice so damn low and filled with fire. "But it sure looks like I can help you."

Not a word is said as my eyes darken with lust. Need slams through me and I take a deep breath, unable to control the pure desperation that has him moving in even closer, his familiar scent wrapping around me.

Grayson reaches down and pulls a knife from his pocket, his eyes never leaving mine. He steps right into me, his chest pressing against my arm as he dips his head down to my ear. The tip of the blade rests against my waist and he slowly drags it across the red latex. "I saw the look in your eyes when I shot that guard," he murmurs, the vibrations from his chest making me squirm below his intense hold. "It turned you on."

"What can I say?" I whisper. "I'm fucked in the head, just like you."

A soft groan pulls from the back of his throat, almost as if my words were exactly what he wanted to hear. He raises his hand and brushes his fingers down the side of my face until they're dropping to my collarbone. He pushes my hair back over my shoulder and then trails over it until the back of his knuckles are sailing down my back, not stopping until his hand is gripping my ass with a forcefulness that takes my breath away.

The knife at my waist travels down the front of my body and I can't take my eyes off it, wondering why the fuck I want him to cut me so badly, but he'd never.

He keeps going down until I feel the cool blade sitting high on my inner thigh. "I'm going to fuck you, Ellie," he tells me, his tone demanding no arguments. "I'm going to slice this fucking dress right off your goddamn body and then fuck you until you scream so loud that the neighbors really do think you're dead. Got it? You're not going to stop me. You're not going to cry betrayal. You're going to fucking take it and you're going to love it."

My knees go weak. It's like music to my ears.

Fuck, I need him so bad, but if it's a boss he wants in the boardroom and a bitch in the bed, then damn him, I'll give it to him.

I don't get a second to respond before he flicks his wrist and the knife between my legs sails right up my body, slicing through the red latex like butter. I suck in a gasp, my heart racing with desire as the dress falls to pieces with not a drop of blood in sight.

I barely get a second to recover before Grayson is at my back, his rough fingers digging into my bare skin so damn tight that they're bound to leave a mark, but hell, if this guy is promising me a night of unbelievable rough fuckery, then I want the marks to wake up to in the morning so I can replay every damn second of it over and over again.

Fuck being mad at him, if this is his way of making it up to me, then I'll take it a million times over.

He pushes me hard and I fall forward, catching myself on a low shelf, but before I can straighten myself up, Grayson's hand is pressing against my back, keeping me bent over as his other hand comes down in a hard, stinging slap on my ass, making my pussy flood with need.

Grayson's hand travels down my ass and between my legs to feel just how ready I am for him. "You like that?" he rumbles, his thick fingers slipping between my folds and playing with everything I have on offer.

I pant, pushing back into him, needing more. "Are you going to play with me or fuck me?" I demand, needing that monster cock slamming deep inside of me and stretching me wide.

His hand slaps down on my ass again and my whole body flinches from the sharp sting. "You'll be fucking patient."

Goddamn it.

His foot slips between mine and without warning, he kicks it out, spreading my legs wide. He groans low and I look back over my shoulder to watch as his tongue rolls over his bottom lip with hunger. His eyes remain locked on my bare ass and as he sinks to his knees, I straighten my fucking crown.

Goddamn. This is going to be good.

His hand remains pressed against my back, keeping me low as my panting increases, the anticipation sending me into a world of unease, until finally he leans in and closes his mouth over my aching cunt.

"Oh, fuck," I whimper, my knees giving out under me, but he doesn't dare let me move. He holds me up as his skilled tongue and warm lips assault my pussy in the best possible way. His tongue circles my clit before going low and plunging inside of me, flicking and teasing me, making me cry out with need. "GRAYSON. FUCK. YES."

His fingers tighten on my skin and he presses harder on my back, bending me so fucking low that my head is nearly at my fucking knees and if I twist my head at the right angle, I get an up close and private showing of his tongue stroking over my clit.

My eyes blaze, completely mesmerized by the erotic show and I get lost in a trance, my body already shaking and quivering under his touch.

Grayson's hand circles over my ass and I press back, needing everything he's got. Without hesitation, he pushes his thick thumb inside. My eyes roll. "Awwww, fuck," I groan low, unsure if I said it out loud or if the words are just bouncing around inside my head.

Grayson pulls back just a little. "You fucking like that, Ellie?" he questions as he pushes a little deeper in my ass. "You like my tongue flicking against your tight cunt while I fuck your ass."

"God, yes," I groan, roaming my hands over my tits and gently pinching my nipples, feeling that familiar pulse of electricity shooting through to my core. "Don't stop."

The pressure on my back eases and I pull up a little to get comfortable but as a ferocious grumble comes tearing from the back of his throat, I lower myself back down. "Don't fucking move or I'll be forced to tie you up, and baby, I know you think you might like that, but I promise you, you won't. Not today."

I swallow hard and nod, and just as I take a deep breath, two thick fingers slide deep inside my cunt, making my pussy clench around them.

I suck in a loud gasp and he leans back in, letting me feel his wicked smile against my burning skin. "More," I demand, squirming under his touch. A soft laugh rumbles through his chest and my knees go weak all over again. "Now, Grayson. Don't make me beg."

His teeth gently nip at my ass cheek as his fingers start to move deep inside me, making me shudder and moan for more. "Baby, you're in no fucking position to be making demands."

The bastard has a good fucking point, but I'm not one to learn from my mistakes. At least, not the life-threatening ones.

"Fucking now, Grayson."

His tongue flicks over my clit, swirling around in tight little circles as he adjusts the pressure just how I like it. It's like electricity building within me and soon enough, I'm going to overload and shut the whole fucking system down.

He gives me just a little bit more and I crumble into a million pieces. My orgasm tears through me and I clench my eyes, the force of it making me weak. I can't take my weight and drop to my knees, tearing his fingers out of me in the process, but with Grayson already on his knees behind me and my orgasm still destroying every little nerve ending inside of me, he plays his cards just right.

I hear the softest little zip before his fingers are digging into my hips and pulling me back.

He impales me, his monster cock slamming deep and stretching me wide as that delicious cold piercing hits the very deepest parts of me. "Ahhhh, fuck," Grayson growls, thrusting forward and stilling for a brief moment, both of us overwhelmed by the instant satisfaction, even more so for me as my orgasm only intensifies. "Those few days were far too long to go without your tight pussy squeezing my cock."

You and me, both!

He reaches around me and rubs his fingers over my clit in lazy little circles, keeping my body right on edge as the intensity becomes too much to handle, his piercing acting like a fucking tease inside me as he slowly pulls back.

I squeeze his cock tight as I desperately try to hold onto it, not ready to come back down to earth. Ecstasy pulses through my veins and he slams back inside of me with a newfound passion. A loud scream tears out of me, probably worrying the shit out of the guys downstairs, but fuck them. If they feel the need to race up here to check on me, then so be it. I hope they fucking watch, and I hope they feel like a bunch of bitches missing out on one of the best fucks of my life. Though I'm not going to lie, having their eyes on me as Grayson makes me come is only going to make it that much better.

My orgasm slowly dwindles but each of Grayson's rough touches has my body quivering, and while I'd do anything to make that one moment last an eternity, I know that with his magical hands and cock, it's only a matter of time before I'm coming all over again.

As I'm coming down from my high, he finally starts to move, and I mean really move. His body rolls back and he takes my hips in both hands, his thumbs stretching right around to my ass cheeks. I drop my chest down to the cold closet floor and look back, getting so much hotter as I watch the way he watches his thick cock moving in and out of my cunt.

His thrusts get harder and harder and my eyes roll back into my head, listening to the sweet sounds of his pleasured grunts that he usually keeps to himself, only this time, he's letting them fly free.

"I fucking love you, Elodie Ravenwood," he spits through his clenched jaw, moving faster and adjusting himself to hit me at a whole new angle. "Everything that I am is yours. Do you understand that?"

"YES," I cry, my pants becoming all too much that the word comes out as more of a harsh yell.

"Do you love me?"

Without hesitation, I respond with my absolute truth. "Yes. Always."

He thrusts even harder to the point of pain, but it's the kind of pain that I'd beg him for every day for the rest of my life. "Then don't ever question my fucking loyalty to you again."

His eyes flick up from my pussy and meet my gaze, holding it for a brief second as I realize exactly what this is. This isn't just about rough sex, this is his version of getting to the bottom of our differences by fucking it out of our systems, and goddamn, I'm so on board with it, especially if it means that we don't have to sit through a bullshit talk about our feelings. After all, Grayson and I have never dealt with our emotions well, even worse when it comes to talking about them.

Grayson pauses, his fingers stilling on my hips and making me clench even harder, missing the motion of his hard, pierced cock slamming into me. "Never again," he says, unable to catch his breath as a light sheen of sweat begins to coat his skin, making him look like some kind of oiled-up model ready for a fucking thirst-trap photoshoot.

"Never again," I agree.

And just like that, he picks up his pace, nodding as a relieved grin stretches across his lips and that darkness in his eyes lifts, revealing the playful Grayson who only wants to make me scream. "I'd never fucking betray you, Elodie," he says through pants. "You and me … we're fucking endgame."

His wicked grin is infectious and I find one of my own stretching across my lips. "You're damn right," I tell him, knowing that from this moment on, everything will return to normal between us and we'll never have to speak on it again. Though don't get me wrong, the hurt and fear that I felt in those woods is all still so true, his words will never take that away, but that can sure as hell ease the pain that resides in my heart—at least, the fraction that belongs to him.

I brace my hands against the wall of my closet and push back against him, my eyes sparkling with excitement. "You missed this?"

"More than you could fucking know."

My gaze darkens and he pauses, momentarily distracted by the challenge in my eyes. "Prove it."

A loud laugh rumbles through his chest and in the same moment, his hand comes down against the soft skin of my ass, the sharp, slapping sound bouncing off every damn wall in the room. I suck in a gasp and let out a loud squeal as he picks up his pace once again, fucking me into oblivion.

"Holy shit," I pant, struggling to keep my brace against the wall as he goes all out, his knees spreading mine even wider as his thumb drags through my wetness and comes back to my ass, teasing me with even more.

A needy groan pulls from between my lips and he laughs. "I fucking knew you wanted this," he says with pride just as he pushes his thick thumb inside of me. "I can't wait to claim your ass again."

"What are you waiting for?" I laugh. "Permission?"

He shakes his head. "You and I both know that I'm not going to sit back and wait for permission. I'd rather wait until you're begging for it."

"Geez, if you're going to be a little bitch about it, then I'll just back up on Cruz instead. I won't even need to utter a damn word."

Grayson laughs, thrusting even harder and making me nearly crash right into the fucking wall. "Watch your mouth, Ravenwood," he demands, adjusting his angle and making me moan low. "Besides, it's not the same as when it's with me. Don't fucking try to deny it."

I laugh, more than ready to deny it until I'm blue in the face, but he has a point. Grayson has a certain advantage over the others, a certain pierced advantage that drives me in-fucking-sane.

My laughs are cut off as his hand curls around my long ponytail and tears my head as far back as it can go, a surprised gasp sailing from between my lips.

He means business and I'm so here for it.

Grayson fucks me hard and fast and just as I knew he would, he works my body right to the brink of exhaustion, my orgasm building so damn hard and fast that I'm positive I won't survive.

My cries sound through my closet and by this point, I have absolutely no doubt that the boys downstairs know exactly what's going on in here, and fuck, I hope they're jealous. I hope it eats at them, sitting on their fucked-up, twisted minds knowing that with every loud thrust that it's Grayson I'm fucking and not them. But more so, I hope the sounds of my pleasure have each of their dicks in their hands, desperately wishing they could be the ones making me come.

I clench down around him, the rapid building deep inside of me almost too much to handle, but Grayson doesn't care. He wants it all. He wants me to come harder than I ever have before, he wants me panting on my closet floor, unable to remember why I was so pissed at him in the first place. He wants me to succumb to his touch like a good little girl, and damn it, he has me right where he wants me and I won't be doing a damn thing to stop it.

His thumb presses harder into my ass and I cry out, desperately wishing that I could reach back and dig my nails into his gorgeously tanned skin. Hell, just running my fingertip over his raven tattoo would be enough, but I'm down on my knees, my face smooshed into the expensive carpet and all I've got is myself.

His monster cock stretches me wide, so fucking wide that I know I'll never feel anything like it again. "Come on, Ellie," he growls, his deep tone shattering that tiny piece of will I hold onto, the will that begs for me to hold on just a little bit longer. "Give it to me. I want to feel you come."

"Fuck, Grayson," I pant, the needy bitch inside of me in full force. My hands curl into fists as they press up against the wall, still trying to brace myself as I push back against it, taking him deeper. My eyes squeeze tight, picturing the way his body would roll with each new thrust.

It won't be long now.

Grayson releases his tight grip in my hair and without wasting a damn second, he curls his arm around my waist, reaches down between my spread thighs and pinches my clit between his finger and thumb before rolling it between his grip.

A sharp, electrifying bolt shoots through me and I come undone beneath his hold. "AHHH, FUCK. YES. YES," I cry out, so fucking loud that I'm sure the walls are shaking, vibrating right along with me as my pussy violently convulses, spasming around his thick cock. Pure ecstasy rocks through me, but it's not nearly as good as the feeling of Grayson pulling out and shooting his hot cum all over my back, his low, satisfied moan making me feel like a fucking goddess.

Chills rush through my body, and as I finally come down from my earth-shattering high, collapsing into an exhausted heap on my closet floor, Grayson comes down beside me. He reaches to my shelf and grabs the closest thing he can find—my favorite black tank—and quickly mops up the mess that threatens to spill down between my ass cheeks.

My face smooshes into the carpet as I stare at him, panting and unable to catch my breath. I can't help but place my hand over that stunning tattoo and feel the rapid beat of his heart. "Who would have known that depriving you of a good time for so long would have you leveling up to beast mode?"

Grayson laughs and reaches for me before pulling me up onto his lap and letting me collapse against his strong chest. "There was no leveling up required," he teases. "I've just been holding out on you, saving it for when I really needed it."

A soft chuckle pulls from my lips and I let out a deep breath, wondering just how long we can stay hidden here in my closet because leaving this space and not letting the moment go on forever would be an absolute tragedy.

Grayson grips my chin and gently raises it until I meet his softening stare and see nothing but a fierce seriousness deep within his gaze. "I love you, Ellie," he whispers. "I don't ever want to be without you."

I nod, feeling that invisible tether that was destroyed in the cabin explosion come back stronger and fiercer than ever. "I love y—"

My words are cut off when his warm lips crush against mine, not allowing me a chance to say what I needed to say, but it doesn't matter anyway because I know he feels it, just as I do. Grayson and I are back, stronger than ever before. But instead of seeing me as the girl who needs his protection, a weak outcast with no hope, he sees me as his equal, a girl who doesn't need his protection, but will dominate with him standing at her side.

# CHAPTER 17

Disappointment floods me as I look over the selections that the heads of Dynasty have offered up as the replacements for both the Scardoni and Harding families. There's not a single female applicant, and honestly, I would have thought that after everything I've fought through and all the strength and courage I've shown to hold onto my position, the men of Dynasty would have already figured out that females are clearly the superior gender.

Well ... not always. When it comes to my four boys and the way they fuck, hands down they'd take first prize every damn time, but when it comes down to leadership, women have proven over and over again, that we've got what it takes. If only men and their egos weren't standing in the way.

The chair scrapes along the marble tile as I drop my ass back into it, letting out a loud, frustrated huff as I go. "What's the matter?" Cruz murmurs, moving in beside me and bracing his hand against the table, scanning over the pages of applicants that are spread out before me.

"Nothing," I grumble, reaching for the next applicant and flipping through the manila folder until I get to the section that holds all of the skeletons this guy was probably hoping to keep locked away until his dying days. "I just … I was hoping this was going to be a little more exciting."

"Then stop," Grayson says, striding into the living room with a small tumbler in his hand, most likely filled with an expensive whiskey and a few perfectly round pieces of ice. "We all know that you're going to go with the guys that King and Carver put up."

"Well, yeah, but don't I owe it to the people of Dynasty to actually take the other applicants into consideration?" I ask. "And besides, I promised that I would narrow the applicants down to five or six for the other heads to vote on, so I need to make sure that the other applicants that I put through are worthy of taking on the role because there's a good chance that King and Carver's selections might not get through."

"It's going to be fine," Carver says, taking the spot on my right and scooping up the application that I just finished with. He leans right back in his seat and props his feet up on the table before flipping open the front page to see the applicant's details. "Our guys are going to get through. You've got nothing to worry about."

I scoff and slam my elbow into his feet, knocking them off the table. "I have a whole fucking society to worry about. If the wrong guy gets voted in, we could be backing ourselves into a corner."

"Which won't happen," King says from the head of the table. I glance up to find his heavy stare on me, his brows furrowed and his stubborn attitude laid out on the table for the world to see, putting me on guard. But what's new? He's been a sour asshole since the second I got home despite not having the right to be, and for that, I do everything that I can to get on his very last nerve. "We've got our bases covered. It's a game of mathematics. Put only five applicants through for the vote and just make sure that apart from mine and Carver's selections, the rest of the applicants are so undesirable that the other heads have no choice but to vote for our guys."

My brow arches and I fix my lips into a hard line, the disappointment clear on my face. "You want me to cheat the vote and have absolutely no respect for the very system that I put in place?"

He shakes his head, rolling his eyes and barely holding onto the scoff that sits on the tip of his tongue. "No, I want you to play the same game that every single one of those heads would have played had they been in your position," he explains, his tone dull, informative, and straight to the point. "Think of it as survival of the fittest. You have to do whatever you can to get a step up in this world, even if it means taking out an enemy before they even get the chance to be one. The numbers have only just stacked up in your favor, but now you need to keep them there."

"You can't deny it," Cruz says, still looking over my shoulder. "The guy might be a dick with a chip on his big ass shoulder, but he has a good fucking point. You can't risk guys like Beckett, Irvine, or Kennedy adding new players this late in the game. They can't be trusted."

"I know," I say with a heavy sigh. "I'm just over trying to figure out who wants to slit my throat while I sleep. I mean, do we even know who's on our side anymore? I think we need to adjust the seating plan at the council table."

The boys flick their gazes around the table, trying to figure out who belongs where in the pecking order. "Well, we know that we have Danforth, Carver, and King who will always have your back no matter what," Cruz says. "Brooks, Winston, Luca, Easton, and Crawford are pretty safe bets. Sebastian Whitman has always pleaded innocent, but he could turn at a moment's notice."

"Daniel Crawford is a bit shady like that too," King mutters. "But for the most part, I think he can be trusted."

"So, who does that leave?" I ask.

Carver jumps in with a list that I'm sure has already been burned into his mind. "Kennedy, Beckett, Rhodes, Irvine, and Montgomery."

"But Matthew Montgomery jumped ship. He announced in front of everyone that I have his loyalty now."

Carver's lips scrunch in thought. "So he says," Carver mutters, his eyes narrowing in distrust. "But he's a fucking slimeball. It suits him to show loyalty now, but that fucker will jump right back to the bad side at a moment's notice. Don't trust him."

I nod, sinking back into my seat and beginning to feel deflated. I've always been one who saw the world as black and white, but here in Ravenwood Heights, they're giving *50 Shades of Grey* a whole new meaning. "Okay, so we have seven safe bets, two more who are a little shady, and five that can't be trusted."

"Yep," Grayson says. "The ball is in your court, Ellie, but if Whitman, Crawford, and Montgomery don't like what they see and settle back in on the dark side, we're back to square one. It's more important now than ever to get these two new applicants on your side. If we had the numbers like that, I can guarantee that Whitman, Montgomery, and Crawford will never be an issue. They only like to play for the winning side. You'll be un-fucking-stoppable."

"Right," I say, feeling the power beneath my fingertips. I grab the applicants' files and start launching them toward the guys. "Then help me figure out who the fuck to put up for this vote."

The boys get to work, all but one who continues to stare at me from across the table. "Can I help you?" I question, crossing my arms over my chest and leaning right back in my chair. I pull out every single ounce of cockiness that resides within me as I raise a brow and press my lips into a tight line.

King just stares at me as the others ignore us, more than used to our back and forth over the last few days, but fuck, the sexual tension between us has been knocking me right off my feet, but neither of us are going to be the one to back down and admit defeat, despite how badly we each want it. I guess that's the downfall of being with someone who's just as stubborn as you are.

"Can you?" he questions.

I clench my jaw, hating nothing more than when he answers my questions with a bullshit question of his own. "I don't know, King. Your attitude has been all over the place that it's too hard to get a read on you now. Did you get your period? Or is this new overly-emotional thing something we should all get used to? I mean, if it was your period, you should have told me and we could have tried to sync our cycles. We could have been blood brothers, though the word sisters seems a little more appropriate. Don't you think?"

King glares across the table, his stare so ferocious that if his eyes were made of laser beams, I'd be dead right about now, but as it is, he's just a regular human like the rest of us, forced to deal with wild emotions whether you're ready for it or not.

A loud huff comes tearing out of him and in the next second, he scoops up the few manila folders in front of him and stands. "Fuck this," he mutters to himself before stalking out of the room, the three other guys still completely oblivious to what's going on around them—either that or they're trying really hard to pretend that they don't give a shit.

I watch King walk away and the anger that I've become so familiar with over the past few days rears its ugly head and I find myself flying out of my seat. "Hey," I snap, racing after him, out of the dining room and through to the kitchen. "You don't get to just walk away."

"Sure I can," he mutters, not bothering to turn around.

I clench my jaw and push myself a little faster until I can finally reach out and grab his elbow. I pull back on his arm and he immediately stops, spinning around and fixing me with that same glare that's come at me since first falling through my bedroom window. "What's your problem?" I demand. "Stop being such a dick all the time. You have no right to be all pissy at me. Now, me on the other hand—I have every fucking right but you don't see me sulking and snapping at you every two seconds."

"Are you fucking kidding me? You've been acting like a spoiled brat since coming home."

"Me? I've been acting like a brat? Take a look in the mirror, asshole."

King groans, throwing his hands to his temples and turning away from me. "You're so fucking impossible."

"I wouldn't need to be impossible if you weren't being so sour over the fact that I've been fucking Grayson and Carver, and not you. You're jealous, King, and it's eating you up inside."

King laughs, spinning back around. "You think I'm jealous?" he asks, the smirk stretching across his face and telling me that he thinks he's onto something. "Babe, maybe you've forgotten that I was the first one to tell you that sharing would be fine. I've never been jealous of you being with the other guys."

I shake my head. "I'm not talking about our relationship. I know you're down with that. I know your soul, King. Out of all the guys, I've been the closest with you for the longest and despite how much you hide your heart beneath all the bullshit, I know it better than I know my own, which is how I know that you've been jealous as fuck since I've come home. I've given the time of day to all of your friends but you, and you sit there every day, getting more and more frustrated by the fact that I haven't come to clear the air with you yet. I've allowed all of your friends the chance to talk it out and explain their versions of events but you, and it's killing you."

His jaw clenches and I realize just how right I am, so I step in close to him, resting my hand against his warm chest. "What you're not realizing is that I've already forgiven you. I was so hurt by your betrayal, but after speaking to Carver and him explaining exactly what was going on right at the start, I understood. I knew you were going to do whatever it took to save your brother and sister, even if it meant sacrificing me to make it happen. It fucking sucked, but I understood it. So, I haven't needed that one-on-one time with you to allow you to grovel because there's nothing to grovel about. If I had a sibling in the same situation, you bet your ass that I would have done the same thing. Sure, the thought of you being the one to set the bomb off was painful, and all the hurt I felt since that very moment will always linger in the back of my mind, but what it comes down to is that I love you, no matter what. And every day that I get to see your siblings running around in their yard and getting a second chance at life, that makes all the pain worth it."

His brows furrow and he moves in even closer, curling his arms around my waist and letting that intoxicating scent wrap around me. "Then why the fuck haven't you been speaking to me?"

A grin stretches across my face and I tilt my head to look up at him. "Because you've been a moody asshole, and you know me better than that," I tease. "If you're going to throw your attitude at me, then I'm going to throw it right back. The only issue is that we're equally as stubborn, so the second this bullshit game started, there wasn't going to be an end, not until you got on your knees and admitted defeat."

King scoffs, his gaze hardening just a fraction. "Then you don't know me as well as you think you do," he murmurs, his lips resting just by my ear. "I don't give in. Ever."

"Really?" I question, dropping my fingers to his thigh and slowly dragging them up his jeans. "So, you just want to go about your day being pissy at me, pushing me away and glaring at me from across tables? There's nothing you could possibly want from me?"

He swallows hard, knowing exactly what I'm putting on offer, but his stubbornness knows no bounds. "Nope. Nothing."

My fingers dip into the front of his jeans and I pop the button before slowly unzipping his fly. "Nothing at all?" I whisper, dropping to my knees while keeping my heated stare on his. My tongue slips out and trails along my bottom lip, the hunger to taste him nearly killing me. "Just say the word and it's all yours."

He clenches his jaw, groaning in frustration as he combs his fingers into my hair, his eyes completely giving him away. "You're impossible, Winter."

I shake my head, reaching inside his undone jeans and freeing his cock, slowly gliding my fingers up and down his velvety skin. I move in even closer, letting my soft breath brush against his cock. "Admit defeat and I'll give you exactly what you want and we can go back to how it used to be, fucking every night, your arms around me and your beautiful cock slamming deep inside me over and over again. Isn't that what you want?"

"Fuuuuck," he groans, his fingers tightening in my hair as he tips his head back, stealing that perfect gaze away from me. "You know that apologies don't come easily to me."

"I'm not asking you to apologize," I murmur, spreading my knees wider on the tiles. "Just admit that I won."

"Babe," he says, his eyes coming back to mine with a newfound eagerness, desire, and overwhelming love. "You won the second you moved to Ravenwood Heights. You had me from the very beginning. There's no fucking question over who won because when it comes to you and me, you will win every fucking time, undoubtedly. I am yours, Winter. I always will be."

Holy. Crap.

Warmth swirls within me and despite how badly both King and I want his cock in my mouth, we need to fulfill this emotional connection first. He bends down and scoops me up into his warm hands and places my ass down on the kitchen counter, his lips coming down on mine in the same second.

He kisses me deeply and as the seconds tick by, he pulls away, keeping his forehead pressed gently against mine. "I wish things could have been different. If there was a way that we could have saved them without hurting you, I would have—"

"Shhhh," I whisper, pressing my finger against his lips. "I know, but there was no other way. Don't beat yourself up over it. You did what you had to do, and I respect the strength it took to make it happen. Those twins will forever see you as their hero. You sacrificed everything that was important to you to save them, and they will never forget that."

"They better not," he mutters as a soft smile plays on his warm lips, enticing me back in. I crush my own against them and kiss him deeply, wordlessly reminding him that we're okay—we all are.

His hands circle my waist and he drags me across the counter until I'm practically falling off the edge, my pussy pressed right up against him. I feel his grin against my lips and it's absolutely everything that I've been needing.

Fuck, I've really missed this playful version of King. He's been so damn serious over the past few days, and don't get me wrong, a broody King is sexy as fuck, but a playful one is everything a girl could need.

His fingers dig into the sides of my sweatpants and just as he goes to tear them down my legs, the softest creak comes from the adjoining living room, a room where absolutely nobody should be.

"Fucking hell," King growls in frustration before tearing away from me and leaving me with an intense case of female blue balls. What even is that? Blue bean? "Go to the dining room. Now."

King flies out of the room and I jump down from the counter, preparing myself for a fight as I run back toward the dining room, my heart racing a million miles an hour, and my mind somehow traveling even faster.

It has to be Paris. She's come for me. There's no other explanation, no other threats that have the stupidity to walk into my home unannounced. She's fucking crazy.

I go skidding into the dining room and three heads snap up in unison, but I don't stop. I keep racing toward the long hallway table that runs directly across from the massive table. "What's wrong?" Carver rushes out, already on his feet.

"Someone's in the house," I tell him, dropping to my knees and grabbing the gun that Grayson hid under here only yesterday. "King heard a noise in the living room."

"FUCK."

Within seconds, the guys create a barrier by the entrance of the dining room, keeping me protected as I stand behind them, a gun in each of our hands. I wait impatiently, my free hand pumping at my side as my knees shake with nerves. I had time to prepare for the raid to get the kids back, but this sudden bullshit really does numbers on my sanity.

We hear loud grunts coming from the living room, but no one moves, knowing that King would call for help if he needed it. The grunts get louder and louder and it becomes clear that King has the intruder in his steel grasp.

"You good?" Grayson questions, his voice sailing out to the kitchen.

There are a few more loud grunts and screeches, telling me that it's definitely a woman but I don't get much more time to think on it as King's voice comes flowing back to us. "Situation is handled," he says as the boys relax before me, their guns going back into their hiding spots. "You're going to want to see this."

# CHAPTER 18

"What the ever-loving fuck is this?" I mutter as my gaze drops to Ida Carver who's currently tied to one of the tall back chairs from beneath my breakfast bar.

Ida's pissed-off stare bypasses me and lands on her confused son who looks as though he has absolutely no idea what the hell is going on, but like … same.

"Oh, Dante," Ida rushes out, her eyes full of fear as she attempts to fuck with Carver's head. "Tell them to get me out of these ridiculous ties. They can't do this to me. I … I … I was just coming to check on you, and this is the reception I received? This is not good enough. I raised you better than this. Release me now. Your father would be rolling in his grave."

Carver's brows furrow as he watches his mother, right along with the rest of us, and without saying a word, he raises his gaze to King who nods toward the kitchen counter. Each one of us swivel our stares to the table to find a small pistol and a knife that looks like it came out of a kitchen knife block.

I suck in a gasp as Ida's eyes widen, realizing just how much shit she's really in.

This bitch did not just break into my home to kill me.

Rage burns within me and I go to move toward her but Carver's hand shoots out to stop me, pressing against my stomach, his arm like a steel pole, completely impassable. "You're fucking kidding me," he says with a disbelieving scoff, looking at his mother with a stone-cold stare that sends chills sailing down my spine. "You really thought you could come in here and hurt my girl?"

Ida's icy stare flicks to me with so much putrid hate that it knocks me back a step, but just as quickly as she hit me with it, it's gone and her stare is back on her son. "That … that little hussy murdered your father and then took you away from me too. I have nothing left, and what's worse is that you're so far up her ass that you can't even see how vile she truly is. How can you stand by her side, knowing her values? She's going to destroy Dynasty and take you down right along with it. Think of your sisters, Dante. Think of their future. Elodie Ravenwood needs to die, and I'm going to be the one to do it."

Carver steps toward his mother and slowly circles her, putting himself at her back where she struggles to see him, so she locks her sick, twisted stare on me instead.

"You're a joke, mother," Carver says, his callous tone darker than

I've ever heard it. "Look at yourself. You used to be the picture of elegance. You were the perfect wife for a man in power, seen and not heard. The other wives used to look at you as a queen among mere mortals, and now they snicker and pity you every time you walk into a room. You're an embarrassment. You're nothing. You will forever chase that same rush that you used to get, but it's long gone. That life is over, and you're desperately hanging on to something that doesn't exist anymore. It's embarrassing."

Ida sucks in a sharp, horrified gasp. "You don't mean that, you horrible boy," she seethes. "I am your mother. Show some respect."

"I am, mother," he says, spitting the word as though it was venom in his mouth. "In fact, I'm showing more respect and restraint than you could ever know. If I truly allowed myself to do what I wanted to do right now, you'd already be bleeding out on the floor."

My back straightens and I watch as each and every one of his words truly sinks in. "Don't get me wrong, mother," he continues as she begins panicking, her chest rising and falling with rapid movements. "If it came down to saving either you or Winter, I would choose her every fucking time."

Ida's stare remains locked on mine and she watches me with such disgust that it makes me uneasy. "You told him," she spits at me, not letting on what she's referring to, but she doesn't need to. I know exactly what she's talking about and so does every one of the guys standing around me.

"How could I not?" I throw back at her. "You threatened to kill his unborn child and slit his throat just as your husband did to my father, and as much as you hate it, I love him. So, what kind of woman would it make me if I didn't share that little snippet of information? You're a monster, Ida. You're a coward, and a low life, and I refuse to sink to your level. I'm not here to play by your rules, I make my own."

She clenches her jaw and my gaze shifts to Carver's as he leans forward, closing in on his mother. "The only reason I haven't thrown you into a cell or ended your miserable life is because my sisters need their mother, but God knows they could do so much better. I won't be the reason they have to grow up without you. I won't be the villain in their stories, but push me, mother, and I swear on your miserable husband's grave that I will see it through. Those girls deserve so much better than what they've got."

"You wouldn't."

Carver laughs and grabs his mother's bound hands and yanks her up from the high back chair. "You raised me," he says darkly. "You know exactly what I'm capable of. You've feared it since the second I was born."

Ida swallows hard and Carver shoves his hand into her back, forcing her forward and making her stumble toward me. I step out of the way and as Carver passes me with his mother, the buzzer sounds for the front gate.

Carver doesn't stop as Cruz pulls his phone out of his pocket and brings up the surveillance cameras. His brows furrow and he stares for a short moment before finally letting us in on the secret. "It's my mother," he mutters, just as confused as Carver had been about seeing his. He buzzes her in and the gate slowly begins to peel back.

The curiosity gets to us all and we follow Ida and Carver to the front door, ready to meet Cruz's mom. Carver pushes her the whole way, his strength at her back making her escape impossible, though that doesn't stop her attempts that each come along with screeching grunts and curses.

We reach the front door and Grayson pulls it open just in time to see Cruz's mom bringing her car to a stop at the bottom of the circle driveway. We all stop and wait, but Carver just keeps going, forcing his mother down the stairs, intent on walking her all the way back to the Carver estate in the most obvious way possible. Hell, discreet has never been a word in Carver's vocabulary, and the more Dynasty members that see her humiliation, the better.

Dianna Danforth steps out of her car—the fancy, expensive one that resides in her garage, not the soccer mom SUV that the boys and I destroyed. She instantly looks up, her eyes going wide as she watches Ida being marched down the stairs. "Do I want to know?" she asks, sucking in a shocked gasp.

Carver shakes his head. "Imagine the worst possible thing a mother could do to their child, and then triple it."

Dianna's eyes go wide and she drops her gaze to Ida in horror.

"Mom," Cruz rushes out, raising his hand and indicating for her to hurry up the stairs, not wanting her exposed to Ida's ugliness any more than necessary. Dianna snaps out of her shocked stare and starts making her move up the stairs, going as fast as she can while still maintaining her ladylike nature.

Her pace fastens as she reaches the top few steps and launches herself at her son, wrapping him into her arms in a rare show of affection—though, I would too if two out of three of my children had just been kidnapped and then returned in less than perfect condition. I'd hold on to them every chance I got. "How are you doing?" she questions, pulling back and meeting his confused stare. "I haven't heard from you since the funeral. Are you well? Eating properly?"

"Yes, Mom," Cruz laughs. "I'm fine. What's going on? Is everything alright?"

"I, ummm, yes," she says, turning her gaze on me with a knowing smile that has my heart racing, trying to figure out what could have possibly brought her here today. "Jackson and Lachlan have finally started talking about the ordeal that Paris put them through and they mentioned that there was a girl who came along with the boys to rescue them. Was that you, Elodie? Did you save my sons?"

I press my lips into a tight line and quickly glance at Cruz who nods. Turning back to Dianna, I nod. "I did what I could to help, but the real heroes are the boys. I was just along for the ride."

Dianna pulls me into her arms. "Thank you," she whispers into my ear before pulling back and holding me by the shoulders. "These boys were raised to fight. Every spare moment they've ever had has been spent in training, refining their skills until they finally reached perfection. They were born to throw themselves into dangerous and unpredictable situations, but you ... you didn't have that same training. You going in to save them shows exactly what kind of situations you're ready to face for the loyalty and protection of your people and it speaks volumes about the kind of woman you're growing into. You're incredible, Elodie Ravenwood, and I will forever be in your debt. Your parents would be so proud of you."

A lump forms in my throat and I try to swallow over it, positive that if I were to try and talk right now, my voice would break and every little emotion that I'm desperately trying to hold onto will come falling out.

Seeing the internal struggle, Dianna simply pulls me back into her arms, holding me tight as her hand rubs up and down my back. I hold onto her a second longer than necessary, loving that warmth she gives me, a warmth that I've always imagined my mother would have had.

Dianna pulls back and her hands capture mine, giving them each a tight squeeze. "Do you have a few moments?" she questions. "There are a few things I would like to discuss with you."

"Of course," I rush out, searching her eyes in confusion as a million things start rushing through my mind, each of them wondering what could be so important that she needs to pull me aside to discuss. I mean, the only thing we really have in common is her son, and as far as I'm concerned, she's all good with our relationship—at least, I hope.

I step back toward the open door and Dianna steps with me, leaving the boys behind, that is until Cruz forces his way between us and stares down at his mother. "What's this about? What's going on?"

"Oh, Cruz," his mother laughs. "You know, not everything has to involve you."

Cruz stares at her blankly, almost offended by her statement. "What are you talking about? I'm Cruz Freaking Danforth, of course everything involves me. I'm God's gift to earth. I'm brilliant."

"That you are, my son," she throws back at him, a smirk on her lips as her eyes sparkle with mirth, playing him at his own game and showing me exactly where he gets it from. "But about a week ago, you, my darling, walked through my front door, looked me dead in the eyes after my sons had been taken from me, and told me that you and your friends had killed Elodie Ravenwood in order to save your brothers. Now, I know you like to forget all those important life lessons your father and I always taught you, but lying to your mother is unacceptable."

Cruz cringes. "Come on, you know why I had to do it."

"I do, which is the only reason that I haven't dragged you out of this house by your ear and locked your ass in your bedroom."

"Mom," he seethes, lowering his voice. "I'm nearly twenty. You can't lock me in my room."

"You want to make a bet?"

Cruz rolls his eyes and huffs. "Fine," he says, "but be honest, aren't you secretly impressed that I was able to get that lie past you? Usually you can see straight through my bullshit."

"Impressed certainly isn't the word I would use for it," she tells him. "You had me thinking that I was losing my edge. I still have two sons to raise and my built-in lie detector has always been my biggest gift. If I were to lose that, I'd be screwed. Now, go and make yourself useful while Elodie and I have a quick chat."

Cruz groans as Dianna and I step around him. "Really?" he calls from behind us, more than ready to throw a tantrum for not being invited to our private chat. "You're really going to hold this against me?"

"Yep."

"For how long?"

"Go and save some more of those poor girls that Sam Delacourt trafficked and I might just consider letting you back into my good graces. Save three in the same week and I might just buy you that new Harley Davidson you've been looking at."

"Is that a promise?" he demands, his voice traveling right up the hallway in his excitement. Dianna doesn't respond as we step through to the dining room that the boys and I had only just been in a moment ago, only now that moment seems like a lifetime. "Fuck. Mom?" Cruz calls out again. "Is it a promise? Shit. Winter? Is it a promise or is she doing that weird smirky thing that she does when she's fucking with me?"

I quickly glance at Dianna to find that she's definitely doing the weird smirky thing and I can't say that I'm surprised. The last time Cruz was on his bike, he ended up flying through the air and crashing into the hood of Carver's Escalade. No mother would willingly buy their son another after that, but Cruz doesn't need to know that, if anything, the extra motivation to help him find those missing children is just what he needs. We've been so caught up with trying to save ourselves that the search has been put on hold, which makes me feel like the biggest dick in the world. But at the end of the day, if we're all dead, then there will be no one advocating for those kids.

I gently close the door behind us, closing out Cruz's desperate pleas before following Dianna to the long table. She quickly glances over the manila folders that are left scattered all over the table before pretending that she didn't see a thing. She takes a seat and I take the one beside her, letting my nerves get the better of me.

"Oh, honey. There's no need to be nervous," she laughs, clearly seeing the look in my eyes. "I've been meaning to talk to you about this since the moment you arrived back in Ravenwood Heights, but every time I feel it's the right time, something happens and I find myself pulling back."

"Oh?" I ask, my bows dropping in confusion.

She takes a deep breath and reaches across the table to take my hand. "I don't know if you knew this, but your mother and I were quite close." I suck in a breath and she gives me a fond smile, nodding as I take in the news. "She was an amazing person, caring wife, and an even better mother. All she wanted in the world was to raise you into the beautiful woman that you've now turned into. I can just picture her looking down on you and knowing that even without her by your side, you've become the woman that she would have always wanted you to be."

Tears fill my eyes and I try to blink them back, but all I manage to do is send them sailing down my cheeks. "Are you sure?" I question. "Because more than ever, I feel like I'm letting them down."

"I'm positive, Elodie," she whispers, squeezing my hand again. "I can't speak for your father, I wasn't as close with him, but your mother prided on strength, courage, determination, and loyalty, and you come fully equipped with all of those traits. You're not afraid to go after what you want and neither was she. Plus, you look just like her. It's uncanny."

"Yeah?"

"Definitely," she says before taking a breath and allowing a seriousness to come over her. "The night of the fire … when Royston—" I nod and she goes on, not wanting to upset me with the constant reminder of what happened that night. "My husband and I had been going through a rough patch back then. We were struggling to conceive after having Cruz and the stress of that was all too much, and your mother, bless her soul, London was kind enough to allow me to stay with her for a few nights to clear my head. I told my husband that I was going for a spa weekend and your father drove us away into the mountains. Your mother sat up front with Andrew while I sat in the back with you, watching you sleep as we drove for hours."

Dianna pauses for a short moment, looking over my face as though she was looking at her long-lost friend. "It was one of the best weekends of my life. London and I sat up all night having cocktails while your father rolled his eyes at our antics and held you in his arms. He would always refuse to put you down, even when your mother insisted that he was messing with your sleeping schedule. They were great parents and you were always their first priority, which is why they were so eager to get away for a few days. There was such an uproar over you being born as a little girl that it was putting a strain on those precious moments they got to have with you as a newborn. All they wanted in the world was to enjoy their baby girl."

She takes a breath as her eyes become watery. "I'm sorry," she whispers. "I've never told this story before and it's … it's so much harder than I thought it was going to be."

"It's okay," I whisper, watching her face and taking in her gorgeous green eyes that are so much like her son's. "Take your time."

Dianna fakes a smile and pretends to be strong, letting out a breath and trying with everything that she is to be encouraging. "I was there the night that Royston broke into your parents' mountain home. It was the middle of the night and I had no idea what had happened until I was woken with flames surrounding my room. I heard your cries and I knew they'd never have left you behind, so I ran to them assuming the fire hadn't woken them yet, and what I found …"

Her voice breaks and she cuts herself off, needing a moment to calm the overwhelming emotions of having to relive that night. "I was the one who took you. It was a miracle that you had survived the smoke inhalation and I couldn't bear anything else happening to you, so I strapped you into your father's SUV and I took off. Tobias King was coming in just as I was leaving and he told me to take you somewhere safe and that he would handle the rest, and he did just that."

My chest constricts, the pain too much to handle, knowing that still to this day, Dianna Danforth trusts that Tobias King had good intentions.

"You were the one who cared for me?" I ask her.

"I was," she whispers. "I moved you into my family's holiday home and hired a full-time nanny who watched you when I couldn't be there, but it was too dangerous. I stayed with you for two months and that time together was enough to bond us and I looked at you as my own daughter, still to this day I think of you as my own, but it was too dangerous. Dynasty was divided. The corruption knew no bounds as everyone fought for leadership. It was a constant battle and I knew that if word got out that you had survived that night, you would have been targeted, and you were too young to fight for your life. I had to send you away, and that decision has crippled me every day since."

Tears stream down my face and it's not until they splash against my hands that I even realize just how much I'm crying.

"I met with Tobias and together we agreed to put you into foster care and destroy any trail so that you could not be found, and I always wondered how they kept finding you, until I realized that it was Royston who had killed your parents. He left you alive, and he was the reason that you spent eighteen years running. Well, he and Paris."

I nod, having already known all about Royston's part in all of this. Hell, I knew so much that I took a dagger and killed him with it—a move that still keeps me warm at night.

"I'm so sorry, Elodie," Dianna murmurs. "I should have told you about it all that first time I saw you at my home with Cruz, but I was in shock seeing your beautiful face. You looked so much like your mom that it just kinda threw me off a bit, and on top of that, I didn't want to upset you. You were so happy with Cruz. It truly was an amazing sight. I'm so glad that the two of you have found one another. Screw the Dynasty traditions. You two together is like a fairytale."

My cheeks flush with the brightest pink and I find myself glancing away. "I've always wondered who looked after me for those few short months."

"Well, now you know," she tells me, squeezing my hand again. "I'm always going to look at you like a long-lost daughter, so it's important to me that you know that you are always welcome in my home. I will drop everything to help you when you need it, all you have to do is ask."

I lean in and wrap my arms around her. "Thank you," I murmur, turning into a blubbering mess as another piece of the intricate puzzle otherwise known as my life finally falls into place, a piece that for once is actually welcomed.

# CHAPTER 19

"You're an even bigger fool than I thought if you think I'm going to vote for that monstrosity," Harlen Beckett roars, flying to his feet and glaring across the wide table at Earnest Brooks, making Grayson groan in frustration at having everybody dealing with his father's tantrum. "That idiot will have the whole organization crumbling and exposed in days. He's never been able to keep his mouth shut."

I moan and drop my head to the table. This bullshit has been going on for hours. I walked in here at ten this morning and after Dianna and Earnest's wife knocked on the door to bring up a platter of wraps and sandwiches, I realized that it was already after two in the afternoon. That was hours ago now.

My ass is cramping and my body is aching to move around. The boys have stuck to their promise of training me to fight and the past few days have left my body aching from my workouts, though the ache is just a reminder that I'm working on myself and that bitches like Paris will never beat me again. But then there are times like this when you're stuck in the same fucking chair for hours on end and it sucks harder than Cruz on Carver's dick. Well, not that I've ever seen that, but I have the vision in my head and that's exactly where I'm going to keep it. After all, we all need something to keep us warm at night.

I wonder what the guys would say if I suggested a little sword fight action. Considering the way Cruz reacted when he accidentally probed his own asshole with the shitty two-ply toilet paper, I don't think it'll go down well, but a girl can always dream.

Fuck. Daydreaming again. That's got to be the millionth time since this bullshit started this morning. I could use a break, but a break is just a delay for when this shit finally wraps up. I just want it done. I'm starting to not even care who gets voted in now.

No. That's a lie. I care more than I should because risking the wrong guy getting in means risking my life, and I'm not about that shit. At least, not today anyway. Generally, I'm really good at putting my life at risk, which the boys are more than happy to remind me of every chance they get. In fact, Carver only reminded me not to accidentally fall in front of a gun this morning. He's so sweet like that.

Crap. I've got to give it a rest with the daydreaming.

I blink a few times while pressing my lips into a hard line and doing my best not to bring attention to the fact that I can't stop yawning. I grab the glass of ice water off the table and cringe at the condensation circle left on the expensive wood table. Oh well, Dynasty has enough funds to replace the table. Hell, they could buy every family in the country a new fucking table if they wanted to.

After taking a sip, I let out a breath and shoot my gaze across the table to Carver who looks as though he's trying really hard to concentrate on the fifth argument that Beckett Sr. and Brooks have had in the span of the last hour, neither of them making very good points at all.

Carver raises a brow, silently asking how I'm doing and I shrug my shoulders, wishing that the time could tick by a little faster. Though, studying his perfect face and his stone-hard body seems to do the trick. Any girl could fall victim to it, get lost in his perfection only to snap out of it an hour later to realize that she's been drooling.

I try to focus, but when Matthew Montgomery gets involved and Mr. Danforth steps in to try and be some kind of adjudicator, I completely give up.

Carver's stare falls away when Matthew Montgomery starts taking shots at his candidate and I scoot down in my chair, the boredom knowing no bounds. My gaze shuffles around the table to the only other face in the room that I have any interest in looking at.

Hunter Mother Fucking King.

He's so gorgeous. He's held his own during this meeting like a fucking pro and every time he's opened his mouth, I've ended up clenching my thighs, even more so now as he catches my gaze and winks, making everything below the border throb with need.

I sink down in my chair even further, my eyes barely able to see over the top of the table. I zoned out of this shit hours ago and haven't had any input, though nobody has exactly asked for it either. They're all too focused on their own opinion. I bet I could get up from this table, strip down to my birthday suit, and walk straight out without a damn person noticing.

That's incorrect. King and Carver would definitely notice, but apart from that, I'd be good.

A soft smirk plays on King's lips and I find myself wondering what else I could do right now that these assholes around me won't notice, and not a second later, I'm sinking down even further, my head disappearing right under the table.

A wide grin stretches across my face as my knees hit the ground and I start crawling, holding back a gag as I catch Dion Luca adjusting his junk under the table.

I put it out of my mind and keep crawling, only one destination in mind. After all, my mouth has been watering for King for three fucking days now, and what better time than the present?

I reach him in no time, my knees already red and sore, but it's so worth it. I sit up on my knees and place my hands on his strong thighs, silently laughing as his whole body flinches in surprise.

King leans back in his chair until he can see me below the table and he stares at me in astonishment, either thinking I'm an idiot for assuming I can get away with this or just pure elation that he has a girl with the balls to get down and dirty at the worst possible times.

I roll my tongue over my lips, letting him see the hunger in my eyes and not a second later, his hands come to his jeans and he frees the impeccable monster that lives beneath.

He's already hard and standing to attention, more than ready for me to take him whole. My gaze shifts around his big cock and meets his heavy stare to see nothing but excitement shining in his eyes. His gaze shifts across the table and judging by the direction they've gone, I can only assume that he's silently letting Carver know exactly what he's missing out on.

But enough time has been wasted and too many days have passed without me getting to taste him on my tongue. Besides, it's only a matter of time before someone realizes that I've literally slipped away.

I shuffle in closer, raising up on my knees until I'm the perfect height to close my lips around his thick cock. I taste the small bead of moisture at his tip as his hand snakes down under the table and knots into my hair.

Fuck yes. This is exactly what I've been craving.

King is usually a vocal kind of guy. He likes to encourage me with whorish little words to let me know when I'm giving it to him right, but right now, the only sign that he's in a world of blissful satisfaction is the way his fingers tighten in my hair, and damn it, it's absolutely everything.

My hand moves up and down with my mouth, doing it just how he likes it as my other slips deeper and cups his balls, giving a gentle squeeze and loving the way his thighs flinch under my touch. My tongue works over his tip as I keep picking up my pace, being absolutely relentless and not wasting a single moment in my quest to taste him on my tongue.

I want him to come and I'm going to do whatever it takes to make it happen as quickly as possible. Knowing that Carver is probably impatiently waiting for his turn only makes it that much better, but Carver will have to wait. I don't think I have time for two right now. Though, if he could somehow kick Matthew Montgomery out of his seat and move in beside King, then I'm sure I could do them at the same time.

The challenge has been thrown down and I keep myself busy, working up and down his cock and absolutely loving the way the tension rises in his body. His fingers tighten in my hair to the point of pain, but I fucking love it. I keep my hands moving, letting him have the premium Winter package, and all too soon his warm seed is shooting to the back of my throat, but I don't let up, wanting every last drop. Though I have to admit, not getting to watch his face as he came undone kinda sucked, but I'm sure it'll only be a matter of time before he makes it up to me.

King tucks his junk back into his pants and peers down at me below the table. He's watching me in wonder with half-closed eyes, his chest rising and falling all too quickly for a table like this. Hell, if the men sitting around it actually gave a shit about anything but themselves, I don't doubt that they would have known exactly what was going on over here.

I make a show of licking my lips and not a second later, I crawl away, heading back to my seat, and just in time as the second I move away from King, his candidate is brought up and he's called to defend the guy for the hundredth time today.

I scooch back up into my seat, having to slide up awkwardly so that my eyes peek up first. I quickly scan the table to see everyone focused on the task at hand—everyone apart from Carver who's watching me with a slight shake of his head and an amused smirk on his lips, though the look in his eyes tells me that it's on tonight, just me and him and a good fucking time.

I slowly slide higher in my chair until I'm fully seated and only then do I stand and look around the table, every eye coming to mine while I silently pray to whoever exists above that I didn't accidentally end up with King's cum dripping from my chin. "This has gone on for far too long. I don't know about you guys, but I'm exhausted and I want to put this shit into motion. You've each had more than enough time to debate your arguments on your preferred applicant, and now it's time to make your decisions. Is everybody's mind made up or do you need more time?"

Mr. Danforth nods. "I'm ready to vote."

"As am I," Earnest says beside me.

Everyone nods and just like that, I get things started. "I am going to name each of the five candidates and you will only be permitted to raise your hand to vote twice. Be sure about your decision, as this is your one shot to make a difference for Dynasty. Tonight we will wrap this meeting with a full house. Is that understood?"

"Crystal clear," Harlen Beckett says. "Let's do this."

Carver nods and I take a deep breath, getting my pen and paper to write down the results, not doubting for a second that someone will eventually question the voting. "Alright, those in favor of Richard

Michaelson Sr?"

Two hands raise and I take my time, jotting down the results before moving on. "Justin Chamberland?" Six hands raise and just as before, I take caution and time writing in the results. I move on to our third dummy vote which gets far too many votes, but not enough to have me sweating.

Leaving Carver and King's applicants till last, I let out a shaky breath and hope this goes our way, but judging by the minimal votes for the first two guys, we should be hitting a home run. My gaze shuffles to King's, knowing he's bound to be feeling the nerves. "Alright, next up, Calvin Huntington," I say. "Please raise your hands if he has your vote."

Hands rise all around the table and I let out a discreet breath of relief.

One down. One to go.

I write down every single name who voted for the Huntington family to step into leadership of Dynasty before finally looking up around the table at the impatient men. "Last but not least," I start. "Can I have a show of hands of those who vote to induct Charles Vandenberg?"

I wait and watch as hands slowly raise around the table, trying not to look at Carver, knowing that the second I do, our whole plan will be given away. So instead, I count the hands, knowing before even glancing down at my paper that we've already won the second seat.

"Thank you," I say after tallying the votes. "That concludes the vote and as of now, we once again have a full house and will accept both the

Huntington and Vandenburg lines into Dynasty. Calvin Huntington will be offered the Scardoni Estate, along with it, the Scardoni seat at this very table. Charles Vandenburg will be offered the Harding Estate and along with it, the Harding seat at our table."

Heads nod all around as everybody rises, more than ready to get out of here. "Earnest," I say before he gets a chance to scurry away and hide in the privacy of his own home, most likely to step into a brand-new diaper. He turns around and raises his brows in question. "Will you ensure that the Harding Estate has been cleared of all their belongings in preparation for the Vandenberg family moving in? They have a young family and I'd hate for them to arrive to a less than stellar property."

"Of course," he says as Carver and King step in beside me. "Is there anything else that I can do for you?"

I nod. "As we discussed earlier in the week, I plan on having a formal celebration to welcome our new families. Can you pass the message along to our main event coordinators? I'd like a big party, every member of Dynasty—past and present generations to be invited. It is a momentous occasion and should be celebrated as such."

Earnest nods and gives me a small smile. "Consider it done." And just like that, he scurries out of the room, leaving me with Carver and King who watch me as though I'm about to fall to pieces. "Wanna get out of here?" Carver questions, slipping his hand into mine and leading me toward the door.

I pull back and the guys stop to look back at me. "What's wrong?" King asks, his brows furrowing. "I thought you would have been dying to get out of this room."

"I am," I say, "I wanted to—"

"Climb back under that fucking table and give me what he got?" Carver suggests, cutting me off.

A wicked smirk stretches across my face. "I'll climb under any table for you," I tell him before dropping the subject and letting them in on the secret. "But I was hoping you guys would come with me down to the cells. I know I shouldn't care, but I wanted to check in on Ember."

King sighs. "You're too pure for your own good."

"I know," I grumble. "And I know that I'm going to regret it, and all it's going to do is cause me pain, but I just need to make sure that I made the right decision."

Carver steps in beside me, his thumb rubbing back and forth over my knuckles. "Is there anything we can say to change your mind?"

"Have you ever been successful in changing my mind?"

"Good point," he mutters, giving my hand a tug and pulling me out into the long hallway. "Let's make it happen."

# CHAPTER 20

The boys remain at the main doors of the cells as I walk ahead, trailing my feet through the long, daunting hallway, each step I take echoing off the walls and rebounding through the empty cells around me. I feel their eyes on me, watching me with concern. They don't want me here and fuck, I don't want to be either, but we need answers. There's no backing out now. I haven't come this far just to turn on my heel and run like a bitch.

This place is creepy and brings back way too many shitty memories of my time in here, though on the other hand, it's mind-blowing to see just how far I've come since then. The world seems like a completely different place now. It's full of hope and promise of a big future, where this cell is nothing but dark and gloomy, and with every passing second, I know I should turn back and get my ass out of here.

Going to see Ember is like volunteering to have her stab a knife right through my back, yet I keep putting one foot in front of the other, determined to see this through. I'm a glutton for punishment. Either that, or just a fucking moron.

Yeah ... definitely a moron.

Laughter comes from the cell up ahead and the noise has my blood running cold. "Wow," Ember says, knowing it's me before even seeing my face. "I didn't think you had the balls to show your face down here after that bullshit stunt you pulled."

I take a few more steps and place myself right in front of her cell, looking in to see her lounging back on the hard bed, looking as though she could be sitting on the most stunning Caribbean beach. *The stunt that I pulled?* I question in astonishment. "You're the one who's been playing twisted little games since the second I arrived. You brought this on yourself."

She laughs again, feigning amusement, but despite the fact that our whole friendship was a sham, I still know her better than she ever wanted me to, and being locked up in this tiny, cold cell is absolutely killing her.

"You're still holding on to that, are you?" she chuckles. "Glad to see my twisted little games left a scar."

"If I was holding on to something, don't you think your bitch ass would have been released from these cells by now?" I question, letting her see just how quickly I was ready to let go of any kind of friendship that we had. Besides, it gives me a chance to flex my callous nature, and what kind of girl could skip an opportunity like that? "I'm simply here to inform you that both the Harding and Scardoni lines have officially been wiped from leadership, so no matter how hard you try, you will never have power in my world again."

Ember stands and throws herself at the bars, clutching onto them with both hands. "What's that supposed to mean?"

A grin stretches across my face and I lean in toward her. "It means that as of ten minutes ago, your whole family line ceased to exist to Dynasty. Everything your father worked for, everything he believed in means nothing now. Everything your bitch of a mother promised you, it will never happen because Dynasty no longer recognizes the Harding line as one of their own. You're out on your own now without Dynasty's protection, so you better be careful. If I ever allow you out of my cells, you're free game. The tables have turned. I have the upper hand and you're the one who's going to spend the rest of your life watching your back."

Ember pulls against the steel bars. "You can't do that."

"I already have," I tell her. "The vote was held this afternoon, and I assume that right about now there are men storming into your home and stripping it bare, preparing the estate for its new owners."

Ember clenches her jaw, the fury and rage pouring out of her in waves. "You can't just take everything away from me. Isn't it enough that you've already killed my father? You have a target on my mother's back, and now you take my home? What the hell is wrong with you? If someone doesn't agree with you, you're just going to trample them out until they disappear, or will you just have your pack of wolves take care of the problem? This is a fucking dictatorship. The power has gone to your head."

I laugh, stepping back and crossing my arms over my chest. "I have absolutely no issue taking out the people who have put their own targets on my back. If someone threatens my life, you better fucking believe that I will deal with it. That's just what life is like in my position. The power hasn't gone to my head because it hasn't even had a chance to yet. I've been too fucking busy trying to keep myself alive so that people like Paris Moustaff can't destroy everything my father and grandfather worked for."

She shakes her head. "You're a joke."

I scoff, shaking my head. "You know what's really sad?" I ask her. "You really had a shot at standing right by my side. All I needed was your honesty and loyalty. Had you come to me and told me what was going down and who you really were, I would have been able to look past it and I would have made sure that you had it all. For so long I thought you were my only friend, but you were too caught up trying to stab the knife through my back. Now look at you, you have nothing and nobody to bail you out. Crossing me was the biggest mistake you ever made."

She shrugs her shoulders. "Maybe it was, but I went down for a chance at a real family, and that's something you'll never get."

"That's where you're wrong," I murmur. "Family is so much more than the people you share blood with. Family is a choice. The boys are my family and no matter what you do or how hard you try, you will never feel that kind of connection."

"You're a real bitch, you know that?"

"Maybe I am," I mutter, taking a breath and moving back a step. "Once you walk out of this cell, you're going to have nothing, no place in Dynasty, no home, and no friends to have your back. So I'm going to give you one last shot to make the right decision."

"What's that supposed to mean?"

"Once Paris is found, I will allow you out of this cell on one condition. You go back home to your adoptive parents and forget that Dynasty ever existed. Forget me, forget Paris, and forget everything that went on here. I will offer you a clean slate provided that you never attempt to step into my world again."

"And if I won't accept that?"

A darkness comes over me and I'm forced to take another step back, hating just how heavy I feel. "If you keep your loyalty to your mother and continue aiding her in her attempts on my life, you will be treated as a traitor to the people of Dynasty and sentenced to life behind my bars for the role you have played against us."

Ember's eyes soften and her hands lower on the bars, and just when I think she's going to take me up on my offer, a sick, twisted grin tears across her face. "If only it was that easy," she says just as a loud BANG sounds throughout the underground cells, the echo going on for miles.

My eyes bug out of my head as Ember howls with laughter and I snap my gaze back at the guys who instantly start running toward me. "WINTER!"

I look back at Ember, quickly backing up. "What was th—"

Another BANG cuts off my question and the walls tremble. My

heart thunders, the sound of my pulse nearly deafening in my ears. "WINTER. RUN."

I don't wait to find out what's going on as I bolt back toward the guys, but as I do, another loud BANG roars through the cells, this one a million times louder. Before the sound has even stopped echoing through the long hallway, a military-grade truck slams through the brick wall and crashes right into Ember's cell, making an absolute joke of the metal bars.

I have no choice but to launch myself through the air to avoid being struck by the debris, and just as my body crashes to the ground, King and Carver are there, desperately trying to pull me to my feet.

I can't help but look back over my shoulder as Ember makes her move, scrambling over the bars, bricks, and rubble before climbing through the open side passenger window of the truck.

As Ember's ass hits the seat, she looks out the window and meets my shocked stare, laughing as the driver of the truck kicks it into reverse. The tires screech against the floor and just as quickly as it came, the truck disappears, leaving nothing but devastation behind.

The walls stop shaking and the boys continue dragging me through the hallway, getting me as far away as they possibly can, unsure how the integrity of the underground cells will hold up now that there's a massive gaping hole in the side.

"How ... how did that ... even happen?" I pant, tripping over my own damn feet as the shock tears through my system. I mean, what the fuck even was that? We're in an underground world. There's no way in here apart from the main entrance which has heavy security.

There's no way that a military-grade truck was approved for access, not to mention all the concrete rooms and structure that the truck would have had to get past in order to get enough speed to tear through the fucking cell walls like that.

My mind whirls with the possibilities as I try to piece together a mental map of the underground world, trying to figure out what rooms that truck would have just smashed its way through when Carver puts my mind at ease. "Tunnels," he explains, sending me straight back in time to the night we raced out of the ball through the tunnels while our world crumbled to dust around us. "There are fucking underground tunnels all through Ravenwood Heights. I was planning the same damn thing when you were locked down here."

We finally reach the main reception area of the underground world and the boys slow their pace, allowing me a moment to actually breathe. "What do you mean tunnels? I thought this was all Dynasty down here."

"It is," King says, still leading me out of here, desperate to get up into the real world and figure out where the fuck Ember went and who she's with. Though I'm sure we can figure that out pretty easily. "But the tunnels were here before we were. Just like the ballroom, we had to build everything around the tunnels and I guess that's exactly what happened with the cells."

"FUCK."

"Yeah," Carver agrees, realizing just how much shit we're in.

"What do we do now?"

"First, we need to get the fuck out of here, and then we need to make sure that whoever's estate is built on top of it isn't going to fucking cave in," Carver says. "After that, we have a fucking big-ass party to organize."

Well, shit. A party is the last thing we need now. We knew a party would lure out Paris, but now that Ember is back in her ear, it's practically a guarantee and we better be fucking ready. Though one thing is for sure, that out I just offered Ember can be shoved right up her ass. I'm done playing nice, and just as I promised, she better be watching her back.

# CHAPTER 21

The deep red strapless gown sails down my body like a second skin and I can't help but feel like the sexiest creature who ever lived, but why shouldn't I? Tonight's party is my first official event after rising from the dead and it's a guarantee that I'll be going all out. I mean, why not? It's a big occasion, one of the biggest that Dynasty has ever had and for the majority of the night, all eyes will be on me.

I step out of Carver's brand-new Escalade into a world of dazzling beauty, absolutely shocked by the sight before me. It's like nothing I've ever seen before … apart from on TV of course, but it's certainly something I never expected for myself.

It's the royal fucking treatment.

There's a red carpet that's been rolled out with people scattered on either side, more than I've ever seen before, each one of them desperately wanting to get a look at every last person who's been deemed important enough to get to walk it. I stare for a moment, unable to move one foot in front of the other as people start screaming my name.

I can't believe my eyes. There were hundreds of people at my fake funeral, but tonight's event just goes to show exactly how far and wide Dynasty spans, and just how many people I have counting on me.

Cruz's arm slips into mine and gives me a gentle tug, kick starting my night. "You're the fucking belle of the ball," he tells me, the pride radiating out of him in waves.

"I shouldn't be," I murmur, smiling at the younger children calling my name and giving small waves, wanting each and every one of them to feel seen and valued, something that I missed out on during my childhood. "Tonight isn't even about me. It's for the new members of Dynasty."

"We could be welcoming Freddie Mercury back from the dead and the masses would still call your name," he says, his eyes sparkling with adoration. "You're their only hope of change. You've declared that you're going to kick Paris' ass, and after news of your involvement saving all of our siblings, you've become a god among us. You're their hero. Elodie Ravenwood can do no wrong."

I press my lips together and shake my head. Clearly these guys need to have a good chat with Karleigh and then I'm sure they'll adjust their high opinions of me, because damn, doing wrong is all I've ever known. "That's taking it a bit far, don't you think? I'm not the girl who should be put on a pedestal. I just want to do what I got to do and then move on. There's nothing great about that."

"That's where you're wrong," he grins. "I bet half the dudes in this place would happily wipe your ass for you if it meant a night alone with the Queen of Ravenwood Heights. You have an air about you. You exude legendary vibes with everything you do and you just happen to look like a fucking goddess while you're doing it. Taking a stand during your own damn funeral—it's shit like that these people will never forget."

"Ugh," I groan, rolling my eyes as we pass through the crowd and approach the main entrance of tonight's venue. "Quit it with the ass-kissing."

"Can't," he laughs. "I don't know if you've realized this or not, but you've fucked everyone since coming home last week, except for me, so you better fucking believe that I'm going to do all the ass-kissing that it takes because I can't hold out any longer."

I laugh. "It's not my fault that you've been out with Grayson saving those little girls' lives these past few nights. You missed your shot. I had no choice but to crawl into King's bed instead, and man, he did me good. Even if I wanted to wait up for you, I had no hope. I've never been so exhausted. Poor Carver. He had to listen the whole time and couldn't help coming to watch the show."

"That's it," Cruz says, his jaw clenched. "Tonight it's you and me. The others can fuck right off."

We reach the doors and I stop, looking up and meeting his gorgeous green eyes as the boys trail behind us, getting just as much love from their adoring fans. "Do you want to make it interesting?" I murmur, keeping my voice low.

Cruz's tongue rolls over his bottom lip. "Do I sense that you're about to throw down a challenge?"

I grin wide. "If you can fuck me during tonight's party, out in the open without a damn soul noticing what we're doing, I'll fuck the guys right off for a whole damn week."

The boys overhear and each come to an immediate stop, crowding Cruz and me in the doorway, desperate to hear what Cruz has to say about my little challenge.

His eyes bug out of his head. "You mean that I'll get you all to myself for a whole fucking week? No sharing?"

"No sharing."

Carver shakes his head. "No. No fucking way," he says, but I keep my gaze locked on Cruz.

"What's it going to be, Danforth? Are you down for the challenge? Can you handle the pressure?"

King looks between me and Cruz, seeing all his hopes and dreams slowly burning in a fiery pit of death. "Duuuuude. Come on. Don't fucking cock block us like this. We're brothers. You can't do this to us."

King's desperation only makes Cruz's grin widen in the most devious, seductive way, his eyes shining with excitement. "You're fucking on."

Grayson groans and before he breaks down in tears in front of all these people, he turns and walks straight through the doors, more than ready to pretend that the next week of his life doesn't exist. Though, that's assuming Cruz can actually pull this off. There are so many people here tonight that this challenge is nearly impossible, but if he still wanted to drag me away and fuck me in private, I'd be cool with that too.

Cruz's arm slips through mine and he quickly adjusts himself before walking forward with newfound determination. His chin is raised and his shoulders held strong, looking like every girl's version of a wet dream which only gets better as my gaze travels down over his impeccable suit.

I keep up with him step for step as King and Carver trail behind us, murmuring to each other about the likelihood that Cruz will choke, leaving me wide open for the taking later tonight, which only prompts a quick round of Rock, Paper, Scissors.

We walk through a long entrance and much like the ball that we never speak of, we're brought to a stop at the top of a massive staircase. My heart thunders in my chest, looking over the spectacular sight.

There are people everywhere in amazing gowns, waitresses weaving their way through the room with champagne glasses, and more security than anyone has the right to see in one place.

The room has been completely decked out in decorations and I find myself sucking in a deep gasp, completely astonished by the effort that the Dynasty event organizers have gone to. They deserve a freaking medal for this shit.

One by one, the people notice us at the top of the stairs and their sharp gazes fall on me, their eyes trailing over my gown. Brows are raised as sly, dirty grins stretch across some of the mens' faces, while their wives scowl at the slit in my gown that trails right up my thigh, not stopping until it reaches the top of my hip. The dress is controversial, but it felt so right that I had no choice but to wear it. I just have to be careful as one wrong step walking down these stairs would have my pussy out on display for the whole world to see.

My impatience gets the best of me and I draw in a deep breath before squeezing Cruz's arm and taking my first step down into the party. He holds me tight and the excitement quickly takes over. Tonight is going to be incredible; I can feel it deep in my bones. Tonight is about a new change. It's about starting fresh and taking back what's ours.

I get halfway down the stairs when a vision of the ball flashes through my mind—me walking down the stairs with my arm in Carver's. His panicked stare. The horror on the boys' faces. The explosion before the undeniable pain and grieving.

The memories flash through my mind like a movie on replay and I start gasping for oxygen, my gaze flicking around the room, certain that tonight is going to be a repeat of one of the worst nights of my life. It's like I took a single step and my whole world flipped upside down.

"You're okay," Cruz says, his tone soothing the fear that lives deep inside me. "The whole room has been swept for explosives. We're safe. Knox can't hurt us, not tonight."

My eyes continue darting around the room and only seeing

the happy faces of the people below, I let out my breath and force myself to keep walking.

One step after another.

By the time we reach the bottom step, I feel a light sweat coating my skin and I realize that after the ballroom explosion, I never got a chance to take it all in, to process everything that happened. I was thrust straight back into my leadership role, trying to figure out who had caused such havoc, but before I was even able to think about it, Tobias King was killed in my living room and the world quickly spun out of control.

"You know, if you want, we can arrange someone for you to—"

"Don't even say it," I tell Cruz as Matthew Montgomery comes racing up to me with a fake smile and a glass of champagne resting in his hand.

He takes my free hand and brings it to his lips, pressing a gentle kiss on the back of my hand. Cruz pulls me tightly against him as a chorus of irritated grunts comes from behind us. "Miss Ravenwood," he beams, putting on a show for the crowd. "You look like an absolute dream. May I be so bold as to ask you to save me a dance?"

My eyes narrow and despite the fact that he vowed his loyalty, I don't trust him one bit and he knows it. "Perhaps you should be asking your wife that question."

A scowl stretches across his face and he quickly presses his lips into a tight line, doing his best to mask his little slip-up, though had we been in private, I'm sure he would have allowed his true colors to fly free. "Of course, Miss Ravenwood," he tells me. "However, the offer still stands."

I nod, more than ready to move along but he presses his champagne flute into my hand. "Anything you need," he murmurs, "just let me know and I'll happily arrange it. I do wish you the night of all nights."

"Uhh, thanks," I say, allowing Cruz to pull me away before Montgomery gets another chance to try and suck up to me. I totally get it though. He wants to look good in front of all these people who have started to doubt him, but he seems too eager to me and the more he tries, the less I trust him.

Cruz and I get all of two steps away before he yanks Matthew's champagne flute out of my hand and tosses it into a nearby planter. The sound of the glass smashing is drowned out by the impressive band that takes up the majority of the stage. Within seconds, Cruz has a brand-new glass in my hands and I eagerly sip at it, knowing it's not a party without a slight buzz. But tonight I'm playing it safe. The real drinking can commence once Paris is securely buried ten feet underground.

We continue walking deeper into the party, saying hi to all the friendly faces who approach us as Carver, Grayson, and King discreetly spread out to keep their eyes on me, having absolutely no idea how to relax and enjoy a party. But seeing as though the whole point of this party was to lure Paris into a trap, I guess I can understand their reluctance to let loose. Besides, as of two days ago, Ember was set free on the world, and a woman scorned is a woman we should all fear. Something tells me that her bite is a lot worse than her bark.

Cruz and I mingle with the guests and stop to say a quick hello to one of tonight's star attractions—Calvin Huntington, who looks more than thrilled to be here. Hell, I couldn't wipe the grin off his face even if I tried. He thanks me profusely and it gets to the point where I have to remind him that it was the group as a whole who voted him in, it wasn't just my doing.

Calvin continues chatting away and I smile at everything he says, but the truth is that after watching Ida Carver slink by me in a pitch-black gown, I haven't heard a damn word. I don't think I've ever seen anyone look so miserable at such a grand party. Hell, a party like this should be Ida's chance at scrambling up her hoity-toity friends' asses. This is her shot to make an impression, and by the looks of it, she's failing miserably.

She bypasses her daughters who are dressed in identical gowns and sitting alone at a table, their eyes slicing around the room in fear, probably wondering when all of their nightmares are going to resurface and they'll be kidnapped all over again.

My heart breaks and I find myself glancing back and searching the faces for Carver. I find him a second later, hanging back near the massive water feature. He meets my stare almost immediately as if he can feel the weight of my eyes on him.

I indicate to his sisters and he follows my gaze. Out of the four guys, Carver has always been the one who's kept his emotions hidden the best, but right now, looking at the fear in his sisters' eyes, his heart breaks for the whole world to see.

He starts moving and the second they see him making his way through the crowd to get to them, they launch out of their seats and their little arms are wrapped around his legs within a mere moment. He's their safety net, their hero, and nothing makes me happier. Though the question stands, why can't Ida offer her daughters that same comfort?

Knowing Carver has the situation under control, I turn back to the conversation that Cruz has effortlessly taken over for me in a way that has Calvin completely unaware that I'd zoned out.

I squeeze Cruz's hand and he wraps up the conversation, then before anyone gets the chance to pull me away again, Cruz leads me across the room and yanks me behind a sheer curtain, managing to do it without a single eye falling on us.

I laugh as the excitement bubbles up within me. I was kinda joking when I set that challenge for him earlier, but he seems to be taking it as seriously as I take my need to fuck all four of them at once. His eyes sparkle with anticipation and I realize just how ready he is. I'd never take Cruz for the kind of guy to get his junk out during a party that his mom is attending, but what can I say? Cruz Danforth is a man of many surprises.

"You sure about this?" he asks as his hands fall to my waist and he pulls me in close. "It's not too late to back out. I don't want you getting caught out and having to explain yourself. We can just tell the guys that we did it."

I shake my head, the grin stretching across my face as my

fingers trail up his thigh, feeling the way his pants strain as his cock demands freedom. "Nu-uh," I tell him. "If you want me for a week to yourself, then you need to come through with the goods, but," I add, "this spot is half-concealed so if this is where you want this to go down, then you need to be warned that you'll only get half a week."

His face drops. "But this is literally the only place we can do it," he insists. "I've been searching the room since the second we hit the top steps." He pulls back a bit and pauses, his brow raising as a dirty, wicked grin settles on his plump lips. "I could always fuck you on top of the bar, but I can't guarantee that nobody will watch the show."

I laugh and pull him back in. "This is your only shot, Danforth," I tell him. "Now shut up and fuck me before someone comes looking."

He doesn't waste a damn second.

Cruz's lips crush down on mine with a passion that I wasn't ready for and I'm quickly reminded that I haven't been with him since my return to Ravenwood Heights, and I can't fucking wait. He's usually so full of emotion. He's the one I go to when I want to feel more than just a hard cock slamming into me. He's the most considerate lover out of them all and that speaks volumes considering that the other three want nothing more than to make me come a million times before even getting close themselves.

Cruz's hand slips inside the high slit of my gown, finding me soaking wet and his lips pull up into a satisfied smirk. "This is going to be fun."

Damn straight, it is.

Without warning, he takes my waist and spins me so that I'm facing the sheer curtain, looking out at the partiers having the time of their lives. Cruz bunches up my gown as he kicks my feet apart, spreading my legs wide and grabbing a good handful of my ass cheek. "I'd fuck you any day with these heels on."

I grin, my tongue running over my bottom lip in anticipation as I look back over my shoulder. "Then what are you waiting for?"

Cruz chuckles and I watch as he frees himself from his pants and not a second later, he's sliding into my slick entrance, making me suck in a gasp, loving how he hits me at just the right angle. "Holy shit, Cruz," I breathe, knowing that keeping quiet is going to be an even bigger challenge than the one we're already in the middle of.

"Damnnnn, baby," he groans low, his eyes closing in satisfaction. He moves in and out with painfully slow movements and reaches around me, slipping his hand inside the slit of my gown and pressing down on my clit, making my whole body flinch before rubbing tight little circles.

I push back against him and despite how slow his movements are, my body is already on the edge. Add the possibility of getting caught and I'm in my fucking zone. My eyes quickly scan around the room, making sure no one is looking this way, but with so many guests scattered around the dimly lit room, it's impossible to tell. Though it doesn't escape me that the eyes of three other men are on me and fuck, they don't look happy. If anything though, their eyes on mine only gets me even hotter.

Wanting Cruz to feel just as good as I do, I clench my pussy, squeezing down around his cock and loving the way his lips drop to my shoulder. "Fuck, Winter. I love you," he murmurs against my skin, making butterflies soar through my stomach.

I turn my head and capture his lips in mine. "I love you too," I whisper. "You and me … I'll never doubt you again."

"You're damn right you won't."

I smile wide and turn back to face the crowd and just as Cruz pushes slowly back inside of me, I find Earnest Brooks searching through the crowd, his eyes scanning the room as though he's searching for someone.

"What's … the … time?" I ask between pants.

"Ten to nine," Cruz says with a clenched jaw, making me realize that it's me Earnest is searching for.

My hand falls to Cruz's on my hip and I squeeze it tight, barely able to speak through the intense pleasure rocking through my body. "We're about thirty seconds from being spotted," I tell him. "Don't make me remind you what will happen if you fail the challenge."

"Fuck."

Cruz picks up his pace and I cry out with soft moans and force myself to bite down on my lip to keep from screaming. His fingers fasten on my clit and my knees start to shake, barely able to keep myself upright.

Earnest inches in closer and it's only a matter of time before he spies the red gown behind the sheer curtain, but I have faith in

Cruz that he'll come through with the goods. What can I say? He's all about performing under pressure.

He leans into me and bites down on my bare shoulder before moving his lips to that sensitive spot under my throat and kissing me there. I groan and clench my eyes, feeling my orgasm rapidly building. "Fuck, Cruz. I'm gonna come."

He's relentless and pushes me further, slamming deep inside my pussy as I squeeze down on him and as he applies more pressure to my clit, I come undone.

My orgasm tears through me and I dig my nails into the back of his hand as I tip my head back to his shoulder. Cruz stills as he comes with me, surrendering to my convulsing pussy. "Oh, fuck, babe," he grunts through his clenched jaw, his eyes closing as he spills into me without a damn care in the world.

I do what I can to catch my breath, desperately trying to come down from my high so I can concentrate on not getting sprung. I search the crowd and find Earnest just a few meters away and Cruz quickly pulls out of me, straightening my gown before tucking himself back inside his pants. He meets my stare as I turn in his arms. He winks. "Mission accomplished with a few seconds to spare."

"You're too cocky for your own good," I laugh.

"And don't you forget it."

Cruz takes my hand and just as he goes to lead me back out into the party, I pull him up short and suck in a breath, feeling everything that he just poured inside of me trailing down the inside of my thigh. "Elodie, there you are," Earnest says, moving in front of me on the opposite side of the sheer curtain. "What on earth are you doing hiding back here? Didn't you check the schedule of events? I need you up on stage to make the announcements now."

My eyes bug out of my head. "I, uhh … I just need to pee first."

"No can do," he says, shaking his head as he gathers up the curtain and ushers me out. "We're pressed for time. Make your way up onto the stage, please. There will be time for a quick bathroom break after the announcement."

I take a step and feel Cruz's cum sliding even further down my leg, hitting just above my knee.

"Now, Elodie," Earnest insists, clearly too stressed for his own good. "What are you waiting for? Get a move on, child."

Well, shit. This is going to be interesting.

# CHAPTER 22

Cum hits my ankles and I try not to cringe as the bright spotlights shine down on me. Applause sounds through the room and I find myself grinning out at the crowd, pride surging through me.

What are the chances that after getting dicked in a room full of over two thousand people, I end up standing on stage with the eyes of the whole organization on me with cum about to drip right into my heels?

I hope Cruz enjoyed himself because as good as it was, nothing is worth the humiliation I'll feel if I get caught out right now. The slit in my gown really doesn't help, and I do everything I can to keep the majority of my body hidden behind the dais. Knowing my luck, his cum is probably spread out all over my dress too. I mean, why keep this shit to myself? It's a party after all.

My gaze shifts around the crowded bodies, trying to search each and every face. This is the moment that we've been waiting for. If Paris is going to show up tonight, then now is the perfect opportunity. I'm standing up here with a light shining upon me. I'm the perfect target, and from the way Grayson and King stand on opposite sides of the room as Carver and Cruz remain close, tells me that they're all thinking the same thing.

I try to remember all the things that Earnest had prepared for me to say, but seeing Cruz's cocky smirk staring back at me, I come up blank and realize that I'm going to have to stick with the good ole Winter tradition of winging it.

After what feels like a lifetime, the applause dies down and I look out at the people before me, so proud to be standing before them and actually enjoying myself. Had I been asked a few months ago if I could see this day ever coming, I would have laughed it off and then punched the person who asked. It's incredible just how much my life has changed, and for the first time, I truly think it's changing for the better.

I stand tall, raising my chin and letting that pride show while unable to avoid searching for Paris in the crowd. "It is my greatest pleasure to be standing here before you all today," I start, watching as Earnest's face drops in horror, realizing that I'm not sticking to his carefully structured script. "It is no secret that over the past few months, we as a community have faced some of our biggest demons and from them, we have grieved. We have suffered, we have feared, and we have fought, and it is with great honor that today we stand victorious."

I pause, listening as the crowd erupts into cheers. "We do not allow our fears to terrorize us, we stand tall knowing that our brothers and sisters will be there to strengthen us in our times of need. Unfortunately, there have been far too many times where we have had to rely on our brothers and sisters to see us through, but those times are no more. We have weeded out those who have held us back, we have ruined those who threaten our future, and we have slaughtered those who dare act out against us. Dynasty is a legacy, Dynasty is our home, our family, and it is with great pleasure that I get to stand before you today and announce our newest family members."

Applause sounds through the room again and I'm forced to wait, which only allows me a second to notice the way Cruz's cum slips down into my heel and spreads out beneath my foot, making my heel far too slippery for my own good.

"I am sure by now you have all heard the whispers, seen the moving trucks, and spoken with your neighbors. It has been well known that for some time the Scardoni seat has remained vacant, but what you may not be aware of is that only recently, Ember Harding resigned from her position, leaving yet another vacancy. So tonight, I introduce you to not one new head, but two, sealing our futures and making Dynasty whole as it should have always been."

I look toward the side of the stage to where Calvin Huntington and Charles Vandenburg stand, their chins raised, each of them seeing tonight as the most important night of their lives. They're proud and so they should be. A chance like this doesn't come around every day.

My gaze drops to the small table that sits in the center of the room and a shudder runs through my body seeing the same dagger that I'd sworn my loyalty to Dynasty on and only moments after that, used it to murder Royston Carver.

The thought has my gaze shifting to Carver's and judging by the emptiness that sits within his eyes, I'd dare say that he knows exactly what's running through my mind, but now is not the time to dwell on the past. We can fuck it out of our systems later … or at least, in a week's time.

"Let's not waste another second, shall we?" I question, my tone hitching with excitement as I address the crowd. Cheers and applause bounce off every wall in the room as I indicate the side of the stage. "Tonight we welcome our new brothers, the new heads of Dynasty and we initiate them into our ranks with the sacred, traditional vows; Calvin Huntington and Charles Vandenburg."

The applause is so damn loud that anyone would think a fucking rocket was taking off in here.

The two gentlemen make their way up onto the stage and look out to the crowd with pride. They shake one another's hand and I take note of the way they seek out their wives and children, speaking volumes about the type of men they are and telling me everything that I need to know about them. You know, apart from already knowing every little intricate detail of their lives.

I move across the stage, hoping to God that I don't slip in my cum heels as I position myself in front of the small table, taking each of the men through the same initiation ritual that I went through only a few short months ago.

The second the dagger is placed back down, Mr. Danforth comes screeching out onto the stage and scoops it up. He gives me a narrowed stare and silently scolds me for what happened last time I was anywhere near this thing, and within seconds, he's gone again, leaving me on stage with the two new recruits and no idea where to go from here.

A laugh bubbles up my throat as Mr. Danforth scurries away, carrying the dagger as though it was as fragile and precious as a newborn baby. I disguise my laugh with a cough as Calvin and Charles both look my way, so without skipping a beat, I indicate to the dais and offer them the floor, giving them each the chance to eat up the spotlight while I give myself the chance to get off this damn stage and clean up Cruz's mess.

Calvin isn't one to skip an opportunity and moves in front of the microphone, quickly thanking me for the millionth time tonight and for taking both he and Charles through the initiation. I give them each a forced smile and make my way off the stage.

I find Cruz in the crowd and nod toward the back of the stage, silently letting him know that I'll be gone for a minute and he nods, understanding exactly what I'm trying to tell him. I take off a second later, hurrying around the back in search of the closest bathroom.

From memory, we're supposed to do some kind of traditional dance following the initiation so I'm going to have to make this quick.

I scramble through the massive state-of-the-art kitchen, not wanting to use the same bathroom as the guests, assuming that I'm going to have to get half naked just to find out exactly where all of

Cruz's yummy goodness has gone. I'm going to have to slip out of my heels, clean my feet, and somehow clean out the inside of my shoes as well. It's going to be a disaster.

The caterers gape at me, probably not used to seeing a gowned moron racing through their kitchen, but fuck them. If they knew the issue I was currently dealing with, I'm sure they'd understand. "Bathroom?" I question, realizing that if they're going to stop working just to stare, they might as well be helpful.

The girl closest to me blinks a few times before pointing to the right of the kitchen. "Through there. Third door on the left."

I nod and keep scrambling, the relief quickly taking over me, knowing that it'll only be a moment longer before I can finally walk in my heels without feeling Cruz's cum squishing between my toes. Don't get me wrong, I absolutely love it when the guys come. In my pussy, on my back, in my mouth or hell, all over my face too, but having it squished between my toes isn't exactly something I ever thought would happen. I mean, there's a reason why I like to race to the bathroom right after they've finished fucking me and it's to avoid this exact situation.

I barge in through the bathroom door and step into a room fit for a king, though in a place like this, anyone should expect impeccable bathrooms. Besides, if Dynasty had anything to do with building this masterpiece, then I can guarantee that the rest of the building is just as flawless. Hell, I can only imagine what the main guest bathroom looks like.

I kick my heels off and tiptoe across the bathroom, hating the feeling of being barefoot in here, but it's a necessary evil. I get myself into a stall and within seconds have my gown bunched up with my ass dropping down onto the heated toilet seat.

It takes far too long to get myself cleaned up and after finishing in the stall, I realize that it's going to take a lot more than just a quick wipe down. I make my way back toward the sink and start searching through the cupboard, feeling the greatest relief as I find a packet of baby wipes sitting high on the top shelf, so fucking high that I have to scale the damn cupboard just to reach it.

Knowing that if I take longer than the guys deem necessary, they'll have no issue barging in here, I do my best to make it quick. I tear the packet of baby wipes open and rip out a handful before scooting my ass back up on the vanity.

Once I have myself feeling brand-new and squeaky clean, I move on to my heels, cringing as the clumps of cum rest right in the bottom of my right shoe. I get busy scooping it all out and go as far as to hold the black stiletto under the hand dryer so that I don't have to slip my foot back into a wet shoe.

Bracing myself against the sink, I bring my foot up and do my best to wriggle it back into the shoe, feeling a million times better. I switch sides and just as my foot comes up, the bathroom door opens.

Not wanting to be that chick who stares at the others using the facilities, I keep my focus down on my foot, concentrating on being fast so that the boys don't end up worrying and coming to look for me.

My shoe slides on easily, and as I lower my foot back to the ground, I straighten up and raise my gaze. Only to come up short as two waitresses move in on me. I suck in a gasp, taking no time at all to realize that these aren't waitresses at all, but Ember and her psychotic bitch of a mother.

Ember holds a dagger in her right hand, a dagger eerily similar to the one I'd used to kill Royston Carver, the very one that not five minutes ago was scooped up by Cruz's father. Though it can't be the same one because I refuse to believe that Mr. Danforth would have handed it over to Paris and Ember. He would have guarded it with his life rather than risk seeing one of our most precious heirlooms slip into their hands.

Ember grins wide as she moves around the bathroom, blocking my escape, but despite the dagger in her hands, she's not my main focus.

Paris holds every ounce of my attention.

The last time we came face to face like this she'd come climbing in through my bedroom window, shocked the shit out of me in the shower, and then tried to stab me. She's fucking batshit crazy. I'm just lucky that Grayson was able to fight the gas and defied all odds by getting his ass up the stairs and into my room before Paris got the chance to kill me. Though, something tells me that she's about ready to try her luck again.

She holds something in her hand and my gaze drops, narrowing on the small flip phone. "You've gotten away from me far too many times, Elodie Ravenwood," she mutters, her chin held high as her usually cocky attitude shines through. "But this is the end of the road for you."

I scoff and start to walk straight past them. "Right," I laugh.

"Good luck with that."

Paris clenches her jaw but I don't hang around, intent on getting my ass out of here and calling for the boys to put our plan in motion, but her hand raises higher, holding the old phone up like some kind of trophy. "If you were smart, you wouldn't take another damn step."

My brows furrow and I look back at her, hating how she wears my mother's face. Irritation soars through me and I drop my gaze over her body, searching for any signs that she might have a weapon on her. She's practically a twig. I could take her easily, but Ember standing at my back with a dagger in her hands creates a problem, but I'm pretty sure that I could take them both out if it came down to it. "For argument's sake, I'm pretty fucking stupid," I say, more than happy to waste time, knowing that the boys will come for me soon. "Tell me, oh wise one, what would happen if I were to take another step?"

Paris moves her hand, slowly reaching up to the top of her jacket and I watch in horror as she drags her zipper down, revealing a row of explosives that have been strapped to her chest. "Take another step and I will set it off," she tells me. "There's enough C-4 strapped to my chest to bring this whole building down, taking out every single mother, husband, and child in this building. Do you really want to be the cause of a mass murder?"

I swallow hard, the fear flowing through my body and crippling me as I make a show of standing as still as possible. "What do you want?" I demand, unable to stop thinking about all the kids who are standing on the dance floor, swaying their hips and celebrating these exciting new changes in our world, completely oblivious to the fact that their lives are currently in my hands.

Carver. King. Grayson. Cruz.

Dianna Danforth, and all the boys' siblings.

One wrong move from me and their lives will amount to nothing but just another number in a long list of mass casualties, and I know without even a second of hesitation that I would hand my life over if it meant saving all of theirs.

"I guess you're smarter than you look," Paris says, flicking her gaze to her daughter and nodding.

I watch Ember through the bathroom mirror as she moves in behind me and shoves the dagger deep into the holster on her thigh. "Hands behind your back," she spits, grabbing my wrists with such force that a sharp sting sails right up through my arm. She takes her time binding my wrists together and I let out a shaky breath, realizing that it was all too good to be true. I was so close and have had targets on my back since the day I was born. My luck was bound to run out at some point, and today, that time has come. I just wish that I'd had the chance to see Paris go down before my luck had run out.

I keep my stare on Paris, watching the delight in her eyes as for the first time in her life, her ridiculous little game is actually going as planned. "Alright," she says once her daughter has me secured. "You're not going to say a damn word. You're not going to raise the alarm, and you're sure as hell not going to alert those boys. Screw up and I blow it. You're mine now. Is that clear?"

"Crystal," I spit.

"Excellent," she says, a smirk pulling at her lips. "Let's go."

# CHAPTER 23

I stumble forward but quickly catch myself as Ember yanks me back to keep me on my feet, though not out of the kindness of her heart. To get away with this, Ember and Paris need a quick getaway, and while Paris has a shitload of C-4 strapped to her chest, I'll be doing whatever the hell they want, even if it means giving up my life.

There's a very real possibility that she's fucking with me and that the explosives aren't even real, but I can't take that chance. I won't risk anyone else's life. Besides, Paris has already caused enough destruction in my world and I will personally see that she chokes on her own damn blood before causing any more.

I'm pushed right to the door of the bathroom and Paris opens it just an inch. She peers out, making sure that the boys aren't about to bust her ass, and after confirming that her insane little plan is going just as she had hoped, she swings the door wide and rushes out.

Ember pushes me along, her hand shoving hard against my back as she forces me to keep up with her deranged mother. We continue in the opposite way from where I came, and after taking a sharp right-hand turn into a small storage room, Paris slams the door behind us and bolts it shut.

Ember immediately gets to work pushing a tall storage shelf aside. It's clearly heavy and she's using everything that she's got just to move it out of the way and I find myself watching the show, taking in the way Paris stands back and refuses to do any of the hard work herself. It must be fucking nice to have minions doing everything for you.

"You're taking too long," Paris hisses, making a sour expression cross Ember's face.

I can't help but laugh. "What's the matter? Upset that mommy doesn't love you?"

Ember clenches her jaw and pushes harder. "At least I have a fucking mother. That's a shitload more than what you could ever say. What happened to her again? Oh yeah, my mother convinced some deranged fucktard to take her out."

Ouch. I'm not going to lie, that stung just a bit.

"Get on with it," Paris snaps. "It'll all be for nothing if we don't get out of here and finish this."

Geez, she really is a moody bitch. No wonder my mother never liked her.

The shelving shifts out of the way and I raise a brow as a long skinny staircase is revealed. It's dark and there's absolutely no hints as to where it leads, but on the bright side, if they were leading me to hell, all the movies suggest that the stairs should be going down, so there's that.

Paris barges past her daughter and skips up the stairs, leaving Ember to slam her hand into my back once again. "Move."

For fuck's sake. How did such a good night turn into such a disaster? Though, it's not like we weren't expecting something to happen. We knew a big party would draw her out but we figured that she'd try to make a show in front of the whole organization. Cornering me in the bathroom with a fucking bomb didn't cross my mind, though it should have.

I get going, moving up the stairs one at a time, making a show of being cautious in my heels and going irritatingly slow in hopes that the boys will come to their senses and come to find me, but so far, not enough time has passed to alarm them.

"Quit the fucking act," Ember spits at my back. "You're not fooling anyone. Move your ass up the goddamn stairs."

I roll my eyes and pick up my pace, but I'm not stupid. I take my time and in doing so, earn the best kind of irritated groans out of Ember.

We hit the top step and I take a quick look around, finding an old storage room that looks as though it hasn't seen the light of day in years.

Paris grins wide as Ember climbs up onto a ledge and opens a small window that brings us back up into the real world, where no doubt they would have some kind of getaway car. "I hope you're ready to die," Paris laughs as Ember disappears through the window. She holds up the phone as though I'd already forgotten about her stupid bomb threat. "Your turn," she says. "And make it quick or else they will all pay for your stupidity."

I narrow my gaze, wanting nothing more than to strangle the bitch, but over the last thirty seconds, absolutely nothing has changed. Their lives are more important than mine, and with that in mind, I turn and start walking for the ledge.

My foot props up onto the ledge and I wobble, not having the ability to grasp anything with my hands bound at my back to help me up. I glance at Paris and indicate down at my hands. "How do you suppose that I do this?"

Paris looks at me like a dirty stain on a perfectly white dress. "Not my problem. Figure it out."

Shit.

Letting out a sigh, I climb up through the window, using the wall as leverage against my shoulder before folding my chest through the window and wriggling myself through. Everything hurts and I'm ashamed to say that in getting myself out the window, I flash everything that I've got with this stupid hip-high slit, though I won't be sorry. It was worth it for the better part of the night.

My hands press against the pavement and I push myself up through the window, coming out on the other side to feel the cool evening breeze against my skin. I quickly realize that we're in the backstreets of the building that the grand ballroom was built under and that there's not a damn soul in sight. Only an hour ago there would have been people everywhere, but now they're all inside the party having the time of their lives, completely unaware that their leader has just been kidnapped by a crazy, psychotic bitch.

Paris comes out a moment later, and before I get the chance to kick her in the face as she crawls up through the window, Ember is at my wrists yanking me back. Paris gets to her feet and all too quickly, we're sprinting through the backstreets and heading around a corner to a narrow alleyway where an old black van has been parked.

Paris tears open the back door and Ember wastes no time throwing me inside, making sure to release my wrists at the last possible second so that I have absolutely no way of breaking my fall.

I land on my side with a heavy bang, the hard floor of the van only making things worse. My face squishes against the dirty ground and just as I'm able to raise it and look back out through the back door for an escape, it's slammed shut, closing me in.

"Ahhh, fuck," I mutter, pulling on my bound wrists and attempting to sit myself up. The windows are blacked out and without a shred of sunlight coming in through the windshield, it's nearly impossible to see anything.

I get up onto my knees just as Ember and Paris come flying in through the side doors, Paris dropping down into the driver's seat as Ember takes the space beside her, slamming her door closed with such ferocity that the whole van shakes.

Ember glances back at me, laughing as Paris jams the key into the ignition and brings the van to life. "You look like a fucking whore in that dress," she says as Paris hits the gas, sending me flying back in the van, my hip slamming into the wheel hub and ripping the slit in my dress even higher. "Point proven," she laughs.

I groan and desperately try to right myself, but with my hands behind my back, it's not as easy as it seems. My ass finally crashes down on the hard ground and I kick off my heels, doing anything and everything that I can to try and give myself an advantage.

Using my leg, I scoop my heel back toward me and do my best to try to get it to my back. I climb up onto my knees, spreading them wide for stability and with Ember and Paris keeping their eyes on the road, desperately trying to attempt their bullshit getaway, I use the heel to claw at the tape around my wrists.

It takes far too long, but with every passing second, it allows the boys to clear the ballroom and get all of our people far away and out of harm's reach. But in doing that, it also takes me further and further away.

My hands come free just as we start approaching the city center, the most populated area in Ravenwood Heights, and despite it being well past ten on a Saturday night, there are bound to be people everywhere. The clubs are only just letting people in as sports bars are crowded for the big game that would have ended a little while ago. Hell, even the theater would be just letting out showings. Now is my only shot to get out of here, but how?

Keeping my hands behind my back, I discreetly inch forward. I have to somehow get that phone detonator off Paris while keeping Ember at a distance, get out of the van, get lost in the crowd, and somehow still have the upper hand.

It should be easy as pie.

I let out a breath. I'm fucked.

What the hell would the boys do in this situation? A laugh bubbles up my throat and I quickly swallow it back down. The boys wouldn't get themselves in this bullshit situation in the first place. They're too good for that. This would be a walk in the park for them. Hell, they'd already be out and calling one of the other guys to come and pick them up by now because screw walking all the way back home.

Fucking hell.

My gaze shifts over the front seat.

Ember still has the dagger holstered at her thigh while the phone detonator rests in Paris' lap. My only advantage being their focus is so heavily trained out the front windshield as they navigate the busy streets. If only I could get my hands on that dagger.

A plan quickly forms and I sit back, a twisted smirk settling over my lips. "So, what's she promised you, Ember? I gave you the perfect out. You could have been freed from all this bullshit."

"You don't know what the fuck you're talking about."

"Don't I?" I laugh. "I've been battling against this psycho bitch for months. You don't think I've learned a thing or two about the way her twisted, fucked-up mind works?"

Ember spins around in her seat, her glare sharp and deadly, but she doesn't quite have what it takes to intimidate me, even with the dagger at her thigh. She's like a fly that just won't go away. "Don't you talk about her like that," she spits at me, the anger building in her eyes and quickly taking control. "You don't know anything about her."

"Both of you fucking idiots shut up," Paris snaps.

"You know, she promised Royston Carver that he was going to rule Dynasty, and then promised Scardoni and Harding the same thing, though we all know it was always her intention to rule. So, what's she offered you? A lifetime of warm, fuzzy mommy/daughter time? Or is it something a little more exciting? It must be for you to throw away a whole safe future with your adoptive parents. You could have had it all, but you chose this. Unless ..." I say, my brows rising as Ember clenches her jaw, "she has something on you."

Ember huffs, struggling to keep control. "Shut up, you don't know anything. She hasn't got anything. I chose this because it's what I want."

Paris snaps her glare up to meet mine through her rearview mirror, knowing exactly what I'm trying to do. Her glare cuts across to her daughter before focusing on the road ahead. "Don't listen to her, Ember. She's trying to get in your head."

I laugh, because why the fuck not? It's working and we all know it.

"She's promised you something, huh?" I question, not even close to wanting to give up. "Tell me, how can you believe a word she says? How could she have promised all those guys that they were going to lead Dynasty? She's a liar. They were all pawns in her twisted game, just like you are. You mean nothing to her. She's known where you were your whole life and she never came looking for you until you were actually of use. She doesn't love you, Ember. She didn't love Harding either. You're going to be tossed aside the second she's got what she wants. Did you watch her shed a tear when I killed Harding? No, I bet you didn't because she didn't fucking care. People like her can't care.

They're not wired for it. Yeah, she was pissed, but only because it screwed with her plan. Face the facts, Ember, mommy dearest doesn't love you. She never will."

Ember screams, her hand flying to her thigh and tearing the dagger out of its holster. She scrambles through to the back of the van and I shuffle back, my hands flying free as she comes for me.

"EMBER," Paris screeches, struggling to focus on both the road and her daughter.

Ember hardly gets a fucking word out before I grab her wrist, holding the dagger away from me and yanking her closer. She screams again, though it sounds more like a strangled battle cry and before I give Paris a chance to bring the van to a stop, my elbow slams down over Ember's temple and I knock the fucking bitch out cold.

The dagger clatters to the floor and I quickly scoop it up, only having a moment to make my move.

Paris slams on the brakes and the van screeches to a stop, but the momentum only has me flying at her faster. My chest hits the back of her seat with a hard thud and I ignore the pain as my hand twists around her, bringing the sharp blade to a stop at the base of her throat.

She scrambles for the phone in her lap, but I beat her to it, grinning back at her through the rearview mirror.

"Checkmate, bitch."

"Do it," she growls at me, her jaw clenching in the same way that Ember's does when she's backed into a corner.

I glance around, trying to figure out where the fuck to go from here.

There are too many people in the streets and they're all gaping at the van that's holding up the traffic. Horns are honking all around us, and if I wait too long, Ember will wake and my advantage will be fucked. So, with so many witnesses, killing Paris tonight is only going to cause me more trouble, and I can't blow her the fuck up without hurting the people around us. I have no choice but to leave her here with her bomb strapped to her chest and hope that I can get far enough away before she has a chance to take it off and come for me.

Wanting this over and done with, I reach for the side, sliding door and tear it open, but not wanting to leave without making it hurt, I bring my hand up and slam it down hard against Paris's shoulder, letting the blade sink low into her shoulder until I feel the dagger penetrating the seat behind her.

She screams in agony as blood begins pouring down her chest and the sound is like music to my ears. Hell, if I had my phone right now, I'd record it so I could show everybody when I finally get my ass back home. Fuck, I'd even make it my ringtone. What a fucking waste.

"I'll see you in hell, you crazy bitch," I tell her, going to move out of the van while grabbing my heels for the walk. I go to step out when I pause in the open door, scoffing at Ember sprawled out on the floor. I hold the phone up and watch as realization hits, knowing that her whole fucking life is in my hands and that the tables have officially turned. "I wonder if you can save yourselves before I blow it."

And just like that, I slide my cum free heels back on and stride right out of the van as though I don't have a care in the world.

The van takes off again and despite all the people standing around watching me, I walk free, holding my head high knowing that tonight, my people will all sleep safely in their beds without having to worry about grieving for loved ones.

Despite Paris walking free, and despite how wrong it felt to let her go, tonight was a win and that's all that counts.

I lose myself within the crowded bodies, weaving and ducking past people as I try to figure out which direction will take me home. I haven't had to come into the city much but honestly, I should know the streets a little better than this. Though, the opposite direction that Paris went is always a good way to go.

The loud honking of traffic sounds again, and I glance back over my shoulder to find the black van parked right in the center of an intersection and without as many people around as there were before, I don't hesitate. I flip open the old phone and press call, watching as not even a second later, the van blows into a million pieces.

People scream and start to run as I look back the way that I was going and keep walking, knowing without a doubt that Paris would have already bailed, but now she knows just how damn serious I was. Though whether she took Ember with her or not still remains a mystery, but for now, my only priority is getting my ass home.

I feel the heat from the explosion on my back and with each step I take, it dwindles to nothing. Twenty minutes later, I'm the only one wandering along a dark and quiet street. My heels hang from my fingers as I walk down the very center of the road, headlights up ahead closing in on me.

The familiar Escalade stops in the middle of the road and I hold up my hands, knowing all four of them are looking back at me. "What the hell took so long?" I demand, letting out a heavy sigh.

All four doors open and not a second later, their gorgeous faces appear as they stand in each of their open doorways. "We went as fast as we could," King tells me. "There were a lot of fucking people and a lot of different places to look."

I let out a heavy sigh, drop my heels in the middle of the road and cross my arms over my chest. "I'm surprised you assholes haven't inserted a tracking device in my arm yet."

Carver raises a brow and discreetly looks across at Grayson. "I mean, would you be down with that? We were only discussing it last night."

My mouth drops, staring at the idiot in shock. "Are you fucking kidding me? Of course I'm not down with that, you big ass moron. You can't be serious right now? In what world do you think I'd ever be okay with that?"

Carver cringes, probably wishing he could be anywhere but here as Cruz laughs, drawing my attention away from Carver, and making me wish that I'd saved the dagger for his shoulder instead. "Geez," Cruz grins, his eyes sparkling and making just a fraction of the irritation I feel for Carver fade away. "Getting kidnapped really fucks with your mood, huh?"

That's it. I'm going to fuck them both up.

I narrow my gaze and huff as I storm toward the Escalade, leaving the heels behind, but let's face it, I won't be able to wear them again without remembering what went down tonight. Maybe they'll end up in some cheap thrift store and they can make some other girl happy.

I scoot into the backseat as the guys all get back in, slamming their doors in unison. Carver hits the gas, and within seconds he's performing a U-turn and speeding back the way he came.

"So, I'm assuming that since you were walking the streets alone that you finally killed her?" Grayson asks, looking back at me from the front passenger seat with a hopeful glimmer sparkling in his eyes.

A scowl pulls at my lips. "Don't you think I'd look a little happier if I finally killed her?"

He presses his lips into a hard line. "Then what the fuck happened?"

I let out a sigh and lean into King's side. "She had explosives strapped to her chest and threatened to blow the whole fucking party if I didn't go with her. Ember was there too."

"No shit," Cruz mutters, his brows raising as he shakes his head.

"Uh-huh. They had this weird little escape route out the back of the party and then the bitches threw me in the back of a van and I swear, my hip is so fucking bruised now, but I fucked with Ember's head, knocked her out and then stabbed Paris with a fucking dagger."

King laughs as he puts his arm over my shoulder. "That's my fucking girl."

"No," Cruz says, yanking me away from King and tucking me into his side. "That's *my* fucking girl. She's all mine for a whole week, remember?"

The guys groan as I roll my eyes. "Half a week," I remind him.

"Wait," Carver says, risking his life by talking to me as he meets my stare in the rearview mirror. "If you were close enough to stab her in the shoulder, why the fuck is she still alive? You just let her get away?"

"It's not that simple," I say as he sails through the streets, taking us back past the main entrance of the underground ballroom that we'd just spent the main part of our night in. "There were too many witnesses. Trust me, I would have done anything to slit her throat or detonate the C-4 around her chest, but I couldn't risk it without other people getting hurt. It killed me to walk away without finishing it, but …"

King's hand falls to my thigh. "You did the right thing. We're not about hurting innocent people."

"Don't get me wrong. I still blew the fucking van to pieces," I laugh. "But I waited until she was further away from the crowd, but by then she'd abandoned the van."

"At least she knows you're not fucking around," Grayson says. "What about Ember?"

I shrug my shoulders as the slightest bit of guilt sails through my system and roots itself deep in my gut, right where it will stay until I know if my actions were responsible for ending her life. "Jury is still out on that one," I tell them, closing my eyes as the exhaustion of my night quickly catches up to me. "Let's just go home, then tomorrow we can work out exactly how we're going to kick that bitch's ass."

# CHAPTER 24

My ass hits the couch as a loud, frustrated huff comes tearing out of me. "So, we have nothing?" I question, looking up at the boys who stand around the table, looking down at the biggest map of Ravenwood Heights that anybody has ever seen, though I guess the map in itself is like nothing anyone has ever seen as our version comes complete with our whole underground world, including every fucking tunnel. I won't be caught out like that again.

"I wouldn't say nothing," King says, dropping both hands onto the table and hanging his head in frustration. "She was heading north of the city so anything south of the point where you left her can be ruled out."

"Can it though?" I ask. "What if she was taking me to some creepy lair, but her actual place is somewhere else?"

"Noooooo," Cruz groans, flopping down on the couch beside me. "We've been at this for hours and we aren't getting anywhere. All this back and forth is giving me a headache. I say we just sit still and wait for her to come to us."

"Are you hearing yourself, man?" Grayson says. "I don't want that psycho bitch anywhere near here ever again."

"I know, but apart from strapping Winter to a dining chair and leaving her out in the middle of the fucking street as bait, we've got nothing," Cruz fires back. "She's not going to play by our rules. She's unpredictable and we have no fucking idea what she's going to do now. All we know is that for the next few days, she's going to be down with that stab wound so at least we have until then to try and figure something out."

"That's not good enough," Carver fires back as though we're not all thinking it.

I look up at the boys around the table, already knowing the answer to my question before it even comes out of my mouth. "Would she have gone to a hospital?"

Grayson shakes his head. "I doubt it. The way bullets have been flying around her, she's bound to have a surgeon on speed dial. We can check hospital records if you want, but I think it'll be a waste of time."

"Shit."

Carver groans. "We have to be missing something. There's no fucking way that we have the technology to find trafficked kids, but yet we can't find one psycho bitch who keeps running in and out of town. We have to be able to track her somehow."

Cruz props his hand behind his head, his bicep bulging beside me. "I don't know what to tell you, man," he mutters, the disappointment clear in his tone. "She's bested us every fucking time. The trail runs cold and we're left with nothing. She must have found some kind of blind spot north of the city."

Grayson shakes his head, his frustration getting all too real. He crosses to the couch and plants himself in front of me, his tall, intimidating body looming over me as his dark grey eyes stare down into my baby blues. "Come."

I look up at him, ignoring his outstretched hand as I raise my brow. "Why?"

"Because."

"Well, shit," I murmur. "What a compelling argument. I don't understand why I haven't already thrown myself into your arms and allowed you to whisk me away with your bullshit one-word responses and that alluring mystery, but you know what?" I add, pressing my lips into a hard line and hating how I sound like such a bitch, but I'm not up for games right now. "I'm gonna pass."

"Elodie Fucking Ravenwood, stop acting like such a spoiled little brat and move your damn ass," he growls, moving his outstretched hand to point toward the front door. "Do you really think that while we're in the middle of this shit that I'm over here trying to play fucking games with you?"

I clench my jaw, hating it even more when he tries to put me straight back into my place. "Then tell me where the fuck you plan on taking me."

"I'm teaching you to drive," he states as my brows shoot straight back up. "Whether you're ready to admit it or not, your inability to get behind the wheel of a car cost you today and you're too fucking stubborn to admit it. Had you known how to drive and were confident in your skills, your first thought would have been to switch places. You should have subdued Paris and turned that goddamn van right around. You had her in the palm of your hand and you let her get away because you're too fucking scared to learn the difference between the gas and brake."

I throw myself to my feet. "Don't you dare do that," I demand, pointing my finger into his stupidly strong chest. "Don't you think I already feel bad enough for letting her get away like that? I was in an impossible situation and chose to save the people around me and live to fight another day. My inability to drive has nothing to do with it."

King chuckles to himself, raising his chin to Carver who digs into his pocket and tosses him the keys to his Escalade. "Sorry, babe," King says, turning to face me while striding out of the room toward the garage. "He has a fucking point and I'm not going to miss this shit. Let's go."

Fuck.

I glance across at Cruz who's been all too quiet. "Aren't you going to do something about this?"

He shakes his head. "First off, you're eighteen. It's a rite of passage to know how to drive, and second, you're the fucking leader of Dynasty who has a string of targets on your back, you should have learned how to drive months ago and that's on us. Consider it righting a wrong, or in the very least, a survival technique."

I gape at him, feeling my heart beginning to stammer in my chest, racing so fast that I'm positive I'm going to pass out. I go to look to Carver for help, but there's no use, I already know what that asshole is going to say, the fucking traitor. We're supposed to be tight now. "I can't. I'm going to hurt someone," I say, considering getting on my knees and begging them, or at least distracting them with some good head.

Grayson groans and rolls his eyes, not down for my arguments, and without a moment of warning, he grabs my hand and yanks me so hard that I fly right off the couch and over his shoulder. He turns on his heel and stalks out of the room before I even know what the fuck is going on.

"Put me down you big ass turd stomper," I demand, barreling my hands into his back, realizing all too quickly that my father never would have had to put up with this shit. "I'm not your ragdoll that you get to toss around whenever the hell you want."

Grayson doesn't respond, just keeps walking out of the room and just as he goes to move into the hallway, I catch Carver's amused smirk, the only one that I'm sure I'll see until we finally have Paris in our grasp. "Hey, little rabbit," he says, getting on board with that stupid nickname again. "Crash my fucking Escalade and I'll take it out on your tight little cunt."

I smirk straight back at him. "Is that supposed to be a threat?" I question, wondering just how quickly he'll collect on my punishment because there's no doubt in my mind that I'm going to crash. I bet I could even have that big ass heap of metal turned into a twisted ball before I even reach the gates at the top of my property. "Because you're sure as fuck going the wrong way about it."

Carver's response is cut off as Grayson steps out through the doorway and leads us out to the foyer. We hear the sound of the garage door opening and rather than cutting through to meet King in the garage, he walks straight out the front door and flies down the front steps, taking them two at a time, making me grip onto the back of his shirt, positive that after everything I've been through, it's this that's going to finally take me out.

As Grayson hits the bottom step, the Escalade comes rolling around the circle drive, pulling to a stop right in front of us. Grayson puts me down and I don't miss the way that his hand remains at my wrist, more than prepared for the disappearing act that I had every intention of attempting.

King gets out of the driver's seat and voluntarily puts himself in the back as Grayson picks me up and physically puts me in the front passenger seat. I'm buckled in and he locks the door before walking around to the driver seat. Within seconds we're flying through the gate, and I find myself watching exactly what he's doing. Don't get me wrong, I know the general idea of what to do, but actually putting it into practice scares the shit out of me. The Escalade is so big and could take out a whole freaking family if I'm not careful, but the Ducati allowed me to zoom past things and avoid everything in my path. I guess there are bonus points for already knowing the basic road rules, so there's that.

Grayson drives for ten minutes and leads us right out of Ravenwood Heights, past my favorite spot under the pier, and into Castlereagh Flats, where there are more than enough empty mall parking lots.

The Escalade comes to a stop and there's silence in the cab as both of the guys' heavy stares fall on me. "What?" I demand when the silence becomes too loud.

A smirk pulls at the corners of Grayson's lips and he does his best to reel it in. "Are you ready for this?"

"Am I ready to wrap Carver's car around a fucking concrete pillar? No. Not even close."

"Perfect," Grayson says, opening his door and looking back at me. "Get in."

Crap.

Knowing that this torture won't end until I at least give it a try, I climb across the center console and drop down into the driver's seat, but with the ridiculous setting the guys need this stupid seat on, I can barely see over the steering wheel.

King laughs and starts helping me make adjustments as Grayson gets into the seat that I'd just vacated. "Alright," he says, watching as I buckle my seatbelt and make sure that it's locked into place. "We're just going to chill, driving around the lot until you get comfortable with the corners, and then we'll venture out into the real world."

I roll my eyes and just when I think I can go, Grayson leans across me and cuts the engine. I give him a blank stare and he shrugs his shoulders as though he's not being an asshole. "What?" he questions. "You need to know all the basics and that includes turning this fucker on."

"Keep crossing me like this and you'll be the fucker that I refuse to turn on."

"Just get on with it," he mutters. "Right foot on the brake, turn on the car and shift into drive. You're going to release the emergency brake and when you're ready, ease your foot off the brake. We're on a flat so the car isn't going to go anywhere until you gently ease on to the gas."

I let out a sigh and do as he asked, thinking way too hard about it despite already knowing the basic fundamentals of moving this big metal beast. Either way, I appreciate him going through every tiny thing so I get the chance to really commit it to memory, but with things like this, the only way to truly get it right is with constant practice.

I ease on to the gas and the Escalade jolts forward, making a sharp laugh tear out of King, only to be terribly disguised as a cough. "You're doing great, babe," he says, his eyes telling me a completely different story.

I zone him out as the wide-open space of the mall parking lot leaves way too many overwhelming options. "Which way do I go?" I rush out, driving dead straight and heading straight for one of those before mentioned concrete pillars.

"There's a whole fucking parking lot," Grayson says. "Go wherever the fuck you want."

"LEFT OR RIGHT?" I panic, my eyes going wide as my heart races.

"Fuck. Left," he rushes out, just moments before grabbing the wheel and yanking it to the left to avoid me ramming straight into the pillar and allowing Carver to take his sweet punishments out on me.

With the first turn out of the way, I let out a breath and relax into my seat, letting out a heavy sigh. "Wow, okay. See? That wasn't so hard, was it?"

The boys just stare blankly as I easily fall into my tasks, quickly getting used to the feel of the steering wheel in my hands and the motion of applying pressure to the gas and brake. I don't know what I was being such a bitch about. At least, that's what I thought until Grayson decided to throw King out in the parking lot to act as a marker for parallel parking.

Half an hour passes and I bring the Escalade to a stop in the center of the lot, needing to pump my fingers after clutching onto the steering wheel as though my life depended on it. Don't get me wrong, the boys have constantly been telling me to relax my grip, but these things just don't happen overnight. Besides, there's bigger issues at hand, like the fact that no matter how hard I think about it, I will never be able to remember which side is which when it comes to the wipers and indicators.

Needing a quick break, I cut the engine and push the door open, letting the breeze flow through to cool me down. Apparently, the stress of driving gets me worked up into a bigger sweat than what the boys do when they're all over me.

The boys open their doors too and I fiddle with the buttons on the dash, turning on the music and chilling out for just a moment, the stress of last night and today's failed attempts quickly catching up to me.

My head falls back against the seat and I close my eyes, desperately trying to channel all that negative energy flying through my mind.

"We'll get her," King promises from the backseat.

I shake my head, looking back at him. "I'm not sure that we will."

King narrows his gaze and a flash of anger shoots through his blue eyes and before I even know what he's doing, he reaches into the front seat and grabs me. He pulls me between the two front seats until I'm straddled over his lap with his lips pressed against the sensitive skin of my neck and his hands gripping my ass, his fingers digging in just enough to let me know that I'm in trouble. "Keep talking like that and I'll have no choice but to fuck it out of you," he warns. "We're getting her and when we do, the five of us are going to fucking celebrate in the way that only we can."

My brows raise. "What's that supposed to mean?"

Instead of giving me the response that I'm looking for, his lips start moving across my neck and I tilt my head to the side, opening up for more, because damn, if he's suggesting what I hope he's suggesting, then I need to prepare myself.

Heat floods to my pussy and I grind against him as he presses up, letting me feel just how ready he is. "We can't fuck in Carver's car," I murmur, my eyes closing in pleasure. "He'll kill us."

A soft chuckle sounds beside me and I glance across to find Grayson standing in King's open doorway. "All the more reason to do it," he tells me. "But if he's condemning us to hell, we better make sure we have fun in the process."

My brows arch in excitement and I glance down at King, seeing that he's on exactly the same wavelength. I bite down on my lower lip and King shuffles us around, sitting sideways on the backseat, his feet propped against the sidestep of the Escalade as Grayson's chest presses up against my back.

Fuck me. A threesome in Carver's car. I can't say this is how I expected my day to go.

Grayson's hands come down on my waist and he clutches the flimsy material of my tank, slowly dragging it up my body. He pulls it over my head and drops it to the hard pavement, disregarding it as though it has no place in this world.

King reaches around me with one hand and unclasps my bra, letting it fall down between us, and without skipping a beat, his mouth closes around my nipple as his tongue flicks against it, sending a wave of fiery electricity pulsing through my body and sailing right down to my pussy.

A gasp pulls from my chest as Grayson takes my chin and tilts my head back to kiss me deeply. His hands work my body, making me feel more alive than I have in weeks. He lifts me off King's lap for just a moment and as he does, King's hands drop to my jeans, unbuttoning them and making quick work of tearing them down my body, taking my thong right along with them, leaving me ready to party while they remain severely overdressed.

King slips his sweatpants down past his hips, freeing his cock as Grayson lowers me back onto his lap. I hear him behind me, unbuckling his belt and the sound sends shivers sailing over my skin, the anticipation almost too much.

My hand curls around King's dick and I pump up and down as I watch him lean back to make room for him to pull his shirt over his head and in doing that, his abs clench and my mouth begins drooling. There's nothing I love more than taking in their bodies. It's like a buffet with endless choices, but all those choices are put out there just for me, and damn, this bitch is hungry.

With his shirt falling to the ground, he keeps lying back until he's laid out on the backseat, looking up at me with one hand at my waist and the other propped behind his head, looking like a birthday boy who's ready to admire his girl as she does all the work, but if that's what he wants, that's what he'll get.

Grayson's hand roams down my body and I watch as King tracks the movements right down to my clit. He pinches it gently before pressing against it and rubbing slow, torturous circles, making desire pool in King's eyes as my fists work up and down his hard cock.

Feeling Grayson's monster cock at my back, I reach behind me and do the same for him. I never want one of my guys to be left out—after all, for what they give me, they deserve the whole fucking world in return.

Rising up on my knees, I guide King to my entrance and groan as I sink down over him, not realizing just how badly I needed to feel him inside of me. I grind my hips against him as Grayson's other hand cups my tit, his thumb and forefinger rolling around my nipple like the sweetest torture.

My hips rock back and forth, going slow to match the rhythm

of Grayson rubbing my clit. My eyes close as I tilt my head back, the pleasure all too good. "Fuck," I pant in a blissful mess of elation. "That's so good."

"You like that?" Grayson murmurs in my ear, releasing my tit and bringing his finger to my mouth. "Open wide."

I let him in and his fingers swirl around my tongue, getting all nice and wet, and when he finally removes them, he trails that wetness over my ass making me groan. He plays with my ass, teasing me with his fingers until finally pressing inside of me, making me gasp and tighten my grip on his cock, my thumb freezing over his piercing.

His fingers dive deeper and I clench my pussy around King's cock, making his fingers tighten on my waist. "Fuck, babe," he growls, our slow, sensual movements already proving too much.

"Are you ready for more?" Grayson asks.

Without hesitation, I lean over, bringing my chest down to King's and meeting his lips with my own, silently letting Grayson know that my ass is all his, however the fuck he wants it.

His fingers come out and as usual, I pause, needing a moment to prepare myself for his monstrous size. I feel his piercing at my hole and I suck in a breath as he slowly pushes inside of me, making King groan into my mouth.

Grayson takes both my hips, holding me still as he gets comfortable deep inside my ass. "Ahh, fuck," I moan, adjusting to his size and taking all of him as I tilt my hips down and arch my back for more.

"Good?" Grayson questions, his tone low and full of desire.

I look back over my shoulder and watch him. "Never been better."

And just like that, he starts to move. I keep myself still as King moves beneath me, pushing in as Grayson pulls out, the two of them working together to make sure my body is getting the premium service, always feeling someone deep inside of me.

I've never been so full. King stretches my pussy, hitting all my walls as I feel Grayson all around me, my ass quickly getting used to the addictive burn that comes along every time that thick beautiful cock fucks my ass.

The boys work me, slowly building the intensity until I lose all control, completely surrendering to their pleasure. Hands go everywhere while lips work over my neck. Sweet nothings are whispered through the cab while devilish remarks are fired straight back.

It's an erotic, blissful heaven and I don't ever want it to stop, but when King pushes up just a little bit more and my clit rubs against his warm skin, the electricity that pulses through me is too much to bear and I come undone, my orgasm tearing through me like a violent lightning bolt.

I cry out, my head tipping back as everything clenches, holding them both there and refusing to allow them to move, but they don't play by my rules, they never have. They both keep moving despite the pleasure tearing through all three of us and with each new movement the pleasure only intensifies. "Ahh, fuck, fuck, fuck," I cry, my eyes watering as my body completely shatters and I become a trembling mess, my pussy convulsing around King's cock as my ass clenches down around Grayson's, his fingers digging into my skin.

It's too fucking much. They need to stop or I'm going to pass out, but fuck, if they were to stop, I think I might cry. Fuck passing out. I'm up for the challenge.

They move in and out of me as I keep grinding my clit against King, riding it out like the fucking cowgirl that I am. Grayson grunts, needing to come but he holds on to it, always a gentleman and never being one to come in my ass. However, King certainly doesn't hold those same reservations and shoots his warm seed inside of me, stilling as the elation takes over his handsome face.

"Holy shit," he groans as I suck in a deep breath, finally easing up on the boys as I come down from my high.

Grayson can't handle it a second longer and pulls out, coming hard into his hand. I'm not going to lie; I miss the warmth of him spilling out against my back, but doing that and risking dripping all over King beneath me probably crosses some kind of silent bro code rule. I'll forgive him just this once.

I sit up on King, feeling him still deep inside of me, and as I do, my eyes go wide. "Shit," I gasp, looking down and meeting his wide stare. "I promised Cruz that I was all his for half the week."

Grayson steps back into me, his warm chest pressed up against my skin. "What Cruz doesn't know won't hurt him."

A grin stretches across my lips as I look back over my shoulder and meet his soft stare. "This is Cruz we're talking about. He'll know. He'll smell you on me."

Grayson laughs and curls his arms around my waist. "You're right," he says. "He definitely will, but if he's going to bust our asses over it, then we better make it worth it."

And just like that, his lips come crashing down on mine and we prepare for round two, knowing that there's going to be a sweet place in hell waiting for us when we get home.

# CHAPTER 25

My ass begs for mercy as it drops back into the driver's seat. "You sure?" Grayson asks. "If you're not ready, I can drive us back. You're fucking exhausted after all of that. No one's judging if you want to spread out in the back."

I shake my head. "No, I want to be in the driver's seat when Carver and Cruz come out to see what took so long. At least this way I can run them over before they figure it out and make us pay for it."

"Babe," King laughs, spreading out on the backseat, his arms hooked over both headrests and his knees wide, more than satisfied to even pretend to care about showing a little class. "We've been gone for nearly three hours, trust me, they don't need to see your thoroughly fucked face and sex hair to know what went down in here. They already know and I can promise that Cruz has been pacing the front steps for at least an hour, thinking of all the ways he can punish you."

Grayson laughs. "Fuck, that dude gets jealous over the funniest things. It's so fucking easy to get under his skin."

"Hey," I snap at them both. "Leave him alone. He can't help it that he still has a shred of humanity left, unlike you dark fuckers. You two wouldn't even be able to find your hearts inside those big ass bodies."

"Good point," Grayson mutters darkly.

I get the car started, dreaming about the way Carver's going to stare at me as I creep onto my long driveway. His eyes will narrow and despite the boys being a bad influence in this particular scenario, he'll look at me as though I had planned it all along. Then I'll hit the gas and it'll turn into a game of chicken with me inevitably being the loser. I don't know why I even bother at this point. He wins every time without fail, but if I stick with it, eventually I'm going to beat his ass.

The Escalade rumbles to life beneath me, the soft hum below my seat making my ass clench as I try to pull up just a bit, needing to avoid any kind of vibrations against it. Grayson isn't the kind to leave a girl needing more, and damn it, today isn't any different. He pushed me to my limits and despite how fucking delicious it was, I don't want to sit down for a week. You know, after this of course.

I ease on to the gas and just as before, I quickly get back into it, my heart racing with fear as I creep toward the exit of the parking lot and force myself to have to face traffic. Those first few seconds will be terrifying but once I get into it, I'm sure I'll be fine.

I get out onto the main road without killing anyone and within just a few moments, I'm keeping up with the traffic and sailing back toward

Ravenwood Heights. My chair is pulled up as close to the steering wheel as possible and I look like an old granny, my eyes wide as I try to concentrate on absolutely everything coming my way.

I take a right-hand turn, trying to take as many backstreets as possible to avoid having to deal with too much traffic. The boys encourage me, offering little bits of advice here and there, and after a few minutes, I think I've really got the hang of it.

We approach an intersection and just as I finally feel myself starting to relax, Grayson's body hardens beside me. He leans forward and studies the side mirror. "Turn left back onto the main road," he tells me, nodding up ahead.

I change lanes and pull up to a stop at the light. "What is it?" I ask as King discreetly looks at the car pulling up behind us at the light.

"Don't know yet," Grayson says, eyeing the black SUV. "Could be something, could be nothing."

I watch it through the mirror, cursing the tinted windows as I come up blank, not even a brief outline. There are no distinguishing features on the SUV, but it's a different style than the fleet Paris hired to chase us through the streets before we made it to King's cabin.

This isn't her, she's still licking her wounds from the ginormous hole I left in her shoulder, though that doesn't mean that it's not Ember, and after I knocked her out cold, I'm sure she has a score that she wants to settle.

I clench my jaw, hating the fear of not knowing. I love to be prepared, and right now, we're at a loss. The light turns green and I sneak forward, my nerves getting the better of me as I turn the corner.

I peer up into the rearview mirror and watch as the SUV follows us around. "Alright, change lanes," Grayson says.

I do as I'm told and sure enough, the SUV copies our movements. Coincidence? It could be, but where my life is concerned, the probability of someone casually wanting to change lanes is a lot lower than the possibility of someone wanting to slaughter me, so yeah, I'm not about to take any risks.

I hit the gas a little harder, propelling me forward into the mess of traffic up ahead but being cautious about it, not wanting the SUV to realize that we're onto him. "Who is it?" I ask, glancing up into the mirror again.

King shakes his head. "No fucking clue," he says, nodding up ahead. "Keep your eyes on the road. You need to concentrate on driving. Let us worry about the tail."

My gaze reluctantly falls back to the car that sits in front of me, wanting nothing more than to throw myself into the back and pummel my fists into King for that comment, but he's right. I'm way too new at this whole driving thing to be thinking about anything more than what's happening on the road around me. Hell, getting into a car chase isn't exactly something that I should be involved in either. Why did I have to go and say that I'd drive? If Grayson were in control, he would have already had us far away from this bullshit.

"Weave into the far right lane," Grayson says, pointing out a narrow route, slipping between two cars.

"Oh, fuck," I panic, my eyes going wide as I focus on the small space, my heart racing, knowing that had I been on my Ducati, I could have slid into that spot without question.

"Now, Elodie," Grayson groans, not appreciating my hesitation.

I clench my jaw and go for it, the move way too jerky and sending the three of us rocking to the right in our seats. I straighten up, putting us in the center of the lane as my gaze flashes up to the mirror just in time to watch the SUV pull into the right lane a few cars behind us.

"Shit," Grayson says, his jaw clenched, clearly seeing that this isn't a position that we want to be in. He pulls his phone out and makes a quick call, putting it on speakerphone so that he can concentrate on both the car and his call.

"What's up?" Cruz questions, his bored tone filling the cab.

"We've got a tail."

"Fuck," Cruz curses. "On my way."

The call goes dead a second later and Grayson drops the phone into the cup holder between us. His eyes remain on the traffic around us, almost as though a game plan is forming in his head. "Speed up as much as you can without hitting the car in front," he says, his eyes flicking between the cars. "You're not going to like this."

I nod, letting out a shaky breath and keep my focus on the road in front of me.

"At this next intersection, you're going to do a sharp left turn exactly when I tell you to, you hear me? Do not fucking hesitate."

"But we're in the far-right lane. I'll never make it through three lanes of traffic, plus the cars coming the other way. It's a suicide mission."

Grayson's hard stare comes back to mine. "Are you up for this or would you prefer to just pull over and let whoever the fuck is in that

SUV take you out? You have three fucking seconds to decide."

"FUCK," I roar. "Shit. I fucking hate you so much right now."

"Elodie?" he snaps.

"Yes, okay," I yell out. "I can do it."

"Good, now wait for me to say so."

I swallow hard as we start approaching the intersection. "Slow down a bit," he says. I ease up on the gas and he nods. "Alright ready …" he says, dragging out each word as the anticipation builds within me, the intensity far more than the bullshit we just did in the backseat. "NOW."

I turn the steering wheel sharp to the left and sail straight through the gap beside me, my heart thundering as my eyes widen in horror. Grayson's hand grips the steering wheel as he helps guide me through the rest of the lanes, each one of them skidding to a stop and creating a mess of traffic behind us.

Horns blare but I ignore every last one of them, determined to make it out of the intersection without a scratch. "Good girl," King praises from the back seat, his hands gripping the backs of both mine and Grayson's seats to keep from flying around the backseat. "He's caught up in the traffic, but it won't be for long. This is our shot to get some distance between us."

We clear the intersection and I breathe heavily, panting more than when I'm with the guys. "Step on it, Ellie," Grayson says. "Go. Go. Go."

I do as I'm told, kicking the Escalade into gear as I fly down the narrow side street, the panic still riding high. I'm definitely not skilled enough to be driving at speeds like this in such a big car. Hell, I'm barely skilled enough to do it on my Ducati. Not that it matters anymore, seeing as though my Ducati was skipped off as scrap metal and technically doesn't exist anymore.

"Take the next right," King says. "There's a long straight after that. We can get you out of there."

I nod, concentrating too hard to figure out what words to get out of my mouth. The right-hand turn approaches and I take one last glance up in the mirror to find the black SUV only just making the turn through the intersection, but the second he can, he hits the gas and chases after us.

"Oh, fuck, fuck, fuck, fuck," I chant over and over again, hitting the brake to slow down enough to make the right-hand turn. The guys have no choice but to hold on to save themselves from flying around the car as I clutch onto the steering wheel, hoping to God that it doesn't break free. The second the Escalade straightens, I slam my foot back down on the gas, sending us soaring down the road.

Just as King had promised, there's a long straight up ahead and without wasting a damn second, Grayson reaches over and unbuckles my seatbelt. "Keep your foot on the gas until the very last second."

I nod as King reaches into the front, curling his arms around my waist as Grayson gets up on his knees. "Ready?" he asks King, glancing back at his friend.

King nods, and like lightning, he yanks me to the backseat as Grayson slides in to take my place, his foot slamming straight back down on the gas. He reaches down by the side of the seat to adjust its positioning, sliding it all the way back until his big frame can fit comfortably behind the steering wheel.

His hands come down on the steering wheel, expertly guiding us down the street, dodging and weaving through the oncoming traffic. Considering we are the only car moving in this direction, I'm pretty fucking certain that King had us turn onto a one-way, and from the looks of it, we're definitely the ones in the wrong.

King laughs, loving our transition, and with me out of the driver's seat with the potential risk of freaking out and driving us headfirst into another car, the boys both relax, now looking at the high-speed car chase as a fucking adventure. "Carver's going to kick himself for missing this shit."

"You're damn right. I can guarantee that the fucker is watching it through the dashcam right now," Grayson laughs, dropping the steering wheel to the left and sending me crashing over the top of King's lap and slamming into the door. "Fuck, sorry, Ellie. You should really be holding on."

"Or you should take your own fucking advice and have a few driving lessons," I mutter before looking up at the little camera. "Do you really think he's watching this right now?"

King nods. "He wouldn't miss it."

I grin wide and fly through the front, draping myself over the center console and grabbing the little camera. I do my best to hold on to the chair to keep myself from flying through the car again as I turn the camera around and grin right into the lens.

"The fuck are you doing?" Grayson growls, far too preoccupied to do anything about it as I reach across him, grab the front of his unbuttoned jeans and shove the camera right down his pants with the lens pointing right toward his monster cock.

"Mind ya business," I call toward his junk, knowing damn well that Carver got my message loud and clear.

King snickers to himself and yanks me back onto his lap just as Grayson takes the turn off the long straight to put us back on the main road. He skids into traffic, barely avoiding slamming us head-first into a red Corolla.

I spin around on King's lap, my stare boring out the back window, waiting and watching with bated breath. We get twenty seconds down the main road before the black SUV comes skidding out, clipping the back of a Dodge RAM and sending it into a tailspin. He goes straight around it and continues after us, making my hands ball into fists.

Before, I was sure that it was Ember, but there's no way that she'd be able to drive like that. It has to be someone else, but who?

I don't get another second to query it when Grayson heads straight for the right turning lane and pulls out onto the highway that leads right out of town. "Where the hell are you going?" I demand, certain that he was taking us back into Ravenwood Heights and to the safety of Dynasty.

"I'm not about to lead this ass back to our homes. I don't want him anywhere near us, especially when we don't know who the fuck it is."

Okay, so the guy has a point.

"He's just pulling onto the highway now," King tells him. "We have to make this quick."

Grayson nods as my brows furrow. "Make what quick?"

Neither of them respond as Grayson pushes the Escalade to its limits, desperate to get some proper distance between us. We drive for a few minutes and when Grayson speeds through the entrance of a darkened tunnel and the automatic headlights come on, he turns them straight off, sending us into complete darkness.

My back straightens.

Something is happening.

"What's going on?" I question, my eyes wide as Grayson drives on pure memory.

King's arm curls around my waist and locks me in like a steel vice. He scoots to the side and presses the button for the window, letting it open wide and as he does, a loud, familiar rumble sounds through the car.

My gaze shoots out the open window, seeing one perfectly round headlight pull up beside us, keeping up with our pace. My jaw drops, watching Cruz Fucking Danforth on my goddamn Ducati, the same Ducati that up until a second ago, I thought was roadkill.

"Ready, babe?" King calls in my ear.

"Ready?" I question. "What the fuck for?"

"Your ride is here," he tells me. "We're getting you the fuck out of here and we'll lose these motherfuckers so you can get away."

"What? But—"

King grins, his hold on my waist tightening as he hoists me up, shoving my head out the fucking window. "Sorry, babe. Too fucking late now."

My eyes widen in horror as my hair whips through the wind and despite my outbursts and objections, King keeps feeding me out through the window until my ass is seated on the edge of the Escalade, half my body in and the other half just moments from falling through the window and becoming a road sandwich.

Cruz moves the Ducati in nice and close, just one wrong move from either Grayson or Cruz and the whole thing is fucked. Cruz's arm curls around my waist and as it does, King eases up on his hold and before I get a chance to tell either of them to go to hell, Cruz yanks me right out of the Escalade and places me down on his lap, straddling him and holding on for dear life, my arms locking around him as my hair comes back and whips me in my face.

King's window goes straight back up and as I flip both King and Grayson off, Cruz takes off, speeding through the tunnel a million times faster than I ever went on this thing, leaving the boys and the tail in our dust.

Cruz passes through the tunnel and takes the very next exit off the highway, bringing the Ducati to a stop behind a sign that warns motorists about the dangers of drunk driving.

The engine rumbles below us and as Cruz looks down at the highway we just left, I pull myself off his lap and straddle the bike behind him, looking up just in time to see Carver's Escalade flying down the road with the black SUV following behind, completely oblivious to the boys' ridiculous little stunt.

Cruz lets out a deep breath and glances back at me. "Don't pretend that I can't smell them on you," he tells me, shaking his head. "We had a deal."

Ah, shit.

I cringe but before he allows me a chance to feed him some bullshit excuse for my bad behavior, he takes off, revving the engine and sending us sailing straight back to the highway, leading us in the opposite direction and taking us back to Ravenwood Heights.

The Ducati rolls to a stop outside my gates to find Carver standing in front of a cop car, not letting the two officers before him enter my property. All three of them turn to look at me and Cruz as we climb off the Ducati and I can't help but feel that there was some kind of showdown about to happen at my front gate.

"What's this?" Cruz questions, taking my hand and holding me slightly behind him as we make our way over to Carver and the two officers.

The cop on the right looks slightly familiar and I try to think back to the day I was arrested at school on murder charges—charges that were miraculously dropped when the boys got themselves involved. This guy was one of the cops who humiliated me by marching me out of school in front of the whole student body, and while I didn't realize that I was holding a grudge, seeing his face now makes it all too clear to me.

"Miss Ravenwood," the cop says, taking a step toward me with his head held high and his arrogance held even higher. "We have witnesses who have placed you at a crime scene."

My brows furrow as I step out from behind Cruz's shoulder, not prepared to take the backseat on this one. The cops have been a problem for me for way too long and I'm not going to continue to shy away from them anymore, especially now that I plan on staying in Ravenwood Heights indefinitely. "What crime scene?" I ask them.

The heavyset cop who stands beside him takes a step toward me making both Carver and Cruz adjust their positioning around both the cops and me, and it certainly doesn't go unnoticed. Even with their guns at their hips, they know damn well that they're the ones in danger here. "We're investigating a car bombing in the city last night," the cop says. "Witnesses have placed a girl matching your description stepping out of the vehicle just minutes before it exploded in a populated area."

I shake my head, laughing. "Of course you immediately assume it was me, right? The troubled foster girl. Well, unfortunately, you've got the wrong person, and quite frankly, I don't appreciate being targeted purely because of my appearances. Do you know how many young brunette chicks live in Ravenwood Heights? Why aren't you knocking on their doors? Besides, it wasn't me," I tell them. "I was at an event last night with over two thousand guests who can confirm my whereabouts."

The first cop narrows his gaze. "We still need you to come down to the station and answer a few questions. You can make your statement and as soon as your alibi can be confirmed, you'll be free to go."

I grin wide and wave my hand to the guys on either side of me. "Ask away," I tell them. "Both Dante and Cruz were at the event and will confirm that I was there all night. Or perhaps you would like to knock on every door on this street. They were all there too. I was the main speaker. My presence was not missed among the two thousand guests and hundreds of wait staff. I didn't get a second to myself all night." The cop glances back down the road at the sixteen other properties lining Ravenwood Estate and I lean back against my gate, crossing my legs as though I have all the time in the world. "Go ahead," I tell them. "I'll wait. I have all afternoon."

Cruz scoffs. "Speak for yourself," he mutters. "I'm stinging for a piss."

I hold back a laugh, knowing exactly what else he's been stinging to do ever since finding out that I accidentally fucked up my part of our deal, and something tells me that I won't be walking away from it without the perfect imprint of Cruz's hand on my ass. Though, it won't be that easy. He's going to make me work to come, that's if he even allows me to. Cruz is usually so sweet, but a bitch better watch out when a man like Cruz Danforth has been crossed. He can be just as callous and cruel as the rest of them and a part of me can't wait to find out.

Buuuuut … on the other hand, I'm sure that I could also bat my eyelashes and give him the sweetest kiss on his cheek, while reminding him how much I love him and everything will be forgiven. Grayson and King though, they're in for a major ass whooping. I won't be surprised if I wake up in the morning to find them both with black eyes for crossing Cruz's boundaries.

The cops narrow their stares on me, looking at me as though they've already decided that I'm guilty while trying to figure out how the hell I could have such a firm alibi. Who knows ... maybe I have an evil twin of my own who's been getting around doing all these reckless, incriminating, and dangerous acts, it couldn't possibly be me. I'm an angel who just happens to love getting dicked ten times a day.

"Don't leave the state," the first cop warns. "We're not through with you."

I wink. "No one ever is."

His nostrils flare and a moment later, the tubby guy turns on his heel and stalks back to the police cruiser as his partner begrudgingly follows behind. The boys don't say a damn word, just stand by my side as we watch the cops reverse out of the top of my driveway.

They finally disappear down the street when Carver enters the code for the gate, letting us back in. "It's not too late," he mutters darkly. "The offer is still on the table. We can pack up our shit and be out of here by morning."

I scoff and go to tell him how ridiculous he is when Cruz cuts me off before I can. "As if, bro," he says, throwing his leg back over the Ducati. "You'd pack your shit and leave your sisters here with your mom? Yeah fucking right."

"Good point," Carver says, knowing more than anybody just how dangerous his plan could be, especially when it's not just us that it affects.

The Ducati roars to life, and as the gate opens to my property, Cruz flies down it, leaving Carver and me to walk the rest of the way.

By the time we reach the top step, Grayson and King are flying down the driveway in Carver's Escalade and I watch in amusement as his gaze travels over his car, checking every last angle for even the slightest scratch or dent.

My hand rests on the door handle and as I go to push my way past him, he stops me with a hand on my stomach. Carver steps right into me, looming over me with that pissed-off stare that I've come to fucking love. That look is the star of my favorite kind of dream. "You ever put my dashcam down someone's pants and have me staring at their junk again, you and I are going to have problems."

I press up onto my tippy toes and brush my lips over his, meeting his stare with a flirty one of my own. "But what if it's my pants that I put the camera down? Would you really say no to your very own private showing of that?"

He groans, his chest rising and falling just a little bit faster as a low breath comes sailing out from between his lips.

Not another word passes between us before Cruz's hand comes flying out the door and hooks around my wrist. He yanks me into his side. "Half a fucking week," he reminds me, narrowing his gaze on Carver who's probably wondering just how quickly I could make a video for him so he has something to do tonight.

Cruz scoffs and drags me toward the kitchen, trying to work out what we're going to do for dinner. After an hour of back and forth arguments, the rest of the guys come striding into the kitchen with Indian takeout.

"Hmm," Cruz grunts, looking over the dishes the guys selected as I stand beside him doing exactly the same thing. "Why didn't you think of Indian?"

I shrug my shoulders, my stomach growling with hunger. "It's not like you thought of it either."

"Both of you fuckers shut up," King mutters, grabbing a few plates and handing them out. "You've been bickering like an old married couple for over an hour. You're doing my head in."

Cruz grins, finding King's insult as the best kind of compliment, making the rest of us roll our eyes at his display. The guys dig into their dinner, scooping food onto their plates until they're almost overflowing.

My hunger gets the best of me and we sit around my breakfast bar, annihilating our dinner. It's not until silence fills the room that I realize the guys are up to something, at least, only a few of them are in on whatever the secret is. All I know is that, once again, I'm on the outside looking in and I can't stand it.

Feeling the tone in the room beginning to shift, Cruz's head snaps up, his attention no longer on the food that's being shoveled into his mouth.

Grayson just grins, focusing his wicked stare on Cruz. "You enjoying that?"

Cruz's face falls. "The fuck is that supposed to mean?" he demands, dropping his stare to his food and searching it as though it has rabies.

"What'd you do to my dinner?"

My gaze falls to the half-eaten plate before shifting to my own, unsure if I should trust the food that's swirling around in my mouth. "Well," Grayson continues. "We know how you struggle digesting Indian sometimes. You know, all that curry always does a number on that weak little stomach of yours. So we just slipped you a little something to help the process along."

Cruz's eyes bug out of his head as he flies up from the breakfast bar, rushing back a step as though just being close to his plate offends him. "Tell me you fucking didn't?" he demands, looking at his friends as though they've crossed the ultimate line. "I'm going to be on the fucking toilet all goddamn night."

King has the audacity to look as though he was just trying to help a friend out. "What's the matter, bro? We were just trying to help."

"FUCK."

I press my lips into a hard line, holding back a laugh, knowing exactly what's happening here and I can guarantee that it has a little something to do with 'If we can't have her, then you can't have her either.'

Fucking pricks. I bet they've been giggling about it all fucking night and were only just holding themselves together as they watched him annihilate his dinner.

Cruz storms out of the room, aiming for the closest bathroom, and within seconds, we all hear as he forces himself to throw up before any of his dinner has the chance to really go through his system and fuck with his whole night.

He's on his third heave when Carver's phone rings in the center of the table, a private number flashing on the screen. Carver stares at the phone ringing, his brows drawn in caution as he only gives his number out to people important to him, and more than that, they're never private calls. He always knows exactly who is trying to reach him and why.

He reaches across the table, all eyes on his phone as silence surrounds us, the only noise coming from the heaving in the bathroom. He hits accept on the call before immediately putting the call on speakerphone.

"Hello?" a familiar voice comes through the phone, though it lacks the flair of arrogance that I remember so well. "Carver? Is that you? Are you there?"

Her voice is a broken and tormented whisper that turns my stomach upside down. "Sara?" My gaze shifting to Carver, wondering why the fuck Sara Benson would be calling him.

She lets out a soft gasp. "Winter? Shit. Is that you? Holy shit. I'm so sorry. Please, I need to talk to you. Please come and see me. I swear, I never meant to go insane like that. Please, I'll do anything. Please come. I'll tell you everything you want to know and I'll never bother you again. I just have to get out of here. I can't do it anymore. I'm begging you."

Carver snatches the phone off the counter and takes it off speakerphone. "What the fuck can you offer us?" he questions, clearly not liking the idea of Sara speaking to me with such desperation, trying to guilt me into giving her what she wants.

Silence follows as Cruz comes striding out of the bathroom with a hand towel and whips it against the back of Grayson's head, only to quickly realize that something is going down. He takes his seat, pushing his plate away from him and taking my hand on top of the counter. "Who is it?" he questions.

"Sara Benson," King says. "She's fucking desperate. She'll probably say anything to get out of that place."

Carver's brows raise and he turns his gaze to Cruz, his eyes full of suspicion. "We'll be there in an hour," he says before ending the call without another word.

"We're going there?" I demand, my eyes bugging out of my head. "I don't know if maybe you've forgotten, but Sara is a fucking psycho. She was stalking me for weeks. She was in my fucking room."

"Trust me, I haven't forgotten," Carver says, his gaze shifting back to Cruz again. "She thinks she knows where we can find Knox, and if she's right, she wants us to get her out on the pretenses that she gets the fuck out of Ravenwood Heights and never comes back again."

Cruz leans back in his seat, rubbing his hand over his face. "She can give us Knox?"

Carver shrugs. "That's what she said."

"And if she's lying?"

Carver shakes his head. "She has no reason to lie," he explains. "She tells us where he is, and if he's there, we get him and she gets her freedom, but if he's not, she stays. She gains nothing from lying to us. But on the off chance she is, what do we lose? A fucking night of looking in the wrong place? What's the difference from every other failed night of searching?"

"True," Cruz says, getting to his feet. "Then let's do this. I've got a fucking score to settle with that bastard."

I'm thrown back to the night, chasing Knox through the thick trees where I chose my own problems over Cruz's need to end him. Knox offered me information on the night Sara abused me and my selfish need to get answers beat any kind of rational thinking. Knox got away and I've hated myself for it ever since. Cruz deserved retribution. He deserved to watch the life fading out of Knox's eye for what he did to him, and I took that opportunity away from him. Now is our chance to even the playing field. Knox won't be getting away from us again.

We leave our half-eaten dinner on the counter and pile into the Escalade, Carver careening down the road like a bat out of hell. Traveling at this speed isn't so stressful when no one is following you. Though, the fact that the black SUV didn't fall into the boys' trap and got out of there before it was too late isn't very comforting. There are so many questions and so few answers.

An hour later after knocking out two security guards and stealing their key cards, the five of us sneak through the quiet, dark halls of the mental institute the boys had stashed Sara in, and with every step I take, an uneasy shiver sails down my spine. It's clinical, creepy, and downright fucked up. It's barely even eight at night and the place is closed up, expecting their patients to go to bed this early. They're probably given sedatives to help them get there and to keep the noise down. No wonder Sara wants to get out of here so badly.

Carver leads, searching the numbers beside each door until he comes to room 162. He swipes the key card over the lock and waits a moment for the red light to turn green. The door is pushed open and the five of us pile into the room.

Sara sits cross-legged on the bed with her eyes closed in meditation. As she hears us enter, her eyes spring open and relief floods her features. "Oh my god," she sighs, looking as though she's on the brink of bursting into tears. "I've never been so happy to see you guys."

The guys form a line at the end of her bed and I plant myself right in the middle of them and her gaze instantly falls to mine. "Winter," she says, shaking her head in disbelief. "I'm so fucking sorry, you have no idea. This place is insane, but a small part of it is actually helpful. They put me on medication and I was able to see how much of a mess I was, and I realize just how fucking crazy I'd been. I ... shit. This is harder than I thought," she says, taking a deep breath and blowing out her cheeks as that same breath comes back out again. "I was infatuated with you, like obsessively infatuated."

"Yeah," I scoff. "I worked that much out."

"Look, I—" she pauses, taking another breath while trying to figure out how to word what she's clearly been needing to say. "You rejected me and I'd never experienced that before and that little thought of not being good enough for you was planted into my head and it was like cancer, constantly growing. I became obsessed with the idea of needing you to want me, and of course, why the hell would that ever happen? I was so awful and you already had these four guys pining for you. You didn't need shallow bitches like me, and everything just spiraled from there. I couldn't control myself. I couldn't function without thinking about making you suffer while also wanting you. My head was such a mess, but I'm better now, and I just want you to know how sorry I am. I … could we maybe be—"

"Friends?" I shriek in horror, reading the words on her lips before they get a chance to come out. "You admitted to wanting to kill me, so understand me when I tell you that respectfully, I decline your offer. We're here for one reason only. I have no interest in building any type of relationship with you. Sure, hearing your apology and knowing that you're getting better is great. Hopefully you'll stick with your medication and continue bettering yourself, but this is where the road ends between us."

"I …" her tongue rolls over her bottom lip as her gaze drops to her hands. She nods slowly, the disappointment rolling off her in waves. "I understand, but that party … what I did. That was inexcusable and I will live with the weight of that for the rest of my life. I know my words will never make up for that, but—"

"No," I cut her off. "You don't get to throw your bullshit fucked-up mental health shit at me. Nothing will ever make it okay. You roofied me. You slipped me a drug and then raped me when I had absolutely no control. I couldn't consent and I couldn't even scream for help. People shrug it off as though a woman raping another woman isn't such a big deal, but it is. It fucking is. You put your hands on me and no, it's not you who has to live with the weight of that for the rest of your life, it's me. I'm the one who was violated. I'm the one who closes my eyes at night and remembers the feeling of someone forcing themselves on me, of not being able to push you off, not thinking clearly. Your words will never make any of that okay, so I suggest you shut the fuck up with your bullshit meaningless apologies and tell us why the hell we're here."

"Sara," Cruz says, drawing her attention back to him, not wanting her eyes on me when I inevitably lose control. "Where's Knox?"

She swallows hard and flicks her gaze to Carver. "Will you stand by your end of the deal? If I tell you what I know, you'll get me out of here?"

Carver nods as I reconsider why the hell we're making deals with this bitch. I know we want Knox but is finding Knox more important than letting someone like Sara free into the world? "As long as your information is good, then we're sweet on our deal, but if you ever come near Ravenwood Heights again, your ass will be coming right back here."

Sara nods. "I swear," she says, her eyes widening. "This place is a nightmare. I never want to come back here again. I'll do anything."

"Right, then tell us what we want to know."

Cruz can't help his anticipation and slowly creeps in closer to the end of Sara's bed. "There's a lot of things I need to come clean about," she starts, her flickering gaze remaining on Carver's as we all wait far too impatiently. "I was the one who trashed your house."

My brows shoot up. "What?" I rush out, remembering exactly what we'd come home to after being away and searching my parents' mountain home. Carver's home was trashed, but that's not all that happened. "You killed Lady Dante?"

Her eyes go wide with fear as my hands ball into tight fists, my brass knuckles tightening against my skin as I picture the sweet sound that it would make when I smash her nose right into the back of her skull. "No, I swear, I had nothing to do with that. The dog was barking at me the whole time. I didn't kill it. I even fixed its stupid automatic feeder because it was jammed. I'm a dog person, I could never, but I know who did." I hold my breath, unable to handle the emotions welling up inside me, and the longer she waits, the harder it gets to control myself. "It was Knox," she continues. "I heard him boasting about it at a party one night. He knew that you and I had our differences and he thought that telling me about the dog would create some kind of kinship between us, but … no. Just … no."

I take three slow, deep breaths, trying to calm myself but have to turn into King's chest and slowly inhale, breathing in his warm, inviting scent while trying to find some level of control.

"Then why the fuck did you trash his place?" Grayson questions, picking up where I left off. "It doesn't make any fucking sense."

"I … for a while, I thought that he was the reason you didn't want to be with me. You wanted him, and I could see how badly and I was so jealous. It made me so mad, especially because before you showed up, he'd show me all that attention. I just … I lost it and trashed his place, but I swear," she says, her gaze shifting back to Carver's. "Everything that's in my trust fund is yours. I feel awful, especially because you have little sisters who are supposed to be living in that home. I wasn't thinking about that shit. I just acted and I'm sorry for that."

Carver shakes his head. "I don't want your money, Sara. I just want to know what you know."

She nods, looking nervously between the five of us, knowing that she's about to show her ace and hoping to God that it doesn't backfire on her. "He's been sleeping in the school," she tells us. "I'm not sure where, but he's there. I swear my life on it."

And just like that, the five of us stalk straight out of her room, that tiny piece of information that we've been needing for so long sitting heavy on my chest and promising that Knox Delacourt will finally get what's coming for him.

# CHAPTER 27

The Escalade tears through the streets of Ravenwood Heights and as we pass straight by my old high school, irritation floods my veins, but we're not running into this blind. There's no way in hell that we're going to allow Knox to slip through our fingers again. We have to play it smart. Besides, there's always the possibility that Sara has bad information. She's not exactly someone that I have any intention of trusting, but her desperation speaks volumes and it's a lead that none of us are willing to sleep on.

All four of the guys look out the window as we pass the school, searching for any lights that shouldn't be on or any signs for whereabout Knox would be staying within the school. Silence fills the Escalade but their thoughts have never been so loud. Tonight is the night. He will die and finally make up for the shit he's put us all through.

It takes two minutes to get from the school all the way back to my home and I have to give Carver credit where it's due; I think that's the fastest he's ever done it. Usually it's a good five to ten-minute drive, though it's quickly creeping toward eleven at night and there's not another car in sight, giving Carver complete freedom on the roads.

We bail out of the Escalade, all doors closing behind us before the engine has even finished rumbling. We wait the painstakingly long few seconds it takes for Grayson to enter the latest security code, and before I know it, we're barging down the door and rushing through my home.

The boys each go their separate directions while I storm straight up to my room, pulling off my clothes in the process while trying to figure out my best bringer of death outfit. After all, I want to look good when sending Knox to his grave, but I also want him to take one look at me and fear the moment he decided to ever fuck with me.

Knowing the boys aren't going to give me long to put something spectacular together, I go for a pair of tight leather pants with a lace up front and quickly grab my black chunky boots to match. After slipping my feet into them, I pull a black cropped halter tank over my head and get busy strapping my holsters around my thigh. Though Knox is only one guy, I can guarantee the boys will go all out.

My feet thud against the stairs as I race back down to meet the boys, and just as the night we went to save their siblings, there are blueprints spread out on the table with all sorts of wraps around it. "How the fuck did you get blueprints of the school?" I question, moving in between Grayson and King.

Cruz's gaze snaps up from the blueprints and travels over my body, his brow raising as hunger flashes in his eyes. "Fuck, babe. How am I supposed to concentrate when you come to the party looking like that?"

A grin settles over my lips as my eyelids lower. "What's the matter?" I ask him, bringing my fingers to my collar bone and slowly dragging them down my body, between my breasts and down past my waist. "You're not telling me that you won't be able to concentrate, are you? Perhaps you need to sit this one out."

Cruz's eyes bug out of his head. "Fuck that," he snaps. "I'm Cruz Fucking Danforth. I don't settle for either or, I get everything I want. I'm going to put a bullet through Knox's skull and when I'm done, I'm going to fuck you in the middle of the goddamn school. How does Principal Torsney's desk sound?"

My tongue rolls over my lip and before I can get too excited about the idea of getting freaky in a deserted school, Grayson steals the spotlight, deciding that we don't have time for this bullshit. "We've had the blueprints since the moment we enrolled there. We told you this, didn't we? We needed to know every inch of that school before you arrived. We don't go into missions unprepared."

A soft chuckle bubbles up my throat. "Funny," I mutter. "Because it seems that going into missions unprepared is kinda my thing."

Carver scoffs. "Yeah, we fucking know."

I roll my eyes and turn my attention back to the table. Despite my reckless habit of running into things without a single thought, tonight won't be like that. My gaze shuffles over the blueprints. "Where do you think he'll be?"

Grayson drops his finger to the papers. "My guess is here," he says, pointing out the utility room in the gymnasium. "From memory, this room has a lock on it. It's close to the locker room where he can shower and shit, and the cafeteria is right next door. He can sneak around and get what he needs to survive without having to risk moving through too much of the school."

King drags his hand down his face. "I don't know, man. It sounds too easy. That's where anyone with basic survival skills would go, but Knox ain't that smart."

"That's what I was thinking," Carver says. "The fucker could be anywhere. I don't want to fuck ourselves in the asses by going all in and storming the gymnasium, only to give him warning and time to slip away. He's fucking slippery. The bastard has a gift for escaping."

"Alright," Grayson says, propping both hands against the table and looking over the blueprints for the millionth time. "Then here's what we're going to do …"

Within the space of three minutes, the guys have gone over the plan, laughed at their own freaking brilliance, hidden all kinds of weapons over all of our bodies, and are now waiting impatiently as the gate at the top of my driveway slowly peels open.

Carver hits the gas, sneaking through the gate as quickly as possible, far too impatient to wait for it to open the whole way. Carver drives way too fast, considering that he's only going to have to stop again when he reaches the main gate into the estate, and when we do finally reach it, we're all left in utter silence, staring out the front windshield in confusion.

"What the fuck is that?" I question, peering through the gate at the lumpy heap that's been dumped on the opposite side of the gate.

Carver creeps just a little bit closer to the gate, letting his headlights shine upon the head. "It's … I think it's a person," Carver says.

"You sure?" King questions. "It looks like someone's just dropped off a fuck ton of blankets."

Grayson pushes his door open before looking back at me. "Stay here," he says, pausing a moment to narrow his gaze. "I mean it. Don't fucking move. Got it?"

I roll my eyes and cross my arms over my chest, but Grayson doesn't hang around to watch me huff and groan about his douchiness. We all watch as he walks toward the gate, leaving the car door wide open so that we can hear what's going on out there.

Carver leans through his window and enters the code for the gate and as Grayson slips through the opening, I lean forward in my seat, my breath held in anticipation.

Grayson slows as he approaches the heap and I don't miss the way that Carver draws his gun, ready to shoot in case this is some kind of threat, but when Grayson begins to crouch down and reaches for the heap, I realize that this couldn't be a threat. There's no way in hell that he would willingly make himself vulnerable by crouching down like that if he thought there was even a slight chance that the heap was going to attack.

His fingers curl around something and he pulls it back, letting the heap roll back toward him and as it does, I realize that Carver was right—it is a person, but what the fuck are they doing crumpled up in a heap in front of the Ravenwood Estate?

Carver's headlights shine on Grayson's face and although he's a little far away, I don't miss the slight hint of surprise that flashes through his eyes. "Fuck," Grayson calls, looking up at the Escalade. "It's Ember. She's been beaten."

A gasp sails out of me and I find myself climbing across King's lap and barreling for the door handle, despite the fact that the boys were all getting out as well. I guess that while I've learned a bit of patience over the past few months, I clearly haven't perfected that skill.

My feet hit the ground and I hurry through the gate, dropping to my knees beside Ember's face. The boys all move in beside me and I look down at her in horror. She's barely recognizable, and although we certainly have our differences, my chest begins to ache. "What the hell," I murmur to myself in disbelief, taking in her swollen eyes and the dried blood matted in her hair. There are trail marks down her face where her tears rolled down her cheeks, dark bruises, and deep cuts. "Is she alive?"

Grayson nods. "Barely," he mutters, his tone dark and thoughtful. "But she won't be if she stays out here much longer."

Fuck.

The guys all look up at me as a million thoughts flow through my mind, but it's King's voice I hear through the dark. "It's your call, babe. We can turn away and pretend that we didn't see a damn thing. She'll die and the threat will die along with her. Or, you can save her and risk that when she gets better, she will go straight back to plotting to end your life."

I clench my jaw as my gaze falls back down to her, absolutely hating that the guys have left this decision up to me. Those fucking pricks. It's times like this that I need them to take the power out of my hands. They should decide because if I make the wrong decision, it could come back and haunt me, and I've already got enough regrets weighing me down.

"Shit," I sigh, looking up at the boys again. "What should I do?"

Carver scoffs. "I know what I would do."

I roll my eyes and look at Cruz, already knowing the right decision, but struggling with actually making the call. "It's okay to want to save her," Cruz tells me. "It doesn't make you weak, and it sure as fuck doesn't make you a pushover. Being able to offer mercy to your enemies shows a kind of strength that none of us were ever gifted with. Besides babe, if you walked away right now, would you be able to live with yourself?"

My gaze travels over Ember's swollen eyes and I follow the bloodied curve of her face down past her chin and over her distorted body. There's no doubt that she has a few broken bones and although she's passed the fuck out, her body would be in the worst kind of agony.

I let out a breath and stand before turning my back and walking toward the Escalade. "Put her in the trunk."

The boys comply and within moments, Ember's broken and bruised body is being shoved into the back of the Escalade. King and Cruz climb in beside me on the backseat while Grayson gets back in the front. Carver takes his time, closing the trunk and getting back in, but instead of hitting the gas and getting on with it, he pauses and meets my gaze through the rearview mirror. "Hospital or here?"

My brows furrow and I go to rush out with the obvious answer when it hits me. If we drop her off at the hospital, we might not get a chance to ask her what the fuck is going down, but if she were at my place and feeling gratitude for saving her life, we just might be able to get exactly what we need out of her.

"My place," I tell him, barely getting the words out before he hits the gas and turns the Escalade around.

We get back to my home and Carver goes as far as to park the Escalade in the garage so that we can get Ember out of here without any of our too-nosey neighbors knowing what the fuck is going on. Though, I doubt anyone is awake at this time of night, but we won't risk it.

The garage door comes down behind us and Grayson moves to the back of the Escalade and scoops Ember out of the trunk. We all make our way into the house, moving up the stairs as one, only Cruz breaks away and heads for the bathroom to find the boys' massive box of first aid supplies.

Grayson lays Ember down in my spare bedroom and I dart into the attached bathroom to grab a washcloth and warm water.

As I come back into the room, I find Grayson and King stripping her out of her bloodied clothes and quickly getting her dressed into something a little more comfortable. I watch them with pride, seeing the respect they have for her despite how they can't stand her. They're gentle with their touch and they don't ogle her body as they dress her. They're the perfect gentlemen and I love them more for it.

I crawl up onto the bed beside Ember and start cleaning her up as Cruz comes in with the box of first aid supplies. The boys quickly start mending her wounds as Grayson doses her up with morphine, taking his role as group doctor as seriously as he can.

There's an odd silence around the room and I can't help but feel that the boys are devastated that they're not storming the school right now and watching as a bullet pierces through the front of Knox's skull, but they will in time. I wouldn't dream of letting them miss out on that kind of fun. That is the kind of shit that makes their dark little hearts race with excitement.

Twenty minutes pass before Ember begins to stir. A pained groan pulls from deep within her chest as she attempts to open her eyes. I instantly pull back on the washcloth as the guys also pull back, not sure how this is going to go.

As if remembering the trauma she's just been through, Ember's eyes fly open and she stares up at the ceiling, hard and fast gasps tearing through her. She quickly looks around, panicking as she tries to figure out what the fuck is going on, but seeing my face, she begins to calm. Though the fear doesn't completely wash away. She doesn't trust that I have good intentions, and right now, I don't know if I trust it either.

"Where … where am … I?" she asks, the words getting stuck in her dry throat and sounding as though each word spoken causes her more pain than she's ever felt in her life, but the morphine should be starting to work.

"My place," I tell her with a blank expression, silently letting her know that while I was the one who allowed her in, she's not exactly welcome. "You were dumped at the Estate gates."

Ember swallows hard and quickly glances at the guys before bringing her stare back to mine. She nods and I watch as tears begin to fill her eyes. "Who did this?" I ask.

Her brows crease and I see nothing but heartbreak written across her face. "Paris," she murmurs, her voice coming out in the softest whisper, almost as though she still can't believe what happened to her. "She blamed me for letting you get away. She … she…"

I shrug my shoulders. "You did let me get away," I remind her. "It is your fault. If you didn't lose control the way that you did, Paris probably would have had her chance to slit my throat. You took that away from her."

The tears fall from her eyes and her heartbreak only doubles. "I thought … I really thought that she loved me. I thought that she wanted to be a family."

"I tried to warn you," I tell her. "I gave you an out where you could have spent the rest of your life with your adoptive family being happy and free. You could have done whatever you wanted in life, but you chose to follow Paris knowing what kind of person she is. You knew all the shit that she did to me, you knew that she kidnapped those kids, and yet you thought that you were different because you share the same blood? Open your fucking eyes, Ember. She's my aunt—the only thing that's left of her twin sister—and she's been trying to kill me since I was born. How could you be so stupid?"

Heaving sobs pull from within her, and with each one, I see the pain that overtakes her body. "I don't know what to do. If she knows I'm alive, she'll try to hurt me again. She had her guards beat me … the things that they …." she cuts herself off with more sobs, surely remembering the way that they touched her. "What am I supposed to do?"

I shake my head. "I'm sorry, but it's not my problem anymore. The second you sided with Paris, you lost all your rights within Dynasty. You know that. I'm not under any obligation to help you, and after what you did, why the hell should I?"

She swallows hard. "Because I know things that you don't, information that could help you."

"What a fucking joke," Carver scoffs and steps forward. "If you think that we're going to barter with you for information in exchange for your safety, you're dead wrong. How about you give up the information in exchange for us not slitting your throat."

Ember's swollen eyes bug out of her head, knowing damn well that the boys are capable of that and so much more. Her brows crease in concern and I watch as she falls into silence, quickly trying to weigh her options.

Grayson quickly gets bored and fiddles through the first aid kit, pulling out a syringe and making a show of filling it with some kind of drug. "Start talking or you'll get to know the effects that a neurotoxin has on the human body firsthand."

Ember's eyes flicker around the room, silently begging for help as she tries to find an escape. "I … what … I … what do you want to know?"

I find myself grinning at her performance, certain that it's only water in Grayson's syringe, though, I could be very wrong. "Where's Paris?" Carver asks, his tone flat and filled with a vicious calmness that sends chills shooting down my spine.

Ember shakes her head, cringing with the movement. "I don't know," she rushes out. "She never let me see where she was staying. She would always come to me."

Carver groans. "Then what's her next plan?"

Ember shakes her head again. "I … she never told me," she rushes out, turning her gaze back to me. "What's going to happen to me? Please, I just want a clean break. Let me go and I swear, you'll never have to see me again."

King scoffs. "You're not going anywhere until you've told us something worthwhile because so far, you've been pretty fucking useless."

Ember breathes hard and presses her lips into a tight line. "Fine," she says, not sounding happy about it as she cringes and turns her stare on Grayson. "Paris has been trying to get your father on board, and she seems to think she's close but I think that your dad is just keeping her around to know what's going on—either way, it's bad fucking news for you guys."

"That's it?" King questions, looking completely deflated and pissed off. "That's your big revelation?"

Ember rolls her eyes and lets out another breath, giving King a hard stare before turning to Carver. "Your mom has been working with Paris for years. She's so deep in her pocket that there's no way out for her. She knew Paris's plan for kidnapping those children and allowed it to happen."

"What?" Carver says, rushing right into the side of the bed and gripping Ember around her throat, pulling her straight up until her knees are dangling over the sheets and she's pulling at Carver's fingers. "The fuck are you talking about? My mother would never do that to my sisters."

"She did," Ember croaks out, her voice breathy and muffled from Carver's hand around her throat. "She said some bullshit about it being an experience that would help shape them. Ida knew the guards were going to raid the party and even helped them take the kids. She all but threw them in their hands while your sisters screamed for help."

Rage burns through Carver and he releases Ember so quickly that she crumbles back to the bed in a broken heap, screaming as the pain tears through her.

Carver storms out of the room, his voice roaring through the quiet house. "She doesn't fucking leave until I say so." And with that, Carver is gone, leaving us all staring around the spare bedroom, unsure of what the fuck will come next.

# CHAPTER 28

## CARVER

My boot slams against the front door of my own fucking home, splintering the wood into a million pieces. The alarm blasts through the house and I have no fucking doubt that my little sisters are flying out of their beds, terrified that their worst nightmares are coming back to haunt them, but once they see my face, they'll understand what's going on. I know they will because as of two minutes ago, I learned that my sisters are going through the same bullshit upbringing that I suffered through and I won't allow it to happen to them the same way it happened to me.

I was tortured, bullied by my own fucking parents, made to believe that I wasn't worth the air I was breathing, not unless I learned how to become someone in this fucked up world, and in order to survive, that's exactly what I did.

All these years, I thought that was my father's influence, but I was wrong—it was her too.

Ida Fucking Carver.

I've always hated her, ever since I was four years old and first learned what the word 'hate' truly meant. She was a pitiful excuse of a mother, but with my father in the picture, I hardly gave it any notice because he was the one to watch out for. It's hard to believe it, but even back then, I had no choice but to look at my mother as my safety net.

I would watch my friends with their doting parents, always wanting them to be the best version of themselves while I was going home to get beaten for not getting the best grades or for getting into fights at school. I always wanted what they had and it wasn't until I was much older that I realized it was never going to happen. I had to create my own light in a dark world. It was the only way to survive and that's exactly what I did.

My only relief came when my sisters were born and they took the attention off me. I was a screw up, I was weak, and every chance they got, they let me know it, and because of that, I always vowed to prove them wrong. I just hate that Winter got the chance to do it before I could, but never again. From here on out, I deal with my problems, they don't get swept under the rug, even if it means taking my own mother's life to do it.

The months at a time when they would disappear used to be the best times of my childhood. I raised myself and I fucking loved it, but then they'd come home and demand to see how I'd improved while they were gone, and the torture would start all over again. I was never good enough, never strong enough, never worthy, even up until my father's last day on earth, he would remind me that I'd never be the kind of head of family that he was, and he was never so right. I was never going to be like him and that's the best goddamn thing about it.

When those words came out of Ember's mouth, I felt fucking sick. I had to do something about it, and honestly, I haven't even thought this through, but I can guarantee that after a lifetime of abuse, I won't be thinking it through calmly. Perhaps Winter's recklessness is rubbing off on me. All I know is that it feels fucking great.

Adrenaline pulses through my veins at the very thought of taking Ida's life. She can rot in hell with her husband, and one day I'll join them there, and that's when the fun is really going to start.

The alarm continues screeching and any normal person would have shut it up the moment they could, but not Ida. She knows better than that. She would be using the noise of the alarm to mask her movements around my house, but while she's had all sorts of training and could kill a motherfucker without hesitation, I'm better, I always have been. Mother and father dearest made sure that I was.

Even through the screeching alarm, I hear my sisters upstairs, running through their bedroom, terrified of who's storming into their home in the middle of the night, but they would have been prepared for shit like this. My parents would have taught them to hide and shut their mouths until it was over, just as they taught me.

I hate that they're scared, but soon enough, it'll all be better. I'll make sure of it. They'll never have to fear again.

I creep through the main foyer, stopping at the bottom of the stairs and listening intently, trying to ignore the alarm as I listen for every other little sound coming from within the house. The girls have settled into their hiding spots, meaning that the only creaks coming from upstairs are those of my mother's.

She walks through the master bedroom and I pause, tracking her movements as she darts across the room to the small dresser and takes the gun out of the drawer. She then hurries across to her massive walk-in closet and pulls the door closed, only leaving it open just a crack. She's too fucking obvious.

Knowing that apart from my sisters, there's not another soul in the house, I make my way up the stairs. My feet ease over the old wood, avoiding every creak and moan that years of sneaking around has burned into my memory.

The girls are my top priority. My fingers curl around their bedroom door and I slowly push it open, slipping inside and quickly scanning their room. They're completely out of sight but their panicked loud breathing coming from inside the closet gives them away, and if I were anybody else, they would have been caught in seconds.

I sneak across the room and slowly push against the closet door, letting it swing open only to find Dominique cowering in the corner, tucked into a tight ball as Danika stands tall, protecting her sister by holding out a gun, aimed straight for my chest. "The fuck?" I grunt, racing forward and taking the gun straight out of her hand as she falls to the ground in relief.

"We ... we thought ..."

"Shhh," I soothe, holding out a hand to both the girls and pulling them to their feet. "I know what you thought. You're both safe. It was just me. Nobody else is in the house. Now, go and sit on your beds and keep the door closed. I will come back for you."

They both nod, intuitive enough to know that something is about to go down but far too innocent to piece the puzzle together, and just as I requested, they make their way to Dominique's bed and sit together, both watching intently as I walk out of the room and close the door behind me. I step away from their room, knowing that the fear inside their chests is still there, but at least they know they're safe.

Making my way down the long hall toward the master bedroom, I ignore the holes in the wall from when Sara decided to help me redecorate. The house still looks like shit, and to be honest, I'm pretty fucking gutted about it. I was positive that my mother would have attempted to fix it up, but the fact that she hasn't tells me that she never had any intentions to stick around anyway, but I won't be letting her leave with my sisters again.

Reaching the master bedroom, I silently slip inside the room, and gently close it behind me, not wanting to step deeper into the room, knowing that if I do, she'll be able to see me from the closet. I need to get the drop on her and I need to make it fast.

I creep across the room, keeping as close to the wall as possible until I'm standing side by side with the closet door. I can hear her labored breath. She hasn't been in a situation where she's had to fight for her life in a while, and I can't wait to make her beg for it.

The alarm turns itself off and I don't doubt that the relentless screeching has woken up every single person who lives in this estate, and I grin to myself, more than ready to tell anyone who will listen exactly what my mother has been up to. She'll never be able to show her face here again, but she shouldn't have to worry about that because I have no intention of allowing her to show her face anywhere ever again.

The softest creak sounds from within her closet and I smile to myself, shaking my head as she begins to move toward the door, assuming the coast is clear. The door slowly peels back, opening the closet but I remain still. After all, why would I go to her when she's so clearly going to come to me?

I see the gun first as she holds it out in front of her, quickly sweeping the room but failing to look all the way around. She steps out of the closet, silently tiptoeing as she goes to move toward the main bedroom door.

I step in behind her like a silent, deadly shadow and only when she catches my reflection in the dresser mirror does she scream and whirl around, her reflexes far too slow for me.

The gun flies toward my chest and my hand shoots out, gripping it tightly and disarming her before her scream has even completely faded from the room. She shrieks as I take her arms, forcing them behind her back and pushing forward until she slams against her bedroom wall, her face squished against the drywall as I spin her gun in my hand, knowing just how easily I could end this. "What the hell do you think you're doing, Dante?" she yells, the disappointment in her voice triggering that lost boy who lives inside of me. But unfortunately for her, I live to disappoint this bitch. "Get off me. This is insane."

I press into her, my fingers on her wrists, feeling the rapid beat of her pulse and knowing that despite the pissed-off glare on her face, she's shit scared. "You know what's insanity?" I question, ignoring her desperate pleas to be released. "A woman who allows a fucking psychopath to kidnap her daughters."

Her back straightens and although she knew she was in trouble before, she's now just realizing exactly how much. "Where did you get such ridiculous information? I would never allow such a thing. Who told you that?"

I laugh, bringing the gun up and pressing it against her temple. "You made my life hell. You and Dad. You were a joke, you still are, but I won't allow you to put my sisters through the same shit that you did to me," I tell her, my finger gently resting against the trigger and making her suck in a deep breath, fear pulsing from her eyes. "Are you or are you not working with Paris Moustaff?"

"Of course not," she shrieks. "That woman is delusional."

"Now, now," I mutter, moving in even closer. "You wouldn't lie to your only son, would you?"

Mom attempts to push back against me but gets nowhere. "This is insane, Dante. Release me now. I'm done with your silly game."

"Face the facts, Mother," I tell her, my voice dropping even lower and letting her know just how fucking serious I am. "I'm going to end you tonight. I'm going to take back my home and the girls and I will never have to suffer through your bullshit again. So, what's it going to be? Are you going to die a liar or are you going to be real for once and show your true colors?"

Ida clenches her jaw, the thought of someone calling her out for being a fraud not sitting well with her, despite the fact that's exactly who she is. "The girls were going to be fine," my mother spits, pulling against her wrists and trying to get free. "They needed to toughen up and Paris offered a perfect solution that helped us all. She was finally going to destroy that whore of yours and make up for what she did to your father, while also teaching your sisters some important life lessons. Everyone is a winner here. Two birds for the price of one. You cannot fault me for that."

"You've got to be kidding yourself," I exclaim, staring at her like a complete stranger. "They are your daughters. Fuck getting revenge for Dad, he fucking deserved what was coming for him, but letting Dominique and Danika get kidnapped? You're fucking crazy. They'll never get past it. They're still suffering. They're scared to be out in public."

"They're weak," she snaps. "Those girls were never going to survive in this world. They're hopeless, just like you were, but look at you now. You're stronger than anyone and you have me and your father to thank for that. We molded you into the perfect soldier for Dynasty just as I'm doing for Dominique and Danika. How dare you question my methods."

I scoff, having heard enough. "You deserve to rot in a fucking prison for the rest of your life, but lucky for you, I won't allow you to get that far." She swallows hard and I press the gun against her temple harder, pausing until she realizes that she's about to take her final breath. "Say hi to Royston for me."

My finger presses against the trigger and just as I go to squeeze down on it, a sharp cry comes from the bedroom door. "NOOOOOOOOOOO," Danika screams with Dominique hiding behind her shoulder, both of their eyes wide as they watch me prepare their mother for death.

Fuck. This isn't how I wanted this to go, but with them standing right there, there's no way in hell that I would ever pull the trigger. "Go back to your room," I tell them. "I told you to stay there until I came to get you."

Their eyes flicker between me and Mom, and while Dominique looks like she wants to run and hide, Danika just stands taller. "No," she says. "You can't kill her because then you'll be just as bad as she is, and you're not bad. You're not like them."

Dominique's head peeks out from behind Danika's shoulder with tears rolling down her cheeks. "Don't kill my mommy."

Fuck. Fuck. Fuck. FUCK.

I shake my head and meet their broken stares. "I'm sorry, girls, but I can't let her go," I tell them as this quickly becomes the hardest conversation that I will ever have. "She's done some terrible things, things that hurt people, that hurt you. I can't just let her go. She has to be punished."

Danika shakes her head and walks deeper into the room. She steps around me and without even a hint of hesitation, she reaches up and takes the gun out of my hand. "You can't kill her because you'll go to jail and we'll be left with no one."

I let out a sigh and keep my hand on Mom, I kneel down and take the gun back from Danika, hating how comfortable she is with it. I wrap her in my arm and pull her against my chest. "That'll never happen," I promise them, glancing at Dominique and indicating for her to come and join us. "So here's what we're going to do. We'll call a council meeting first thing in the morning and tell them what Mom has done, and the decision will be theirs. They may choose to put her in the Dynasty cells or they may decide to take her life, that's out of my hands, but just know that you two will always have a home with me. Always. Is that understood?"

The girls nod and I stand. "Alright then," I say, pulling my mother back away from the wall and looking down at the girls. "Go and pack your bags. You're going to stay with me."

# CHAPTER 29

My foot hits the bottom step and I turn into my kitchen to find Dominique and Danika Carver sitting at my breakfast bar, their older brother standing directly across from them as he pours them each a bowl of Lucky Charms. "Ummm …" I cut myself off, not really knowing what the hell I was going to say.

All three of them turn to face me and I can't help but notice the way the girls' eyes widen with excitement. "Dante said we could stay here," Danika rushes out, bursting away from the breakfast bar and racing toward me. "Oh, please let us stay. It'll only be for a little while until we can get our place fixed up."

"I … ummmm." I look up at Carver, my brows furrowed in confusion. "What?"

He smirks back at me, still going about his kitchen duties, popping a spoon in each of the bowls. "They kinda walked in on me with a gun to Ida's head and convinced me that she should stand trial instead of being executed on the spot. Soooo …. we sorta have a few house guests. At least, if that's okay with you. If it's too much, I can take them back to my place. We don't want to impose."

I stare at him blankly. "It's six in the morning," I say. "I haven't even had coffee."

Carver laughs and steps around the breakfast bar, walking straight into my arms and all but barging his sister aside as Cruz comes striding into the kitchen, not even noticing the two new miniature guests. "I don't want you to feel pressured into letting us stay. If you need some time to work it out, then that's fine. It's just … I'm all they've got now, but the thought of being away from you …"

"It's fine," I murmur, stretching up on my tippy toes. "I was just surprised to see them in my kitchen. No one heard you come in last night so we figured that you stayed there. If I knew you were bringing them back here, I would have stayed up and made up some rooms for them."

Carver pulls back and searches my eyes. "Are you sure?" he questions, his eyes filled with desperation.

I nod. "I've been the girl with nowhere to go. I know what it's like to lose everyone and not have a home to go back to. I don't want that for your sisters, but I also don't want you to be doing it alone. Little girls are hard, and it's going to be worse for you because there's two of them, but we'll figure it out."

Carver pulls me in close, his arms wrapping tightly around me as Cruz sails right up to the breakfast bar to find one of the cereal bowls ready to go. He grunts to himself as though he's just stumbled upon the best find of his life. A stupid grin pulls at his lips and he drops down at the breakfast bar and starts eating Dominique's Lucky Charms.

"Hey," she squeals, racing back to the breakfast bar and pummeling her fists against his thigh. "That's mine."

Cruz's eyes bug out of his head as he glances down at Dominique, looking at her as though she just came out of nowhere. "Where the fuck did you come from?" he rushes out, his head whipping up to find Danika by my side. "Fuck, there's two of you. Have you been here all morning?"

Danika grins wide and her eyes sparkle as though she's got the biggest crush in the world. "Uh-huh. Elodie said we can stay here now."

Cruz raises his brows and looks up at me in surprise before glancing across at Carver with a questioning stare. "I'm assuming that means things didn't go so well last night?"

Carver grunts, shrugging his shoulders as he moves back to the breakfast bar to make another bowl of cereal for Dominique. "Things were going fine until these two stopped me," he explains. "Ida admitted everything and I was ready to end it, but the girls didn't want me to be like them. So, Ida's down in the cells and will face trial instead."

King appears from the other side of the room, his bare chest dripping with sweat and his shirt dangling out of his pants pocket. "You realize that means they could vote for an execution," King mutters, clearly having heard the whole conversation as he stops by the fridge for a bottle of water. "Whether or not it was their decision, they will always feel guilty for that and that's a lot of weight to put on their shoulders."

"It wouldn't be on their shoulders," Carver explains. "Always mine, and I'm okay with that. Besides, we talked about it last night and they understand that their mother did some bad things, and when they're old enough, if they still want to know, I'll explain it to them."

The boys nod, realizing that there are about to be some pretty big changes around here, but they're changes for the better.

I make my way into the kitchen and step in behind Carver, wrapping my arms around his waist and plastering my face against his back. "So, does this mean I should call you 'Daddy' now?" I tease, a grin stretching across my face.

"No," Dominique says. "Dante is our brother not our daddy."

I laugh and shuffle myself beside Carver, leaning onto the counter and stealing a piece of toast that's been left in the middle of all the bowls. I glance up at Dominique and wink as an even wider grin stretches across my lips. "Speak for yourself, girl."

Her brows furrow but the conversation is dropped when Carver slams his hip against mine, sending me flying halfway across the kitchen and smacking right into King.

Grayson comes into the kitchen, dragging his feet in annoyance. "What's all this fucking noise? It's ..." his gaze sweeps to the little digital clock on the front of the oven and his eyes bug out of his head before irritation crosses his features and he starts to mope. "It's barely even six in the fucking morning."

"There, there, big guy," I laugh, resting my hand against his raven tattoo and giving him a pity pat. "If the rest of us are up, then you're up too."

"It was my one day to sleep in," he mutters as I pass him, his words fading into silence as he sees the girls sitting up at the breakfast bar, fighting with Cruz over who has the biggest spoon, though if they really want to know, it's Grayson, always Grayson. "Umm … we have new friends?"

Carver restarts the long-winded explanation that I feel like I've already heard a million times by now, and as I cross the kitchen and find my brand-new coffee machine, I feel a little hand on the bottom of my tank, giving it a yank and demanding my attention. "Do we really get to stay here with you?" Dominique asks me, making Danika's gaze shoot to mine, her curiosity far too great.

I give Dominique a soft smile and crouch down while pointing at Danika and telling her to get her little butt over here. The girls stand before me and I study their perfect little faces, assuming that if Carver and I were ever to have kids that they'd look just like this. "Do you two really want to stay here?" I question, watching as their faces light with excitement.

Danika nods her head so violently that I fear it might fall straight off. "We do," she tells me. "We really do."

"Well you should know that I have a few rules at my place," I explain, watching as the excitement quickly drains from their faces, but they remain standing before me, determined to know the new rules that they'll be living by. "Number one," I start, nodding toward their big brother. "He needs to be woken up at five in the morning every single day to make us a fancy breakfast."

Their grins quickly return and they each step in a little closer, more than ready to know the rest of my house rules. "Number two," I continue. "I need to have at least three in-house fashion shows a week and I better be included because I have a killer closet with a million new outfits and no excuses to wear them."

The girls giggle, gaining all the guys' attention and leaving them more than curious about our conversation. "What was I up to?" I ask them, the boys' stares instantly distracting me.

"Rule number three," Dominique reminds me.

"Right, rule number three," I say, fighting a smile. "Now, this is the important one, are you listening carefully?" I pause and watch as they nod, their eyes wide with anticipation. "Rule number three is that any and all tantrums must be taken to Grayson."

They both laugh and shoot their little stares back at the guy in question. "Why Grayson?" Danika asks.

I indicate for them to come in nice and close so I can whisper in their ears. "Because he'll never admit it, but Grayson is actually really scared of girls."

Their eyes bug out of their heads and they crack into undeniable laughter. "So, if you can stick to my three rules, then I don't see why we can't all live here as one big, happy family. Do we have a deal?"

The girls nod and instantly rush back to Carver, pulling on his pants and telling him all about my rules to all the boys' horror, but as they're just starting to explain rule number three, my phone rings on the table and my gaze shifts to Carver, already knowing what this is about.

I grab the phone and bring it to my ear. "Hello."

"Miss Ravenwood," Earnest Brooks says. "I'm sorry to disturb your morning, however we have issues that need tending to."

"Issues?"

Earnest lets out a deep sigh. "Ida Carver has shown up in our cells this morning with a horrifying confession that needs to be discussed. I suggest that we get this over and done with quickly before news of this begins to spread through Dynasty."

"Of course," I tell him. "I'll get King and Carver and we'll meet in the council chambers in twenty minutes."

Earnest ends the call and I look up at Carver, concern flooding my gaze. "Are you ready for this?" I question, not needing to explain what was said.

His gaze flashes to his sisters who remain completely clueless to the tension now spreading through the room. "I just want it done," Carver tells me before finishing his glass of orange juice and stalking straight out of the room.

Twenty minutes later, I sit in the council chambers, my gaze skirting around the table that's actually full for the first time in months. I'm not going to lie, both new guys look way too fresh and excited to be here. If only they knew what was about to happen.

"Thank you all for being here so early in the morning," I say, noticing that more than just one of the men around me look as though they've just rolled out of bed. "However there have been some startling revelations overnight and this meeting simply could not wait."

Earnest stands, prepared to explain what he saw this morning when I hold up a hand to silence him. "If you don't mind," I say, indicating for him to take his seat. "I am already completely up to date with the situation and I believe it only to be fair that Dante Carver be the one to run this morning's briefing."

Earnest clenches his jaw, hating not being the one running the show as he reluctantly turns his attention to Carver who stands and glances around the table like the true leader that he is.

I press my lips into a tight line as Brooks sulks beside me and I'm forced to look away to avoid laughing at his pitiful display, only I catch King's stare who perfectly reads exactly what's going through my mind and only makes my struggle harder.

Carver's gaze falls back to mine and just like that, it's all business. "Roughly six hours ago, Ember Harding was found beaten and bruised by the main gate of our estate. She was taken back to the Ravenwood mansion and her wounds were taken care of. She explained that she had been beaten under the instruction of Paris Moustaff, her biological mother, after a failed attempt on Elodie's life."

"How is this relevant?" Harlen Beckett questions. "Ember Harding is no longer our problem."

Carver's irritated glare snaps to the man who is no doubt going to cause us problems one day. "If you had a little patience, you would find out. Your interruption is only wasting everyone's time, including your own."

Harlen glares straight back at him and if we were anywhere but here, I don't doubt that he would have pulled a gun on Carver for the way he spoke to him, but it wouldn't have done him any good anyway. Carver would have just turned the situation around and had Harlen on his knees, begging for his life.

Carver continues. "In exchange for her life, Ember offered up what little information she had. In doing so, she brought my mother, Ida Carver, into the mix."

"How so?" Mr. Danforth questions, his chin raised and eyes narrowed in curiosity.

"Ember explained that my mother has been working with Paris since the beginning, just as my father had been." Gasps sound around the room but Carver doesn't stop. "My mother was accused of knowing that the kidnapping was going to take place and voluntarily helping in the process."

Earnest shakes his head beside me. "That doesn't make sense. Her own children were taken."

Carver nods. "I'm very well aware of that and refused to believe it myself. However, I have a whole childhood of abuse which suggests that Ida Carver is more than capable, and when confronted about it last night, she didn't just confirm Ember's accusations, she insisted that it was for her children's own personal growth."

"That's absurd," Mr. Danforth demands, flying to his feet in anger. "My sons are struggling to sleep at night. They have been scarred from the whole experience. How on earth was that supposed to encourage personal growth? Her girls are still babies and barely able to understand what happened. It would have terrified them."

"It did. They haven't been adjusting well at all. Public outings have them scared, they can't be alone in the dark, and they have had to learn the hard way that sometimes the people we love are capable of the worst actions against us," he says, making my heart break for everything he's had to go through during his childhood. I had it bad, jumping from home to home, but sometimes it's the ones who we think have it all who are suffering the most. "Late last night, I stormed the Carver residence and confronted my mother. After her confirmation of her involvement in the kidnappings, I had every intention of executing her, however my sisters were there and refused to allow me to do so. They begged to allow their mother the chance to stand trial and I refuse to give them a reason not to trust me."

"So, you were the one who broke into our cells and deposited Ida?" Earnest questions.

Carver nods and not another word is said about the cells.

"Alright," I say as Carver takes his seat. "I don't believe that Ida is entitled to our time this morning. Her confession has already been made. Does anybody disagree?" Heads shake all around the table and I continue on. "Very well, then we shall take a vote on how to deal with the situation. Do we adopt that same callous nature and execute her for her involvement with Paris Moustaff and the recent kidnappings, or do we show her kindness and allow her to live the rest of her miserable life in our cells? I'll give you all a moment to consider the options."

A minute passes and then another. "Is everybody firm with their decision, or do you need a few more moments?"

"Ready to go, Miss Ravenwood," Matthew Montgomery says from across the table.

No objections come from around the table and I quickly get on with it. "All in favor to allow Ida Carver to spend her days in our cells, locked up until we decide otherwise?"

Hands begin rising around the table, heads flicking from side to side as everybody tries to gauge how one another is voting. Carver's hand remains down, as does King's, Mr. Danforth's, and Harlen Beckett's, all the men whose children were affected by the kidnappings. I keep my own down, wanting to stand by Carver in this, but the numbers are against us and even before continuing, we all know how this is going to go.

"Thank you," I say. "All in favor of a private execution?"

The five hands, including my own, raise high and we quickly lower them back down. "The votes are in. Ida Carver will remain in the cells until we, as a group, decide that she should be let free. That concludes this morning's meeting and you may all be excused to go back to your families."

I turn to Earnest who packs up the papers that he'd prepared for today, the papers which definitely weren't needed. "Please see to it that Ida has the basic necessities that she requires for a long-term stay in our cells and ensure that we have a guard on duty around the clock."

"Yes, ma'am," he says, and just like that, scurries away to get it done.

I stand and find Carver still seated at the table, looking completely deflated. I make my way over to him and prop my ass against the table as King discreetly leaves the room, giving us a moment of privacy. "You were hoping for a different outcome?" I question, picking his hand up off the table and holding it in my lap.

Carver shakes his head and lets out a deep breath. "I honestly have no fucking idea what I was hoping for. I want her dead for the things she's done to me and the girls, but—"

"No matter how you look at it, she's still your mom and it makes you feel like the worst kind of human being for wishing her dead."

"Yeah," he mutters. "Something like that."

"You've got to look at the silver lining," I tell him. He raises his chin and meets my stare with a look of disbelief etched across his gorgeous face, clearly believing that there's no such thing as a silver lining in this situation. "Despite how you voted, your sisters' wishes were honored, and I know you don't see it now, but in five or ten years they're going to come to you wanting to know more about what went down here. They're going to want answers about why she got locked up and they're going to go through all these shitty emotions that you're going through now, and when that happens, you'll be able to offer them retribution."

He watches me for a moment, his brows furrowed. "That's why you kept saying 'until we decide otherwise.' You added a loophole."

A smile stretches across my face and I watch as Carver stares back at me in awe. "I don't know what you're talking about."

He shakes his head and stands, laughing as he pulls me into him, wrapping his strong arms around my body and holding me close. "Fuck, I love you," he says, crushing his lips on mine. "You never cease to amaze me."

He pulls back and I grin up at him, my eyes sparkling. "Right back at ya, asshole," I tease. "Now, do me a favor and hold on to all that pent up rage because we've got a date at the school tonight and I've never been so excited."

Carver's hand drops to mine and he leads me out of the room, holding the door open for me. And as I pass by him, a questioning look flickers through his eyes. "Do you think Cruz will do me a solid and let me take the big finale into my own hands tonight?"

King laughs, waiting for us on the other side, catching the tail end of our conversation. "Not a fucking chance."

# CHAPTER 30

Dianna Danforth barges through the dining room doors as I'm tightening the leather holster around my thigh. Her eyes narrow on the blueprints spread over the table. "Do I want to know why you have blueprints to Ravenwood Heights Academy?"

Cruz laughs, jamming a gun into the back of his pants to his mother's dismay. "Trust me, it's better for your sanity if you just pretend that you didn't even see us tonight."

Dianna rolls her eyes and meets her son's stare. "Be careful, Cruz. I've already filled my funeral quota this year. I don't need to attend anymore." She strides past me and squeezes my hand. "Same goes for you, Elodie. You didn't come this far to allow their stupidity to catch you out. Play it safe and when in doubt, duck."

I laugh and give her a warm smile. "That sounds like the best advice I've gotten since coming here, but you don't need to worry about me. I'll be safe. I've got too much to lose."

Dianna looks between me and Cruz and a warm smile settles over her lips. "You sure do," she says, walking back the way she came. "Now, do you have any popcorn in this house? I'm not going to be able to rest until I know you're all home safe and a girlfriend told me about this new show everyone is raving about on Netflix. What was it called again?" she muses, murmuring to herself. "Ahh, yes. Sex/Life. Apparently, it's a lovely historical romance. I thought I could watch a few episodes of that while the girls slept."

My brows fly up and Cruz nearly dies of embarrassment. He's well aware of the show I forced the guys to watch with me last week. "Oh yeah," I tell her, knowing damn well that it's so much more than just a lovely historical romance, well it's not historical at all, but if you want to be technical, the characters do talk about the past a lot, so really, there's no need to correct her. "I've seen that. It's perfect for a night home alone. You're going to love it, though be sure to really pay attention in episode three."

Cruz turns his back, hanging his head as he tries to become one with himself, breathing slowly and desperately trying to control his urge to go and wrap his mother in bubble wrap and not allow her to live any kind of life outside her respectable housewife duties.

Dianna walks out of the room, determined to find some popcorn before divulging in Sex/Life and corrupting her sweet, pure mind with the realities of great sex. Though she's married to Cruz's father and if he's anything like his son, then perhaps Dianna already knows a thing or two about great sex.

The boys and I get our shit together, getting everything we'll need for tonight and going over our plan one more time before slipping out of the dining room and making our way toward the door, going as quietly as we can so as to not wake the girls upstairs.

My fingers curl around the door handle when a soft voice cuts through the silence. "Where are you going?"

We all freeze, catching our breath and slowly turning to find Dominique standing behind us, her long nightgown skirting against the marble tiles as her teddy hangs from her hand.

Carver looks down at her, trying to figure out a nice way to explain that we're about to go and put a bullet in someone's head, just as we should have done last night until I decided to take pity on Ember. "Uhh, we … ummm. We're just going to deal with a bad guy."

Her gaze travels over my tight leather and her eyes widen as though she's just figured out a secret. "Like The Avengers?"

"Yeah," Carver laughs. "Exactly like that, but we can't go unless I know you're tucked safely in bed."

She nods quickly and turns on her heel, racing back up the stairs, going so fast that I worry she's either going to wind herself or fall face-first into the hard steps, but she makes it to the top and within moments, we hear the loud thud of her bedroom door slamming closed. "I'M IN BED," she yells at the top of her voice, the sound traveling through the whole damn house and surely waking her sister.

"Shit," Carver cringes. "We should get out of here before the other one comes looking for me."

The five of us scurry out of the house and hurry down the front steps until we're barreling into the Escalade. Carver starts the engine and within moments, we're racing down the long drive toward the gate. Cruz sits beside me, hardly able to sit still in excitement as King sits on my other side with a smirk stretched over his delicious lips.

There's no doubt about it—tonight we're getting our hands dirty and I can't fucking wait.

The drive to the school takes no time at all and by the time we're approaching the familiar front gates, I've hardly had a chance to calm the wild excitement pulsing through my veins. Carver turns off his headlights, concealing us under the cover of darkness as he bypasses the school and brings the Escalade to a stop on a side street.

The guys pour out of the car, and as I go to follow Cruz out the door, Grayson reaches through from the front seat, gripping my wrists and pulling me back. "Have you got everything you need?"

My hand falls to my thigh, feeling the knife that was stashed there before we left, then I check my opposite hip for the gun that the guys insisted on. "Yep," I tell him, nodding as I take a second to breathe and push the excitement aside. Despite what's going to happen tonight, it's still a life-or-death situation and we have to be cautious. "I'm ready."

He nods and releases my wrists. "Good."

I scoot out of the Escalade and close the door behind me, and without another word, the five of us take off toward the school. I break off with King, heading right for the front gates, while the others all split off in opposite directions, making a wide grin stretch across my face. This is going to be too good.

The main lights of the school are all out, but the pathways, front gate, and security lights are all shining brightly around the school, so we're forced to stick to the shadows.

King and I reach the front gate and I can't help but notice the way that his sharp gaze travels around the school, taking in our surroundings and making sure that we're the only threats here tonight. The gates are chained and bolted just as we expected. Without hesitation, King bends down and makes a brace with his hands.

My foot slips into his hands and he catapults me up the gate. I grab hold and hoist myself over the top, dropping back to the ground with a soft thud, and not a second later, King comes down beside me with a cocky smirk playing on his lips. He winks and I roll my eyes knowing that he's only seconds away from mentioning how he was able to get over the gate without someone else's help, but before he can, I take off, dashing toward the massive school.

We keep close to the main building and King points out toward the student parking lot where we can see Grayson rushing across the pavement and heading toward the back of the school. I blink a few times, watching him go in amazement. "Fuck, he's fast."

"Mmhmm," King murmurs, keeping his tone hushed as we reach the closest classroom. He immediately starts working the window, jimmying it open just enough for us to slip inside. "Carver and Cruz should be just getting where they're meant—" A light flashes toward us and a devilish grin cuts across King's face. "Uh-huh, there they are."

I look up ahead and find Carver standing by the back entrance of the building furthest away from the gymnasium while Cruz approaches the midway point. Grayson hurries into position, and with us standing at the top of the school, we have all exits covered. We're almost positive that Knox is staying in the gymnasium to be close to the amenities and food, but we're not about to fuck this up by not double checking the rest of the school first.

"Let's fucking do this shit," I tell King, and just like that, King takes my waist and all but launches me up through the open window.

We make quick work of our search, not leaving a single classroom unchecked. The bottom floor is cleared and we meet Grayson at the stairs. Carver and Cruz take the rear stairs and as one, we make our way up to the second level.

We check all the classrooms as Carver and Cruz move further down the hall toward the staff areas and quickly disappear. Trusting them to do their thing, we finish our search, and after what feels like far too long, King, Grayson, and I finally start making the trek back to the gymnasium.

It's late, and assuming Knox doesn't have a whole artillery of entertainment to keep him occupied into the late hours of the night, I'm assuming that he's already tucked himself away into his makeshift bed, probably spooning a fucking basketball.

The gymnasium has three exits. Two that lead out into the world and one internal exit that leads toward the locker room, so the boys and I cover the external ones. I stick with Grayson as King rushes around the outside of the building.

There's a heavy chain sitting on the floor by the door and I meet Grayson's stare, a devilish smirk cutting across my face as Grayson holds back a grin of his own. "Ready for this?"

"Hell yeah."

We don't waste a second. Grayson curls his fingers around the handle and presses his hip against the huge door, creating a gap just big enough to slip inside.

The gymnasium is massive, and with bleachers rising to the ceiling on both sides, the acoustics are perfect for spirited ballgames and graduations. Though now, as the cold and cavernous room is shrouded in darkness, it feels like another world entirely.

There's nothing to suggest that Knox has been staying here other than the fucking chain on the ground by the door. I'm sure he had some grand escape route planned for that unlocked exit, but he's not the sharpest tool in the shed.

A sliver of dull moonlight shines across the gymnasium, lighting up the basketball hoop at the end of the court. I glance up just in time to watch King slip in through the other entrance. He meets my stare and nods before silently closing the door behind him and letting the gymnasium fall into complete darkness.

My gaze shifts toward the storeroom and the anticipation burns within me. I can't fucking wait.

The power to the school is cut and I grin wide, knowing that Carver and Cruz are exactly where they're meant to be. I flick my stare between the guys and keep my voice down low. "Let's haunt this motherfucker."

Without another word, both Grayson and King's hands curl around the massive locks on the door, shoving them hard and letting the heavy metal slide into place. The sound is like nails on a chalkboard as the locks fall into position with loud BANGS that echo through the gymnasium, the sound rocking right through me.

The storeroom door swings open and Knox comes tearing out wide-eyed. "WHO'S THERE?" he wails through the gymnasium, his tone bouncing off the walls and echoing around the open space.

We remain silent, and without skipping a beat, King hits play on his Bluetooth speaker, and a woman's loud, ear-piercing scream tears through the gymnasium. She cries and shrieks, her tone so terrifying that it sends chills down my spine.

Knox panics, backing up against the door he'd just come barreling out of, his gaze flicking around the room but coming up blank.

He runs to the door that Grayson has just bolted and grips the lock, desperately trying to pull it back, but it's no use. It won't budge. He turns around, frantically trying to figure out who stands around him in the dark, but we're giving away absolutely no clues.

The screeching woman intensifies as a low shallow laugh tears through the room, sounding like a fucking horror movie. The man catches up to the woman and the scream that tears out of her is enough to make me want to throw up.

He laughs louder and the sound is absolutely chilling. "WHO'S THERE?" Knox demands, the panic in his tone making everything seem so freaking right in the world.

All at once, the guys and I reach into our pockets and hold the little LED strobe lights that Cruz had lying around in his garage, and as we turn them on, we start running. Light bounces off every corner in the room, a horrifying contrast against the darkness as the sound of our shoes slap against the basketball court.

Knox's head whips around, unsure where to look and only now just realizing that there's more than one person in the room. "WHO'S THERE?" he wails again, his terror making me feel all kinds of good inside.

King's speakers kick up a notch and the laughing only gets louder as the woman tries to fight him off. There's one big BANG and everything goes quiet. We stop moving and the strobe lights turn off, sending the room back into complete darkness as the silence surrounds us.

I grin wide, struggling to hold back my sick laughs, and just when Knox pushes off the door and goes to bolt across the room, the horrifying sound of the man butchering the woman sounds through the room, her screams fading as she chokes on her own blood. "NO," Knox yells. "LEAVE ME ALONE."

All at once we move again, the bright white strobe lights flashing through the room. Knox screams and runs for the third exit, the one we left open for him. We chase after him just as the man over the speaker was doing to the woman.

As we cut through the narrow hallway leading to the locker room, we cut our lights and the sound, letting Knox hear nothing but the noise of our feet slapping against the linoleum as we race behind him, quickly gaining as he looks back over his shoulder, desperate to figure out who's here, but if he hasn't worked out who's after him yet, that's his own fault.

Knox breaks into the boys' locker room and we come to a silent standstill as we listen to his loud panting that bounces off the walls. King stops behind me and grabs the metal door, letting it clang shut with a loud BANG, and again, I'm more than impressed with the acoustics of this school.

I take the knife from my holster and press the sharp tip against the closest locker and step up onto the bench that lines the row of lockers. Putting one foot in front of the other, I move along the bench, the tip of my knife dragging along the metal, the sound chilling and cold. Knox backs up toward the showers, his hands pressing against the wall behind him to feel his way through the locker room.

King and Grayson begin to stalk him, their own low terrifying laughs echoing deep into the room and making me thankful that it's not me on the receiving end of this because I sure as fuck would have shit my pants by now.

The scraping of my knife gets louder, and as Knox takes another step back, the shower behind him turns on, the water shooting out on full pressure. Knox's head whips to the showers, straining to see through the darkness, but not a moment later, a second shower turns on, and then a third and fourth. One by one until all eight showers are on, their combined water pressure vibrating through the walls of the boys locker room.

Knox frets, hyperventilating with each quick and ragged pant as he makes a break for it and runs back through the locker room, realizing just how outmatched he is.

Grayson catches him by his arm and throws him right back where he was and I drop down from the bench, sticking my landing with a low thud in front of him. "Someone's been a naughty boy," I taunt, keeping my voice low as I move forward and continue to stalk him with the boys, forcing him back toward the showers until I feel the spray of the water bouncing up and hitting my legs.

"Please," Knox begs, his voice breaking as sobs overtake him. "I'll do anything. Please."

Cruz and Carver step into his back, each of them gripping his arms and yanking him back into the heavy spray of the water. He screams, absolutely terrified and making my darkened little heart shine with joy. "Begging is not going to help you now," Cruz tells him, his tone filled with a sick happiness.

Four spotlights shine through the showers, lighting up Knox like a performer on stage and creating the perfect canvas.

"I swear," Knox sobs as the water streams over his face, plastering his hair to his unshaven jaw, the light finally allowing us to see just how deep the fear runs. "I'll make it up to you. I'll do anything you want."

Cruz looks up at me, his eyes sparkling with excitement. "I believe you have a score to settle too?"

I grin wide, letting the love pour out of me as I look back at Cruz. I wasn't expecting such a nice surprise tonight. I thought I was just along for the ride and to show my support of Cruz as he finally gets even. I settled my score months ago when I beat the living shit out of him for offering me up to his uncle, Sam Delacourt. I was kidnapped and trafficked, but the guys saved me, other girls though, they weren't so lucky. Yet here Cruz is, offering me to settle that score all over again, and I don't think I have the heart to say no.

I step up in front of Knox, my gaze shifting over his body as I try to work out what exactly I should do to settle my score. "Winter, no," Knox begs. "Please. Don't do this. I don't want to die."

Carver rips his arm straight back and Knox cries out. "You don't get to talk to her."

Knox swallows hard and I step in a little closer, a sick grin stretching across my lips. "Don't worry," I murmur. "This isn't going to hurt … much."

I spin my knife between my fingers and reach up toward Knox's wrist and Grayson hovers in close behind me. "Careful," he warns. "You don't want to get the artery because he'll bleed out and we want this to last all night long."

I study Knox's wrists. "Where then?"

Grayson leans around me and uses his fingernail to trace exactly where I should be slicing. "Right here," he tells me. "Not too deep, though. Just make him bleed."

I nod and concentrate on what I'm doing, feeling like some kind of medical student taking notes from her superior, and once I've gone over it a few times in my head, I slash out with my knife, letting the sharp tip slice through Knox's skin like butter.

Knox cries out and blood pours from the wound, splashing to the ground and mixing with the water. "Wow," I say, watching the swirls of crimson dance around the drain. "Look at all that evidence just disappearing right down the drain."

Carver and Cruz hold him still, and as I move toward his other wrist, I notice the hungry way that the guys watch me, and fuck, I don't think I've ever been so turned on.

Cruz holds his other wrist out, offering it up to me like a gift. I don't hesitate as I bring my knife down again, watching as the blood splatters from the wound. I suck in a breath, the blood flow is too much. I whip around to Grayson. "Did I get the artery?"

He nods. "Yep," he says as Cruz adjusts his grip on Knox's wrist to plug the wound and keep the bastard alive for just a moment longer, at least until we're finished playing with him.

I turn back to Cruz and cringe. "Sorry, I got a little too excited."

He winks. "It's fine, babe," he tells me. "It was the fucking sexiest thing I've ever seen. You can make it up to me when I get you home."

"Really?" I smile, all but batting my lashes as blood mixes with the water at our feet, creating quite the show.

The guys grin, and realizing that we're going to have to speed up the process, they get to work beating the shit out of Knox while Cruz plugs the wound just enough to keep him from passing out. When Knox can barely keep himself standing, Cruz releases his wrist and moves in directly behind him, the excitement in his eyes making me come alive inside.

Cruz takes Knox's head in his hands and slowly begins to turn, pushing it past its limits as we all watch in anticipation. Knox cries, knowing what comes next, but the few times that I've seen someone's neck being snapped, it's been a quick process. I've never quite seen it like this, and damn, it's almost like Knox gets to come along for the ride, feeling every last moment as death pounds on his door.

"NO. DON'T DO IT," Knox cries, his eyes wide as Cruz turns his head just that little bit further, snapping the tendons and ligaments that line his neck. He screams in agony, the sound bouncing off the walls of the showers, and just as Cruz has drained every last ounce of fear out of Knox, he violently twists, nearly spinning Knox's head right off his shoulders and snapping his neck like a fucking twig.

# CHAPTER 31

Knox's body falls to the ground, the bloodied water splashing up around us as I breathe heavily, staring at Cruz as though I just discovered a whole new part of him that I never knew existed. "Holy shit," I pant, barely able to control my reaction to him. "That was hot."

Cruz grins and moves directly under the spray of water, letting Knox's blood rinse from his skin. "You liked that?"

I move toward him, stepping right over Knox's fallen body, completely enraptured by Cruz's dark side. My hand falls to his chest, feeling the rapid beat of his heart, but something tells me that it's not racing because of the guy he just killed, but solely because of the way I'm looking at him as though he's my whole damn world. "Loved it," I whisper, raising my chin.

Cruz's lips crush down on mine and I kiss him deeply, our bodies pressing together as Grayson and King move in behind me and lift Knox's limp body out of the water. They disappear out of the shower area and I hear them around the side, opening and closing lockers. There's a strange gurgling sound but I ignore it and let it fade into the distance as Cruz's hand trails down my back and squeezes my ass.

I moan into his mouth, needing him like never before, but all too soon, his hands are at my waist spinning me around, pressing my back against his chest as his lips fall to my neck.

I tilt my head, allowing him better access as his hands wrap around my body, one hand moving up to grip my tits, cupping and squeezing as his other sails down the wet leather and slides between my legs. His fingers rub against my pussy and I grind down against them, desperately wishing that I was already stripped bare and his thick cock was slamming inside of me.

A third hand plays at my collar bone and slowly trails down between my tits and I open my eyes, finding Carver standing before me, his gaze focused heavily on my body. I keep grinding against Cruz's hand and Carver watches, the hunger in his eyes telling me that I won't be going anywhere tonight until he's come hard and had my taste on his tongue.

The undeniable pleasure rocks through me, and I close my eyes, needing nothing more than to just feel their hands on my body. "Touch me," I beg Carver.

He doesn't hesitate, moving in closer and letting me feel his warmth washing over me. Carver reaches out and grips my tank in both hands before tearing the fabric right down the center. A soft gasp pulls from deep within me and my eyes fly open, watching as he peels the tank away and drops it into the bloody water at our feet. He doesn't waste a second, stealing the knife from my thigh and slicing straight through the center of my bra to free my tits.

Cruz grinds behind me, snaking one hand up and pinching my pert nipple between his fingers, rubbing and teasing as fire builds within me, each touch sending a jolt of electricity shooting straight down to my aching cunt. "Fuck," I breathe, tipping my head back to Cruz's shoulder as his tongue works over the sensitive skin on my neck. "I need you both to fuck me. I don't want to wait."

I feel Cruz's smile against my neck as Carver's fingers dig into the front of my pants, working the complicated clasp with ease. I kick my boots off, sending them sailing across the locker room and the second they're gone, Carver yanks the tight leather down my legs, letting me feel the cool air against my pussy.

I gasp, the anticipation quickly building inside of me. I reach for Carver's shirt and pull it over his head, loving the sight of his perfect tanned body against his low riding jet-black pants. Add that fucking sexy as sin smirk and the hooded gaze and I'm a fucking goner.

I reach back and grip Cruz's shirt, not able to pull it off from this angle, but he reads my thoughts as though they're stamped across my skin. "Lose it," I demand. "I need to feel you."

His shirt is gone before the words are even out of my mouth and as his chest presses back into me, I feel the tight ridges of his abs against my back.

Cruz reaches between us and unbuckles his belt, but he doesn't need to do much more than that as the weight of his pants pulls them straight down, freeing his cock against my back. His fingers trail down the front of my body and I groan as they press down against my clit. He rubs tight little circles as I catch my breath, his touch making me flinch as the pleasure rocks through me.

Carver shuffles back a step and I watch as his hands fall to his pants, completely mesmerized by the sight before me. As if in slow motion, he pushes his pants down past his narrow hips and his thick, waiting cock springs free, aiming right at me like a fucking arrow desperate to find its target, and fuck me, I've never been so happy to be a target.

Cruz grips my ass and bends me over, the anticipation almost killing me as he takes his time sliding his thick fingers deep inside my cunt and mixing with my wetness. As he pulls them back, a soft cry escapes my lips. But within a moment, his fingers are against my ass, teasing and preparing me for what he has in store.

I groan as he adjusts himself behind me and presses the tip of his cock against my ass. My eyes remain on Carver's, and despite him not being able to see what's going on behind me, he knows, and fuck, the way his tongue rolls over his lips as he watches me gets me so fucking hot.

Not being able to wait, I push back against Cruz and gasp as he enters me, stretching me wide and filling me completely. His fingers find my hips and he squeezes hard as I straighten myself up, spreading my legs wider to feel him right where I want him. "Fuck, Winter," Cruz groans through a clenched jaw. "I fucking love your sweet ass."

His words send a smile soaring over my lips and I look back over my shoulder, needing to see the satisfaction on his face. "Then fuck me, Cruz."

He starts to move and as Carver steps back into me, I grab hold of his shoulder, needing something to brace myself against. "Oh, fuck," I moan, but it only gets better as Carver drops to his knees on the flooded shower floor, nearly all the blood completely gone.

His eyes linger on mine and I watch his tongue rolling over his lips, knowing that whatever the fuck he does to me now is going to blow my fucking mind. Carver leans into me and his mouth closes over my clit as Cruz pounds into my ass, fucking me as the high of Knox's death pulses through his veins.

Carver's tongue works my clit and I dig my fingers into his shoulders, the pleasure making my eyes roll back into my head. Cruz's strong arm curls around my waist, holding me up as the water rushes down over us. "Holy shit," I gasp, the intensity coming out of nowhere and shooting through my body. "Fuck, fuck, fuck. YES."

Gasps, pants, and breathy cries come tearing out of me as I clench my eyes, needing everything they've got. But hell, I'm not even sure I can handle everything they've got. They're fucking gods and my body is their religion, and fuck, they love to worship.

Carver's tongue flicks over my clit going back and forth, around and a-fucking-round, but it doesn't stop there. His lips and teeth get in on the action, making reality fade away and leaving me riding high as I drown in endless pools of pure sensual pleasure. I glance down and I can't help but notice the way his fist is wrapped around his cock, slowly stroking as his relentless tongue works my clit. I'd give anything to replace his hand with my own, hell even my mouth, but it'll have to wait. Besides, there's no rush. We have all the time in the world. No one is looking for us here.

My hand crushes down over Cruz's at my hip as he groans my name, the sweetest sound I'll ever hear, and as Carver's tongue flicks over my clit again, two figures appear by the entrance of the shower, their brows arched and their cocks straining through the front of their pants.

Holy. Fuck. Are we finally going to do this? All five of us together? This has been my ultimate dream from the very moment I met them, but surely I'm not that lucky. Surely it couldn't get any better than what they've already offered me.

I don't doubt that Grayson and King heard everything that's been going on in here as they've been dealing with Knox's body. Waiting has probably killed them, but if they don't hurry up and get in here, it might just kill me instead.

King doesn't hesitate. His shirt is gone in seconds, and as he moves toward us, his hands fall to his belt. King moves in beside me, his eyes lingering over my skin, mesmerized by the soft bounce of my tits as Cruz fucks my ass. His cock is in his hand in moments, squeezing his tip before sailing his tight fist all the way down to his thick base.

"Let me," I pant, the words coming out as a strangled cry.

I reach down and take his thick cock in my hand and his fingers curl over mine, controlling the speed as we sail up and down his velvety skin together. King groans and I can't help but notice the way that he watches both Cruz and Carver as they work my body from both the front and back.

Grayson on the other hand, he likes to watch. He likes to take in all the sights before divulging in our wicked little games, but that doesn't stop him from stripping down and putting that beautiful raven tattoo on display as his heavy cock springs free from his pants and dangles low between his legs, his piercing softly sparkling against the harsh bright spotlights.

Grayson moves in close, but not close enough to touch, and for the slightest moment, I want to curse him until his dying days, but Carver's tongue twitches against my clit and I scream out, my eyes rolling back as my grip tightens on King's cock.

King groans and I feel Carver's grin against my clit, the fucking prick. Then as if my body isn't already wound up, his fingers slip in below his chin and before I even know what he's doing, his thick fingers are pushing up inside of me, massaging my walls and finding my G-spot almost immediately.

My eyes roll to the back of my head and my body gives out, unable to hold on to it anymore. I shatter around his fingers as I clench down around Cruz, my pussy violently convulsing as my orgasm tears through me. King groans, the softness of the sound wrapping around me and only making it that much more intense.

Carver doesn't let up on my clit and my whole body goes weak. Without Cruz holding me up, I'd be a fucking puddle on the ground. It becomes too much and I have no choice but to press against his wide shoulder and push him back just a bit. If he were to keep going, I know I would crumble, and I'm not nearly finished with them yet.

Realizing that I need a moment to find myself, Cruz eases up and slows his movements, giving me a chance to come back down to earth. His fingers rest around my waist and slowly creep back up to my tits, the soft movement against my skin sending goosebumps sailing right over me.

As I come down from my high, I press back against Cruz, taking him deeper, but as Carver gets off his knees, a darkness flashes through his eyes. He's only just getting started. He steps in closer to me and pushes me back against Cruz, making him lean back against the shower wall.

Carver grabs my thighs and lifts me up, going slowly so as to not break Cruz's rhythm. He spreads my legs wide as I watch Grayson's eyes drop to my aching pussy. Carver pushes straight into me, slamming deep inside my cunt as the water slams down over all of us, my leg hooking right over his shoulder as my other wraps around his waist.

"Fuck," I cry, taking them both.

Carver thrusts into me, his hips forcing my legs wider as he and Cruz find a rhythm that works for us all; hell, even making it possible for me to keep working King's cock with my hand.

Grayson can't take it anymore and moves in closer, grabbing my chin and forcing my head to him. He strokes his monster cock and it rubs up against my leg as his warm lips crush down on mine, swallowing my gasps and groans.

"Fuck," Cruz mutters behind me, his teeth clenched as a ferocious growl rumbles deep in Carver's throat, both of them right on the edge.

Grayson's piercing rubs over my leg and my mouth waters for

it. "We need to take this down," I pant, pulling away from Grayson's warm lips as my fists keep working up and down King's cock. I look back over my shoulder at Cruz before looking ahead at Carver. "I don't know how, but you guys have got to get me down on the ground."

Carver's brows furrow as his pace slows. "Why?"

"How the fuck else am I supposed to get Grayson's big cock in my mouth?"

The boys grin and in a tangled mess of arms and legs, Carver drops to the ground and stretches back, his hands digging into my thighs as I sink down on top of him. A long groan escapes his lips as he feels Cruz still moving inside me, both finding a comfortable pace and fucking me from both the front and back as my world turns to sweet bliss.

I don't dare release my grip on King as I turn to my left to find Grayson's glorious monster now right by my lips. I can't help but feel like a fucking cock burrito. They're coming at me front, back, left, and right. Hell, some even high and low, and I don't doubt that soon enough, I'll be getting all that delicious sauce right along with it.

Cruz wraps his arms around my hips as he thrusts into my ass, supporting my body as I reach out and grab Grayson's cock, my tongue roaming over my lips to wet them in preparation for just how big he is.

His piercing hits my bottom lip and I guide him inside of my mouth as my gaze falls to Carver's, loving the way that he watches me in return. My pussy clenches around him and he grins, loving that secret little message between us.

I start working Grayson's cock with my mouth, my lips moving over his sweet velvety skin as my tongue roams over his piercing. I glance up past his raven tattoo to meet his dark eyes that look down at mine, satisfaction written over his face, but as both Cruz and Carver move in and out of me, my rhythm is bumpy at best.

Grayson quickly tires of me losing my motion and curls his fingers around my soaking hair, gripping it tight and keeping my head still so that he can fuck my mouth instead. He moves in and out, his piercing slamming the back of my throat, and if I wasn't so practiced, I'd probably be choking by now.

My other hand grips King tighter as I move faster, keeping up with Grayson and within moments, Cruz is freezing behind me. "Ahhh, fuck," he groans low, the satisfaction clear in his tone as his fingers dig into my skin. He pulls out of me and pours his warm seed all over my back, letting it quickly wash away and mix into the now clear water below.

Without Cruz behind me, I start falling backward but Carver's strong arms wrap around me, holding me still. I adjust myself to get comfortable and before I know it, I'm riding him like a fucking cowgirl, but as usual, Carver needs to be the one in control and without Cruz invading my ass, Carver gets free reign and fucks me just how he likes it—hard, rough, and fast.

My eyes roll in my head, my pussy clenching around him as that familiar burn builds within me, warning me that I don't have much time left. I groan against Grayson's cock and the vibrations are enough to make his knees go weak. His grip in my hair tightens and as his roughness turns me on even more, King's hand over mine speeds up, squeezing my hand even tighter.

Carver groans low, gripping my ass and squeezing tight as he looks up and watches me working his friends' cocks. I can hardly take it but when I rock my hips over him and my clit grazes over his warm skin, my body explodes.

My pussy convulses around his big dick and I clench my eyes, my orgasm tearing through me at a million miles per hour. My whole body freezes, and just as a loud moan rips from my chest, Carver's hot seed shoots up inside of me.

I feel like a fucking goddess as he pours inside of me, his eyes closing with intense pleasure, but before I can even take a moment to breathe, both King and Grayson finish with loud grunts of their own. King's warm cum shoots against my tits, spreading all over me, and I feel Grayson in the back of my throat. I swallow him down, and as he draws out of my mouth, I collapse forward, catching myself on Carver's strong chest as all the evidence of King's orgasm washes off me.

"Holy shit," I breathe, barely holding myself up.

"Yeah," Carver grunts, completely out of breath.

King reaches down and grabs my waist, pulling me up into his arms until my legs are wrapped around his hips. "You're a fucking queen," he tells me, standing me more directly under the shower spray and roaming his hands up and down my sore, used body.

I smile as he gently presses his lips against mine. "I hope so," I tell him. "I've been waiting for that since the moment I met you all."

His brow shoots up and he pulls back to meet my stare. "Really?" he questions. "How'd we do?"

I shrug my shoulders. "How do you guys feel about double penetration?"

Cruz laughs from across the massive communal shower. "Someone has been spending too much fucking time on Pornhub."

I whip my head around, grinning back at the smartass. "Are you going to deny me?"

"No fucking way," he says, grinning right back at me.

I focus my attention back on King as the guys begin to creep back in, all of them hardening before my eyes as the idea of DP flutters through their minds, exciting us all. I feel King's cock against my pussy and he presses me up against the cool tiles of the shower.

I slowly grind my pussy against him and feel that familiar wetness dripping out of me. "You're ready for more?" King murmurs, dropping his lips to my neck.

"You know I am," I tell him before a wicked grin stretches over my lips. "But this," I say, rocking my hips, referring to the warm arousal he feels spreading between my legs. "This is just Carver dripping all over you."

Carver laughs behind him but King doesn't find it all so funny as he pulls his hips back, lines his heavy cock up with my cunt and slams inside of me. My head tips back as the three other guys, all with their thick, long cocks in their hands move in closer, more than ready to rock my world all over again.

# CHAPTER 32

Carver's arm wraps around me, pulling me in close as I attempt to sleep. Today was fucking exhausting and now my brain is too fucking fried that I can't even turn it off, making sleep almost impossible. I barely made it out of the school alive. I knew that when King and I launched ourselves over the front gate that there was a possibility that we might never come out of there, it was a small possibility, but that's just the risk you take when you play games with guns. I never expected that it was going to be four dicks that took me to the grave instead.

I mean … what the fuck just happened? I've been fucked from every damn angle I could ever think of, hell, positions that I didn't even know existed. The guys have either been watching too much porn or their little brains are far more creative than I ever gave them credit for.

Who would have known that there were so many different positions to fuck with a group of five?

Sure, Knox didn't get the chance to kill me, but fuck, I still died all the deaths tonight. Sorry Dianna, I guess there's one more funeral to attend in the very near future and it's for my fucking pussy because she's long gone. There's no reviving this bitch ... at least for a few more days. The boys are going to have to be patient with me because I'm down for the count, but it was so worth it.

I grunt and groan as I try to roll over, getting as close to Carver as possible. My pussy has been aching since the second we got home, but that's expected after everything it just went through. I'm going to be spending most of tomorrow on the couch with an ice pack shoved between my lips.

I wonder if I can make a dick icicle for my vag, but I guess the bigger question is which of the guys I can convince into making a life-size mold for one. Actually, if I were smart, I could make a whole bunch of molds and sell them to thirsty bitches like me and make a few extra dollars on the side. Don't get me wrong, I don't need the extra cash anymore, but it would be an interesting side hustle.

Hmm, I'll have to google if there's a type of oil that I can massage into it or if there's some kind of anti-swelling cream, but that's a whole new risk in itself. There have been too many times that I've been caught out with a cream only for it to instantly start burning and paralyzing me with instant regret and self-loathing.

Don't get me wrong, the night was fucking awesome. Watching Knox die was only the beginning and it just got better from there.

Though what I did learn is, despite what I think of myself, I'm not actually superwoman, and I'm definitely not ready for double penetration. That was a mistake, a big motherfucking mistake, but it gives us something to work toward and look forward to which is always a bonus.

I roll again and Carver grumbles, pulling me in tight and trying to get me to stop fidgeting, but he'll never get it. If anything, his dick might be limp for a few days, but he's not going to feel the same kind of discomfort that I feel. I mean, I knew I was going to be sore when I agreed to go for the fourth round, but we finished and I felt great. It was only the late hour that forced us to get our asses out of there. If I'd known that it was going to swell like this, I probably would have called it quits after the first round. On the bright side, I now know that the guys are like stallions, always ready to go, no matter what.

My discomfort gets all too much and I sit up in bed, throwing the blankets off me and making Carver groan as I climb over him. "The fuck are you doing?" he grumbles in that deep, sexy sleepy tone that I love so much, his hands coming to my waist as I straddle him. "Damn, again? Fuck babe. Okay, but just give me a second to wake him up."

I groan and pull myself over him, cringing at the feel of his hard body beneath me as I climb over him. "Don't even think about it," I tell him. "Send that soldier straight back to the deepest pits of hell. I'm not fucking anything for at least a few days. I'm sore. I need to get a dick-sicle."

"A what?" he questions, straining to open his eyes, probably going over my last comment a million times to figure out what the fuck I'm talking about.

"You know, a dick icicle," I mutter, my sleep-deprived mind not understanding why the hell he can't just read my thoughts. "I need something cold to shove up there. My fucking pussy is swelling from getting dicked too hard and now I can't get comfortable."

"Ahh, fuck, babe. I'm sorry," he murmurs, rolling over in bed to watch me as I climb out and cross his room. "Why don't you lay down? I'll go get you some pain killers and your fucking dick-sicle."

I shake my head, grabbing a blanket and pulling it over my shoulders. "It's fine. Go back to sleep. I couldn't shut off anyway."

I don't give him another chance to try and change my mind as I walk out the door and gently pull it closed behind me, leaving it open just a crack so that I don't wake him when I come back in. I drag my feet as I walk down the hall, passing the main bathroom and wondering just how awkward it would be to fill the bathtub with cold water and sit in it with my legs spread wide for an hour or two.

My room comes up next and I peer into it to find King sprawled out over the covers and I grin to myself. We'd all been so exhausted when we got home that after sending Dianna home and thanking her for being here with the girls, we'd all broken off to our own beds and crashed almost immediately. I couldn't sleep and as usual when I have trouble sleeping, I find myself in Carver's arms, but tonight, the old trick didn't work. King on the other hand must have had trouble sleeping too and found himself in my bed. I just hope he wasn't too disappointed when he got there and realized that I must have been sleeping in another man's arms. Though from the looks of it, he seems to have found comfort from just being in my bed, even if it is without me.

Making my way down to the kitchen, I find myself some painkillers and shove my head into the freezer, searching around for something I could use to ease the pain. After coming up with nothing but perfectly round ice cubes, I realize that I'm screwed. I mean, technically I could shove them up there but the freezing ice against my bits is probably going to burn me alive, plus I've already been leaking enough tonight from the boys' special … deposits. I don't need to add another reason for something to be dripping out of me.

Giving up, I grab an old-fashioned ice pack and a paper towel before starting to shuffle my way through to the living room. I get myself set up on the couch and grab a bunch of remotes that live in the coffee table drawer. I start pressing buttons until finally, I find the one that has a jaw-dropping fire spreading through the fireplace. It takes a moment to warm the living room, but when it does, I realize how much of an idiot I've been for not utilizing this space more often.

I snuggle up with my blanket, laying my head back on a cushion as I wrap the ice pack in a thin layer of paper towel before gently placing it between my lips. It's awkward as fuck, and for the first time in a while, I've never been so happy not to have one of the guys hanging around. They'd completely understand my predicament, but they'd also want to see, and some things a woman just can't share. For me, an ice pack shoved between my lady lips would be it.

The painkillers finally start to do their thing and I close my eyes, feeling the calm starting to spread through my mind. I zone out and allow my brain the silence it's deserved all night and finally drift off into a peaceful sleep.

I don't know how long I'm out for but when I roll over and the ice pack launches halfway up my vag, my eyes spring open and I quickly realize that my ass turned off the fireplace and now I'm freezing, my neck is aching from the cushion, and on top of that, my tank is so twisted that both my tits are hanging right out, one where my arm is supposed to be and the other protruding out the neck hole.

Just fucking great.

I sit up and cringe but having the ice pack on me for so long seems to have helped a little. Scooping up the little blanket, I wrap it around myself and make my way back up the stairs, more than ready to scoot down into my own bed and sleep until this time next week.

Carver will forgive me for not coming back while I'm sure King wouldn't mind the company at all. Though, if the fucker starts breathing in my face, he's out. I love my guys but I'm so down for a little peace and quiet.

I reach the top of the stairs and move toward my bedroom door, but a soft creak in the floor has my gaze shifting down the hallway. Cruz and Grayson's bedroom doors are closed and as I can still see King hanging off my bed, I realize that it must be Carver.

His door is propped open a little further than I'd left it and guilt instantly sails through me. If he's been up this whole time waiting for me to come back for him, I'm going to feel like a colossal bitch. Though, I also wouldn't put it past him to have been the one to come downstairs and turn off the fire so that I would freeze and be forced back upstairs to his bed. He's a dick like that.

Letting out a sigh, I tighten the blanket around me and make my way toward Carver's room, more than ready to either apologize for keeping him waiting for so long or call him out on his standard douchebaggery techniques. My hand presses against his door and as I swing it open, the light from the hallway spreads through his room and I find Ida Carver standing over him, her hand raised high in a dramatic arc with a knife that sparkles against the intrusion of light.

My eyes bug out of my head and as her hand begins to lower, I scream. "CARVER!"

His eyes spring open and I start to run but I'm too far away, I'll never make it in time, but Carver's reflexes are like lightning bolts. He rolls out of the way and springs up to his knees just as his mother's knife plunges deep into his mattress, right where his heart used to be.

I hear the familiar sound of the guys flying out of their beds and racing down the hallway and I come screeching to a stop, my eyes wide as I watch Carver, his chest rising and falling with rapid movement. He stares at his mother in shock, the betrayal tearing across his perfect features and making me want to strangle her for darkening his soul like that.

Ida sucks in a sharp gasp, realizing just how much trouble she's in, and as the guys barrel into Carver's room behind me, his hand flies out, wrapping around his mother's on the hilt of the knife. "What did you do?" he spits, his eyes filled with the worst kind of venom.

She shakes her head, desperately trying to pull her hand out from under his grip, but he's too strong, even in a foggy, sleep-deprived state. He yanks the knife out of the mattress and steps off his bed, forcing his mother back against the wall, leaving her nowhere to go and absolutely nowhere to run as we all watch on in horror.

The knife remains between them, the question of how she was released from her cell silent in the air around us.

"You put me in a cell to rot," she sneers through a clenched jaw. "After everything that you've done to me. You allowed your trailer trash girlfriend to take your father's life, you took my home, and then my children. How could you do that to me? I am your mother, I bore you in my womb, and you have done nothing but ruin me. I gave you life and in return, you disrespect mine, but I will see this through, Dante. You do not deserve the Carver name. You will never amount to anything and I will see to it that the Carver name returns to the great glory that it once was. I swear on your father's grave. You have let me down for the last time."

Carver pushes into his mother, overpowering her and turning the knife on her, the tip pressing against her stomach. "And how will you do that when you're rotting in hell beside him?" he questions, not flinching, not blinking, hell, not even fucking breathing.

Ida sucks in a breath, her eyes flashing down to her stomach and staring at the tip of the blade that pierces through her clothing. "You wouldn't do it," she spits. "You've always been too weak. Now, cut the act and release me. I'm tired of your lackluster performances. You already proved that you don't have what it takes."

Carver doesn't move as he presses harder against the knife, piercing her skin. Ida sucks in a breath, her eyes going wide, realizing just how much she underestimated her son. "DANTE," she hisses. "THAT'S ENOUGH."

I go to take a step toward him, but Grayson's hand curls around my wrist, pulling me back. "He needs this," Grayson mutters in my ear, so softly that I doubt Carver would hear us. Though, he's so damn focused on ending his mother's pathetic existence that a bomb could go off right now and Carver still wouldn't move.

The knife slips just a little deeper and Ida's gaze flicks around the room, silently begging for one of us to save her as her son uses her own fucking knife to slaughter her, but she'll get no help from us. This has been a long time coming and after how many times we've caught her slipping up, she's lucky that we haven't already ended her.

The knife slowly pushes deeper inside her stomach and blood trickles from the corners of her mouth as she turns her stare back on her son's, looking at him with such deep betrayal. She trusted that no matter what, the bond between mother and son would have saved her, despite coming here to end his life while he slept—the same way that her husband had murdered my parents.

"Dante," she breathes, choking on her blood as it starts to fill her lungs. "Dante, please."

Carver is relentless, and instead of easing up on her, he plunges the knife deeper, giving her only moments to live. "Who let you out?" he demands, his tone low and terrifying, so fucking low that I shrink back a step and press myself up against Cruz's chest.

Ida opens her mouth, trying to say something but she chokes on her own blood, the words gurgling in her throat.

"WHO?" Carver orders.

Tears fall from her eyes and I don't doubt that it's out of pain, not the million regrets that are bound to be rushing through her mind. "H … Har … Beckett. Harlen Beckett," she finally manages as her eyes begin to fade away.

Grayson straightens beside me, his fists curling at his sides as his jaw clenches in rage, but he doesn't dare move, giving Carver this moment to do what should have been done months ago. "You were wrong, mother," he tells her, standing tall with pride. "It wasn't me who was unworthy of the Carver name. It was you, you and Royston. You've both brought shame and embarrassment down upon me and I will have to carry your burdens for the rest of my life. But don't be fooled, I will resurrect the Carver name in my own image and my sisters will soar under it. Ravenwood blood will pulse through my childrens' veins and one day, Dynasty will cease to exist as the corrupted, bloodthirsty joke of a society that you and your husband molded it to be. Dynasty will rise again, and when it does, it will be in the image of Elodie Ravenwood, and the people who follow her."

My heart races at his words but I keep my mouth shut as Ida shakes her head, real fear shining in her eyes as life continues to fade from her eyes. She attempts to speak but all we hear is her blood blocking her airway. She goes limp in Carver's hold and just to finish it off right, he slams the knife the rest of the way in, the angle making it impossible for the blade to have missed her heart.

Carver releases his grip on the knife and steps away from her, letting her lifeless body sprawl out on his bedroom floor, and just as he turns to face us, wiping his mother's blood onto his bedsheets, the first rays of sunlight stream through his bedroom window.

# CHAPTER 33

We storm in through the underground cells, all five of us looking around and trying to figure out exactly how Harlen Beckett was able to free Ida, and more so, why? It doesn't make any sense.

Considering the complexity of Ida's case and the fact that she wasn't intended for a short-term stay like most of our cell guests, the keys weren't readily available for the sixteen heads of Dynasty as they usually are. Only I had a key, and only I knew where it was, but as the boys scrubbed the blood out of Carver's bedroom carpet and I raced down the hall to the secret room, filled with all the little details of my life, I realized that the key was nowhere to be seen.

We've always known that Harlen was going to be a threat one day, but we didn't expect him to make a move so quickly, and honestly, it's frightening. It's always the silent ones you have to be wary of. People like Paris are easy to read. I know what she wants. Hell, she fucking screams it from the rooftops every chance she gets, but Harlen goes about his business in secret. No one knows when he might strike, and that's proven in the way that Grayson hasn't said a damn word. He's been lost inside his own mind, trying to figure out his father's game plan but so far, he's got nothing.

Carver passes me, walking right up to the cell that his mother was staying in up until only an hour ago and grips on to the bars as though there's some kind of hidden message left behind in her cell, but it's as empty as it was before she was put in there.

The guys begin pacing, everyone caught inside their own minds, and as Carver tries to assemble the puzzle pieces he doesn't have, my gaze shifts down the long hall to the destroyed cells at the end. It's been a matter of days since I stood down here talking to Ember through the bars when that military truck drove straight through here, destroying everything in its path. I didn't know who was driving the truck, and while my gut is screaming that it was one of Paris's guards, I can't help but wonder if it could have also been Harlen Beckett.

I'm questioning everything that I know to be true and it's fucking with my mind. "Come on," I tell the guys, turning and walking out of the cells, hating being down here in the first place from the memories it brings of my own time locked up. "We're not going to find anything in her cell. We should be barging down Harlen's door and demanding answers."

"No," Grayson says, moving in beside me. "He'll be expecting that and he'll have some bullshit response already lined up. He's the kind of man who doesn't risk anything. He would have had an alibi sorted and people who could back it up. We need to catch him out and going in blind isn't the way to do it. We wait."

I let out a sigh and nod, hating the impatience that pulses through me. "Do you think he's working with Paris?" I ask as Cruz and King follow us out, leaving Carver a few steps behind, dragging his feet as he comes to terms with just how fucked up his morning has been.

Grayson shakes his head. "No. No fucking way. He wouldn't. He values himself and has always been able to see through Paris' bullshit. If his goal is leadership, then he won't bother with Paris. To him, that's just an extra step to the top."

"Shit," I mutter, curling my hands into tight fists and getting high on the feel of my brass knuckles tightening over my skin. "I thought we'd be able to chill for a while before another fucking threat came at us. I mean, FUCK. We're so close to taking down Paris. I can feel it in my veins, and now this. Why does life always have to be so fucked up around here? All I want to do is swim in my fucking pool without an assassin trying to drown me, get drunk with my boyfriends without someone kidnapping everyone's siblings, and fuck in a goddamn cabin without it blowing into a million fucking pieces. Why can't I just have that?"

"You're thinking too much into it," King tells me as we walk back through the long hallway. "Harlen has been making moves for months. He's been having secret little conversations with all the heads, trying to campaign and win their trust. Even Montgomery outed him on your return, but you have the numbers on your side. Beckett has nothing without those numbers and he knows it. They won't follow him. You're the fucking star attraction, and besides, he doesn't know that Ida spilled about his involvement in her freedom. We can use that to our advantage."

"How?" Cruz mutters.

King shakes his head. "I've got no fucking idea. It sounded good in my head, and I bet it went a long way in making Winter feel better about it."

I glance back over my shoulder, fighting a stupid grin as I roll my eyes. "I mean … it kinda did."

King winks and my stomach flutters with butterflies and the thought flies through my mind that those butterflies would feel a shitload better going through my stomach than the knife felt going through Ida's.

Shit. That was dark, even for me.

I shake the thought from my head and concentrate on getting my ass out of here.

Carver scoffs behind us, killing any attempt that King had made of getting my mind off the bullshit. "You're really trying to make light out of this?" he questions, his comment thrown straight at King's back, piercing through his skin just as his bullet had pierced through mine … and well, the blade through his mother's stomach. I guess Carver has a knack for inserting things where they really shouldn't be. Like his bullshit opinion right now.

King stops and spins just as we break out into the main foyer of our underground world. "You got a fucking problem, man?"

I study Carver's stare as he looks back at King and I groan, recognizing that look so damn well as it's one that usually rests on my own damn face. He's looking for a fight and he doesn't care how he gets it, even if it means tearing down his friendship just to feel the adrenaline of his fists pummeling against bare skin.

I shake my head and move forward, only just slipping away from Cruz as he reaches out to stop me. "No," I growl, forcing my stare onto Carver and pushing in front of King who would have been more than happy to go a couple rounds with Carver. "You don't get to do this. Yeah, you've had a shitty morning and your world just imploded on your ass, but you don't get to preach to me about self-control and then go pick a fight with your friends. If you want to beat the shit out of something, there's a perfectly fine punching bag in my home gym with your name on it. Got it?"

Carver narrows his gaze, hating when people use his own bullshit against him, but he knows I'm right. Either way, he doesn't move an inch as King stands at my back, ready to push me out of the way if Carver decides to go against all his basic urges. I step in close to him, raising my chin. "What's it going to be, Carver? Either walk away now or use me as your punching bag, the same way that you do for me." I watch as his eyes widen just a fraction, completely horrified by my suggestion, but I don't pause or give him even the slightest chance to cut me off. "But just know, that if you lay a single fucking finger on any of my guys, I'm coming for your ass, and trust me when I tell you that you won't like it."

Carver's gaze narrows and as he goes to step into me, Grayson's hushed tone sails through the foyer. "Hold up," he murmurs, moving in closer to us. "We're not alone down here."

Without hesitation, Carver reaches out and grabs my wrist, he yanks me behind him as the guys move in on Carver's other sides, their protective instincts knowing no bounds. Grayson points toward the opposite hall, our eyes landing on the dull light shining from within the filing room.

I've been in there once when Tobias King was giving me my induction tour, taking me around and showing me all the ins and outs of Dynasty, and now that I know where his true loyalties were, it's hard to figure out if anything honest ever came from his lips.

The guys' gazes shift around our small group, silently putting a plan into place and within moments, Carver's hand is in mine, slowly moving through the underground world, his tantrum a thing of the past. Our feet shuffle across the expensive marble and despite there being five of us, not a damn sound is heard until we're standing right outside the filing door, listening to the soft thud of drawers opening and closing.

I meet Grayson's stare and my brows furrow, a silent question between us asking if he has any idea what the hell is going on in there, but he shrugs his shoulders, just as clueless as the rest of us. His gaze shifts to Carver's whose shifts to King's and then Cruz's and with a sharp nod, the door is pushed wide and we throw ourselves through the entrance, the five of us standing as an impenetrable force.

Matthew Montgomery sits at a long table, his reading glasses crooked on his face as his head shoots up from the piles of papers that aren't his to be going through. His eyes bug out of his head and before letting us get a single word out, he drops his gaze back to the papers as though he didn't just get caught out doing something that he really shouldn't be doing.

King steps forward, his brows furrowed as he approaches Montgomery with caution, never knowing what could happen when you approach a crazy man. "Uhhhh … the fuck, dude?" King says. "What the hell are you doing?"

He holds his hand up, his pointer finger out, a silent message asking King to shut the fuck up for just a second. "I think I've … I think I know where she is."

"What?" I rush out, pushing past Carver's shoulder and moving in beside King, only to have his arm shoot out to stop me from getting closer. "You know where who is?"

"Paris Moustaff," Matthew rushes out, not bothering to raise his head as he shuffles through the papers before him. "I've spent countless nights down here trying to figure it out and I think I finally have something."

Cruz cuts in, stepping straight up to the table. "What do you mean? We've been searching for information for months and came up blank."

"I know," Matthew says, finding a property sales contract and holding it out to Cruz. "The day you guys mentioned that you went down to the Ravenwood's mountain property and found that's where Paris had been staying, a memory sparked inside my head from years ago and I couldn't quite figure it out until this morning."

Carver moves in beside me as Grayson hovers close by, not trusting

Matthew one bit. "What memory?"

Matthew shakes his head, standing from behind the table and stretching his neck. He pulls his glasses off and rubs his hands over his eyes, looking just as tired as I feel. "Umm, when I was around nineteen or twenty—fifteen or so years ago—I made some pretty fucking stupid choices and got myself in trouble with substance abuse. I got high, stole a fucking car and went joyriding through the streets. I thought it was a great time, but when I came down from my high, I learned that during my ride, I killed a man and I didn't even know. The cops were after me and Dynasty made me a deal to spend my days down here sorting out the fucking mess this room was in while I got sober, otherwise I could do a few years in prison."

Grayson nods. "It's true," he says, making Matthew's head snap up in shock, thinking that he was spilling a secret that he's kept close to his heart for all these years. "I make it my business to know this shit, but how the fuck does this have anything to do with Paris?"

Montgomery lets out a sigh and drops his gaze back to the papers. "I had to sort through all the paperwork and file it all away. There were years of backlog and I got through it quicker than I thought, but I hadn't done my time yet, so I came here day after day and I went through each of these files. Given, I was trying to find dirt on the men who I would one day lead Dynasty with, and while I certainly found plenty of shit about the men we live and serve by, I also found more useful information than I could ever know." Matthew's gaze falls to me. "Your father for example, did you know he was in the property market? He was an avid purchaser, a collector if you will, but always had issues reselling."

I shake my head. "No, he wasn't," I say, positive that Matthew has his wires crossed. "I've been through his property portfolio. He has his estate here, the mountain estate which burned down, and a few smaller properties littered around the globe but nothing substantial."

"That's where you're wrong," he tells me, indicating the contract in Cruz's hands. "You've been looking in the wrong places. Check out the name on that contract."

I take the contract from Cruz and glance over it, seeing a name that I wasn't expecting to see—The London Moustaff Family Trust. My brows furrow and I flip through the pages, having absolutely no idea what I'm looking at. "What … what is this?"

"Your father wanted to keep all his properties separate from his Ravenwood title so he had a family trust drawn up under your mother's name and together, they purchased as many properties as they could. They started off small, buying properties that needed a bit of love. But right from the start, they never sold any of their projects. Instead, they were rented out to people in need."

My gaze lifts back to Matthew's. "And you just know all of this information?"

He shrugs his shoulders. "It's amazing what a bit of light reading can find you."

"Holy shit," I breathe. "So they have hundreds of properties?"

"Yeah," he says. "Hundreds, maybe thousands. I don't know everything, but what I do know is that you are the sole surviving member of the London Moustaff Family Trust and those properties are now yours."

"What does this have to do with Paris?" Cruz questions, getting bored of storytime.

Matthew indicates to the hundreds of filing cabinets labeled 'Ravenwood' and glances back at Cruz. "Because Paris is obsessed with her twin sister. She went out of her way to live in her mountain estate and when that was compromised, she had nowhere to go, and if I know this information about London and Andrew, then how many others do? Tobias was Andrew's closest friend. Is it possible that he knew of these properties and told the wrong person in passing? Who's to say that Paris hasn't been staying in one of these properties this whole time?"

I glance around at the boys. "Do you think he could be right?"

Grayson rubs his hand over his face, deep in thought. "I don't fucking know. This is the first I've heard of all these properties, but it's also the only fucking lead we've got."

Matthew nods and points back down at the contract in my hands. "That right there is the contract that I've been trying to find for weeks," he says. "That's the closest property the Trust owns and it's right here in Ravenwood Heights, just to the north of the city center. I was going to gather all the information I could find and bring it to you this morning."

My heart starts to race as I look a little closer at the contract. It's a penthouse property at the top of a high-rise building, one of the biggest in the city and just that in itself means that raiding it is going to be a little difficult.

I don't doubt that the boys are thinking of a game plan as well, but as I glance up at Matthew, another thought crosses my mind. "I've been here for months, desperate for information on my family. Why didn't you come to us with this sooner?"

Guilt flashes through his eyes and he swallows hard. "Look, I'm going to be honest with you," he starts. "At first, I didn't like you. You came in here with an attitude. You were reckless and had a million threats working against you. The odds weren't in your favor and I'm a winning kind of guy. I don't give my loyalty easily, and from where I stood, you weren't going to be around for long. It's always been a cutthroat world out here and you keep the information you have close to your chest until you find some way of advancing your game. Then one by one, you defied all the odds and eventually you were coming out on top, winning everyone's hearts and votes, and by the time I realized that, you were already the heir that everybody needed you to be. I didn't tell you because I knew that even without this information, you were still going to come out on top, but I also run the risk that the information I give you is no good. I'm working on a hunch here and I don't want to be the reason anyone gets hurt."

Carver steps in behind me, glancing at the contract over my shoulder. "How positive are you on this hunch?"

"I'd weigh my life on it," Montgomery tells us. "I know it's been difficult to hear, but when I told you that you had my loyalty, I meant that. I was only a kid when your father was in power, and to be completely honest, I didn't like him. He wasn't my cup of tea, but you've proven yourself over and over again and I know that you're going to be the one who can turn this sinking ship around. I know you're just a kid yourself and it's a lot of weight to put on your shoulders, but I trust you, which is why I need you to take out this threat once and for all so we, as an organization, can work on bettering our future for not only ourselves but our future generations."

"I couldn't agree more. Now, give me everything you've got," I tell him, slamming the contract down on top of the pile of papers. "Assuming you're right, this bitch is going down today."

# CHAPTER 34

The door is practically kicked in, our arms loaded with files as we barge into my home, more than ready to figure this shit out. If Paris is staying in my parents' city apartment, I want to know about it.

My blood boils as my heart races. Could we really be onto something here? Is this finally the end? But more so, has the fucking bitch been that close to us this whole damn time? It infuriates me. She's been right under our damn noses and it makes me feel like a fucking fool. I bet she's up in that apartment, living off my parents' fortune—my fortune—her feet up, enjoying every last second of it, laughing at us as we scramble for answers and never get anywhere.

Not anymore. The fucking game is over and I won't stop until her head is hanging from my hands.

Fuck, that was morbid. Maybe it's about time that I at least attempt to find a tiny shred of control. Every second we waste gathering files, searching through documents, and painstakingly going over our plan is just more time that she has to get away, and damn it, every second that we waste only pisses me off more.

How could Montgomery just sit on this information for so long? Those children were kidnapped because he wasn't open about his hunch. We could have looked into it and gotten answers so much sooner. We could have saved those children from a lifetime of nightmares. The boys could have avoided blowing up the cabin and betraying my trust, and I could have felt true freedom for the first time in eighteen years.

I barely get through the door and into the dining room, ready to drop all the heavy files onto the table when a soft, sleep-filled tone sounds at our backs. "Where'd you go?"

Dumping my armful of files on the table, I turn around to find Danika standing at the entrance of the dining room, rubbing her eye as her face twists moments before a yawn comes tearing out of her.

Danika's eyes squeeze shut as Carver crouches down in front of her, his hand dropping to her shoulder. "Are you only just getting up?"

He bypasses her question like a pro, putting on a cheery tone for his little sister despite the turmoil raging through his mind. It's only seven in the morning, but it's already been a fucked-up day, one I'm sure that he won't be forgetting anytime soon, though fingers crossed that the rest of the day can turn around in a big way. Nothing would suck more than going on a raid only to find that we were wrong and Paris was never there to start with. The place we were looking for was north of the city center, somewhere she could stay without leaving a paper trail, and somewhere close enough to keep an eye on us undetected. The penthouse apartment is perfect for that.

All this time, we've been searching for a rundown property, something she would have forced her way into, but she outsmarted us once again. The penthouse is the exact opposite of what we've been looking for, and the more I think about it, the more I want to scream.

Danika rubs the back of her hand over her nose and nods, a soft pout settling over her lips. "I … I had a bad dream where I thought I heard Mommy, but I didn't want to upset you so I just went back to sleep," she explains, breaking my heart and making me so damn grateful that she didn't have a change of heart and come searching for Carver while his mother was lying dead on his bedroom floor.

"You know you can always come to me," Carver tells her. "Where's your sister?"

"She wanted to talk with the broken girl, but she wasn't there," Danika says, shrugging her shoulders. "So she stole the candies that King hid in the cupboard and now she's eating them under her bed."

My brows furrow and I step in behind Carver, sailing straight over King's hidden candies. "The broken girl?"

"Yeah," Danika says, a smile pulling at her lips, loving the idea of being helpful. "The girl who's been sleeping in the bed at the end of the hall. We were playing doctor with her yesterday. She let us put bandages on all of her ouchies and give her a check-up like when we visit the doctor with Mommy. Dominique wanted to be friends with her, but she wasn't there anymore."

Carver's gaze shifts to mine, a silent message passing between us, and without a word, I slip out of the dining room and head for the stairs. I sprint up them, two at a time, determined to check on Ember before rushing back downstairs and getting our 'end Paris' plan into motion.

My hand presses against the spare bedroom door at the end of the hallway and just like every other time I've pushed through to this room over the past few days, I brace myself, not wanting to be here one bit.

The door glides open and I glance up to find an empty bed, just as Danika had suggested. Suspicion takes over me. I've learned from my mistakes that trusting Ember isn't something anyone should ever do, so as I step deeper into the room, my gaze sweeps the wide space. Knowing my luck, she's probably standing behind the door with a vase, ready to smash it over the back of my head, and I am not down for taking a risk like that, especially on a day like today. I want to be clear-headed when I take out Paris. There is no room for concussions. Besides, a head injury would surely have the guys chaining me to my fucking bed, determined to find any little excuse as to why I shouldn't be going with them today. But fuck that. I'm a woman on a mission, and no one will stand in my way.

Confident that the room is safe to step into, I look over the rumpled sheets on the bed as I make my way across the room to the adjoining bathroom. My knuckles wrap against the closed door. "Ember?" I question, keeping my voice low as she's bound to still have a nasty concussion. Though it beats me why I'm making it a priority right now. "Ember? Are you in there?"

Getting no response, I knock again, my voice hitching a little higher as irritation spreads through me, hating being ignored. "Ember?"

I get nothing and taking a deep breath, I twist the handle and push my way through to an empty bathroom.

The fuck? Where the hell could she be?

My brows furrow and I move back toward the bed, glancing over it again. The pain killers that were laid out for her are still on the bedside table, but at least some of the water has been drunk, though that very well could have been Dominique when she snuck in here this morning.

I let out a sigh and turn to walk out of the room when a piece of paper catches my attention. It's torn from a book and resting just down the side of the bed, stuck between the mattress and the bedside table. She must have left it on her pillow and when Dominique came in, it flew right off.

I lean against the bed and scoop down, the movement making me cringe as that same dull ache that I suffered through all night reminds me that it's still there. Capturing the paper between my fingers, I drop my ass to the bed and glance over it.

There's text printed all over one side and as I flip it over, I find Ember's familiar handwriting scrawled across a blank page.

*Winter,*

*I don't know how to thank you for taking me in. I didn't deserve your kindness after the way I treated you. You offered me a way out and I laughed in your face. You deserved better than that.*

*I've done terrible things for Paris, things that will weigh on my heart for the rest of my life, but I truly believed that she loved me. I thought we were finally going to be a family, but I was fooled. I should have known better. You tried to warn me and even though I saw all the signs, I chose to ignore them. I'm not trying to make excuses for my behavior, I just wanted you to understand where my head was. I know, it's fucked up, right?*

*I know that I will never be able to make it up to you, and I'm sure that you don't even want me to try. The Winter that I knew would just want to beat the shit out of me with her brass knuckles and tell me to fuck right off.*

*I've clearly made some big mistakes but I'm smart enough to know that you just want me gone, and after everything that I've put you through, it's the least I can do. I want to be away from here. I want to have a chance at a real life and if I don't slip away now, I don't trust that those guys of yours aren't going to shove me right back in that cell.*

*I know that I deserve it, but I won't go back there. That place is a living hell, but I guess you already know that.*

*I'm going to get out of here and you will never have to see me again. I just … I wanted you to know how sorry I was. I really do wish that things could have been different, but despite how awful he was, you killed my father, and it's only a matter of time before you kill Paris too. A friendship between us would never have worked out.*

*For what it counts, I hope you take down Paris and I hope you make her suffer. My eyes are open now and I see her for who she really is, and that's someone that I don't ever want to become.*

*Make her pay, cousin.*

*Ember*

I stare at the note for far too long, wondering why the hell I still care so much. Ember burned me in the worst possible way. She was my first friend here, at least that's what I thought. I gave her all my trust and I opened up to her in a way that I've never done with a girlfriend before, and even now, the betrayal still stings, but knowing that once I walk out this door, I will never have to think about her again makes my world seem like a much simpler place.

Getting up from the bed, I curl my fist around the note and walk into the bathroom before searching through the cupboard for the small packet of matches that lives beneath the sink. I light one up and a sick joy spreads through me as I dip the edge of the page into the flame.

Fire licks up the paper, getting closer and closer to my fingers until I have no choice but to drop the paper into the sink and watch as it burns, leaving the last piece of Ember Harding behind, and hopefully I'll be doing the same to her mother before the day is out.

Making my way back downstairs, I let out a deep breath, not missing the way that each of the boys glance up, curiosity flooding through their eyes. "She's gone," I tell them, not wanting to waste time talking about the note when there are more important things to be focusing on. I nod toward the table at the mess of papers, contracts, and blueprints. "What have we got?"

Grayson rubs his hand over his face, his gaze dropping to the printout of the building's floor plan. "Here's how I think we should do this …"

Grayson only gets halfway through his plan before King is shaking his head, disagreeing with absolutely everything that's said and starting an argument that seems to go on for hours. He clearly has his own ideas on how this needs to go.

Carver and Cruz immediately get involved, everyone's opinions, ideas, and insults being thrown around the room. Hell, even I get in on the action.

Plans and opinions fill the air, each of us considering every point. We're all terrified of missing a single detail that could lead to Paris escaping again.

Our plans depend on knowing everything about the building's surveillance, from the placement of staff and cameras to the time it takes the elevator to go all the way from the bottom floor to the penthouse. Hell, gaining entry into the penthouse is a whole new situation on its own.

No stone is left unturned and by three in the afternoon, the boys and I know every last detail of how today is going to go. Hell, we know how it will go if she is alone, if she has guards, or even if the elevator breaks down and we have to leg it up the fire escape, but all that matters to me is two things—that the boys don't get hurt and that I get to be the one to end Paris' miserable life and personally send her ass straight to hell.

# CHAPTER 35

Ravenwood Estate hovers in the rearview as Carver flies through the gate. It's been one hell of a long day, and it's about to get a shitload longer. The girls were dropped off with an overnight bag at Dianna's house and the heads of Dynasty were put on notice, ready to protect our community if things were to go south.

My heart races, each beat bringing a new wave of terror pulsing through my veins. I feel fucking sick, but at the same time, I've never been so ready. This is the moment we've all been waiting for; this is the moment I've lived for, the day where I will finally give my parents the sweet vengeance they deserve.

Today, Dynasty wins and the Ravenwood name will shine for all to see. Today, I become the true deity that my people deserve. Retribution is ours, and in doing so, I will hand-deliver Paris Moustaff to the deepest, darkest pits of hell.

Carver drives manically through the streets, his tires screeching around every corner as we race toward the finish line, only this last hurdle isn't going to be easy. It's going to be downright terrifying, and I'm almost certain that one of us is bound to get hurt. The risks are too high, but the reward is too great to even think about passing it up.

We reach the city center within ten minutes and we all stare ahead at the massive building as Carver slows his speed, far too many people loitering around to keep traveling this fast. The city-goers line the streets, spilling out onto the road and making Carver groan as he constantly hits the brakes.

As we finally approach the building, Cruz slips out of the Escalade and jogs toward the main entrance of the underground parking lot, keeping his head down. He disappears inside and by the time Carver is pulling in and coming to a stop by the security barrier gates, Cruz is there, swiping a key card and gaining us access.

Cruz slips back in beside me as the arm raises and once it's all the way up, Carver drives on through as though we have every right to be here. Though, considering my parents own the penthouse apartment at the top, I guess we kinda do.

As Carver descends each level, the lighting seems to dim and flicker into complete darkness. He eases the Escalade into a shadowy parking space on a lower floor, the Black SUV barely even a ghost through the lens of a cheap security camera.

We have to assume that Paris has eyes all over this building, hell, all over Ravenwood Heights, but if this is her home, the place where she allows herself to be vulnerable, then she's bound to have this place locked down like a fortress. The elevator security systems would be hacked, she'd have control of the fire escape cameras, and I can guarantee that the people who walk in through the main entrances are being monitored.

We have to play this smart. The boys' usual brute strength tactic isn't going to work, at least not yet anyway.

The guys and I slip out of the Escalade, being discreet so that we don't draw attention from the other people walking to and from their cars. I assumed that the inside of the building was going to be packed with bodies as it's home to many businesses, restaurants, and a number of conference rooms scattered throughout, but I hadn't considered the parking lot. There are people everywhere, but they're all preoccupied by their own lives that they don't even notice us as the boys step around the back of the SUV and empty it of the big cart that's locked and loaded with every type of weapon we should need.

A white tablecloth hangs over it and I can't help the grin that stretches over my face as King reaches into the back and grabs a white chef's coat and pulls it on. Hell, he even goes as far as adding one of those tall chef's hats to complete his look.

King winks, making butterflies swarm through my stomach before glancing at the guys, double-checking that everyone knows where they need to be and when, then not a second later, he nods. "Wish me luck, boys," he mutters before grabbing hold of the cart and striding away, whistling as though he has all the time in the world as he pushes his cart through the parking garage toward the back restaurant entrances.

He looks perfect for the role he needs to play and will effortlessly roam over the whole building without a single person glancing his way twice.

Carver grabs my big coat and hands it to me as Grayson pulls a tired suit jacket over his shirt. My arms slip into a soft material, and before I know it, the clothes I wear beneath are completely concealed and I fit straight in with the other women walking through the garage.

"Alright," Carver says, glancing down at his phone. "Ten minutes exactly."

Grayson nods and slips a small pair of scissors into his suit pocket. "Got it," he says, and before giving any of us a chance to say another word, he slinks off into the parking garage.

My gaze sweeps to Carver, feeling the nerves beginning to rise in my chest. "You know what you need to do?" he questions as Cruz steps into a maintenance guy's uniform and hands me the same key card he'd used to get us through the gate.

I roll my eyes and grab the stack of random papers in the back, completing my businesswoman look. "I literally have the easiest job out of us all."

Cruz laughs. "We could switch, but something tells me that you have absolutely no idea how to shut down the power for a building like this without electrocuting yourself."

"Geez," I mutter under my breath. "The lack of trust you guys have in me is astonishing."

Cruz and Carver chuckle to themselves, but I don't hang around to waste precious seconds. I technically have plenty of time to do what I need to do, which is pretty much nothing, but there's always the risk that something could go wrong, and I don't want to be the reason that this doesn't happen.

I break away from the guys, slipping behind the parked cars beside the Escalade and making my way toward the exit of the underground parking garage. As I walk past the security barrier gate, I can't help but glance back over my shoulder to watch as Carver steps into the service elevator and Cruz pulls open the door for the fire escape.

It's fucking showtime.

I burst through the main entrance of the parking garage, stepping onto the sidewalk with the rest of the busy city people and allowing myself to blend into the fray of bodies. My heels click against the pavement and I hold the stack of papers close to my chest, doing my best to play the part.

The key card rests safely in my pocket and I'm more aware of it than anything I've ever been aware of before. I can't afford to lose it. It's everything. It's our way in.

I keep my head down, not risking getting caught by any of the hundreds of cameras around and within moments, I reach the main lobby entrance of the impressive building. I walk on through the big revolving door and approach the security check where I dump the stack of papers onto the conveyor belt and scan the access key card before stepping through the metal detectors.

The guard on duty gives me a bored nod clearing me to pass, and before I've even stepped across to grab my stack of papers, his attention has fallen on the guy behind me.

Acting as though I'm here every weekday of my life, I walk straight past the reception area at a quick pace. I mean, if I'm going to play the role, then I want to at least appear a little important to the people around me.

Continuing through the lobby, I come to a wide corridor with three elevators on either side and I lean toward the button, swiping the access card before pressing the call button and stepping back. All of the elevators are in use so I have a little bit of a wait, and as the seconds tick by, more people come to stand around me.

Friendly colleagues partake in light conversation while pompous men bark orders into their phones. But the only thing that holds my attention is the gorgeous man who steps out of the mens' bathroom and joins the crowd of people waiting by the elevator.

Grayson keeps to himself, standing toward the back of the group as I remain up front, pretending that I don't want to throw myself at him and screw him in front of all these people.

What is it about a man in a suit that has me acting like a complete idiot?

The elevator dings and we wait as the doors slowly peel open and a bunch of business minded people come pouring out. It takes far too long, and by the time I step into the elevator, my nerves are completely shot.

My fists pump at my sides as I hit the button for the thirty-fourth floor, the highest business level that this elevator will allow us to go. Everybody piles in around me and Grayson's fingers gently brush past mine as he takes his space in the very back corner.

The doors close and moments later, we're doing the rounds,

stopping at each floor and letting people off. Second floor, fifth floor, eighth floor, thirteenth. It goes on and on until I watch the little digital 19 turn to a 20 right before the elevator plunges into complete darkness, jolting to a sickening stop.

I grin wide. Gotta love Cruz Danforth.

The women around me panic, screaming as the arrogant businessman on the phone curses. "Shit, power's out," he mutters, trying to calm the women, though I think it's for his own sanity rather than for their benefit. "That's exactly what I needed."

A woman across the elevator sighs. "Does this building have a backup generator? Does anyone know? Or are we stuck here until emergency services can free us?"

"It better have a backup generator," Mr. Arrogant Jerk spits. "I have a meeting with my investors starting in four minutes. I don't have time for this."

I roll my eyes as they carry on with their bullshit, but a second later, a hand grabs me in the dark. At first, I think it's Grayson until the hand yanks me out of the way and a strong whiff of mens' cologne wafts around me. "Out of the way," the dickwad says before I hear him slamming his fist down over every single button on the elevator.

The need to knock him out flies through me as I'm pushed toward the back of the elevator but the feel of Grayson's calming fingers brushing down my arm has me coming back down. "You do it?" I murmur, my voice so low that I doubt he can even hear me.

"Sure fucking did."

A moment later, the power comes back on and the lights flicker throughout the elevator. The gears strain and for a second, I truly fear that the whole elevator is going to drop straight to the ground and kill us all, but it pulls through and relief pulses through my veins as the elevator dings and the doors open wide on the twentieth floor.

Everybody scrambles out of the elevator, not risking staying in there a moment longer, and as the doors close, I'm left with just Grayson and the privacy to do what we need to do.

With everybody off the elevator and the system completely reset, the elevator takes off, shooting up through the floors and bringing us closer and closer to level thirty-four. I can't help but glance up to see the small USB drive that Grayson shoved into the back of the security camera when the power went out, and a grin settles over my lips knowing that if Paris really is here and has eyes on this elevator, all she would see is an endless loop of people getting on and off.

The Elevator reaches the top floor and as the doors slowly slide back, I can't help but wave my hand toward the exit. "Ladies first."

Grayson rolls his eyes and mutters under his breath as he steps out in front of me. "You're such a shit."

"You wouldn't have it any other way."

We walk side by side through the long corridor, keeping our heads down to avoid the array of cameras scattered throughout the building. People pass us, deep in conversation, completely unaware of the havoc we're about to bring down over their fancy as fuck building.

A big black door with gold letters reading 'penthouse' passes on our right and my gaze shifts over it, taking in the complicated tech that keeps it locked. It's not the main entrance of the penthouse. There's a private elevator that leads straight to the front door, but getting in through that way proved far too complicated. So this is our best bet.

We continue past the door, and a moment later, King rounds the corner up ahead, strolling through the long hall as if he were catering to the many businesses on this floor. He stops by a private conference room and swipes a key card, shouldering his way through and pulling his cart along with him.

The blinds are drawn, the lights are out, and the room is sheltered in complete darkness.

King is already in the process of yanking the white cloth off his cart and exposing the treasure beneath, and as the door falls shut behind me, movement across the room has a soft gasp sailing from my chest. Carver sits in the darkness, somehow already here and looking as though he's been waiting a lifetime for us to show up. He stands and crosses to King's cart, scanning through the weapons and loading his tactical belt with everything he could possibly need.

King, Grayson, and I start pulling off our stupid disguises, and as my big coat falls to the floor, a soft knock sounds at the door.

King steps toward it, peering through the closed blinds before gripping the door handle and opening it. Cruz barrels in out of breath and catches himself against the table. "Fuck, do you have any idea how many steps it takes to get to the thirty-fourth floor?"

A laugh pulls out of me, realizing that in order to have time to cut the power and make it all the way up here at the same time that we did, he would have had to run … fast.

Grayson scoffs, more than amused by Cruz's lack of fitness, which is saying a lot because Cruz is one of the fittest guys I know. "Shit, bro. Guess it's time to get back on the treadmill, huh?"

"Fuck off," Cruz laughs, straightening as he does his best to act like he was just exaggerating. "I'm fine. I could whip all your asses in a race."

Carver grunts to himself, still loading up on weapons, and as he finds the specific gun they'd packed for me, shit gets real. The boys fall into silence and we get busy loading up. It takes us two minutes, and the more weapons I attach to my body, the more my nerves come alive.

It's like preparing for a war that you're not sure you're going to win, but we've got this. It'll be an ambush with the knowledge of complete freedom keeping me going.

There's no backing out now.

Worst case scenario, we destroy an empty room, but on the other hand, we could take out Paris and never have to fear for our lives again, never have to fear for our people, family, or friends. We would never grieve horrendous losses, and we'd never have to watch our backs so closely.

Fuck, I'm so worked up that I'm going to be pissed if she's not here. I mean, it's just my luck that she's out doing her groceries right now. Hell, I never thought that I'd see the day where I would be annoyed not to see Paris Moustaff because, for the first time in my life, I want to see her more than ever before.

King grabs his cart as Grayson opens the door and peers down the hall. He holds up a hand, telling us to wait a moment, and then all too soon, it's go time.

We rush out of the conference room and barrel down the hall toward the big black door with gold writing. Grayson sticks himself to the wall and reaches up, cutting the wires to the security camera and the second his hand comes back down, King pushes past him with the cart, grabbing everything he needs.

Explosives are wired to the door and I stand back, knowing that this could go wrong, but King is trained in this shit. He knows what he's doing.

Grayson moves to block me from the explosion as Carver moves in closer to the door, his gun raised, ready to go. If Paris really is in there, she's bound to have a guard stationed at this door 24/7 and Carver is going to make sure that the fucker doesn't get a chance to fight back.

I bounce on my toes as King moves back, the detonator in his hand. "Ready?" he questions.

Everyone nods and I reach down to my hip, pulling a gun out of the holster, holding it tight and readying myself for Paris' epic takedown. I breathe heavily, knowing that if there isn't a guard on the other side of this door, it was all for nothing. But King doesn't allow me the chance to think on it as he hits the button, sending the big door flying off its hinges and rocking back inside the penthouse emergency exit.

The sound echoes through the hallway and we only have mere seconds before people come rushing out, needing to know what the fuck is going down in here, but my hopes are that none of them are stupid enough to come in here. In a perfect world, they'll all run for the fire escape and get the fuck out of here before they get themselves hurt.

Carver races in ahead of us and the one shot that flies from his gun tells me everything I need to know—Montgomery's hunch was right.

Paris Moustaff is going to die today.

With the guard down, we race in after Carver to find a narrow stairwell that leads up through the floors and hopefully right into the center of my parent's penthouse apartment. The noise from the explosion should have Paris' guards already preparing themselves, and I don't doubt that by the time we hit the top of the stairs, they'll already be bearing down on us.

Despite not needing help, Cruz's hand curls around my upper arm as he flies up the stairs, taking them two at a time and practically dragging me along with him, terrified that I'll get left behind. While I hate the feeling of having someone pulling me along, I'm grateful. The guys' long, powerful legs are twice the size of mine, and while I've been training hard, I don't hold that same kind of explosive power to shoot up the stairs the way they can. Even on my best day, I simply can't keep up with them.

Carver is barely hitting the last step before the door at the top is kicked in and at least three guards hover inside the entrance, their guns out, locked and loaded.

The four boys split. Carver and Cruz go to the right, gluing themselves to the wall as Grayson and King fly to the left, pushing right up beside the railing and instantly returning fire, not skipping a damn beat.

Both King and Cruz drop to a knee behind Carver and Grayson, hitting the guards at all angles as I fold myself in behind the boys, avoiding every one of those bullets that come flying toward me.

I'd give anything to shoot back at them, but there's only one narrow door and four boys to get that bullet past before I'd have any hope of actually taking any of the guards down. If they lost the fucking guns though, I bet I'd be able to kick a few asses.

Bullets ricochet off the concrete walls, flying past my face, and I don't miss the way Cruz shields me with his body, though I'd give anything for him to not. Having his body angled like this just puts him at risk and I'd hate for him to get clipped with a bullet because he was too busy trying to protect me.

The boys' aim is impeccable, and while the guards are raining bullets down over us, the boys only need a handful to take out the guards, Grayson even going as far as sending a clean bullet right between the eyes of the guard to his left, but what can I say? We're not here to make friends and we sure as hell don't want to take out a threat only to get kicked in the ass by them later on. When a threat goes down, we make sure they stay down. We've been burned by people rising from the dead and we won't get caught out like that again.

They all go down as the sound of gunfire eases from the small stairwell, the echo taking a moment longer to fade completely and giving me the chance to hear myself think, but there's no time for that. Every second we're stuck in this stairwell is another opportunity for Paris to escape.

Carver creeps to the open door, his gun entering the penthouse first. He goes slowly as Grayson steps in behind him, the boys creating a line with me right at the end. When Carver finally steps over the threshold, his gaze sweeps the room, just the way he's been trained to do.

His shoulders relax just a touch and he walks deeper into the penthouse, letting the rest of us know that this space is cleared for now, but who the fuck knows where there could be more guards hiding in this place.

We have no way of knowing how long Paris has been staying in my parents' penthouse, but she's got the advantage of knowing the layout much better than we do. We've seen the apartment through images and floorplans while she's had time to figure out all the hidden secrets of this home. She knows all its little hide-outs and crevices and because of that, we can't let our guard down. Any corner, cabinet, or wall could pose a threat. We need to be careful and have each other's backs even when we think we're in the clear. Hell, who knows how many more guards Paris has been keeping here.

We step into hollow silence, moving past the dead guards at the door and creeping through the living room, and fuck, it's eerie. I don't see another soul, but my gut is telling me that she's here somewhere.

The main elevator entrance is to the right and the little lights on the digital screen are telling me that the elevator hasn't been used. It's sitting at the penthouse level, which also tells me that the last time it was used, it was coming and not going.

The elevator is the main point of entry for the penthouse. There's the emergency stairwell that we just came through and the fire escape, which is on the opposite side of the building. But no matter which way she goes to make her escape, she has to cut through here first.

We split into two groups as we sweep through the wide living space. Carver and Cruz go to the left while Grayson, King, and I go to the right.

My heart thunders with each new door that's kicked in and we quickly move through the kitchen, butler's pantry, and dining room, while King and Cruz clear the staff quarters, home gym, and bathrooms.

Confident that the downstairs area is cleared, we make our way up the stairs, but with each step we take, my stomach drops, twisting with unease as the top portion of the stairs puts us straight into a blind spot where we can't see anything that could be waiting for us, just the bland artwork that sits off-center at the end of the hallway.

The boys make their way up the stairs in formation, and as usual, they leave me at the end, not trusting my skills despite already proving myself time and time again.

My gun rests comfortably in my palm, and lately, it's been starting to feel like a permanent fixture to my hand. Carver and Grayson hit the top step and pause, listening intently. Not a sound is heard through the big apartment and they take that as their sign to forge on, but as they step onto the landing, two guards step out from around the corner, dropped to their knees with their guns out, ready to go.

Bullets sail straight toward the boys, the sound echoing through the apartment, but Grayson and Carver have been trained for this shit. Grayson pulls back, folding himself against the wall as Carver all but sails across the landing, dropping into a low roll and putting himself right in the entrance of a bedroom, giving him a much wider view of the upstairs area and the guards who dare aim their guns toward us.

He starts shooting, instantly getting the upper hand, and as his bullets rain down through the landing, he calls out to us. "Go, go, go."

We don't hesitate, bounding up the rest of the stairs and moving down the hallway. As King rounds the top of the steps he stops, dropping on one knee to assist Carver in taking out the two guards who lie in wait.

Time is ticking all too fast and the second the two guards are down for the count, we get a move on as every second passed is another second we're wasting.

The upstairs area is huge, and fuck, it's absolutely stunning, but now's not the time to appreciate my parents' taste in apartments. We're surrounded by floor-to-ceiling windows that span the whole apartment, giving a 360-degree view of the city and the rest of Ravenwood Heights. I can only imagine how stunning this must be right as the sun is going down.

There are rooms littered all over the top floor and if I hadn't spent a good portion of my morning studying the layout, I'd be lost and disorientated, but I came prepared, and because of that, I know there are two main bedrooms behind us while the rooms up ahead are the ones we need to focus on.

We make our way through a second living space and quickly clear a home theater room, and as we continue down the long corridor, movement out of the corner of my eyes catches my attention. I stop walking and turn toward the open door of a spare bedroom. "In here," I murmur to the guys, my stomach twisting with unease.

King and Grayson break off from the others and follow me into the bright room, and at first, it looks completely empty, but I know better. I nod toward the adjoining private bathroom. "There."

Grayson nods and gives me a hard stare, telling me to hang back as he goes to check it out. King backs him up and I hold my breath, my fingers swelling from gripping my gun so tight.

Grayson inches toward the bathroom and he glances back at King, making sure he's ready and then with one hard kick, the bathroom door is splintered into hundreds of pieces. "Don't shoot. Don't shoot. Don't shoot," a guard begs from inside, his gun laying on the tile as his hands shoot up in the air. "Please. I have a wife and children. I only took this job because I need cash so my kid could do dance lessons. I didn't sign up for this shit. Please man, I want to see her fifth birthday next week."

Grayson stares down at the guy, not trusting him a damn bit as his leg sweeps out, drawing the abandoned gun back toward King. "I'm not going to kill you," Grayson says, his gaze narrowed. "But you understand that I can't just let you go, not now."

The guard nods and Grayson steps toward him. "Sorry man, this is going to hurt," he says and rears back before his fist flies free, soaring toward the guy with an undeniable power that has my mouth going dry. Grayson's punch finds home and the guy is instantly knocked out cold.

King rushes in and kneels down beside him, dragging him toward the toilet and wrapping his arms around the base. He's chained to the toilet and I nod toward Grayson, proud of him for taking the high road and letting him live.

With still so many rooms to clear, I take a step back, and just as Grayson's eyes go wide, a hard body presses into my back. A burly arm snaps around my chest as I see a flash of a gun, but there's no way in hell that I came this far just to be shot down now.

My fingers grip the strong arm and before Grayson can even raise his gun, my ass slams back into the guy and I throw my body down. The guard goes toppling over the top of me, his back slamming down hard against the expensive flooring.

His eyes bug out, not having expected such a big move from a girl, and before he even gets the chance to fight back, my hand flies out, my finger pressing down on the trigger as a perfectly round bullet sails straight through the front of his head.

I stand tall, watching as the life fades out of him and as Grayson and King come rushing out of the bathroom with pride shining in their eyes, I know that we're going to be alright.

The nerves and anxiety that's been plaguing me since the second we arrived disappears and I stand just a little bit taller, feeling that familiar adrenaline pulsing through my veins and making me feel as though I can do just about anything I want.

I meet the boys' stares, making sure that I'm not about to freak out. A wide, twisted grin stretches across my lips. "Let's do this."

They smirk back at me, excitement bubbling in their eyes. They walk toward me and King hooks his arm over my shoulder as we walk back out of the big room. "Fuck yeah," he murmurs before pressing a kiss to my temple. "Do you know how fucking hot that was? I'm fucking hard."

"Just as you should be," I laugh, but as we approach the door, his arm drops from my shoulders and we fall straight back into business mode.

As we join Carver and Cruz in the hallway, they glance over me and I don't doubt the the sound of the single gunshot is weighing on their minds, wondering what the fuck went down in the spare room, but they won't ask me now. All that matters is that we're all still breathing, and so far, no one is hurt.

As one, we continue down the hallway until there are only two rooms left, the massive master bedroom and the attached private office.

Chances are that Paris is in the master bedroom with guards at her disposal so Cruz stands guard at the door and we quickly clear the private office, which isn't hard as it's absolutely tiny. We make quick work of it so we can move onto the reason we're here, the fucking main event.

Just as we thought, the office is empty and we come back out of it and take the few steps to the master bedroom at the end of the hall. The big double doors are closed and I don't doubt that the moment we kick them down, bullets are going to rain down over us.

"Get behind me," Carver murmurs, his stare trained heavily on the massive double doors, and it goes without saying that his comment was meant for me.

Now not being the time for arguments, I slip behind him, letting his big frame block me as King discreetly adjusts his stance, covering my side as well. Carver nods at Grayson and his gaze flicks back over everyone, making sure that we're all ready for what's about to go down.

With us all locked and loaded with determination on our side, Grayson goes for it. He slams his foot straight into the doors and they fling open as though they were made out of the cheapest wood. We storm through the double doors, guns held strong.

The guys fan out, covering all our bases, but we're met with absolutely nothing. "The fuck?" I question, my gaze sweeping through the room as Cruz storms toward the attached bathroom and comes back with nothing.

Carver grunts, his frustrations getting the better of him. "Where the fuck is she?"

"We must have missed something," Cruz says, his brows furrowed as I just know that he's going over the last fifteen minutes, making sure that we checked every last space.

I walk back toward the door and look out into the hallway. There's no way that she could have gotten away. We checked every room; we swept this place clean and the elevator was here waiting. Hell, King even had the elevator doors opened just in case she thought that hanging out in there was her best option.

But something isn't right.

I pull my phone out and scan over the picture I'd taken of the floorplan while mentally picturing every last room that we've been in. Everything looks right. We've checked every last room. "Is there an attic or outdoor space that we missed? A balcony or … I don't know. Did she get out into the fire escape?"

Cruz shakes his head. "I jammed her access to the fire escape," he says as I continue glancing over the picture, studying it like it was my only lifeline, "and there was nothing in the contract about an attic or manhole."

"There's always the roof," Grayson suggests.

Carver sighs, shaking his head. "The roof would be fucking stupid, but it's all we've got."

My fingers press to the screen of my phone and I zoom in on the picture, my gut telling me that there's something here that we've missed, and as I take in the attached office space, the room right beside where we're standing, my brows begin to furrow. "Check this out," I murmur, realizing that the floorplans have the office nearly twice as big as what it was. "That office was way too small to reflect what's on this floorplan."

King and Cruz snap their gazes up, barging past me and not bothering to look over the picture. "There's a fucking false wall," King mutters.

Carver goes with them as Grayson comes up behind me and takes the phone from my hand. We all walk into the private office and Grayson studies the image, trying to figure out which wall needs to be removed, but Carver and King don't have that same patience.

Carver walks around the room, his fingers brushing over the drywall for some clue as to where the hell she could be hiding, and then all too soon, he takes something off his belt, punches a hole in the drywall, and shoves something inside of it. Then before I can even see what it is, the guys are barreling out of the room, King grunting in shock. "Oh fuck, oh fuck, oh fuck."

Carver grabs my hand and yanks me out of the room as Cruz slams the door shut behind us. We race down the hallway and just as a loud BANG sounds through the apartment, I'm thrown to the floor with Carver coming down on top of me. "WHAT THE FUCK?" I screech, my face pressing into the hard floors.

"Are you good?" Carver rushes out as the explosion echoes through my mind.

"Get off me you fucking dipshit," I screech. "Tell me that you didn't just blow up the office without giving us even the slightest bit of warning. FUCK."

"Are. You. Good?" he demands, getting to his feet and pulling me up behind him as the boys start moving back toward the office.

I brush off his hold and narrow my glare on him. "I'm fine," I hiss, stepping around him and following the guys back to the office to watch as Cruz slips his hand inside his black shirt and uses it to help open the door, no doubt because the door handle would be boiling hot, assuming Carver's little stunt didn't just melt it right off.

The door comes free, falling right off its hinges and the boys don't hesitate, walking straight into the room. Smoke fills every corner but is quickly escaping through the shattered window, though my attention falls only to the panic room that was hidden behind the false wall, a wall that now ceases to exist.

Carver grins wide, looking at the panic room. "I guess blowing the room wasn't such a bad idea after all."

I roll my eyes and let King get to work, attaching explosives to the door of the panic room and leaving Paris with absolutely no escape. Though hopefully King has a little more sense than just throwing a grenade at it and hoping for the best.

"Cover yourself," King says a moment later, and like clockwork, Carver moves in front of me, crushing my body to the charred wall and covering my face. A moment passes before another loud BANG sounds through the apartment, but at least this one is far more controlled.

The door comes flying off its hinges with far more force than the small explosion should have allowed, and not a moment later, five guards come pouring out of the room, bullets shooting from their guns, the smoke masking their view and sending their shots wide.

"FUCK," Carver spits, falling away from me and spinning around to take care of business.

With my gun raised, I open fire, desperate to help neutralize the threat, but the room is far too small for us all to be moving around so rapidly. A guard jumps at Grayson, a knife gripped tightly in his hand, but Grayson doesn't have time for this shit.

His arms swing in a low arch, bringing his gun up against the guard as he comes down over Grayson, and without hesitation, Grayson pulls the trigger and takes the guard down before the guy has even finished falling.

Carver shoots straight at the guard that stands in front of the shattered window. As the bullet pierces his skull, the momentum sends him falling backward, his ass hitting the full-length window, right where the glass used to be. The guy falls straight out, plummeting to the pavement thirty-four floors down.

A flash of brunette hair cuts across my vision, and I watch as Paris slips through the smoke, darting out of the home office as though the world wasn't imploding around her. "FUCK, THERE SHE IS," I call to the boys over the noise of the rapid-fire bullets.

I dart after her and the boys curse as I fly out of the room, but with the guards still bearing down on them, they have no choice but to let me go, having to trust that I'll be okay.

# CHAPTER 37

Paris sprints down that hallway and my feet slam against the hardwood floors, racing after her. She catches the railing of the stairs and swings herself around, flying down them two at a time. She cries out, clutching onto her shoulder as she runs, and I can't help the grin that stretches across my face, the unbelievable satisfaction coursing through my veins nearly enough to send me into euphoria.

"Where are you going?" I call behind her, barreling down the stairs. "Stay and play. We have so much to catch up on."

Paris hits the last step and as she races through the living room, she whips around and points a gun directly at me. I don't dare stop as the shot rings out through the house and I dart away, screaming as the bullet catches my upper arm. "FUCK," I cry, crushing my teeth together and trying to channel the pain.

Tears sting my eyes, but knowing this could be my only chance, I push through the pain and keep putting one foot in front of another. As she creeps closer and closer to the back door that we'd broken our way through to get in, I raise my gun and take one clean shot, determined to keep her in the apartment.

The bullet shoots straight through her waist, and as she drops like a sack of shit, her hand clutches her side, blood spilling out onto the floor. Her gun skids along the ground, sliding straight under the cabinets and making this game all that more interesting.

I let out a breath, knowing that I have her right where I want her. She rolls on to her back, her eyes clenched as the pain rocks through her. "Fuck," she spits, "you're a little whore just like your mother."

"You're awfully obsessed with my mother," I laugh as I reach her, and not giving her the chance to get away, I grip her wrist and give a hard yank, practically dislocating her shoulder—the same shoulder that I'd stabbed a knife through only a few short days ago.

Her tormented scream echoes through the big living room as I drag her across the floor. I can't help but love every second of it. Maybe I'm twisted and sick myself. Maybe I need therapy or need to be locked up like Sara. At least, she will be until the boys can find a spare moment to release her after she held up her end of the bargain.

I give an extra hard pull as we reach the heavy dining table and laugh as her body skids to a stop, her ribs slamming into the leg of the table. Not wasting a precious moment, I pull cable ties from my pocket and get to work tying her down.

She thrashes against me. "You better fucking hope that you kill me," she hisses, "because if you don't, I'm going to hunt you down and skin you alive for this."

Fuck, she's funny. I really should have taken the time to get to know her because damn, this bitch really knows how to make me laugh.

I don't stop tying her up until her back is flat on the cold floor, her arms above her head and her legs strapped to the other end of the table, leaving her body wide open for anything that I might have in mind.

I get to my feet and survey my handiwork as I holster my gun, preferring a different tool. After all, a bullet to the head would be too easy. This woman has stalked me for years, sent assassin after assassin, she orchestrated my parents' murder and then had the audacity to move into their home. My life has been a living hell, and it's all because of this woman.

My gaze travels over the face that looks so much like my mother's, but as I look at her, all I see are the seven children who she kidnapped and tortured. I see the two little girls who scream in the middle of the night when the nightmares overwhelm them. I see Cruz's brothers who have lost the youthful spark in their eyes, and I see King's little brother and sister who haven't dared step out of their home, locking themselves in the safety of their bedrooms because they're too afraid of the monsters who lurk outside. Hell, Grayson's brother is the only one who looks remotely okay, but it's all an act. When nobody is around, I can see him shrinking back, the fears circling his mind on repeat.

My fingers curl around the hilt of my knife, freeing it from the holster at my thigh. For those seven children and for the lives that Paris has destroyed along the way, I'm going to take my sweet time.

I step over her, and in one quick movement, I drop down to my knees, straddling her hips as I stare down at her. She curses, the sudden weight of my body tearing at her open wound. I press my finger to the tip of the knife and spin it before lowering the edge to the bullet wound at her waist.

Inching my blade into the bullethole, a twisted smile spreads across my lips as she screams. "I bet this hurts, huh?"

She doesn't respond, but I didn't expect her to, so instead of bothering with conversation, I dig the knife a little deeper and listen to the sweet sounds of the gunshots above fading to nothing.

"ELLIE?" Grayson calls out. "YOU OKAY?"

"More than okay," I say, my stare lingering on Paris.

The boys thunder down the stairs and my gaze shifts over each of them, seeing they're all perfectly fine as they do exactly the same to me, picking up their pace as they see the blood trickling down my arm.

"You're hurt," King rushes out.

"It's fine," I tell them, turning back to Paris and yanking out the knife. "It's nothing a few stitches won't fix."

They reach the bottom step and make their way toward me, but before they can even ask my plan of attack, I slam the knife down hard against her stomach, plunging the knife deep until I feel the tip digging into the floorboards beneath. "THIS," I cry, "IS FOR MY FATHER."

The knife is yanked out and blood spurts from the wound, but I'm only just getting started. "AND THIS," I yell, "IS FOR MY

MOTHER."

The knife comes down again, closer to her chest and I revel in the feel of the blade sinking lower and lower. Nothing has ever felt so good.

The guys stand back and watch, Carver and Grayson both with sick smirks on their faces, loving it more than any sane-minded person should. King looks chill with the situation while my precious Cruz looks as though he's about to call the therapist on my behalf, but he'd never dream of taking this moment away from me.

The instant satisfaction that tears through me at the thought of getting retribution for my parents makes me feel like they're here in the room with me, guiding my hand as I take from Paris what she took from them, but I'm not nearly done.

I bring the knife down seven more times, one for each of the boys' siblings that suffered at her hands and just when life begins to fade from her eyes I look up at King and indicate for him to come closer.

His brows furrow, unsure of why I would need him when I clearly have the situation handled, and as I reach to his belt and take a grenade from him, understanding dawns. The guys move back, caution spreading through their gazes, but I keep my resolve strong, determined to end this the best way I know how.

Glancing back down at Paris, she follows my movements as she sees the grenade in my hand, she knows she's fucked. "No, no," she whispers, her voice breaking in despair.

My knife clatters to the ground beside me and I don't miss the way that King presses his foot over it and slides it back across the ground to the guys, making sure that when we make a run for it, we're not leaving anything behind.

The cops are bound to be here soon, along with the whole Ravenwood Heights Fire Department. There's no way that the gunshots, explosions, and the body falling from the window would go unnoticed by the public. We only have a matter of minutes to get this done and I'm going to make them count.

Keeping my stare on Paris, a soft laugh bubbles out of me. "You never had a shot at Dynasty. You were never going to win and look at you now. It was all for nothing. You killed your own flesh and blood for nothing, you beat your daughter and tortured your niece. You could have come forward as my mother's twin sister and I would have made sure that you never wanted for anything, but you don't deserve to live. You deserve the most painful, excruciating end, and I'm more than happy to make it happen."

I glance down at her bloodied stomach and I finger the wound right in the center, stretching it wide as she screams in agony. Then all too soon, I push the grenade down inside the stab wound, watching as her eyes roll to the back of her head in agony. "And this," I tell her, tearing the cap off the grenade. "Is for me."

King doesn't allow me the chance to stay back and watch the show as he grabs me under my arms and yanks me back. The boys turn and run and as my feet hit the ground and I finally start to move, the explosion rocks through the apartment and I'm thrown to the ground, King's heavy body slamming down on top of me.

His arms circle over my head as the shock blasts through the apartment, shattering every last window and sending strips of flesh flying through the room.

The BOOM echoes through my head over and over again as I blink, trying to focus my eyes. I peer through the gap below King's arm to look back at Paris but my view is blocked as something drops to the ground beside us.

King's body shuffles around on top of me, and before I know what's happening, his hands are at my arms, pulling me to my feet and gripping me tight. "WINTER. COME ON. WE HAVE TO GO."

I blink a few more times, but as reality grips me, I see the flames quickly spreading through the apartment, and understanding dawns. We have to get the fuck out of here and we have to do it now.

I go to take off after the boys, but the object at my feet catches my attention and a wicked grin cuts across my face. Knowing there's not a moment to spare, I scoop up the bloodied and broken hand and laugh as I race out of the apartment right on King's heels.

We barge out through the small stairwell and out onto the thirty-fourth floor. The cart is abandoned as we fly through the fire escape, and as we bound down the stairs, no one asks me about the hand and I don't bother offering up an explanation. All I know is those pretty rings that don her fingers are going to be the best kind of souvenirs. Besides, I'd bet everything I have that they're probably my mothers.

Granted, a hand isn't nearly as good as a head, but it'll do. I could have it put into a jar and shoved up on the mantelpiece above my fireplace like a damn trophy to serve as a constant reminder that nobody will hold me down. Besides, I'm sure I could find a million and one ways to fuck with the boys using it.

My legs ache by the time we hit the bottom but we don't dare stop until our asses are crashing down into the Escalade.

Carver fires up the engine and he carefully pulls out of the underground parking garage, going slow and making a show of looking up at the smoking apartment just as all the other people who stand out in the street are doing.

Carver navigates through the crowd, and just as he's able to really hit the gas, the cops come screeching in the opposite direction, flying straight past us and spilling out into the crowd to figure out what the fuck just went down.

And just like that, I relax back into my seat with King's hand still in mine, knowing that from here on out, I'm finally free. My parents have been avenged and the sweetest revenge has been taken for the boys and their siblings. Paris Moustaff is finally dead, and we will never have to fear her reign of terror again.

# CHAPTER 38

Champagne flows as the people of Dynasty celebrate their freedom, cheers, laughs, and joy spreading far and wide through our incredible community.

Ravenwood Estate has been set up perfectly, and I have no one but Dianna Danforth to thank for it. Hell, I think I'm going to make her the official Dynasty event coordinator. She's just that good, and even more, she truly loves organizing this shit, and it shows by how incredibly well she's been able to put it together.

We'd barely gotten back in Carver's Escalade when Cruz's phone started screeching through the car with his mother demanding to know that we were all alright. Cruz had told her the great news and by the time the Escalade was rolling through the gates of Ravenwood Estate, the plans were already in motion.

It's crazy to think that it was only less than three hours ago that I was ending Paris Moustaff for good, and now, I'm at a fucking street party with hundreds, if not thousands, of our Dynasty members flooding the road.

The street glistens with the canopy of fairy lights draped overhead, a stark contrast to the night sky peeping through the glittering strands. Layers of party decorations surround the mob of people, all of them dressed in their best suits and gowns for our last-minute celebration. Dianna offered the caterers five times their regular paychecks to ditch their plans and cater for us, and after one call to a gossipy wife, everything fell into place.

Children dance freely to the music flowing through the streets, and I finally feel like I'm home with my family behind me, right in front of the house where my parents had planned to raise me. It's the most dazzling sight I've ever seen.

I truly have found a home in Ravenwood Heights and I don't think I will ever leave here. This is where I will one day marry, hopefully in this very street with these same incredible fairy lights. One day, I might just raise a family of my own, though how that would actually work with four different guys … I don't know. That's a battle I can face way, way down the road.

I step up onto the little stage, which I'm pretty sure is just somebody's dining table with a fancy black cloth draped over it, and take a few shaky steps toward the small podium. The DJ sees me and slowly fades the music down, announcing to the street that their leader is demanding their attention.

All eyes fall toward me and people slowly begin creeping in, plastering themselves right in front of my temporary stage. The microphone rests just in front of my lips, but I wait for the stragglers that are making their way in.

The boys stand to my right in the most gorgeous suits, making my mouth water like never before. I know that it was only this morning that I woke up with an aching pussy after giving myself to them over and over again last night, but something tells me that I'm going to be demanding an instant replay the second we're behind closed doors.

Danika and Dominique stand in front of Carver, his arms encasing both of them as King's little sister stands by his side, clutching onto his hand. Just seeing their faces as they stare up at me, idolizing me as though I'm supposed to be something special makes me want nothing more than to earn it, over and over again.

I don't ever want to let my people down. I want them to be proud of me. I want them to go home at night and talk to their families about how my return to Ravenwood Heights has been one of the best things to happen to Dynasty, but more than that, I want to make my parents proud. I'm never going to get that validation, but I'll never stop trying for it anyway.

All my favorite faces linger in the crowd, and happiness spreads through me as they stand proudly, finally accepting me as their leader. But today, I truly earned my position here and proved to the people of Dynasty that I will do whatever it takes to keep them safe. It's because of me that their children are able to run free through the streets without the fear of being taken.

Right now, not only do they accept me, but they follow me. They want me here; they want the change that I can promise them, and because of that, we can all see a much healthier and happier future for the generations to come. Corruption is a thing of the past.

A soft chant starts from the crowd and quickly picks up. "ELODIE. ELODIE. ELODIE."

I can't help but laugh, seeing the joy on all of their faces, but a part of me wishes they were chanting for Winter instead. Don't get me wrong, the more I live with my new name, the more it grows on me. My parents gave me the name Elodie, heavy with their dreams and expectations of the life they never got to see. So even though I will always hold the name Elodie Ravenwood dear to me, it will never be who I truly am. I will always be Winter, the kid without a home, the girl with a chip on her shoulder and everything to prove. If going by Elodie means leaving those haunting years behind, I couldn't do it. I am who I am today because of those experiences. And I'm not going to lie, hearing the name Ellie slipping through Grayson's lips gets me hotter than I ever have the right to be.

My gaze shifts over the chanting crowd and as I raise my hand to silence them, a familiar face stands out to me and I hold back tears.

Karleigh is everything to me, and when I called her this afternoon to finally tell her that I was alright and to explain everything that's happened since the day I barged down her front door, she broke down in sobs, telling me just how proud she was. I had no choice but to invite her here tonight to finally get a real glimpse into my world, but in doing that, we had to organize a quick helicopter ride for her and her beautiful foster kids, and up until right now, I didn't know if she had taken me up on the offer.

Karleigh smiles up at me and then raises her brows before making a show of dropping her gaze down my body. I hold back a laugh, knowing damn well that she's taking in the plunging neckline of my black gown, but what can I say? At least I don't have a slit that comes riding right up to my hip like the last gown did. She should be grateful that I don't have my pussy out on display, scarring her kids' precious minds. Plus, my tits look great in this. Why not show them off? You know, the whole *if you've got it, flaunt it* bullshit.

Karleigh shakes her head, attempting to be serious, but in all honesty, I look fucking amazing. My hair is down in soft curls, making me look more girly than I ever have before, but damn, I feel like a freaking princess and the boys definitely seem to approve. Did I mention that my gown has pockets and a freaking train? It's absolutely everything a girl needs.

Karleigh's attention is stolen away by one of her kids, and I focus back on the patient crowd, their eyes boring into me and waiting to hear what I have to say, so I give them exactly what they want.

"PARIS MOUSTAFF IS DEAD."

Throwing my fist into the air, my brass knuckles point toward the dazzling lights and Dynasty erupts into loud cheers. Hands shoot into the air, men are wolf-whistling, and kids are hollering and chanting, turning this already awesome party into a fucking rave.

I wait a moment as the crowd finally begins to settle down. "Tonight, we celebrate for everything that we've lost. Paris has taken from us over and over again. She has stolen our hearts, our loved ones, our safety, but never again. We will rise back up and we will dominate knowing that not even her horrendous evil can hold us down. We are stronger than ever before. WE. ARE. DYNASTY."

The cheers start all over again and I watch as the crowd moves, jumping up and down with elation. I've never felt so good in my life. Getting to tell these people that they don't need to fear ever again is like handing them the whole world and telling them that they can do whatever the hell they want with it.

When they finally settle down, I move on to the more important topics like what happens now and offer all of the heads of Dynasty the chance to return to their normal lives away from here. Their children can return to their normal schools and their wives can get back to their normal lives, but a big part of me is kinda hoping that they'll all stay.

We've created a family here and it would be a shame to see anybody leave, but I understand the need for normalcy in your lives, especially when those lives come jammed packed with children to care for. I'm only just learning that myself now that we have Danika and Dominique staying with us. I've suddenly gone from the cool friend who hangs out with their older brother to the closest thing they have to a mother. It's daunting, but I'm taking on the challenge and will happily look at those girls as my daughters ... or at least my closely related little stepsisters. I'm way too young to be looking at myself as a mother of two pre-teen girls, but I can't wait to help mold them into the strong women that they'll one day become.

I close out my speech by reminding everyone to enjoy this night, even if they're not big partiers because tonight is one hell of a good reason to celebrate, and after a third round of cheering, I walk to the side of my little dining table stage and meet Cruz. He raises his hands to my waist and helps me down despite the shifting little stairs that were erected beside the table.

I come down on my feet and Cruz pulls me into his arms. "You were amazing."

"Speak for yourself," I murmur, loving the way he steps in even closer and presses the sweetest kiss to my temple. "I've hardly been able to stop looking at you all night."

"I know," he teases, that too confident, cocky attitude shining bright. "It's because I'm a fucking god, sexy as sin with the ability to fuck like the devil, plus I'm in my Beckham suit."

Well damn. He ain't wrong. He looks like a fucking meal and I plan on devouring it the second I can.

The partiers disperse around me, dragging me back into the crowd and showing me the time of my life as the guys watch me from the sidelines, dancing with the younger generations of Dynasty and finally allowing myself a chance to get to know them.

It's an hour before I finally find Karleigh standing by the bar and I can't help but race up to her and throw my arms around her. "I'm so happy you came," I tell her, the joy radiating out of me like a ray of sunshine. "I wasn't sure if you'd be able to make the trip. It was very last minute."

"I wouldn't have had it any other way," she tells me, stepping back to really look at me before frowning as she catches sight of the chunk Paris took out of my arm today. "Do I even want to know what happened there?"

I shake my head. "Some things are better left to the imagination."

"And what do you suppose I imagine?"

"Definitely a shark bite," I tell her, glancing down at my arms. "You know, because I recently took up surfing lessons. I'm a survivor."

"Ahhh," she says as the bartender hands her a drink and then hurries to fill my glass of champagne. "How strange. I could have sworn it looked like you got swiped by a stray bullet, but now that I look at it, it's definitely a shark bite. I don't know why I ever thought of anything else. You're lucky to be alive."

I laugh and raise my glass to her. "You don't know how right you are."

Karleigh's eyes bug out of her head and she quickly takes a long sip from her drink. "But that's all over now?" she questions. "You called your surfing instructor and canceled any future lessons? No more shark bites?"

I shrug my shoulders. "I mean, I've canceled my lessons for now, but I really do love surfing and I'm actually really good at it so I can't promise that I won't get back in the water, and I sure as hell can't promise that there won't be any more shark bites, but for now, I'm happy to give it a rest."

Karleigh shakes her head and takes another drink "Holy shit, kid. You're going to be the death of me," she tells me. "You have no idea how worried I've been about you since you fought that guy in my driveway."

My eyes bug out of my head as horror takes over me. "You saw that and didn't come to help me?"

She shrugs her shoulders and grins back at me. "It wasn't my fight to be involved in," she explains. "And besides, you looked like you had it handled … until you didn't."

I groan and lean into the side of the bar. "Why am I not surprised?" I ask her, rolling my eyes as I dig my hand into my pocket and produce some papers. I let out a breath and I watch as she picks up on the seriousness growing in my gaze. "Look, I'm really happy you were able to come tonight," I tell her as her brows begin to furrow in curiosity. "You mean the absolute world to me. You gave me a home when I had nothing and if it weren't for you and the way you taught me to have faith in myself, I think I would have given up a really long time ago. I owe that all to you."

"Don't be ridiculous," she says. "You had it in you all along. I just helped you to see it."

"You did so much more than that," I insist. "You taught me what it means to feel love for the first time in my life. You were a mother to me and you taught me that trusting another human being is possible. I'm a better person because of the time I spent with you, and I want to say thank you for that."

I hand her the papers and she glances down, confused about what the hell I could possibly be giving her. She unfolds them and scans over the documents. "What the hell is this?" she asks, wondering why the hell she holds the deeds to a big home in Santa DeClara, just an hour from her home now.

My eyes well with unshed tears and I hold them back, determined not to break during this. "Just this morning, I learned that my parents were in the property market. They invested in homes, studios, businesses, factories, even penthouse apartments in the most expensive cities, and this here," I say, indicating down to the papers. "Was one of them."

Karleigh shakes her head, having a hunch where this is going. "No, Winter. If you're doing what I think you're doing then you better stop it right now."

"I want you to have it, Karleigh. I don't need it. My parents invested in hundreds of properties, and this one right here is exactly what you've always dreamed about. It has seven king-sized bedrooms with a pool, tennis court, and a billiards room that can be transformed into some kind of cool playroom for the kids," I tell her. "I'm going to have a meeting with my lawyers to have the property transferred to you and make sure that everything is brand-new. I'll have all the rooms decked out for the kids and make sure that I replace that stupid TV that you've been holding over me. I have so much in this world that it would be a crime for me not to share it with you. You're doing such great work, Karleigh. Imagine how many kids you could take on. You could sell your current home and get a nice big wad of cash to your name, plus no more mortgage. You wouldn't even have to work."

Karleigh laughs, unable to wrap her head around it. "What's the catch?"

"There is no catch," I tell her. "I just want you to keep helping these kids and giving them a home like you did for me. I have the money to get them off the street, but not the time to show them the care and affection that they need. I don't have that motherly touch the way that you do, and with everything that I have to do for Dynasty, I'd be far too distracted. Hell, do you want to open a shelter? We can do that. My parents have places all over the world. We can have them renovated into homes and get some really great people running them. We could call it the Ravenwood Foundation after my parents."

Karleigh blinks, staring at me as though I've completely lost my mind, but perhaps she doesn't understand just how much money comes with this lifestyle. I need to do something with it because right now, it's just being wasted when I could be helping so many kids who are just like me. "I … um. Slow down a second," she tells me. "Are you being serious?"

"I'm so serious," I tell her. "Do you want to partner with me in all of this? We can do it. I can speak with my lawyers and get it all started as soon as this party is over."

"I … yes," she squeals. "This is insane. Do you really think we can do it?"

"A thousand percent," I laugh as she throws her arms around me and pulls me in. "As long as we have you, we're going to be just fine. You're my secret weapon and I want to share you with the world."

"Stop," she hisses. "You're going to make me cry in front of all these people."

"Consider it payback for not coming to help me in your driveway," I mutter, letting her see the smirk that stretches across my face. "But it's settled. I'll put you and the kids up in a five-star hotel for the night, and come tomorrow, we can start planning this new business and get the first shelter approved and opened within a few months. Though, I think I should introduce you to Dianna Danforth. She won't want to miss this."

"This is insa—"

Karleigh cuts herself off as four imposing men in the most jaw-dropping suits step in beside me, each of them greeting Karleigh with a silent nod before turning their attention to me. King's hand slides across my back, his touch sending goosebumps sailing down my body. "It's time," he murmurs.

I glance back at Karleigh to find her mouth hanging wide. "Shit, Winter. No wonder you got yourself in so much trouble."

I can't help but laugh as I take her hand and give it a firm squeeze. "I have to slip away for a moment, but I'll find you afterward and we can talk. This is going to be really incredible."

"You're damn right it will," she tells me before turning back to the bartender and asking for a refill, more than ready to celebrate her new home and business that's bound to help children all over the world.

I slip away with the boys, hiding in the shadows as they lead me right to the top of the street. We make our way down the narrow road that leads to the lift down into our underground world and slip inside. I take Grayson's hand in the darkness of the lift and don't let go until Carver is pushing the door of the council chamber wide open to a full table of men.

I walk in with my head held high and pride resting on my shoulders. Earnest stands and pulls my chair out before helping me into my seat, my gown making life just that little bit harder.

King and Carver take their seats as Cruz and Grayson move into their favored positions behind my chair. "What's this all about?" Harlen Beckett questions, annoyed to have been pulled away from the party where there are countless men gathered in the street, all of which he was surely planning to sweet talk into following his lead.

"Thank you all for slipping away tonight," I tell them, ignoring his question and sticking to my original plan. "It's certainly been an eventful day, but it's not over yet. First off, I just want to say thank you to all of you for being on guard today. Had we failed in the penthouse apartment, the protection of our people would have fallen on your shoulders and each one of you stepped up just as I knew you would."

I take a breath and slowly trail my gaze around the table, meeting the stare of every man who sits in my chamber. "Now, the reason I've brought you all here tonight is because a situation has arisen. Well, if I'm honest, I've known about this situation right from the start. However it was lying dormant for so long, up until recently, and that situation is Harlen Beckett."

Harlen flies to his feet, his usual temper flaring as Grayson flinches behind me. "What is the meaning of all this? I have been nothing but a loyal servant to you and your leadership," he demands as men scoff around the table. "I have only ever looked out for Dynasty and what is best for our people."

"Indeed," I say. "I did not say that you haven't."

"Then what are you talking about?"

I glance back at Grayson and nod, and without hesitation, he moves to his father's side and slides his phone on the table before him, pressing play on the security footage of Harlen breaking Ida out of the Dynasty cells. "You wiped the security footage, father, but you forgot about the cloud. It took only seconds for Cruz to find it."

Harlen falls back into his seat, his eyes wide, knowing how I like to handle traitors, but in this case, it's different. Harlen has never stepped out against me and has never taken an attempt on my life, though I'm sure he would given time. Freeing Ida was a mistake, one done with the intention to gain followers, but he's clearly not smart enough to pull it off.

"You freed Ida Carver while fully aware of her connection to Paris Moustaff. I would ask you why, but your reasoning is pretty clear, seeing as though you have been campaigning for leadership since the very beginning."

"I ... I have not. I campaigned during the time I thought you had passed."

I raise a brow and glance around the table. "Can anybody confirm that Harlen Beckett has not attempted to gain their loyalty since finding out that I was alive?" Not a damn hand raises and I look back at Harlen. "I think it's pretty clear where their loyalty lies."

"I ..." he starts, shaking his head, not knowing what to say. "I don't know what to tell you, Elodie. You're right. I have been aiming for leadership and with Royston and Scardoni out of the way, I thought I had a fair chance. And to be quite honest with you, the threat from Paris was looming over our heads and the likelihood of your survival wasn't great. I was simply preparing for what could have been. However, you are right. I did release Ida from her cell, but no ill will was intended for you. I wish to take your position, not see you dead. I can see the respect and loyalty you receive from our people and I could not risk losing that by being the reason for your untimely death. That would not look good for me."

"Indeed it wouldn't," I tell him. "However I have already taken this into consideration and the men sitting around you have already had the chance to come to a conclusion about your future as a head of Dynasty."

His brow arches and he glances around the table, looking at each of the men around him as though he's just been stabbed in the back. "Dare I ask what they have decided?"

"Of course," I say. "You are lucky that despite your harsh attitude and ability to throw tantrums, the men at this table have respect for you, and considering that no harm was brought to me or any of the other heads of Dynasty, bar Dante who was nearly murdered by his own mother, we have decided that effective immediately, you will step down from your position as head of your family, and your son, Grayson, will resume your duties."

Harlen looks at his son as though he just took a knife and stabbed it right through his back. "This is outrageous."

I scoff. "What's outrageous is that despite your betrayals against Dynasty, your son has pleaded for your life and managed to keep you out of a cell, so I suggest that you take this as the blessing that it is and use this newfound time to travel with your wife. Buy a yacht and learn how to sail. Consider it early retirement, and in exchange, not a word of this will be uttered to the people of Dynasty. You will maintain your reputation, however, if you decide to put up a fight or step out of line, I will be inclined to change my decision and put you in a cell. Now, I don't know about you, but it seems like you're getting the better end of the deal here."

Harlen lets out a breath and slowly nods his head as he stands from his seat. "Understood," he says as the other men around the table stand, letting him go peacefully, but not before he stops by his son and pulls him into his arms. "Don't embarrass the Beckett name," he says. "Your mother will be thrilled. She's always wanted to spend a year traveling."

"Sounds good, Dad," Grayson says, clapping him on the back before pulling back. "Think of it as a bonus. There's a party going on and this gives you the perfect opportunity to announce your retirement and put the spotlight back on you."

Harlen raises a brow in interest. "You know, that's not such a bad idea." And with that, he walks out of the council chambers, leaving the empty seat at the table for his son and giving us all one more reason to celebrate tonight.

# CHAPTER 39

It's after five in the morning when the boys and I call it quits on the party of the century and make our way back to my place. The girls were far too excited about their sleepover at Dianna's place and begged her to still have them for the night even though their brother was finished with work. But those girls come fully equipped with the skills to pull any damn strings they want and somehow end the conversation with Dianna begging for them to stay. I swear, there's just something about those big, dark eyes and those gorgeous smiles that have grown ass adults caving to their every desire. There were no complaints from me though because it left me and the boys with the whole house to ourselves.

I wonder what we could get up to. The possibilities are endless.

Carver, Cruz, and King walk ahead as Grayson walks in beside me, his arm thrown over my shoulder and his hand slipped inside the front of my gown, cupping my tit. As the door closes behind us, he spins us around and pushes me right up against it, my chest flush with the door as a soft breath escapes my lips, the guys walking on ahead, having absolutely no idea that we've stopped.

Usually I see his moves coming, but I've had a few drinks and my reflexes are off tonight. I guess that's just the downside of alcohol. On the plus side though, if Grayson's down for surprising me all night, then I'm in for the long haul.

"You were a fucking queen tonight," he growls deep in my ear, brushing my hair back over my shoulder and dropping his warm lips to my neck. "I've been hard for you all night. Seeing you dominate that stage and put my fucking father in his place … fuck, Ellie. You take my breath away."

My knees go weak, his words wrapping around me and reminding me why the hell I love him so damn much, but then as if to prove his point, he presses his body against mine, plastering his chest to my back and letting me feel his monster cock grinding against my ass. And damn it, the guy doesn't lie. He's not just hard, his cock is straining against his pants, desperate for a release, and I'd be a liar myself if I said that I didn't want that release all over my body.

I glance back over my shoulder and he raises his head to meet my hooded gaze, and while I plan to say something along the lines of 'well, hurry up and fuck me then,' it's certainly not what comes out of my mouth. Instead, a breathy whisper slips from between my lips. "I love you so much," I tell him, meaning every damn word.

Grayson's dark gaze softens and his hands fall to my waist and slowly turns me in his arms. "I love you too, Elodie," he tells me, leaning into me and letting me feel his lips brushing against mine. "You have my whole heart in your hands. Everything that I am is yours."

Fucking hell. How is a girl supposed to live with those sweet words bouncing around inside her head? I don't know what it is about Grayson, but when he turns the tables on me and tells me something so damn sweet that my knees go weak, I turn to slush in his hands.

His lips press harder against mine and he kisses me deeply, soft at first before applying just a little more pressure and sinking into me. His warm tongue roams against mine, both of us fighting for more.

I'm so immersed in his kiss that I don't even notice him bunching up the long skirt of my gown until I feel his calloused fingers against my smooth skin. His hands fall to the top of my panties and he hooks his fingers inside before pushing them down over my hips. I step out of them, and as I do, I press my hands against his wide chest and slowly push up to his shoulders, letting his suit jacket fall down his strong arms.

Grayson throws the jacket off and I can't help but study his body. He's still far too dressed but seeing the top of his raven tattoo sticking up over his collar bone reminds me of the day I went with him to complete it. It's one of my favorite memories that I share with him, but every single moment since then has only gotten better.

My fingers start working the little buttons of his dress shirt, and he lets me take my time, soaking up every little moment of this rare time that we get alone. His shirt falls open as I release the final button and I get the perfect peek of his strong chest and abs, which only gets more intoxicating when I slip my hands inside and push it open, just as I'd done with his jacket.

The soft material falls to the ground and I don't waste any time roaming my hands over his body, feeling the sharp ridges of his abs before trailing over his wide pecs, his tattoo, and up over his shoulder before trailing down his strong arms.

His skin is sizzling, so warm and inviting. It's like drowning in a sea of bliss, but when it comes to Grayson, I can guarantee that bliss will quickly turn into a river of molten lava. That's just the kind of lover he is. He can't help himself and it's absolutely everything a girl needs.

He presses against me and slides his hand down around my bare ass, giving it a firm squeeze as he grinds against me. His other hand comes up and brushes against my collar bone, sending electric pulses sizzling through my body. His fingers trail down to the narrow strip of material over my shoulder and he gives it a gentle push, letting it sail down my arm and exposing the soft curve of my full tit, my nipple straining and begging him to touch it.

Not being able to wait, I reach for the front of his pants and free his monster cock, knowing that tonight there's not going to be time for foreplay. I need to feel him stretching my walls. I need that hypnotic piercing dragging through my cunt and pushing deep within me, and I need to feel it now.

Screw the fact that every step I've taken has been accompanied by a dull ache right up in my pussy after my wicked night with the boys at the school locker rooms. I deserve this. Besides, my swollen, sore cunt can rest when I'm dead. Tonight is for the living, and living is exactly what I intend to do. Grayson will take care of me and I bet that from the moment I feel him stretching my walls and that incredible adrenaline starts pulsing through my veins, I won't even remember what my problem was.

My arousal spreads between my legs and I groan against him as he lifts me up and presses my back against the door, my legs wrapping tightly around him. I reach down between us and wrap my fingers around his cock, feeling that delicious bead of moisture sitting right at his tip.

My thumb rolls over it before trailing down his thick shaft, feeling the angry veins that have been waiting far too long to get me alone.

Grayson's mouth drops to my nipple and his tongue swirls around it, teasing and taunting me with the promise of what's to come. "Please," I whisper, my day being far too long to be made to wait.

I feel his soft smile against the curve of my breast and taking pity on me, his mouth closes down around my nipple and he sucks it hard, letting his tongue wreak havoc over my body. My hand continues moving, and as it does, my fingers brush past my clit over and over again, making me shudder with need. And rather than making me wait, he reaches between us, takes the tip of his large cock, and guides it to my entrance.

He pushes into me slowly, and my pussy stretches around him, welcoming him home like a long-lost friend. "Oh shit," I breathe, burying my face into his neck and kissing him there.

Grayson groans and slowly begins to move, pushing deeper before pulling back and making us both moan as the undeniable pleasure overwhelms us. He starts to pick up his pace, and I grip his shoulder, holding on as my head tilts back against the hard door.

I close my eyes and focus on nothing but the pure pleasure of him moving in and out of me, hitting deep inside and driving me wild. The soft groans that rumble through his chest vibrate against my nipple, and as his fingers slip in between us and his thumb presses down over my clit, I die.

A noise sounds behind Grayson and I open my eyes, looking over his shoulder at Cruz who comes to a standstill, watching the scene before him, and I can only imagine how delicious it would be, watching Grayson's perfect ass clenching as he thrust into me.

"Started without me, huh?" Cruz questions, the corner of his lip pulling up into a soft smirk.

My tongue rolls over my bottom lip as I watch the front of Cruz's pants begin to strain. He slides his suit jacket off his shoulder and it falls to the ground in a heap. "You know how I like to reward eagerness, and what can I say? Grayson gets a gold star every fucking time."

Grayson releases my nipple and brings his face up, his fiery gaze meeting mine. "You down to share?"

I raise my chin and brush my lips over his. "Always."

Grayson grins and drops his hands back to my ass before taking my weight into his hands and pulling me away from the wall. Keeping himself buried deep inside of me, he turns and walks straight through to the living room with Cruz heavy on his trail.

My ass is placed down on the edge of the glass coffee table and

Grayson kneels, lining himself up perfectly with my needy cunt, and within moments, I feel his fingers at the back of my gown, slowly dragging the zipper down my back and letting the material fall open and gather at my waist, freeing my other tit.

Not wanting to pull out of me, Grayson bunches up the gown and pulls it up over my head, tossing the black fabric into a dark corner. His hands drop to my thighs and spread my legs wider, wanting to watch as his cock comes out of me, glistening in my arousal.

Cruz steps in beside me, his cock bouncing by my face, and just when I think he's going to ask me to take him in my mouth, he drops to his knees and curls his hand around the back of my neck, laying me back against the glass table.

His fingers start at my collar bone and slowly trail down my chest, brushing over the curve of my breast and skimming over my waist, making me flinch as his soft touch tickles, but it only lasts a moment before I feel him dipping between my spread thighs, his fingers trailing low and circling through my arousal. He comes back up just a bit, and I suck in a breath as those same two fingers press against my clit.

"Oh, fuck, Cruz," I breathe as his fingers torture me with a sensual dance, slowly rubbing tight circles as he leans over me and collects my pert nipple into his mouth. I can't help but to reach down beside the table and take his cock in my hand, slowly moving up and down, matching the tortuous movements that he makes against my clit.

Cruz groans low and I can't help but draw him toward my mouth, my new position on the table perfectly matching the height of his cock as he kneels beside me. Cruz is all too eager and I lick my lips, preparing myself just moments before I feel his thick tip pressing against them. I open wide, letting my tongue trail over his cock as I take him deep, my fingers curling around his base and working him up and down.

I feel Grayson's eyes on my mouth and I glance up at him as my other hand trails over the curve of my tit. I flood with need, absolutely loving the way the guys like to watch me with their friends.

"Yo, where'd you fuckers go?" I hear King hollering through the house and a wicked grin stretches across my lips.

Cruz meets my stare with his brow arched. "Yeah?" he questions.

"Mmhmm," I moan against his cock, loving the way his eyes roll with pleasure.

"Both of them?" My grin only widens and he doesn't bother waiting for a response, though I'm sure he wouldn't mind.

"You guys coming to the party or what?" Cruz calls out, and I feel joy spread right through my chest, chipping away at the darkness that overwhelmed it. "I'm down for you guys to wait your turn, but I think our girl's feeling a little adventurous."

Damn right, I am.

Carver and King practically skid into the living room, not ones to miss out on a good time, and if my mouth wasn't so damn full, I'd be laughing at the way their eyes become hooded, filled with undeniable desire, and their clothes start falling off of them.

Carver meets my stare and the familiar darkness swirls within his depths as he strides toward me, standing over the coffee table and looking down at me with Cruz's cock deep in the back of my throat and Grayson stretching me wide.

King joins him, both of them watching my body being worked, and as their heavy cocks are taken in their calloused hands and gently stroked, I feel the butterflies going crazy in my stomach, this particular angle making their cocks look like fucking mountains desperate to be climbed.

Seeing that things are going to get difficult, Grayson reaches down and slips his arm around my waist, lifting me off the coffee table and dropping down on the couch, resting back and bringing me with him as I straddle his hips and pick up where he left off, feeling that piercing hitting me at a new spot that has my eyes rolling in my head.

Cruz turns and kneels beside Grayson on the couch and I draw him straight back into my mouth as King moves in beside me, dropping to his knees at Grayson's feet and reaching down between my legs to feel just how wet I am.

His fingers swirl in my arousal and he draws them up to my ass, gently pushing his thumb inside and getting me ready. "Fuck, babe," King breathes, pressing the tip of his wide cock to my ass as I slow my movements on Grayson. He pushes inside of me and I groan low, loving that initial tight burn as he stretches my ass around his impressive size.

I push back against him, taking him deeper, and in doing so, grind against Grayson, making both of them groan, which only has a moan pulling from the back of my throat and Cruz dying in pleasure.

King starts to move and I hold still, letting him do his thing as I rise to my knees and give Grayson the space to move up into me, matching his rhythm with King.

My gaze shifts to Carver who stands back at the coffee table, still watching the show as though he's mesmerized by everything that's going down, but it's unlike him to not already be involved and taking control.

His dark, lingering gaze shifts up to mine and a million silent messages pass between us, but it's all he needs to kick himself into gear and come join me on my other side. He kneels just as Cruz is and I can't help myself to pull back on Cruz, gripping him with my hand instead and turning toward Carver. I take him in my mouth, gripping him at his base just as I'd been doing with Cruz and I work my hand up and down as my tongue rolls over his thick tip.

I take him deep in my throat and he knots his fingers into my hair, holding on tight, but he doesn't dare steal my control. He gives me free reign and I take it all, giving him exactly what I know he needs.

The boys move in and out, fucking me slowly like a human pin cushion, their hands a mess of limbs as they travel over my body with soft sensual touches. Grayson sucks my nipple into his mouth, teasing me with his tongue as Cruz lightly pinches the other, letting a bolt of electricity fire through me.

"Holy shit," I pant, knowing I won't be able to handle this intensity for long, but from the echoed chorus of groans, grunts, and moans, I don't think they will either.

King pushes deeper into my ass and the guys pick up their pace, Grayson moving deep inside me, stretching me to my limits as Carver fucks my throat.

The familiar burn builds within me and I clench my eyes, but when

Cruz's hand drops from my tit and flicks over my clit, I fucking lose it. My orgasm tears through me and I come hard, squeezing down around both Grayson and King, convulsing violently as my body shatters around them.

"Ah, fuck," King mutters, squeezing both my ass cheeks as Cruz moans, watching the euphoria spreading over my face.

My grip tightens around him and I move my thumb over his tip, making sure he knows that I haven't forgotten about him as I ride out my high, but his finger continues working my clit and my orgasm just keeps pulsing through me, absolutely destroying me as a slow groan travels up my throat, vibrating against Carver's strong cock.

"Shit," Grayson mutters, his jaw clenching. "I'm gonna fucking come, but if I don't get to shoot my load all over these pretty tits …"

"Damn," King mutters. "I'm down for that."

I raise my brow at Carver and a twisted smirk cuts across his face and within moments, King curls his arm around my waist and pulls out of me before lifting me off Grayson and leaving me no choice but to release both Carver and Cruz.

I'm placed back down on the coffee table, my legs spread as the boys move in front of me, each of them with their cocks in their hands. Cruz isn't there yet and drops back to his knees, slamming deep inside my cunt and fucking me hard and fast as Grayson groans low and comes hard against my tits, his warm seed hitting the curve of my breasts and sailing down my stomach.

King and Carver watch, their eyes darkening with desire, and before Grayson has even finished emptying himself, they blow with him, their warm seed covering my tits and winding me up all over again. "Fuck, Winter," Carver mutters through a clenched jaw, the pleasure taking over his face making me want to go all over again.

Feeling my pussy tightening around him, Cruz's hand comes down against my clit and I cry out, a sharp groan tearing from the back of my throat. I tip my head back, feeling the cum sliding all over my tits and dripping down onto my toned stomach just as a second, intense orgasm tears through me. Cruz comes hard, shooting his load deep inside my cunt as I explode around him, my body completely exhausted and shattered.

Grayson appears back at my side with a warm washcloth and wipes me down as I collapse back against the coffee table, struggling to catch my breath.

I close my eyes and listen to the sounds around me as I feel fingers trailing over my tired body, slowly working up and down. A second set of hands join in and soon a third is between my legs, gently rubbing at my clit and enticing another orgasm to build within me. My breath comes in hard, sharp pants, but I don't dare open my eyes, intent on just feeling, and fuck, it's the purest thing I've ever experienced.

Lips press against mine as my breasts are gently caressed, and within moments, the sweetest orgasm is pulsing through my body. Before I even have a chance to open my eyes, Carver is scooping me into his warm arms and crashing down onto the couch.

My body fits against him perfectly and a warm blanket falls over us, the boys murmur softly as they settle into their places around us. Someone crashes onto the end of the couch, pulling my feet into his lap and rubbing gently at my heels.

"Love you," I mutter, not even knowing who I'm speaking to. All I know is that the words are true for each of the guys in the room.

Carver's arms tighten around my waist as I hear the sweetest, "Love you," rumbled like a chorus around the room, four evenly matched men, each who have stolen my heart in their own perfect way and given me a life that I never even dreamed of.

I feel fingers trailing through my hair as my world is fading to darkness, a deep sleep claiming me. I know that from here on out, with every threat neutralized and Dynasty thriving, my life is only going to get better.

Every single moment is bittersweet, and I can't fucking wait to experience all of them with these four men at my sides.

Silence falls around the room and all too soon, Cruz is at my side, shaking my shoulders. "Are you coming?"

"Huh?" I grumble, the word getting caught in my dry throat as I realize that I've not only been snoring, but I've had my mouth hanging wide open. "Coming? What's going on? Where are we going?"

"Got a hit," he tells me. "Eight-year-old girl just out of state."

I sit up on the couch, only now just realizing that Carver is no longer plastered to my back and the sun is shining brightly through the front window of my parents' beautiful home. "Are you serious?"

"Would I lie when a new Harley is on the line?"

"Good point," I laugh, getting up, only to have my favorite leather pants, a pair of panties, a cropped black tank, and my favorite boots thrown onto the couch beside me.

"Get dressed," Cruz says as Grayson saunters through the living room. "And make it quick. I have a bet with Carver that you can't get dressed and ready in under thirty seconds." My mouth drops and he grins. "He thinks you'll need at least four minutes."

"Well fuck him," I laugh. "You guys are about to see something incredible."

Exactly twenty-five seconds later, I'm stepping through the internal door of the garage and passing by my Ducati as the excitement builds within me. I haven't had a chance to drive her since she returned from the shop and I've been dying to throw my leg over the smooth seat and feel the vibration right between my legs.

I slide into my designated spot in the Escalade, knowing that we're in for a long drive as the guys climb in and close the doors, locking us in. I can't help but glance up at Carver through the rearview mirror, determined to get him back for underestimating me. "You never told me what kinky shit you saw Earnest Brooks getting his rocks off to," I remind him, grinning as his stare darkens. I make a show of glancing down at the non-existent watch on my wrist. "We've got about seven hours of downtime together, so let's hear it, what tickles his fancy?"

Carver's glare hardens through the mirror and I let out a satisfied sigh, leaning back into my seat as he hits the gas, knowing that for the next seven hours, Carver won't be able to get the intrusive thoughts out of his head.

It's going to be a fucking beautiful day.

# EPILOGUE

## 4 YEARS LATER

Water swirls around me as I dive into the shimmering water of the private island Cruz booked for us. It's been a long time coming and we've been waiting for this day with bated breath.

Yesterday morning, the five of us flew to Georgia, and after one hell of a showdown, we saved the very last girl from Sam Delacourt's ledger and the second we did, I crumbled to the ground and cried, feeling the weight of their tortured years at the hands of their abusers falling off my shoulders, and Dynasty is a big part of that.

We worked our asses off to turn shit around and we've come full circle, even the FBI worked hand in hand with us, helping to locate missing persons and I've never been so proud. Dynasty has turned into the kind of organization that I know both my father and his father before him would have been proud to run. Hell, I don't doubt that they're looking down on me now, shaking their heads as they try to figure out just how I defied all the odds.

I break through the surface of the water, feeling the blistering sun bearing down on my skin and know without a doubt that I'm going to end up with the sweetest tan, though if I'm not careful, I'm going to burn and give the boys another reason to try and keep me sheltered.

It'll never happen though. They've been trying for nearly five years and all they've managed to do is help me to figure out new ways to get under their skin and I absolutely love it.

I roll onto my back, floating in the water as I look up at the boys, coming to a stop on the edge of the deck, looking down at me as my arms and legs gently tread through the clear water of the sea as the stunning turtles swim around me. "Get that ass over here," Cruz tells me, the grin that lights up his face making me melt for the millionth time today. It's impossible to deny him, but I'm not one to shy away from a challenge.

"No," I call back. "You guys get your asses over here."

Grayson scoffs. "Don't make me come and get you."

"Is that a promise?" I challenge, laughing at him.

"So, I guess that means you don't want to see what we got you?" Carver says, raising his brow and waiting for me to silently freak out.

"You got me a present?"

King rocks back on his heels, his gorgeous grin nearly tempting me to swim all the way back, even if they're just fucking with me. "We could always take it back if you don't want it."

"What?" I rush out, my eyes widening, trusting completely that he'll follow through on his threat. "No, I want it. I'm coming."

I start swimming back, feeling the soft tickle of my string bikini brushing against my skin. It's been a crazy few days. We saved that girl yesterday morning and while we've been hating ourselves for just how long it's taken to find her, it was also bittersweet. The moment we reunited her with her family, Cruz turned to me and the boys and demanded that we book a vacation, and here we are, halfway across the world having the time of our lives on a private island. You know, after spending countless hours on a plane and then a private boat to get here.

It's the most incredible place I've ever seen, and since the moment we arrived here, I've been kicking myself, wondering why the fuck we haven't done this sooner. Though, I'm not going to lie, the jet lag is killing me. But I'm sure by tomorrow morning, I'll be perfectly fine, more so knowing that we have this island for as long as we want.

I approach the side of the deck and Grayson reaches down and scoops me straight out of the water as Carver drapes a towel around me, but with the blistering sun, I only need the towel for a quick moment before my body is dry and my bikini begins to soak up the rays, warming my body.

King takes my hand and the guys lead me back toward the massive resort until we're standing out front looking over the beautiful shore with the shade from the palms looming over us.

Nerves flow through me, having no idea what this could be about but when the guys step in front of me, each of them looking at me with love shining in their eyes, I realize that this is the good kind of present, not the kind where they surprise me with a new position that they saw in a cheap porn movie.

"What's going on?" I question, my tone filled with suspicion. "What did you get me?"

Grayson's hand digs into his pocket and he walks over to me with a big velvety box and places it into my hands. "Why don't you take a look for yourself?"

The curiosity gets the best of me and I open the box and suck in a shallow gasp as a beautiful set of knuckles stares back at me, the diamonds glistening in the sun and telling me that this right here didn't come cheap.

"What the hell?" I breathe, my eyes widening as I lift it out of the box and take a closer look at the diamonds that completely cover the four finger holes. I slide my fingers into place and it fits me like a glove, but as I turn my hand over to look at the bottom half, I find all four of the guys' names carved into the metal. "It's beautiful," I whisper, feeling my emotions begin to overwhelm me. "But what's it for? It's not my birthday."

Seeing me about to cry, King steps into my side and presses a kiss to my temple. "You need to have a birthday for us to buy you things now?"

"Definitely not," I laugh, glancing back down at the knuckles. "but this one just feels … different."

"That's because it is," Carver tells me, stepping into me and taking my hand, looking down at the array of diamonds covering my fingers.

"We all love you, you know that," he tells me. "But because of our … unique situation, we haven't been able to give you the things that most girls want out of a relationship, and I know that even though you'll never admit it, a wedding was always something you wanted for yourself."

"But you know that I—"

"I know," he says, cutting me off, his voice softening. "We know that you don't want to commit to just one of us in marriage and then not be able to do the same for the others, and that's fine, we get and respect that, and quite honestly, I don't think I could hack it if you were to marry one of these other guys and not me."

I laugh and a wide grin stretches over his face as Cruz moves in and takes my other hand. "We wanted you to get to experience those things so this is our version of telling you that we are completely committed to you. Each of us would marry you in a heartbeat, but just because we can't doesn't mean that you should miss out on all the perks."

I laugh and glance down at my hand again. "Is this my version of an engagement ring?"

"It sure fucking is," Grayson smirks. "Four fingers, each covered in diamonds to represent each of us. We had it made from titanium instead of gold because gold is weak and you deserve something that reflects who you are."

My heart flutters with the amount of thought the boys have put into this, but then Carver goes and opens his mouth. "Besides, your favorite pair of brass knuckles are starting to look a bit ratty, so it was time."

I roll my eyes and glance at Grayson as he goes on like Carver never even spoke a word. "We want to give you the world just as you've done for us," he tells me. "You worked so hard getting your business off the ground with Karleigh, and over the past four years it's flourished into something incredible. You've given your all to your shelters, but now it's time to think about you."

Joy overwhelms me and I lean into Cruz, loving the feel of his other hand resting against my lower back as his thumb trails over the back of my hand. "You guys are insane," I tell them. "I just wish I had something as awesome to give back to you."

"You give us you and that's enough," Cruz tells me.

"Fuck that," King teases. "Speak for yourself. I want a fucking diamond ring if one is on offer, but if the option is out there, I wouldn't mind a diamond-encrusted Rolex. Now that would be sweet."

I roll my eyes and laugh. "Way to ruin a good moment," I tell him.

"Uh-uh," he says, grabbing me around the waist and lifting me right into his arms, stealing me away from the guys and walking out toward the shore. "There's no such thing as ruining a moment when you're on vacation," he says as the guys follow behind.

"Maybe not," I laugh as he walks straight down into the water. "But there's certainly such a thing as making a moment even better while on vacation."

"Oh yeah? And what's that?" he grins, already knowing where my mind has taken me, but wanting me to say the words anyway.

I press my lips against him before pulling back and spying the guys just behind us, moving in even closer. "Well, I just think that we have all this wide-open space to ourselves and we haven't fucked in a single part of it yet."

"Well then," he says as Carver moves in even closer, grabbing the soft string of my triangle bikini and giving it a gentle tug until it comes free. "I guess we better get started," and just like that, he kisses me deeply as Cruz and Grayson move in, more than ready to show this island something it's never seen before.

The early morning sun shines through to our villa and directly into my eyes as though it didn't already know that I only went to sleep an hour ago. After all, we put on one hell of a show for the island, but something tells me that it hasn't seen anything yet. We're only just getting started. Hell, the only reason we had to stop last night was because of the chaffing I was getting from the sand creeping up between my lady bits, prompting a 5 am swim in the ocean. It was so much better than I could have imagined.

Needing to pee, I slip out from under Grayson's arm and climb over Cruz before accidentally backing my ass up into Carver's face, but what can I say? That's just the risk we take sleeping with so many in a bed, though at home we're a little more spread out. We can't keep up with this five in the bed thing. It's too much so we keep it for special occasions ... or those nights when we're all too exhausted after being together that we all crash without bothering to get dressed ... nights like last night.

My feet hit the ground and the second I straighten, my stomach squeezes and I bolt for the bathroom, feeling everything sloshing around inside of me. I barely get through to the bathroom, having no choice but to leave the door wide open as I crash down on the ground, my knees hitting the cold tiles just in time for me to hurl into the bowl.

The need to pee remains strong and I have no choice but to shove my hands between my pussy to keep it all in as my violent heaves take over me.

"Babe?" King rushes out, storming into the bathroom behind me. "What's wrong? Are you sick?"

"Obviously I'm fucking sick," I growl at him. "Now get the fuck out."

He comes rushing at me, grabbing locks of hair and pulling them out of the way and I don't get another chance to tell him to fuck off again before more vomit is flying out of me, decorating the toilet bowl in the worst possible way.

"What's going on?" Carver asks, the next to come through the door, closely followed by both Cruz and Grayson, their eyes wide.

Carver just stares as Cruz rushes to my side to pat my back like I'm some kind of child in need of help, while in reality, I'd like nothing more than to be alone. There's nothing worse than having four guys watching you at your absolute worst, but at least Grayson is actually helpful and grabs a cool washcloth and a glass of water.

"You good?" Grayson questions, handing the glass to Cruz who lifts it to my lips and attempts to make me drink, only I pull away, my stomach rolling with the thought of swallowing anything. "Is it finished?"

I shake my head, feeling absolutely helpless. "I … I don't know what it is. I haven't eaten anything weird. I mean, I don't think I have. I ate the same as you guys, and you're all fine."

"Could you be pregnant?" King suggests, his question silencing the other guys who all stare at me wide-eyed.

I roll my eyes and let out a heavy sigh, slowly taking the glass from Cruz and dropping the lid of the toilet seat before shuffling up and sitting on it. "Not possible," I tell them, watching as they all sigh, though those sighs don't exactly look relieved. "I've got this thing in my arm, remember? I can't get knocked up until it's been yanked out."

Grayson shakes his head and moves back to the bathroom cupboard, searching through it as he begins to interrogate me. "When was the last time you had it replaced? Aren't they supposed to be changed every three years?"

I nod as my brows furrow, thinking back to the last time I stopped by my doctor's office to have my birth control updated, and while I remember the awkward visit vividly, I can't exactly remember when it was. "I, umm. Shit, I can't remember."

Grayson rolls his eyes and a moment later, pulls a little pink box out of the cupboard and starts tearing into it. "Here," he says, handing me a pregnancy test. "Couldn't hurt just to check."

Knowing he's right, I pull the cap off the test and as I rise up off the toilet and lift the lid, it becomes pretty damn clear that none of the guys have even the smallest intentions of leaving the bathroom. "The fuck are you waiting for?" I ask them. "An invitation? Get the hell out. Let a girl pee in peace."

They all grumble and reluctantly move out of the bathroom but judging by their murmured conversation, they didn't go far, but I'm not surprised. They're a bunch of over-protective asshats who would do absolutely anything for me. Asking them to leave while I'm sick was like asking them to build a rocket, fly to the moon, paint themselves blue, and wiggle their dicks at each other.

Realizing that their patience won't last forever, I shove the test between my legs and get to work pissing all over my hand, and the moment I can, I dart over to the sink and get cleaned up. The test rests against the vanity as I scramble through my things for my toothbrush and by the time I'm spitting into the sink and rinsing out my mouth, the test is ready to go.

I drop my toothbrush back into my little toiletries bag before glancing down at the test and feeling the earth shifting under my feet.

Well, fuck.

I let out a sigh and turn on my heel, storming out of the bathroom with the test held tightly in my hands, my head spinning with what's to come. "WHICH ONE OF YOU FUCK KNUCKLES KNOCKED ME UP?"

# PLAYLIST

Blood // Water - Grandson
Evil - 8 Graves
11 Minutes - Yungblud Ft. Halsey & Travis Barker
Hate The Way - G-Eazy Feat Blackbear
Control - Halsey
Play With Fire - Sam Tinnesz
You Should See Me In A Crown - Billie Eilish
Everybody Wants To Rule The World - Lorde
Courage To Change - Sia
You Broke Me First - Tate McRae
Yellow Flicker Beat - Lorde
Sweet Dreams - Marilyn Manson
Wicked Game - Daisy Gray
Nobody's Home - Avril Lavigne
Stand By Me - Ki: Theory
Paparazzi - Kim Dracula
Bringing Me Down - Ki: Theory (feat. Ruelle)
Therefore I am - Billie Eilish
I see Red - Everybody Love An Outlaw
In The Air Tonight - Nonpoint
Tainted Love - Marilyn Manson
Saviour - Daisy Gray
I Put A Spell On You - Annie Lennox
Heaven Julia Michaels
Heart Attack - Demi Lovato
Dynasty - Mia
Weak - AJR
Redemption - Besomorph & Coopex & RIELL
Legends Never Die - League of Legends & Against the Current
Time - NF
Rumors - NEFFEX

# THANKS FOR READING

If you enjoyed reading this book as much as I enjoyed writing it, please leave an Amazon review to let me know.

https://www.amazon.com/gp/product/B0924X4K6M

For more information on Boys of Winter,
join me online with the rest of the stalkers!!
I swear, I don't bite. Not unless you say please!

----------

Facebook Reader Group

Facebook Page

Instagram

TikTok

Threads

Newsletter

# MORE BY SHERIDAN ANNE

www.amazon.com/Sheridan-Anne/e/B079TLXN6K

## DARK ROMANCE STANDALONES

Pretty Monster | Haunted Love | Darkest Sin

Midnight Stage | War Games

## DARK CONTEMPORARY ROMANCE SERIES - M/F

Broken Hill High | Haven Falls | Broken Hill Boys |

Aston Creek High | Rejects Paradise | Bradford Bastard

## DARK CONTEMPORARY ROMANCE - RH

Boys of Winter | Depraved Sinners | Empire

## NEW ADULT SPORTS ROMANCE

Kings of Denver | Denver Royalty | Rebels Advocate

## CONTEMPORARY ROMANCE

Play With Fire | Until Autumn | Remember Us This Way

## HOLIDAY ROMANCE

The Naughty List | Santa's Dark Secret